INDEPENDENCE DAY

CRUCIBLE

INDEPENDENCE DAY

CRUCIBLE

NOVEL BY GREG KEYES

BASED ON THE SCREENPLAY BY
NICOLAS WRIGHT & JAMES A. WOODS
AND DEAN DEVLIN & ROLAND EMMERICH
AND JAMES VANDERBILT AND THE STORY BY
DEAN DEVLIN & ROLAND EMMERICH AND
NICOLAS WRIGHT & JAMES A. WOODS,
BASED ON CHARACTERS CREATED BY
DEAN DEVLIN & ROLAND EMMERICH

TITAN BOOKS

Independence Day: Crucible
Print edition ISBN: 9781785651304
E-book edition ISBN: 9781785651359

Published by Titan Books
A division of Titan Publishing Group Ltd
144 Southwark Street, London SE1 0UP

First edition: May 2016
10 9 8 7 6 5 4 3 2 1

A CIP catalogue record for this title is available from the British Library.

Printed and bound in the United States.

For Karen Hunt Spangler

PROLOGUE

JULY 7

1947

Corporal Jackson Hardy knew the alien wasn't dead. When he was helping Reynolds stuff it into the body bag, his hand touched the smooth, mouthless face. He jerked back as if stung, every inch of his six-foot-two frame tingling in alarm. He felt like he'd just kissed a copperhead on the lips.

Reynolds laughed at him nervously.

"Least you know it can't bite," he said.

That was what Jackson's grandfather used to call laughing in the graveyard. However well hidden, every man on the detail was battling at least some amount of terror. Jackson didn't have anything more than a high school education, and someone might have been able to convince him that the crashed ship was a government prototype, or a Soviet spy plane, or a Chinese weather balloon. What did he know about that stuff? But no amount of convincing could explain away the things in it. No way they came from the same world that had produced Jackson Hardy. Not the creature he and Reynolds put in that body bag.

A spider was closer to being human.

It was alive, too. He wasn't sure how he knew, but he did, and with absolute certainty. His fingers prickled long after the thing was taken away. He worried a little that he might be infected with something, but as the day wore on the sensation faded, and with it, his apprehension.

*   *   *

The next day they went back to the site, with a lot more men, and cleaned everything up. Where the higher-ups took the ship and the scraps, he didn't know and didn't want to know. Like most of the other soldiers Agent Leigh had picked for the mission, Jackson had worked under military intelligence before, and knew how to keep a secret. That started with not asking questions, even in your own head.

At that point, he figured the whole thing was done, and he could start packing this mess in with all of the other nightmares he was trying to forget from his tour in Europe. But the next night he was loaded into a truck with a bunch of the other guys and driven out through the desert.

When Jackson stepped out of the truck, it was beneath a waning gibbous moon in a New Mexican sky. At least he assumed they were still in New Mexico. Even in the dark, he could make out that there wasn't much but sand and the scrubby cacti locals called *cholla*. It was a thoroughly inhospitable landscape, an alien world compared to the lush subtropics of Louisiana where he had been born and raised.

Made all the more inhospitable for what he'd seen in the past few days.

Still, there wasn't anything particularly alien about the ranch house and its little scatter of outbuildings and corrals, the sheep bleating in the darkness, the yard dogs sounding their canine alarms as the soldiers invaded their territory. Agent Leigh hadn't explained what they were doing on the ride over, and he didn't explain now. He sent

Jackson and two privates to check out the barn.

Jackson rarely had nightmares. His old flame, Irene Clay, had chalked that up to what she called his thorough lack of imagination, but the night after touching the alien, he'd had a night terror. He didn't remember the details, but it had left him shaken.

It was like being back in the war, where death seemed to hide around every turn taken, in every shadow entered. If not his own death, then the sightless eyes of other men, and sometimes women and children. But now there was more, a deeper kind of dread. Like the world he knew was just fresh paint on a house already gone to rot.

In Belgium and Germany, the monsters had at least looked human.

Despite nearly giving him the shakes, the barn didn't contain anything out of the ordinary, so they took positions around it. Fidgeting a bit, Jackson got out a cigarette and a book of matches. As he was shaking the match out, he caught something in the corner of his eye, something that sent a shiver up his spine. He turned a little.

The moon was behind the barn, and he was in its shadow. He stared into the darkness, alert for any motion, while he took another match and struck it.

The barn wall appeared in the fitful yellow light, and he saw what had startled him. Someone had painted a big circle on it, and then painted a line through the circle. Jackson took a step back and nearly jumped out of his skin when he bumped into Reynolds.

"What the hell is that supposed to be?" Reynolds said.

"I don't know," Jackson said, "but I don't like it. Not one damn bit."

PROLOGUE

JULY 3

1996

Mr. Marshall was in the lead, and he came to the top of the big hill first. He stopped and motioned for them to stay back, and then stood still for a moment, looking down the other side. After a minute he turned back to them, and Jake saw tears running down his face.

Jake's father cried the day Nana died, but Jake was five then, and only understood a little bit about what was going on. He was older now, and had watched his goldfish, Tuna, die, twisting in the water, trying to right himself, moving less and less and finally not at all. They had buried the fish in the backyard, and now—at seven—Jake knew that when someone died—like Nana and Tuna—you never got to see them again, at least not until you died and went to heaven yourself.

Sometimes his mother cried, but when that happened Jake almost never knew why, and that was worse, because he didn't understand at all.

What he did know was this—that when grown-ups cried, it meant something really bad was going on, usually something Jake didn't understand.

Jake had never seen Mr. Marshall cry. He was a big man, with curly red hair, a big smile, and white teeth. He cracked his knuckles a lot and called everyone "sport."

He always knew what to do.

Except now he was crying and it scared Jake, a lot, so much so that he was on the verge of tears himself. He wanted to be home, watching TV, wrestling with his dad, helping his mom make cookies. Anything but being up here, on this hill, where something bad was happening.

Hank—Mr. Marshall's son—started walking forward. He was twelve, one of the oldest of the kids there.

"Stay where you are, Hank," Mr. Marshall said. "All of you, stay back. You don't need to see this."

"It's true, isn't it?" Hank said. "It's all true." He began walking uphill again, even with his father waving him back, and this time some of the others followed him.

Before the hike, Mr. Marshall had counted heads—fifteen including his own. They had taken the bus from camp to the trailhead and spent all morning hiking to reach this point. It had been awful—Jake's legs were chapped and his feet had blisters on them. Mr. Marshall was the only adult with them. The rest were kids between the ages of six and twelve. Jake was one of the youngest.

Usually when Mr. Marshall said to do or not do something, the kids listened. Not this time, and though he kept waving them back, Hank and the older kids just walked right around him. A girl named Marisol took Jake's hand. She was ten. She had long black hair and was nice to him, although she treated him like a little kid, which bugged him sometimes.

He walked with her to the ridge top, and he saw the spaceship.

The camp wasn't supposed to have a TV, because camp was supposed to be about being outdoors and fresh air and all of that stuff, but Mr. Marshall had one in his cabin, and several of the kids had radios, so they knew about the spaceships. Everyone was talking about them, how big they were, wondering why they were here. Some of the talk Jake didn't understand, but he could tell the adults were scared. Some of them left the camp and didn't come back. Some of them took kids with them. Then, all of a sudden, Mr. Marshall turned off his television and took all of the radios, and everyone that was left at camp was loaded onto the bus.

And now they were here.

"It's not as big as I thought," Jake said. It reminded him of a manhole cover, except that it had a sort of fin on one side. He felt better now, because although it was a little weird-looking, it didn't seem to him that there was anything to cry about.

"Because it's so far away," Marisol said.

Black smoke rose from beneath the spaceship and spread along the ground, curling into the sky and darkening the horizon. The sky was a weird reddish color in that direction, but when Jake looked behind him it was blue, like a normal, sunny day.

"It's all gone," Hank said. The older boy was crying now, along with most of the others. Jake still didn't understand why.

"The city," Marisol whispered. "It's gone, see? They burned it all up. See all the smoke?"

"That's the city?" Jake asked. "That black stuff under the ship? I thought it was its shadow."

"That's not a shadow," she said.

"You mean L.A. is burned up?" Jake said. "The whole city?"

Around the smoking area, he saw what looked like roads and buildings, all made tiny with distance, and he finally started to understand how huge the ship really was.

"Most of it," Marisol said.

"What about my house?" Jake asked. "Can you see it?"

"I don't know where your house is," she said, "but it

doesn't matter. I can't tell where anything was. It's all too different."

"I bet my house is okay," he said.

All of the kids were talking now, yelling, some screaming hysterically, and Jake suddenly felt tears in his own eyes, because it was all really confusing and scary and *wrong*.

"I want my mom," he said. He started crying harder. Marisol put her arm around him, but it didn't help. He started to shake.

He'd been crying a lot lately, but this was different.

Jake hated summertime, because summertime meant camp—sometimes more than one. His parents said it was because they had to work in the summer, but he didn't have school, so he needed to go someplace fun while they were working. The problem was, they had a weird idea of what was fun.

Day camps weren't so bad, because in the afternoon he got to go home, and Mom would read to him at bedtime, and Dad would sing him a song or two. But last year they decided he needed an "outdoor" experience, and sent him to a camp in the mountains, where he didn't get to go home at night, where he had to share a cabin with a bunch of other kids for two weeks. He told them he didn't want to go this year, but they didn't care. It felt like they didn't care about him, like they just wanted him out of the way. Like they hated him.

So when they made him get out of the car, and took his stuff out, it was like he couldn't breathe, and he told them.

"I hate you," he said. Because he thought it would make them understand how he felt, and make them change their minds.

It didn't change anything. They hugged him, told him they loved him, and left him there.

"I won't say it again," he sobbed, gazing down at the

smoke. "I won't ever say I hate them. I'll just say nice things from now on." He turned to Marisol. "Tell Mr. Marshall to call them so I can tell them I didn't mean it."

"Do you see a telephone around here?" she asked.

"When we get back to camp, then," he said.

"I don't think we're going back to camp," Marisol said.

He stared at her.

"Then how will Mom and Dad know where to come get me?" he demanded.

"Jake..." she began, but broke off and looked away. Mr. Marshall and some of the others were pointing.

Mr. Marshall took out his binoculars.

"Fighter jets," he said. He suddenly didn't sound as sad. He sounded stronger, somehow, like he usually did. It made Jake feel better. "F-18s, I think. They're going after the bastards!"

Jake saw them too. They didn't look much bigger than flies at this distance, and compared to the spaceship they were tiny, but everyone seemed excited now, yelling and cheering like they were watching a ball game or something.

He knew what a fighter jet was. He had a model one in his room. He'd been to a Blue Angels show last year, watched the planes do all sorts of crazy stunts. He'd even been thinking he might want to be a pilot when he grew up.

"The aliens are sitting ducks," Hank said. "God, I hope they blow it to pieces."

So did Jake. He watched, feeling like something was missing. If this were in a movie, there would be music, the roar of aircraft engines, all kinds of noise, but from here it was like watching with the sound turned down. With a really, really big screen.

"They hit it!" Mr. Marshall said, watching through his field glasses. Everyone cheered. Even without the binoculars, Jake could see the little yellow explosions, like matches striking on the side of a matchbox. Everyone kept yelling like crazy, as more and more flashes of light appeared on the huge ship.

Then Jake noticed Mr. Marshall slowly lowering the field glasses. He said some words Jake knew, and knew he wasn't supposed to say.

"I don't think they've damaged it at all," Mr. Marshall said.

All of a sudden, something came swarming out of the spaceship like a cloud of gnats. The jet fighters broke out of their neat formations and started flying around like crazy. Bursts of red and orange began to bloom all over the sky, and in moments burning aircraft fell like a fiery rain. Jake wanted to think he was seeing it wrong. Surely the alien ships were the ones exploding.

Eventually it was clear even to him, though, that not a single alien craft had been shot down. No one was shouting anymore. They just watched silently as the F-18s grew fewer and fewer in number. Finally, the remaining planes flew away, pursued by the alien fighters.

"We lost," Hank whispered. He said it really low, but since no one else was talking, everyone heard him.

"They didn't even have a chance."

That wasn't how it was supposed to be, Jake knew. The good guys were always supposed to have a chance. They were supposed to *win*. When someone blew a city up, they weren't just supposed to get away with it.

"I want my mom and dad," Jake said.

"Me too," Marisol said. "Maybe..."

She didn't finish.

Mr. Marshall put away his field glasses. He wasn't crying anymore. He looked sort of sad, but he also looked determined, the way he did when he wouldn't take no for an answer.

"Come on," he said. "We've got to go."

"Where, Dad?" Hank said. "Where can we go?"

"Someplace safe," Mr. Marshall said.

1

JULY
1996

When London was destroyed, Dikembe Umbutu was in Oxford with Brian Aldridge, a mate from university. They had started the previous evening at the Old Tom Gristle, a favorite pub of theirs. On any other day they probably would have been discussing football, politics, girls—their antics as seniors—but like everyone else in the place, today their eyes were glued to the television. And not because a game was on.

Typically, the media coverage focused largely on the ships over Western European and American cities, but there was a brief report about the monsters hovering over Lagos, Nigeria, and Dakar, Senegal, which for Dikembe were closer to home.

Of course, the one overshadowing London was nearer to *him*, and everyone else in the Old Tom.

Closing time came, but the owner didn't shut down. The place became more crowded with people who didn't quite believe what was going on. One older gentleman insisted that it was all a hoax, à la the *War of the Worlds* radio broadcast. The idea caught on, and drinking games were invented. As dawn approached, Dikembe switched from beer to coffee and bought a hot breakfast.

Halfway through the meal, the television showed the

torching of London. He and Brian watched, unbelieving, as some of the world's greatest cities were laid to waste in an instant.

Dikembe finished his coffee and stood up. He stuck out his hand for Brian to shake.

"I'll see you, old fellow," he said. "I have to go."

"What?" Brian said. His face was so drained of color, it nearly matched his cottony hair. "Where do you think you're going?"

"Home," Dikembe said. "May I borrow your bicycle?"

"You can have it, mate," Brian said, "but you'll have to pump the tires way up to cross the Channel."

"I'll deal with that when I get there," he said. They shook hands and parted company, as around them the world unraveled.

The bicycle proved the way to go. The main roads were packed, not so much with refugees from London— there weren't very many of those—but with people fleeing every other city, fearing they were next.

*   *   *

In some cases, they were right. Birmingham and Liverpool were annihilated within the next day. News of the rest of the world was hard to come by on the road.

He stopped for a sandwich and some crisps at a roadside convenience store whose owner still had the stones and the greed to remain open. Everything was double price. He didn't flinch about it though, guessing that the ten pounds he'd paid would be worth slightly less than dog piss in a day or two.

He rode south and west toward the coast, skirting very wide around where London used to be, often going cross-country when the roads were too mad. He wasn't sure what he expected—squads of aliens on the march, fliers murdering people from the air—but if the world was ending, the scenery didn't know it in the fields and meadows of the West Country.

He first thought to go to Portsmouth, but remembered there was a Navy presence there the aliens might be interested in blasting, so he went farther west to the little resort town of Weymouth. He reached it, exhausted, about eight o'clock in the evening. He couldn't find a room, but he did find another pub, where he ate and watched the television, which had maddeningly little to say, especially about his homeland. In England and Europe, the pattern was clear—each ship destroyed a city and then moved on to the next. So Lagos was finished. What about Kinshasa? Was it now a smoking ruin like London and Paris? From what he gathered, the first targets had been chosen by size, and some military installations had been targeted, as well.

"Is this seat taken?" someone asked.

He looked up from the well of his thoughts and saw a young woman with slightly wavy flaxen hair and a dimpled chin.

"No," he said. "Please." He stood and pulled out the chair for her.

"Oh," she said. "A gentleman." She craned her neck in an exaggerated way. "A very tall gentleman. You don't see that a lot these days. The gentleman part." She was about his age, maybe twenty-five. Her eyes were gray, and she had a nice smile, judging from the single one she had let slip when he pulled the chair out.

"I still can't believe it," she said, looking up at the television. "It's like science fiction. So unreal."

"It's—difficult," he said.

"Did you have anyone—in any of the cities?" she asked.

He shook his head. "Not really. Not that I know of. Where I'm from is pretty far from any major city. And you?"

She nodded. "I'm from Atlanta," she said, a little sadly. He had noticed the American accent, but had declined to ask about it. People were always making assumptions about him and where he was from, or else fishing to find out. He generally tried not to do the same, and found that people usually wanted to tell you about themselves anyway.

"Atlanta had time to evacuate," he said.

"I know," she replied. "I hope they made it out. They would have tried, but there's no place to call, you know? Even if the phones were working."

"I know," he said. He had tried placing a few calls, to no effect. "Look, my name is Dikembe. And you are?"

"Oh," she said. "Sorry, misplaced my manners. I'm Hailey. Pleased to meet you."

"Hailey, may I fetch you a lager?"

"Yes sir," she said. "You certainly may."

He pushed his way politely through the crowd at the bar and ordered the drinks from a young woman with purple hair wearing a railroad engineer's cap.

"So what brought you to Weymouth?" Hailey asked when he returned.

"Yesterday I was in Oxford," he replied. "Now I'm trying to return home."

She nodded. He thought she would ask him if his home was Africa, as if it was a country instead of a continent. He got that a lot.

She surprised him.

"Why Oxford then?" she asked.

"School," he said.

"Oh," she said, dipping her finger in the foamy head of her beer. "College man. What did you study?"

"Art," he said. He took a drink.

"Art," she repeated. "Every parent's dream, right? An art major at an expensive school."

Dikembe smiled.

"My father did not approve," he admitted. "Drawing and painting aren't fit pursuits for a man, especially an Umbutu man. I finished my degree two years ago, but I could never quite bring myself to go home. I've been working up to a gallery exhibition…" He trailed off, realizing.

"What is it?"

"Well," he said. "My studio was actually in London, in Earl's Court. I was just visiting a friend in Oxford."

"Lucky you," she said. "Best visit you ever made."

He thought about the paintings, two years of work…

"Sure," he said. "Lucky me."

"And you choose to go home now?" she said. "Why the change of heart?"

He gestured at the television, although at the moment it displayed only static. "Why do you think? I should have returned a long time ago. Now I may have waited too long."

She took a lingering sip of her beer, looking thoughtful.

"I came over here to go to school too," she said, "but it didn't turn out to be my thing. I ended up working on yachts instead."

"Yachts?" he said. "That must be interesting."

"It's a living," she said. "The travel is fun—I've been a lot of places I never imagined I would see—and the owner is almost never on board, so we're pretty much left to do our own thing. I'm still young, footloose. Surrounded by luxury, even if it doesn't belong to me. Yeah, it's kinda cool."

"Why own a yacht if you're not going to be on it?" Dikembe wondered.

She shrugged. "He'll call and say, 'Take the boat to Marseilles.' Or Sydney, or wherever. Then he'll fly in, throw a big party on the yacht for his very important guests, and then fly out, leaving us to clean up and have a few parties of our own."

They had a few more drinks. She told him about working

for a Russian mobster and he told her about growing up on the savanna, and for a little while they almost forgot what was happening in the world around them. Yet it crept back in. Dikembe mused that his handful of paintings weren't the greatest loss to culture.

"The Louvre is gone," he said. "The British Museum. The Prado. The Met. MOMA."

"The house I grew up in," Hailey countered. "The World of Coke. My parents, maybe." She sighed. "The two of us, tomorrow or the next day, if things keep going this way. They're beating the hell out of us. What do they want?"

"I don't know," Dikembe said. "Maybe they just don't like cities."

"We're never going to get this off our minds with that thing on." She waved at the television. It was now replaying footage of London going up in flames.

"What do you suggest?" he asked.

"There's booze on the boat," she said. Her expression was somewhere between shy and artful. He wasn't sure which was affected.

* * *

Lao Lei climbed into the cockpit of the Shenyang J-8, familiarizing himself with the controls as quickly as he could. He had trained and flown somewhat more modern jets, most of which were now piles of wreckage near the ruin that was once Beijing.

"That's okay," he said to the plane. "You and I, we're going to be friends." He started through his checklist, just as the others in his squadron were doing.

Lu, one of the ground crew, looked up at him.

"Do you believe it?" Lu asked him. "Do you think the American plan is real?"

Lei shrugged. "I don't care," he said. "Real, or not real.

Maybe they can bring down the shields. Maybe it's just wishful thinking. My job is to fly and fight, and die if it comes to that. I know myself, I know my enemy. I fear nothing."

"Sun Tzu?" Lu said.

"I may be paraphrasing," Lei admitted.

Lu nodded. "What have you named this one?" he asked.

"*Meifeng*," he said. "Beautiful Wind."

"That's a good name," Lu said. "A little odd—"

The radio crackled. It was time.

Lu bowed to him. "Good luck," he said.

"And to you, my friend," Lei said.

* * *

As the monstrous ship loomed on the horizon, everything seemed to slow down. They were coming from the east, and the sun was setting beyond the ship, so its shadow rose toward them. There was a bit of chatter, but most of the pilots were silent.

It seemed to take a long time to reach it, like walking toward a distant mountain.

Lei's anger and grief were so closely tied together that he could not tell them apart, and both had been gnawing his soul away from the inside out. Now he felt almost quiet. He remembered his wife, brushing the lock of hair from her face. He remembered when they met, how young they were, how alive the world had seemed.

He thought of Rain, his daughter, of singing a lullaby to her as he held her by the light of a candle. Some part of him had been disappointed, of course. Under the one-child policy, a daughter meant the end of his father's line—but she had been so beautiful, so quick and intelligent, that any discontent on his part had vanished, and he thought only of the years ahead, of watching her unfold, reveal herself, become who she was meant to become.

If they failed today—if *he* failed—that would never happen. His wife was already entombed in the ashes of Beijing. He would never know her touch or see her smile again, and maybe he would never see Rain again either.

But Rain was going to live. If he had anything at all to say about it, his daughter would grow to be a woman.

He was carrying missiles, so he had something to say about it.

"Fighters!" someone shouted, and ahead he saw flickers of green light as the alien craft disgorged from their carrier and began attacking the slender Chinese force.

"Come along, *Meifeng*," Lei said. "Come along, my beautiful wind." With a clear heart and terrible purpose, Lao Lei accelerated toward the enemy.

* * *

Dikembe awoke to cheering. He sat up, rubbing his eyes, wondering if he was still in some sort of dream.

"What the hell?" Hailey swore. She looked pleasantly disheveled and slightly cross.

But she smiled when she saw him.

"Hey, you," she said. She looked around. "Not dead yet."

He remembered Scotch and the sea air, and holding her. Her standing on tiptoe to kiss him…

Someone banged on her cabin door.

"Hailey, get out here," the someone yelled.

Dikembe put on his shirt and slacks as Hailey drew on a T-shirt and blue shorts. Then they made their way to the deck, where a party was in progress, and fine champagne was flowing freely.

"What's going on?" Hailey asked a young man with unfortunate sideburns, who was handing her a flute of Dom Perignon.

"What's going on," the fellow said, "is we kicked their asses."

"The aliens," Dikembe said dubiously.

The fellow pointed to a large-screen TV set up on the deck. It displayed images of the huge spaceships, crashed and burning. A glance around the little port revealed revelers in the streets.

Sideburns offered him some of the bubbly, and in a bit of a daze, he took it.

"Cheers," he said.

*   *   *

The euphoria following the defeat of the alien fleet had a half-life of hours. Estimates put the death toll in England alone at more than four million, and more than a million were now homeless. The government was in a shambles, as were most governments everywhere.

Global mortality was guessed to be in the billions, and the aliens hadn't been entirely defeated.

At least not all of them.

Their ships seemed to have all been destroyed, but in the areas where they crashed, reports were on the rise of encounters with armed survivors. In England that was mostly in the north, which only meant more refugees were headed for the south and for Europe, where many hoped things might be better. So Dikembe knew he had to work fast. The docks were already starting to get crowded. He needed to stay ahead of the next wave of refugees, or he might drown in them.

Hailey had disappeared. He spent a few precious minutes finding her. She was in a deck chair near the bow, well on her way to being drunk again.

"Hey, end-of-the-world buddy," she said. "What's up?"

"I just wanted to say goodbye," he said. "I need to find

passage to Europe before everything fills up."

She stood a little shakily and kissed him.

"Umm, last time I checked," she said, "you were already on a boat."

"Of course," he said. "But I couldn't ask—"

"You didn't," she said. "Anyway, we heard from the boss, who seems to have survived. We're headed for Greece, but we're not in a hurry. I think we can drop you somewhere convenient on the way. Algiers, maybe?"

"That would be—really good," he said. "Thank you."

"Cool," she said. "You can bunk with me in the meantime. If you want. If you can handle the company. Or I can find you a stateroom."

"I would be happy to share with you," he said. "If you can stand the company."

* * *

Mr. Marshall looked at them across the small fire. For a while, it seemed like that was all he was going to do, but finally he cleared his throat and began speaking.

"So I know some of you are scared," he said. "So am I. I've been thinking what the best thing to do is, and for right now, I think we should stay right here. We're about as deep in the national forest as we can get, and from what we've seen of the aliens, they seem mostly interested in cities. At least, that's where they started. Up here, I don't think we'll draw their attention."

"How do you know?" Hank asked. "We don't even know what they want." He massaged an ankle and winced as he spoke. He'd gotten tangled in some barbed wire on their hike back down the mountain.

"That's a good point, Hank," Mr. Marshall said, "but until we have more information, it just seems safer up here. We still have gas in the bus if we need to leave. In the meantime, we need to focus on surviving, on living off the land. There's fish in the lake and food in the woods, and we have some supplies. We're going to be alright."

Jake raised his hand.

"Jake?"

"Mr. Marshall, how are my parents going to find me way up here?" he asked.

"Oh, jeez, kid," Hank said. "Grow up."

"Hank," Mr. Marshall said. "There's no need for that." He turned his attention back to Jake. "I don't know the answer to that. I only know that your parents would want me to keep you safe. Do you understand?"

Jake just stared at him. It was like no one grasped what he wanted. But he didn't say anything.

Later he helped gather wood and drew water to be boiled for drinking. At night, they slept in the bus. The older kids managed to catch a few fish, but the food that was supposed to be in the woods seemed to be pretty well hidden.

Meanwhile, Hank was getting sick. His leg swelled up and he slept a lot, although he yelled in his sleep. When Jake was close he noticed that the leg smelled really bad. Mr. Marshall got more and more worried, and after five days he called them back together and told them they were getting back on the bus. He said there was a small town nearby that should have a hospital.

Jake was happy to be back on the bus, to watch the trees go by as it bumped along. If they were going to a town, maybe his parents would be there. If not, he might be able to use a phone to somehow find them. It was better than being in the woods, starving.

They drove a few hours, and then Mr. Marshall stopped the bus. He got out, and after a minute everybody else followed him.

They were still in the hills, but down below they

could see the small town Mr. Marshall had been talking about—just a few buildings and a water tower. Only now the town was completely surrounded by cars, vans, and campers. Dozens of big green tents stood along one edge, near the highway.

"There must be thousands," Mr. Marshall said. "Tens of thousands."

"Aliens?" Marisol asked.

Mr. Marshall shook his head. "They must be refugees, like us," he said. "See those tents? Those are army tents. So we still have an army."

"That's good, right?" Jake said.

"Yes," Mr. Marshall said, looking out over the makeshift settlement. He didn't sound completely convinced, though.

Still on the bus, Hank moaned.

"Back on the bus," Mr. Marshall said. "Let's hope they have room for a few more."

2

AUGUST

"Oh, no you did not," Steve Hiller shouted, banking hard to the left as a surface-to-air missile tore through the space where his F-18 would have met it, had he not noticed it in time. He needed to yank the stick back immediately to avoid colliding with the pilot who was supposed to be his wingman, but who was apparently oblivious both to the missile and Hiller's maneuver.

"Wake up over there, Williams," he shouted. "Do you see what you almost did? Do you see? Nearly banged up my sweet ride."

"I'm sorry, Knight One," Williams came back.

"Sorry, huh? Oh, well, that's okay then. I ain't mad."

"Sir," Williams said. "I—"

"It's *alright*," Hiller said. "We're all okay. Just—try and have a little situational awareness over there. Know what I'm saying?"

"Yes, sir."

Just then a spray of green energy stuttered by, nearly hitting his wing, and Williams turned hard to the left, even though he was in no danger from the attack.

"Newbies," Hiller muttered under his breath. Most of the experienced pilots were long gone, killed trying to take out the destroyers—alien ships fifteen miles in diameter surrounded by energy shields that could stop a nuke. He had been among the first to attempt to take one down, and it hadn't gone so well, but when it became clear it was a pointless exercise, the president had called off the attack.

Here, in Russia, they hadn't accepted defeat as quickly, sending squadron after squadron at the alien craft, so by the time the city killers were finally taken out, they had no air force left to speak of.

That might have been one thing if their July 4th victory had been complete—but it hadn't been. It still wasn't certain how many aliens the ships had carried. Based on what he had seen in the mother ship, it might have been millions, and of those millions some fraction survived the crash, at least in some cases.

So his vacation—damn, his *honeymoon*—had lasted less than a day. Pilots were just too few and valuable to be idle.

Fortunately, the aliens that survived were pretty poorly organized, and with a little air support the infantry had mopped them up fairly quickly back in the States, killing or capturing the vast majority of the aliens in just a few days.

Other places—like here—things weren't going as well. The city killer that destroyed Moscow had moved on to a more-or-less secret military installation, a holdover from Soviet times. A few thousand of the aliens were dug in, and without air support the Russian infantry was having a hard time cracking their perimeter. The destruction of the mother ship had deprived the enemy's aerial fighters of power, but hadn't affected their small arms, so they were still shooting green shit at him. That he was used to, but the surface-to-air missile—that was new.

They must have learned how to use human weapons.

He circled back in time to see another missile rise up from a mobile launcher.

"Gotcha," he said. He painted the launcher with a laser and then fired an air-to-surface missile.

He watched it detonate with a satisfying bloom of smoke and flame.

"Okay, fellahs, let's make another pass," he said. As they made the turn, the surface-to-air fire intensified exponentially, becoming a hard green sleet. He heard Alvarez swear.

"Hang in there," Hiller said.

"I can't see anything," Alvarez said. "My cockpit is compromised."

"Pull up," Hiller advised. "Get clear."

"I can't—" the other pilot's voice cut off abruptly, and off to Hiller's four o'clock, he saw Alvarez's plane shred apart.

"Damn it!" he snarled, launching another missile into one of the buildings from which much of the enemy fire seemed to be coming. Then he pulled up. "Everybody get clear and regroup," he said. "We need to think about this here for a second."

"Knight One," Control said. "Be advised. You have incoming."

"Incoming? Incoming what?"

"Medium range surface-to-air missiles. Big ones, Krugs maybe, four of them."

He checked his radar. "Yeah, I see 'em. Damn, talk about big guns."

"I've got visual," Williams said. "Holy crap."

"One's got a lock on me," Knight Four said. He was trying to keep the panic out of his voice and not doing a great job of it.

"Keep your head," Hiller said. "You've got a brain, it doesn't."

"Yes, sir."

"See," Hiller said. "One has a lock on me too. You

don't hear me gettin' all panicky, do you?"

In fact, he didn't feel too good about it. The damn thing was *fast*.

He made a hard break down and back toward alpha target, deploying flares as he did so. With any luck, flying back into the maelstrom would confuse whatever guidance system the thing was using. It also increased his odds of being fried by alien energy weapons, but at the moment that was the lesser threat.

He went so low he nearly plowed into the ground, then pulled up so hard the g-forces put black spots dancing before his eyes. It was worth it, though, because the damn thing went off in an airburst that leveled half of alpha target.

"Yeah," he shouted. "*That's* what you get!" His elation was short lived, however, when he realized that two more of his pilots were gone.

"Alright," he said. "Where'd that come from?"

"Near the big hangar, your beta target," Control informed him.

"Yeah, well beta just became alpha," he said. He turned and sped toward their second target, about four klicks away. He was halfway there when another missile leapt up to greet him. "Well, this is gettin' *way* too real," he said.

He got a lock on it, launched one of his air-to-surface missiles, and broke hard to the right. This time he really did almost pass out, but he knew he couldn't stop pushing. Without knowing exactly what the other missile was, he couldn't be certain of its capabilities—but it was big, much bigger than his Maverick, which meant that it should be slower and less maneuverable.

It also had a head start.

He banked again, as he saw the blips on his radar rush toward convergence. Then he knew he had to eject. He was reaching to do it when the concussion hit him.

His first thought was that it was all over.

His second was that he was still thinking, and the F-18 was in the air, albeit completely out of control. He managed to kill the roll, but the stick was half dead in his hand, and the plane was becoming increasingly less responsive. He was in a dive and had a date with the dirt in about ten seconds.

Cursing, he ejected, knowing he had probably waited too long.

Jasmine, he thought. *Dylan*.

There hadn't been enough time.

* * *

"Okay, Munchkin," Patricia's father said gently. "I think it's time for bed." He reached for the remote on the bedside stand.

"Please, Daddy," she pleaded. "Just one more?"

"You've already said that twice," he said, "and I've given in twice. Anyway, you've seen all of these ten times."

That was true. Patricia remembered that, not so long ago, there were all sorts of things on TV. Now they just had a few video tapes they watched over and over again. She liked it anyway, and looked forward to nightly TV with her daddy, because it made her feel safe. Like nothing had changed.

Even though everything had changed.

He turned off the television.

"Can I stay in here with you?" she asked. "I don't want to go to my room. I don't want to be alone."

He nodded, sighed, and tousled her hair. "Sure," he said.

"And can we leave the bathroom light on?" she pleaded.

"Yes ma'am," he said. He got up and turned off the bedroom light, turned on the bathroom light, and half closed the door.

"Daddy?" she said. "When do we get to go back to our old house?"

"Patricia," he said, very gently. "Haven't we talked about this?"

"I know," she said, "but I really want to go back there. I'm tired of being underground."

"But we can't, sweetheart," he said. "Not yet. Our old house is gone—but you know what? We're going to build a new one, right where it was before. You just have to wait a little while."

"How long?" she asked.

"I don't know," he said. "I've already talked to some very important people about it, and we should get started soon."

"Nobody is more important than you, Daddy," she said.

He smiled. "Well, I'm glad you think so, but everyone is important, you know. Now get some sleep."

She settled under the covers, closed her eyes and tried to imagine what their new house would be like. Maybe they could have a trampoline room this time. But no matter what else the new house had, there was one thing it wouldn't have.

Mommy. Because Mommy was asleep, and she wasn't going to wake up.

Patricia wept a little, but quietly. She was tired, and soon fell asleep anyway.

What woke her, she wasn't sure at first, but then her father screamed again, and she knew. He was sitting straight up in the bed, and his eyes were open, like he was staring at something horrible, but there was nothing there.

"Daddy!" She grabbed his arm, and felt her heart pounding in her chest. He didn't look at her, but he didn't scream again—he just sat, breathing hard, looking at nothing. His lips were moving a little, but he wasn't saying anything.

Someone knocked on the door.

"Are you okay, sir? Sir?"

"Daddy!" Patricia said again.

He blinked, and put his hand to his forehead. He looked down at her, and over to the door.

"It's okay," he said. "Just a nightmare. I'm alright." He patted her arm. "I'm okay," he said.

*　　*　　*

Hiller was still trying to sort up from down when something tried to knock all of his guts out. Everything went very white, like an overdeveloped photograph, and for a moment he couldn't remember what was happening. Then it came back to him and he groped for his sidearm. The air was thick with the stink of burning jet fuel.

As his sight came back and the spinning in his head slowed a bit, he managed to detach his parachute and begin to get his bearings. With any luck, he had come down on the Russian side of the situation.

No, it seemed he'd used up a lot of his luck escaping the alien mother ship.

He had landed on the roof of a two-story building, which was probably the only reason the ETs weren't swarming all over him. He lay flat, trying to assess the situation. The air was so full of smoke, there was at least a chance he hadn't been seen yet, and he wasn't in a hurry to help them spot his location.

He didn't see any F-18s. He hoped they hadn't all been blown out of the sky.

Through the smoke, he saw aliens, lots of them, decked out in their exoskeletons. Still no sign that they knew of his whereabouts, or that he had even survived. Maybe he hadn't used up all of his luck after all. Now all he had to do was travel unseen through a few hundred aliens, reach the perimeter, and not get killed by friendly fire.

All good.

He scooted closer to the edge of the roof for a better look, and found himself looking down on the roof of a lower part of the building. For a few seconds he wasn't sure what he was seeing. Part of it was an anti-aircraft rocket launcher—not an alien weapon, but Russian-built. The launcher and its operator were facing away from him, but as the weapon swiveled to the right, he understood.

The operator was human, but an alien crouched behind him, holding him with the tentacles that sprouted from the back of its exoskeleton.

In 1947, an alien craft had crashed near Roswell, New Mexico, and for forty-nine years scientists had been studying the alien craft and the bodies of the creatures that had piloted it Because the creatures lacked vocal cords—and for several other reasons—the investigators early on speculated that they communicated by some sort of voodoo-telepathy bullshit.

They were only too right.

Not only could the aliens use it to communicate, they could use it as a weapon. The alien Hiller himself captured had nearly killed President Whitmore and put the lead scientist on the project—Dr. Okun—into a catatonic state he still hadn't recovered from. This one was flat-out controlling a guy, like a puppet master.

He reconnoitered the rest of the rooftop and found that the other four sides presented him with a two-story jump. He was banged up enough as it was, without risking a twisted ankle or even a broken leg. He would do it if he had to, obviously, and the clock was ticking, because it was already well past noon. The aliens could see better at night than he could, due to night vision built or grown into their suits—the science guys were still trying to figure that stuff out. So he had to make a move sooner, rather than later.

*   *   *

He'd been waiting no more than ten minutes when he heard jets coming. When he saw them, he felt like whooping for joy, but then he noticed that of the nine they'd had at the start of the day, he now counted only three.

He was a little less excited when it occurred to him that they were coming to finish the job they had begun before the missile attack—and he was sitting pretty much on the bullseye. Moving quickly, he checked his sidearm and scrambled over to where he could see the anti-aircraft gun and its hybrid operating team.

The "crew" was in motion, tracking one of the approaching Knights.

"Oh, no, I don't *think* so," he said. He dropped the ten feet down to the lower roof and started sprinting toward the launcher. It felt good—he was tired of hiding. The alien started to turn at the last second, whipping a tentacle toward him, but he already had it in his sights. He put four bullets in its face before it went down.

The man slumped to the rooftop. Hiller was afraid one of the rounds had hit him, but the Russian was still alive, and Hiller didn't see any wounds. He grabbed the fellow and started dragging him across the roof. When he got to the far edge, he heaved the soldier onto his shoulder.

"This is gonna hurt," he said, and he jumped just as the F-18s screamed overhead. A missile took out the rocket launcher and most of the building. Hiller hit the ground with the weight of two men—a sharp pain in his ankle caused him to buckle and fall. Debris rained down, but he and the Russian were protected from the explosion, which hadn't taken down the far end of the structure.

"I knew it," he groaned. "I *knew* that was going to happen." He rolled over and tried to stand, hoping the ankle wasn't broken.

The Russian was already on his feet. His eyes were wide, ice-blue. His hands were gripped into fists.

"*Tchort*!" he screamed. "*Tchort v moi golovye*!"

Then he backed away, turned, and ran.

"Yeah," Hiller said. "You're welcome."

The F-18s had made their pass—smoke and flames were everywhere. Hiller began to limp as fast as he could toward the allied lines. After about a hundred yards he hunkered down behind what was left of a wall and looked back.

The flash of green energy that disintegrated the concrete about six inches from his face wasn't encouraging, and he ducked way down. He couldn't be sure how many were following him, but thought he'd spotted as many as three.

"It's a cakewalk," he said. "Ain't nothin' but a cakewalk."

He sprang up and ran for the next cover, a cluster of buildings another twenty yards away, trying to ignore the grinding pain in his ankle. If it wasn't broken, he thought it was doing a damn good imitation.

He came under fire just as he ducked behind the nearest structure. He looked back and saw them coming over the first wall, about ten of them. They were gaining on him.

"Oh, no, fellahs," he said. He picked one and started squeezing off rounds. His first two kicked up the dirt, but then he got two solid hits on one of them, and it staggered. The others came on.

He looked toward the United Nations positions. All that separated him from them was about two hundred yards of open ground. About a hundred and ninety-nine too many.

He changed clips and waited for the aliens to get closer, determined to take a few more with him.

Then he heard the thunder of low-flying jets. He threw

himself flat behind the building as the oncoming enemies vanished in a blaze of napalm. Even with concrete protecting him, the heat was shocking. He smelled something burning and realized it was his own hair.

When it was over, he climbed painfully to his feet and continued toward the Russian lines, turning now and then to make sure none of the aliens had survived to follow him.

They hadn't and they didn't.

As he approached the allies he lit his cigar, thinking that lately he had spent way too much time walking away from fires.

3

AUGUST

The sea the Romans had once called "Our Sea" had been a busy place for millennia, but now it was dangerously awash with craft from aircraft carriers to rafts made of plastic jugs strapped together.

Dikembe shuddered to think how many hundreds or thousands must be dying daily there on the Mediterranean, fleeing death and destruction only to encounter more. The captain of the yacht, a Belgian named Jaan, gave orders to rescue those nearest to drowning, but drew the line at a hundred, a quota they quickly filled.

Without Hailey and the crew, Dikembe was acutely aware that he would probably be among those masses doomed to reach the bed of the Mediterranean rather than the farther shore they sought. When it was time for him to go, he expressed his thanks to her as best he could.

"You could just stay on with us," she suggested.

"I appreciate that..." he said, "and everything else. But—"

"You need to get home," she said. "I know. If I knew where my parents were, I'd be there so fast..."

"I truly hope they're okay," he said.

"Me too," she said. She leaned up and kissed him.

"Okay," she said. "I've got a little present for you.

It's not really mine to give, but in the shuffle, I don't think it will be missed."

The "present"—to his delight—turned out to be a motorcycle.

* * *

Algiers was rubble, so they dropped him in Tunis, where he began the dangerous, dubious business of crossing the Sahara.

The days blurred together. Few of the roads he traveled were paved for any great length, and many were little more than tracks. Finding fuel was at times challenging. He had American dollars, in addition to his pounds, which some people were still accepting. At other times he had to perform chores to fill up. On those occasions he felt more honest.

Most of the great cities on the African continent were on or near the sea, so the interior hadn't been as severely affected, especially the rural regions. Life went on for many people as it had for centuries. In some villages he was met with great hospitality and offered food, drink, and shelter, even when the people had little for themselves.

There were hot spots, places where old tribal grievances were stirring up, just as there had been before the aliens came. Some borders were virtually unmanned, others were heavily guarded, and a few seemed to have shifted. On the way he heard a great deal of rumor and few facts. Nairobi had been destroyed, and Kinshasa, of that he could be fairly certain. The rest he took with a grain of salt.

At the end of a week, home was close enough he could almost smell it. The last of his journey took him through a mosaic of woodland and savanna. It was well into the wet season, and the enormous sky was always changing. Rain and wind bent the tall grass in long waves, like a restless pale green sea. Golden spears of sunlight struck through the charcoal hearts of the clouds. Come early afternoon, a double rainbow arced across the heavens. In the far distance, amongst the storm clouds clinging to the horizon, he thought he made out a peculiarly regular shape, almost like a vast, shallow dome. He thought that it might be the smoke of a massive grass fire, obscured by the clouds and distance.

On the downside, when the rains let up he plowed through swarms of mosquitos and gnats so thick that he and the bike were thoroughly, unpleasantly coated in spattered bug.

He realized how unconsciously claustrophobic he'd felt in England, how constrained. He had never known until now what a claim this place had on him, that his blood and bones were the rainwater and bedrock of this country. Even his name, his beloved name. He was beginning to understand his father's obsession with it.

Umbutu was this place as much as it was a word.

He rolled into a village he knew, where he hoped to learn something of current events. He found it savaged and abandoned, most of its few structures burned to the ground. The wet char of it had a sharp smell of lye. He didn't see any bodies, thankfully.

He pressed on as the deep of the sky darkened. The tall grass and isolated trees rustled in a hot, inconstant breeze, and he smelled something else, another burnt scent, but this one more industrial, somehow, as if a chemical plant had exploded or a load of polyester slacks had been set aflame.

As the sky shifted from gray to gunmetal, he saw lights in the distance. It was hard to tell, but he thought they might be automobile headlamps. Then something big moved in the grass off to his right. He couldn't tell what sort of animal he had disturbed, but it probably wasn't good. He pushed forward on the throttle, glancing back, trying to get a better look, but all he saw was a shadow— following him, and at terrific speed.

Something was off to his left as well, and he abruptly realized he was being driven. By what? Wild dogs? Hyenas? He bore down on the gas, but they began closing in, whatever they were. The light from his lamp picked out one ahead of him, and with a sudden chill as from fever he saw a mass of tentacles writhing about, like a nest of snakes all striking toward him at once.

"*Merde*," he yelped.

Then there was a flash of light and something struck the front wheel of the bike. With an awful rush the vehicle flipped end-over-end. He heard a sort of demented chattering, felt bubbles of nightmare forming in his brain. Then he bounced on the hard-packed savanna dirt.

Hurting in every bone and muscle, Dikembe scrambled to his feet in time to see it stoop over him. He had seen a few images. He hadn't expected them to be so big. Tentacles reached for him and he backpedaled, balling his fists. The noise in his head grew louder, more insistent.

Suddenly something went hurtling past him from behind. It rolled between the weird, bent-the-wrong-way legs of the monster and then sprang up at its back, the shadow of a giant. The scene was instantly flooded with light, also coming from behind him. An intense, ammonia-like smell burnt its way into his nostrils.

The alien tried to turn to face its attacker, but it was too late. Its assailant was a man, a big man wielding a pair of machetes, and he had already cut off most of the thing's tentacles. Although mouthless, the creature somehow managed to scream. More men came running by him, also armed with machetes, uttering war cries as they went at the aliens in the tall grass.

In a few moments, the creatures were all down. The

man who had saved him stood up from the twitching remains of the thing and grinned. Dikembe recognized the face.

It was his own, or very nearly so.

"Nice work, big brother," the man said. "You led them straight to us."

"Bakari?" he gasped.

"Don't be so surprised," Dikembe's twin said. "Didn't you think we could get along without you?"

* * *

Bakari and his men took Dikembe to a temporary camp on some high ground about a half a mile away. There he had meat for the first time since leaving the yacht, unless he counted caterpillars. It was probably bush meat of some sort, but he didn't ask what kind.

By the flickering fire, watching the sparks rise like star seeds, Dikembe listened as his brother told him of the war.

"Mom was in Kinshasa, on a shopping trip," he said.

"Oh, no—" Dikembe began.

"Easy," his twin said. "She made it out. The ship that hit Lagos went to Kinshasa next, but it took a bit of time. Dad sent a helicopter."

"You might have started with her being okay—" Dikembe said "—to spare me the cardiac arrest."

"He tried like hell to get hold of you, too," Bakari said. "We thought you died in London."

"I was visiting a friend," Dikembe said. "I tried to call, but the lines were all tied up." He poked at the fire. "How is the old man?"

"Stubborn, as usual. The whole world is turned upside down. It's not even clear who is in charge, nationally. All Dad knows is, that this is his territory, Umbutu territory, and he won't budge. He was stubborn enough when we had a working government, such as it was. Now... well, we've had a few offers of help in troops and materiel from other places."

"How did that go?"

"He didn't chop the emissaries' hands off before sending them packing, at least, but he's not letting anyone in."

"So where is the ship these things are coming from?" Dikembe asked.

"Northeast, near Little Babale."

"That's not far," Dikembe said.

"No it isn't," his brother agreed. "It's far too near. If it was light now, you would see it. I'm surprised you didn't notice it coming in."

"There were clouds covering the horizon," Dikembe said, but he remembered the vague dome shape.

"That wasn't all clouds," Bakari said. "It's... big." He reached into a bag and pulled out a bottle of Scotch. "You were supposed to bring the Scotch, remember? When you finally returned."

Dikembe smiled and nodded his head.

"I'm sorry," he said. "Getting a good single malt wasn't exactly the thing on the top of my head. I only wanted to get back here, even if only to die. Bakari, I've never felt anything so powerfully in my life."

"And here you are," Bakari said. "You and I, reunited for our drink. Though we'll have to make do with a blend."

"I think I'll manage," Dikembe said. He took a sip from the bottle. "Good," he said.

"It isn't bad," Bakari said.

"So how did you shoot it down?" Dikembe asked. "The spaceship. I mean, where was it going? I heard a different ship was taken down near Nairobi?"

"Oh," Bakari said. "We didn't shoot it down. We're pretty sure it just fell, and not from far up. It may even have landed."

"So how many aliens...?"

"We've killed more than two thousand," Bakari said. "They just keep coming, and we've lost..." He sighed and shook his head. "A lot. They're everywhere, and they do things to our minds. I know it sounds strange to say."

"No," Dikembe said. "I felt something, just before you killed them. Like insects in my skull."

Bakari tapped his head. "They can get in here, make us do things if they get those tentacles on us—sometimes when they don't, if they're close enough. And they can feel us, track us the way a dog can follow a scent. It's hard to surprise them, but we're figuring it out. And we have some artillery, which they don't. We've also managed to capture some of their energy weapons, although they're a little strange to use."

"Plus you have your very high-tech machetes," Dikembe said.

"Machetes don't jam or run out of ammunition," Bakari pointed out. "In some ways they work better than guns—there's a sort of seam in their armor—well, you'll learn." He took another drink. "If I had tried to shoot it, I might have killed you."

"Very thoughtful," Dikembe said. "I appreciate it." As he took another drink, he noticed something on his twin's arm—it appeared as if a series of hash marks had been tattooed there.

"What's that?" he asked. "The number of hearts you've broken?"

Bakari uttered a sharp, humorless bark of a laugh.

"In a sense," he said. He pulled the short sleeve of his shirt up to reveal his shoulder. Above the hash marks was tattooed the image of an alien head.

"Oh," Dikembe said. "I see."

"You'll have your own tally soon enough," Bakari said.

Then his brother patted him on the shoulder. "You look like a man who could use some sleep. Share my tent. Tomorrow I'll take you home."

*　*　*

When morning came, Dikembe saw the ship. It dominated the savanna like a mountain. He had seen footage of the ships in flight, of course, as well as crashed. Like Bakari said, this was neither. Instead, it was opened up on the bottom like a flower, each vast petal supporting the ship well above the ground. Beneath was shadow, of course, but within it lay a deeper umbra.

"We haven't been able to get that close," Bakari said, "but it appears they were digging a hole of some sort."

"A very big hole," Dikembe said.

It took two hours bumping along unpaved roads to reach his father's compound. Word had gone ahead, however, and Dikembe received a greeting that was nothing short of royal. In the village outside of the compound, children lined the streets, waving and cheering. Young women, as well, most demure and a few dressed to be noticed.

He was caught off-guard by how good it was to see the house where he had grown up. It was old and rambling, a colonial structure that went back to Belgian times. It was raised up three meters on thick wooden columns, both to keep the first floor higher than mosquitos tended to fly and as a precaution against the floods that sometimes came in the rainy season. Wide stairs led to a long veranda, with the doors to the interior just beyond. An upper story jutted up from the middle, with a peaked roof and a little tower on the very top.

An honor guard in faultless uniform met them on the dusty plaza in front of the house. More military were assembled in the compound, along with his mother, the female servants in their blue-gray dresses—and of course, his father.

Upanga Umbutu was a big man in every dimension— even his fingers were thick, and Dikembe had forgotten how bone-crushing his handshake could be. After the grasp, his father pulled him in for a hug, then turned to the crowd that mostly was soldiers and held up Dikembe's hand as if he had just won a prize fight.

"The eldest son of Umbutu has returned to us!" he shouted. "It is a sign, as you all can see. Our victory is near at hand." There followed a cheer that sounded a little flat and ragged to Dikembe's ear. He was noticing that many of the "soldiers" seemed to be no more than fourteen or fifteen.

His father wore military attire, as well, with several decorations Dikembe did not recognize. He continued his speech for a few more moments, then put his arm around Dikembe's shoulder and walked with him toward the house.

"I had almost despaired of you, boy," he said softly, "but now I see you understand at last where your true loyalties lie. It is good you have returned."

"Thank you, Papa," he said. "It is good to be back."

"Let's have some breakfast, and you can tell me of your journey."

The morning meal felt more like a debriefing. The only women present were the serving girls—even his mother was excluded. His spirits rose when he saw his childhood friend Zuberi across the table and he was bemused to see he had somehow risen to the rank of colonel in the few years Dikembe had been gone.

When he was finished relating the somewhat expurgated tale of his return, his father began rambling about the war with the aliens. It wasn't anything he hadn't learned from Bakari, although the slant of it was quite different, much more optimistic in tone.

After breakfast broke up, Zuberi came over and clasped hands with him.

"Dikembe, old man," he said. "Trust you to run toward the fire, rather than away from it."

"Had I known there was a fire here, I might not have been so hasty," he replied.

"Well, it's good to have you back," Zuberi said.

"How is Eshe? The kids?"

"They are well," Zuberi said soberly. "The reason I fight, my friend."

"I can think of no better motivation," Dikembe said. "We need to catch up, old friend—but I haven't seen my mother yet."

"I understand," Zuberi said. "Soon, though."

* * *

He met his mother on the veranda. It was raining, and water was pouring in sheets from the eaves. A small, round-faced woman, she was sitting next to a table, a cup of tea in front of her.

"It's good to see you, Mama," he said.

She rose and embraced him.

"I didn't think I would see you again," she said. "The signs were all against it."

"Well, I'm glad to say the signs were wrong," he replied.

He saw she was weeping, and took her hand.

"What's wrong, Mama?" he asked.

"I wish you had not come home," she said.

"Why?" he asked, surprised.

"Because I fear you have only come here to die."

* * *

The next day, his father summoned him to his office, which had largely been furnished by taxidermists. As a younger man, Upanga Umbutu had been fiercely proud of his hunting prowess. Growing up, Dikembe and Bakari had often accompanied him, but Dikembe had never felt particularly proud of the pursuit. The animals were always at such a disadvantage, it hardly seemed fair, but he had loved being with his father, and valued the memories of their time on the trail and in camp.

"Dikembe," his father said. "I am considering what rank to begin you at."

"What?" Dikembe said. "Father, I am of course willing to fight, but I need not have any rank."

"You're an Umbutu," his father insisted. "You're my son. It will not do for you to possess no rank in the national army."

"National army?" Dikembe said. "What do you mean?"

"The army of the Republique Nationale d'Umbutu."

For a moment, Dikembe was at a loss for words.

"Father," he finally said. "There is no such country. This is a province."

His father's chin lifted a little from his chest.

"Son, at the moment there is no government other than what you see sitting in this chair. One day, hopefully, that will change. Until then, we must defend ourselves."

"Against the aliens, you mean," Dikembe said.

"Against everyone," he said. "In times like this, there are those who will take advantage. I will not let them."

"Bakari said you had been offered aid against the aliens," Dikembe said carefully.

"Aid," his father replied dryly. "Aid in the form of foreign troops. Planes in our airspace—and who is to say that when the war is over, this 'aid' won't stay here and continue to 'help' us? I know the lessons of colonialism, son. We can—and will—do this ourselves.

And you, I think, will start as a colonel."

"Papa," he said, "don't you think that will anger those who have earned their ranks?"

His father regarded him silently for a moment. He cut the end from a cigar and lit it with a pocket lighter, then took a puff. For a long moment he remained silent.

"It's no secret I was unhappy with your choice of studies," he said. "I did not ask that you become a military man, like me, only that you bring some contribution to our country. You could have been a scientist, an engineer, a city planner—a physician. Not so far from here, there is a spacecraft from another world. They came here to kill us all, and they are still trying. But they also have advanced technology, weapons of great power. Some sort of alien plant is breeding at incredible speed, displacing our native species. Do you have the faintest idea how useful it would be to have a scientist or an engineer standing before me right now? Instead I have a… a *scribbler*. Can you paint our enemies away, Dikembe?"

"I could not plan my life for an event that no one could have foreseen," Dikembe said.

"Yes," his father said. "You could have. So much of what happens in the world is unforeseen. That very fact requires us to have skills of universal usefulness."

"Humanity is bettered by art," Dikembe said.

"That is an argument of the elite," his father snapped. "Go ask a poor villager, whose children have died from drinking polluted water, what use the Mona Lisa is. Ask the survivors who lost entire families in the cities." He sighed and rubbed his head.

"I'm sorry," he said. "I did not mean to begin this, not now. Not when I'm so glad to have you here. You must understand, however, I know my business. The people love you. You and your brother are like princes to them. They will want you to have a substantial rank. They will require it, and one day, when it is your time to succeed me—it will be important then, too."

"But surely this is a democracy," Dikembe said.

"Democracy, like art, is not something we can afford at this time. One day, we can hope—but not now. Then, if there is by some chance a vote, they will vote for you."

We'll see about that, Dikembe thought, because if there was one thing he was certain of, it was that he would never be the ruler of this or any other "republic."

4

David Levinson paused to stare as the guards at the gate checked his credentials.

"He's okay, boys," Connie said. "He's with me."

"Yes, ma'am," one of them said. He studied David. "Hey," he said. "You're that guy."

"Yes," David said. "Absolutely. I'm that guy." Turning, he crooked a forefinger at the ongoing construction ahead of him. "Honey, am I... Are they making it bigger?"

Connie squeezed his arm. "A little bigger," she said.

"How much bigger?" he asked.

She looked down and pushed a stray lock of hair from her face.

"You know—about twice—ah, as big."

"Right," David said. "Of course. A bigger target, that's what we need. That's our national priority."

"David, be nice," Connie said.

"You two can go on up now," the guard said.

"Thanks," David said. He took Connie's hand, felt the ring there, and smiled a little. It had taken saving the world to get her back, but it had been worth it.

"It's just... unreal," he said. David had seen a lot of strange things in the past few years—the guts of an alien mother ship, for one—but this was right up there.

The fence they had just passed through and the structure coming together in front of him stood in the middle of an ash field around eight miles in diameter. Here and there, the slumped, melted forms that had once been buildings and monuments thrust up from the dust. Weeds had begun to repopulate the wasteland, but the predominant color was still gray.

Except right here, where a carefully manicured lawn grew. And beyond the lawn, the scaffolded, half-formed building.

"White House 2.0," David said.

An aide and a secret service agent met them at the door. He remembered when he had last been here, frantically trying to find Connie, to convince her to leave.

Well, no, not here. That White House had been vaporized.

The only part of the new building that seemed to be completely in the dry was the West Wing, and that's where they led him, into a room very much like the Oval Office he had been in before but—bigger.

"David. Welcome."

"Mr. President," David said. "Nice to see you again."

Whitmore looked a little older, a little less boyish, which was to be expected. Even in good times presidents seemed to age faster than most people, and the last year or so of his administration hadn't generally been what could be considered "good times." But if he had lost a bit of youthful appeal, he had become a much more decisive, confident, proactive leader. He was a man with a mission, and he didn't mind saying so.

That mission was nothing less than the unification of humanity. In the past, David had disliked the man for both political and personal reasons, but he had come to truly admire him since the events of the Fourth.

General Grey was also present, along with several

other people he didn't know but assumed to be freshly minted cabinet members or advisors—and Stephen Bell, the vice-president.

He did a round of handshaking, then sat in the chair Whitmore indicated. There was a little chitchat, someone brought coffee, and then the president got down to business.

"So, David," Whitmore said. "What have you got for us? What do you need?"

"Well, uh—let me see," he said. "Money, and a good deal of it."

There were a few chuckles, and then silence.

"That's it?" Whitmore finally said. "I read the last budget Area 51 submitted. I expect Congress to approve it."

"Sure," David said, frowning slightly. "Maybe I started in the wrong place. Area 51 was created for a rather limited purpose—to study, basically, one ship and three bodies. I know there was some other stuff, but, you know—that would be quibbling. The amount of material we're in possession of now is astronomical, to say the least. A lot of it is literally sitting on top of us.

"We need more than one facility—we need dozens, and more than that, we need a coordinated approach to eliminate redundancy and waste. We need a centralized method to the study—and maybe more to the point to the application—of alien technology. When I say a centralized, I mean an international agency of some sort." He paused, but no one seemed ready to fill the silence.

"I think this is urgent," he added.

"You think more of these ships are on the way," Bell said. He was a pleasant-looking fellow with wispy auburn hair and a round face. He seemed terribly young for the job he now inhabited.

"Maybe they are, and maybe they aren't," David

said. "We can't take chances. I've been studying their last transmissions. There was a burst toward the end. I can't be sure what it was, but if I had to guess—given the timing and the energy involved—I would venture to say that it was a distress call."

"Yes," Whitmore said. "I read your memo."

"Well, then…"

Whitmore smiled. He appeared genuinely amused.

"You didn't think you were going to get an argument from me, did you, David?"

David blinked.

"Well," he said, "it's just that I know money is tight, right now, and when I see how some of it has been allocated…" His eyes darted around the reconstructed Oval Office.

"*David*," Connie said under her breath.

"You don't approve?" Whitmore said.

"I… no, I didn't say that," David said. "Why wouldn't I approve? It's—you know—so big."

Whitmore chuckled. "I'm not sure I approve myself," he admitted. "To even deign to call what we have right now an economy is laughable, but here's the thing. New York, L.A., Houston—those cities won't be rebuilt. Eventually, maybe, but we've lost so many people—it's easier to build a new life—or continue an old one—where there is working infrastructure. This place, however— this place is different. The White House wasn't just a building, it was a symbol. So was the Capitol building, and we'll soon get to work on that. This is the one place in this country that *must* be rebuilt. We need people to understand that we didn't just not lose—we *won*. That we'll carry on."

"Okay," David said. He wasn't sure he bought it, but he hadn't come here to argue. Or actually, he had, but things seemed to be going well, and by the way Connie was digging her nails into his arm he realized he had set them off on an entirely unnecessary and probably counterproductive tangent.

"Okay," he said. "About the center…"

"The other side of the equation," Whitmore said, "is that people need to feel safe. You're not the only one who worries about the next invasion. We have to show them we're working on that, learning how to turn their own technology against them."

"Yes," David said. "Exactly. And there are other, non-military applications for the technology that can make all of our lives better too. For instance—"

Vice-President Bell interrupted.

"That may be," he said, "but I think that sort of thing is for the private sector to deal with. Every dime the government spends on this should be on military applications, period, full stop. Because if more of them do come, and we aren't ready, no one is going to care if they have a zero-gravity coffee maker or what have you."

"Well, I wasn't thinking about coffee makers, specifically," David said cautiously, "but—"

"I'll cut to the chase, David," Whitmore said. "You're going to get your center for alien technology. You're going to get your funding. I've run a similar suggestion past the Speaker, the Senate majority leader, and other key members of Congress. I've never seen such a unified government in my lifetime. Congress is ready to write a bill. We just need you to tell us what should be in it."

"Well, that's—that's great," David said. "May I start with the big one? We need a base on the moon, and soon as possible."

"Why is that?" General Grey asked.

"Well, you know better than I that commanding the high ground is important. I think in a few years we can build—or grow, actually—energy cannons based on alien technology. On the moon—in the lower gravity—we can make them big, really big, and we won't have to fire them through our own atmosphere."

"But the cost—" Whitmore began. "The Apollo missions cost twenty-six billion, if I remember correctly."

"Twenty-five point four," David said. "Yes, but the technology we're now working with—we're within a decade of having spacecraft based on their technology. Anti-gravity. Fusion drives. Once we make that initial investment in the technology, space travel is going to be cheap, and there's no reason we have to foot the whole bill. Like I said, I think this should be an international effort."

"Are you sure that's a good idea?" Grey said.

"Russia, China—everybody is working on this right now," David continued. "That's what I meant by reducing redundancy. The better we task this out, the faster it gets done."

"I agree," Whitmore said. "I've been in talks with the leaders of some of those countries, about something I'm calling the Earth Space Defense initiative. I won't go into a lot of detail, but it will involve consolidating our own military organizations and working across the globe with others. Research and development, of course, will be a big part of that. You lay out everything you want, in writing. Let me worry about international negotiations."

David absorbed all of that for a moment.

"Well," he said, finally, "now that you mention it, there's one negotiation that really can't wait."

"And what's that, David?"

"This guy in Africa, Umbutu. Reports are that he's got a nearly intact ship. We've got to get in there."

"Mr. President, if I may?"

The speaker was a dark-skinned woman with short, curly hair, probably a couple of years south of forty.

The president nodded. "David, this is Francine

Pinckney, my advisor on foreign intelligence."

"Ms. Pinckney," David said.

"The region you're talking about wasn't exactly stable when the aliens showed up," she said. "Now it's much less so. Umbutu was a provincial authority, but now he can probably be better characterized as a warlord. In fact, he's renamed his province the Republique Nationale d'Umbutu. They have a flag and everything."

"Classy," David said. "Humble guy."

"Because the ship was intact, many more aliens survived there than elsewhere. Because of that, and because Umbutu wouldn't accept any outside help—not even air support—the ground war there has dragged on almost a year. We've heard almost nothing from the regime. One thing is clear, however. Umbutu refuses to let anyone representing any foreign power or agency into his 'country' for any reason. He's made it clear he considers the alien ship to be property of the state. Short of a military invasion, there's no way to get to it."

"There will be no invasion," Whitmore said. "We're trying to bring the world together, not pull it apart. And before anyone suggests it, covert action is also out of the question. In the present environment, diplomacy is our most powerful tool. There must be something this guy wants. We'll find it. Besides, you have nearly three dozen other wrecks to work with."

"Yes," David said, "but this one isn't a wreck."

"Does that make such a big difference?" the president asked.

"Well, I don't know," David said. "It might. We can't know until we check it out."

"I'll take it under advisement," Whitmore said. "So, for now, let us know what you want, and we'll get what we can."

"Well, it's not just what *I* want," David said. "I'm

just the messenger. I drew the short straw. I'll talk to Isaacs and the new guys and we'll have a proposal in—I don't know, a matter of days. One thing I think we can do immediately is improve SETI, the search for extraterrestrial intelligence, fine-tune it to be more sensitive to their signals."

"Good," Whitmore said. "Just—write it down."

"Okay," David said.

"One more thing," Whitmore said. "The Earth Space Defense will largely be a military organization, but I think it needs a civilian director. I want you to be that director. I want you to run it."

"Yeah, right," David said, grinning.

But none of them smiled.

"Oh," he said. "You weren't kidding. Ah—run it? Not so fast. Look, that's not—that's not me. Let someone else do that and let me, you know, do my thing. I've got ten projects going right now. I'm not—*clearly* not—the leader type. Evil counselor, I can do, you know, the guy plotting in the shadows, Cardinal Richelieu and so forth—"

"David," Whitmore said. "You're a hero, and like this building, you're a symbol. You *beat* them. People will feel more confident if they know you're in charge."

"Because they don't know me," David replied. "I just—I'm sorry, no. I'm happy to help build this thing, make it work, pass it along. Give me a fancy title. Just don't put me in charge. I'm the guy who tells the guy in charge what's wrong with what he's doing. I can't do that if—well, you get the picture."

Whitmore studied him for a moment, then sighed.

"I wish you would reconsider," he said, "but I can't make you do it."

"I'm honored," David said. "Really."

* * *

Patricia watched as David Levinson shook hands and left with his wife. Mr. Bell seemed to want to talk about something, but her dad sent everyone out of the room. Then his shoulders slumped. He closed his eyes and leaned back in his chair.

"Is something wrong with your dad?" Dylan asked.

The two of them were hiding up on the unfinished second floor. They had begun the day when Dylan's mom dropped him off so she could go to nursing school. It was their summer routine. Then it was playing on the lawn, pretending to be explorers in an ancient ruin. The new favorite game was giving the secret service woman who was supposed to be watching them the slip, so they could slide down the newly finished banisters, pretending to be fighter pilots, blowing aliens out of the sky.

And sometimes eavesdropping on Dad.

"He's just tired," she said. "He works all the time."

"Mom says everybody needs a good night's sleep," Dylan said. "Of course, she's up late studying, too." He scratched his head. "So what now?"

"I feel like ice cream," Patricia said.

They snuck back downstairs to the kitchen. There were a couple of people doing the dishes from breakfast, and Chef Cortez was in a huddle with his staff, probably talking about lunch. Dylan kept watch and she stole into the walk-in cooler and emerged with a container of rocky road. Then the two of them retired to the garden with a pair of spoons.

"That's good," Dylan said.

"Yeah," Patricia replied.

"I like hanging out here," he said. "I'm glad my dad moved us to D.C."

"Me too," Patricia replied. She took another bite, kept it in her mouth while it melted.

"He wakes up at night sometimes," she said. "He has really bad dreams."

"What?"

"My dad. You asked if there was something wrong with him."

"Oh."

"I still have nightmares about all that stuff too," Dylan said.

She nodded. "He misses Mommy," she said, "and he's tired a lot. He says it will get better."

"Well, that's good," Dylan said.

"Yeah," Patricia said.

5

Bakari stopped short of the top of the hill.

"You feel them?" he whispered.

"Yes," Dikembe said.

If he had to explain it to someone who didn't understand, he would probably describe the sensation as similar to hearing a swarm of bees or the pins-and-needles feeling when his foot went to sleep. Yet it was neither a sound nor a feeling, but a thing inside of his head.

It had started small, but as the months of the war dragged out—as the aliens hunted them with their minds, like bats used sonar to find insects—a sort of feedback loop was beginning to develop. Their human minds were somehow adapting to the alien mental probes and attacks. It was becoming easier to know where they would be, sense a trap, know when they were at your back. Some were more sensitive than others. Dikembe, as it turned out, dealt with them better than anyone.

"It's only a few of them," he said. "On the other side of the hill."

"Okay," Bakari said. "Let's do this then." He signed for the flanks to move around, and began to move the middle up. At the top of the hill, Bakari pulled the pin from a grenade and hurled so it cleared the top and fell downslope on the other side.

An explosion, then Dikembe felt their anguish, their pain, if it could be called that. Green energy began spearing up from below, and five of them crested the ridge. They never had a chance, as thirty-four soldiers opened up on them, but as they died, Dikembe felt something... different.

"*Merde*," he swore. "I think..." He closed his eyes, trying to concentrate. The gunfire continued, as the rest of the alien force died.

It was nearly over. In the early stages of the war, the aliens had expanded away from the ship, foraging for food—and breeding, planting cocoons in stands of trees and lowland marshes, spreading their own insidious vegetation. The cocoons contained fetal aliens which absorbed the vegetation around them for nourishment.

Not long after Dikembe returned, the tide had begun flowing the other way. The cocoons were hacked to pieces, the alien flora burned, the perimeter of their occupation pushed steadily back. Now the creatures had been driven back almost to the ship.

For Dikembe and Bakari, their present mission was to reconnoiter the west, to make certain they wouldn't have any nasty surprises when they made their final push, which was planned to begin a few days from now.

But something was wrong.

Dikembe stepped to the edge of the slope they had just come up, and looked down.

At first he thought it was nothing, just the wind rustling the grass.

But it was no wind.

There were hundreds of them, maybe every single remaining alien, and they were coming from every direction. The mass of them had kept their distance, so he had only sensed the nearer ones. The bait.

They swarmed up the hill in a constricting ring. It looked

as if someone had kicked open a termite mound in reverse. The aliens ran up the slope, and they died by the dozens. Dikembe fired his rifle until it felt like it was going to melt in his hands, until at last a mass of aliens breached their lines, screeching and scrambling over soldiers, the viridian flash of energy weapons everywhere. He dropped his rifle and drew his machetes. Hitting an alien in the middle of the head, he split it open, revealing a smaller, more delicate head inside. He slashed his weapon into it.

Bakari was behind him, cutting like a dervish.

The thing to do was to get behind them, cut their tentacles off at the source and then split the unseen seam of their exoskeletons. Dikembe had become quite good at it, but now the press was too great to maneuver.

He and Bakari managed to rally the remaining men into a fighting square, a formation at least as old as ancient Greece. Those on the front of each line knelt and cut at the aliens' legs, while the second rank slashed at the horrid, mouthless faces. Still there were too many of them. They plucked men from the square and hurled them back to their comrades behind them. They snapped arms and broke necks. Bodies piled so thickly that footing became first difficult, then impossible.

Eventually, the square fell apart, and it was Dikembe and Bakari alone, back to back.

Suddenly, the aliens drew back, leaving the two brothers panting, standing amid the foul-smelling corpses. To his horror Dikembe looked around and saw that everyone else was dead.

Then he realized that wasn't true. Two other men still lived. Both were wrapped tightly in alien tentacles. One of them was Pierre, a man from Gara village. The other was Zuberi. Pierre opened his mouth. What came out was a human voice—Pierre's voice—but with a distinctly alien intonation.

"You are alike," Pierre said.

Two dozen energy weapons were trained on them.

"We are twins," Dikembe answered.

"Don't," Bakari cautioned. "Tell them nothing."

"Two minds, much alike," the possessed Pierre continued. "Sons of the leader."

"Why aren't we dead?" Dikembe whispered to his brother.

"I don't know," Bakari said, "but I don't like it."

"The leader must die," Pierre said.

Bakari frowned. "I don't like this at all," he said. "Are you ready, brother?"

"I suppose," Dikembe sighed.

"I love you, Dikembe," Bakari said. "I'm proud to die with you."

"What do you mean?" Dikembe said, lifting his chin and waving contemptuously at the enemy. "Look at them. They don't stand a chance."

"Of course not," Bakari agreed. "I'll see you after, then. You bring the Scotch."

Then they charged the aliens.

They didn't get far. Dikembe's mind filled with a thousand voices screaming for him to stop in his tracks. His mind fought, but his limbs succumbed. Then, mercifully, everything seemed to dissolve.

*   *   *

He woke surrounded by aliens, but he had been moved into the shade, on flat ground. In the distance, he saw rain moving across the savanna, slanted streaks of gray against a yellow sky. Nearer, a herd of wildebeest grazed as if nothing unusual was happening.

Then he understood what was casting the shadow.

The ship, rising above them, unimaginably huge.

If he didn't know what the alien craft looked like from television—if he hadn't seen this one from afar—he knew he would never even be able to guess at its shape, any more than a flea in the folds of an elephant's skin could comprehend the appearance of the entire animal. They were near one edge of it, and from there it seemed like a vast gray sky that faded in the distance behind them.

Bakari sat to his left, Zuberi across from him.

"What's going on," Dikembe groaned. "What are they doing with us?"

"Waiting for us to wake up, I think," Zuberi said.

The words had hardly fallen from his mouth when Dikembe felt a tentacle wrap around his neck. He grasped it with both hands, but it might as well have been made of steel for all that it gave to his strength.

His entire body suddenly felt pins and needles.

Then the pins and needles pushed all the way to his bones, and he was distantly aware of his own voice, a thing apart from his body, a scream that was like a living thing. The pain was like nothing he had ever felt before; it was total, without relief. His blood vessels were rivers of fire, his marrow was magma. He felt his skin splitting like an overcooked sausage and his flesh liquefying. A thousand voices mocked him, insisting he was nothing, lower than the lowest worm. He hoped only for death, for the release it would bring.

When oblivion finally arrived, he was grateful.

*　　*　　*

He woke, still in the shadow of the ship. His body was whole, untouched, but he still remembered its destruction.

Bakari was awake also, starring at him, glassy-eyed.

"Why?" Dikembe managed to wrench out. His throat was raw, and when he spat, his phlegm was bloody.

"They tortured all of us," Bakari said. "And then they released Zuberi."

"They're trying to make Papa come here," Dikembe suddenly understood. "They think if they kill him, this will end, and they will be unopposed."

"I believe you're right," Bakari said.

"He'll know it's a trap," Dikembe said. "He won't be stupid enough to come himself. The smart thing would be to use our remaining surface-to-surface missiles to take all of this out."

"That would kill us, too," his brother said.

"We're dead already," Dikembe replied.

Bakari started a reply, but instead his eyes went wide.

"No!" he said. "Not again!"

Then the tentacles wrapped around their necks once more, and the pain became everything.

*   *   *

David managed to keep it in until they got home and he had mixed himself a gin and tonic. When Connie came in to sit with him, he had to let it out.

"You knew!" he said. "You knew they were going to ambush me with this."

"I hardly think asking you to be the director of the organization you want them to build for you constitutes an 'ambush,'" she said, sipping her Scotch calmly.

"It's not about me," he said. "That's the point."

"Oh, David, come on. You're like a kid in the biggest toy box in the world. You're loving it."

"Sure," he said. "But director? That's politics. That's bureaucracy. That's red tape. That's not the toy box." He frowned. "Is this the thing again? You always wanted me to be a part of something bigger, more important. I have to be director of an international agency now?"

"David," she said, "I'm not pushing you into anything. You saved the world. I don't think you have anything to prove to me or anyone else. But I do think you would make a hell of a director."

He absorbed that, feeling a bit sheepish.

"You did know they were going to spring this on me, though."

"I suspected," she said. "I didn't know."

"You should have told me," he said.

It wasn't often he couldn't read Connie at all, but this was one of those times, and he was suddenly very, very worried.

"Well," she said quietly. "You won't have to worry about that anymore."

He sat up straighter. "What? About what?"

"I quit my job," she said.

"I may be having a stroke," he said. "It sounded like you just said you quit your job."

She smiled and shifted forward in her chair. "David, whatever issues you ever had about me working for Tom—you should have gotten over that by now."

"Over, yes, completely," he said.

She gave him the look.

"Okay," he said. "Some reservations. About the secret stuff."

She smiled and nodded. "I've been ready to move on for a while," she said, "but after the Fourth he needed me more than ever. Everyone was gone. But now…"

"Now what?" he asked. Then he saw it.

"Wait," he said.

"What?"

"Oh, no," he said. "It's the look. You've got the look."

"What are you talking about?" she said. "There's no look."

"There is most certainly a look, and you've got it right now."

"Damn it," she said. "How do you do that?"

"Native intelligence," he said. "Long years of practice. Spill. Before you explode."

"Okay," she said. "Don't make too much of this, but I was talking to Alice Tillman this morning—she asked me to coffee—and she said that they had been discussing me."

"Discussing? Discussing sounds good. Discussing how?"

She was actually flushed. He hadn't seen her like this in years.

"They think I should run for the Senate," she said. "Crazy, huh?"

It hung there for a moment as David processed it.

"David?" Connie said. "Say something."

"No," David said, snapping out of his daze. "Not crazy. Not even mildly deranged. It's terrific. You'd do a hell of a job."

"Do you really think so?"

"Absolutely," he said. "Just think—I could be Mr. Senator Levinson. This calls for a drink. In fact, this calls for champagne. Which, ah—we don't have, but I can go get some. Or better, let's go out."

She grinned, and her eyes flashed.

"I wasn't sure you'd be this happy," she said.

"Seriously?" he said. "Why wouldn't I be? I've finally found my calling, so to speak. You found yours years ago. Like you said, it's time to move on. If you want my opinion, I say go for it."

"You know what?" she said. "I think I will. Thanks, David."

"You never needed my permission," he said.

"I never asked for it," she replied. "I just wanted your blessing."

"So blessed," David said. "Now, where should we go for that champagne?"

"I've got some in the fridge," she said.

"Of course you do," he said.

*   *   *

How long it went on, Dikembe did not know. His brain began to refuse signals. Thoughts would not cohere. His existence became binary—pain, rest, pain, rest. The rest only because they did not want to kill him.

Yet.

And then, something changed.

He felt pain that was not his own.

In a red haze, he realized that he heard gunfire, and the aliens were screaming.

He also realized that he wasn't in the grip of a tentacle anymore.

He came swaying to his feet, although his body was numb and he had trouble controlling his limbs. Across the squirming sea of exoskeletons he saw his father, standing upright on top of a tank, flanked by soldiers, many soldiers.

He must have brought them all, Dikembe realized, every single man and boy in arms, and those men—his people, his soldiers—were dying in ranks, stepping over their own dead, moving implacably toward the knot of aliens clustered around him and his brother.

He felt a tentacle at his neck, and despaired. He knew what they were going to do. They had what they wanted, his father in front of them. He felt their minds all bending in the same direction, toward the *leader*.

He heard a savage cry, and realized it came from Bakari, who bodily threw himself at the alien attacking Dikembe. Bakari slammed his head into the alien mask—once, twice, again. It staggered back, and Bakari went after it, his eyes empty of sanity, fists swinging like sledgehammers.

Bullets began to spray all around them. Dikembe desperately tried to pull his twin down, but Bakari was pushing the monster back, slamming it to the rough earth of the savanna. An alien reaching for Dikembe staggered as bullets smacked into its exoskeleton.

"Bakari!" he shouted. He finally got hold of his brother and pulled him to the ground. A mortar shell went off, not too far away.

Dikembe rolled over and saw an alien weapon pointed at his face. He lurched up, finding more strength than he thought remained in him, and took hold of it, pushing it so the blast went over his head. He hurled the monster back and staggered away as AK-47 rounds chewed it up.

Then all of the aliens near them—all of the aliens, period—rushed toward the army, toward his father. Dikembe sagged back against the spaceship and slid down to the ground.

"Brother," Bakari wheezed. He was lying on his back, a hand on his chest. Blood was leaking through his fingers.

"Bakari!"

"Hold my hand," Bakari said.

Dikembe did so, although his own was trembling. He glanced at the front, where the aliens were piling into Umbutu's forces.

"Let me try and find a medic," he said.

Bakari only gripped his hand more tightly.

"Papa is wrong," he said. "There is use in beauty, in creation. Leave this place, big brother. Go far away. Do what you were meant to do."

"Maybe we should go together," Dikembe said. "I know a good pub in Oxford…" He trailed off, feeling helpless and numb.

Bakari nodded, but he didn't say anything else. Blood frothed on his lips and Dikembe sat with him, his heart breaking, afraid to leave him.

Long before the fighting was over, Bakari's fingers relaxed and began to grow cool. The rain came, gently.

6

AUGUST

Steve Hiller was just giving the sauce another stir when Boomer lazily pricked his ears up and offered a muted *woof*.

"Ah, yeah," he said to the yellow Labrador. "Is it that time?" He glanced at the clock, then went to the front door and opened it just as Jasmine and Dylan were getting out of the car. Dylan made a beeline for him. Hiller scooped him up and spun him around. He felt a twinge in his ankle, a souvenir of his time in Russia and the last active fighter mission he'd flown.

"Ah, shoot," he said, setting him down. "What's your mama been packing in your lunch, bricks? I can hardly pick you up anymore."

Back on the ground, Dylan looked around with a slightly worried expression—probably hoping none of the kids in the neighborhood had seen him hugging Hiller. He was getting to be that age, wasn't he?

"Go on in and put up your backpack and lunch box," he told Dylan. "Do you have any homework?"

"Yes sir," he said.

"Take an hour of downtime, okay? And then we're on that sh—*stuff*. You and me. Okay?"

"Okay," Dylan said, and he scurried off.

"I hope it's not sentence diagramming," he told Jasmine as she put her arms around him. "It really ain't my strong suit."

She kissed him, and he gave his full attention to that for a bit—and he didn't care who was looking.

"You're home early," she said. "I wasn't expecting you until Tuesday."

"I could tell," he said. "That dude I found here when I showed up was surprised, too. I had to put a whoopin' on him."

"Well, good," she said. "I'm glad to know you'll still fight for me."

"Every time," he said.

She crinkled her nose.

"What's that I smell?" she asked.

"Mama Hiller's house special spaghetti," he said. "Figured you've had a long day and might appreciate the evening off."

"You've got that right," she said. "My thoughtful man."

"And how about you, young lady?" he asked. "Do you have homework?"

"Actually, I do," she said. "Anatomy and physiology."

"Now that's what I'm talkin' about," Hiller said. "I've got an advanced degree in that. I can think of several topics to assign you right off the top of my head."

"Really?" she said. "You think you can just bust in here, givin' out assignments—you best go stir that spaghetti sauce, or it's gonna burn."

"I'm gonna stir somthin'," he said, but then he smelled the char in the air. "Shoot," he said, and he hurried back to the stove.

"It's all good," he said, stirring. "That's how mama did it. Brings the flavor."

He turned off the burner.

* * *

After homework, they had supper. The sauce was a little burnt, but no one complained. Dylan claimed to like it better that way. When they finished eating, he and the boy did the dishes, while Jasmine did her reading.

"I can't get over it," Steve said, rinsing a plate and handing it to Dylan to dry. "You're shooting up like a weed. Can you dunk yet?"

"Not really," Dylan said.

"Well it won't be long," Hiller told him. "Then watch out. So how do you like third grade?"

"It's okay," he said.

"Okay? How bad can it be? You know, back in my day, if you couldn't answer a question you got blasted by a fire hose."

Dylan grinned. "I don't believe that," he said.

"Well, it was way harder back then," Hiller said. "Let's just leave it at that. You have a girlfriend?"

"Dad!" he said. "No, man! Girls are nasty."

"Really?" Hiller said. "Nasty, huh? Does that include Patricia?"

"That's different," Dylan said. "She's my best friend, not my girlfriend."

"Yeah, you two get along, don't you," he said. "That's good. Have you worked out what you wanna be when you grow up?"

"Well, sure," Dylan said. "I want to be a pilot, like you."

Hiller felt a swell of pride, but he tamped it down.

"That's one choice," he said, "but I want you to know that you can be anything you want to be, son. You don't have to follow in my footsteps, or anybody's. And as long as you do what you choose with passion, and conviction—I will always be proud of you."

"Thanks, Dad," Dylan said.

Hiller smiled. Back when he and Jasmine were dating, Dylan always called him "Steve," and that was okay. They got along, and it would have been weird if the kid had called him anything else. Even after they got married, the boy kept calling him Steve, and he didn't give it any thought. Neither did Jasmine.

Then one day, a few months ago, they had been on a playground, and Dylan introduced him to another kid as "my dad." Afterward, on the way home, he said, *"Thanks, Dad. I had a good day."*

It had almost taken his breath away, shaken him up in a good way. It wasn't that he loved Dylan any more after—he already loved him. He couldn't explain how it had changed him, even to Jasmine, but it had, and even though he had been in outer space, his world now seemed infinitely bigger.

He let Jasmine do the good-night stuff—he was gone a lot, and Dylan liked the routine he was used to. Afterward, Jasmine joined him at the kitchen table.

"Okay," she said. "Let's have it. What's going on?"

"What makes you think anything is going on?" he asked.

"Because I know you," she said. "You've got something on your mind, and you're being shy about it."

"Yeah," he said.

"So let's hear it."

He cleared his throat. "Okay, well, see—there's this new thing they're starting. The Earth Space Defense—"

"I watch the news," she said.

"Well, see, one part of the program involves developing aircraft with new… capabilities."

"Like that thing you flew up into space," she said. "The one you crashed and nearly died in."

"Pretty much exactly like that," he said. "Since I'm the only one that's ever flown one, they thought I might have some valuable insights."

She leaned back and folded her arms.

"You mean you're going to be the monkey they put in their experiments," she said.

"No," he said. "Well, yes, eventually—but it's gonna be years before we have anything ready for a test flight. Meanwhile I'll be working with the program, helping with development, working out training programs for pilots and all of that."

"And where will all of this be happening?" she asked.

"Nevada, mostly," he said.

She sighed.

"I know," he said. "You're in school here. That's great—"

"It's not about me," she interrupted. "I can get my nursing degree anywhere. But Dylan—he's in a good school. There aren't many of those these days, what with everything going to the military. I want him to get into one of the STEP schools, and here he has a shot at that. I don't know about Nevada."

"Well, I checked," he said. "It's not a good situation for kids his age. They say there's gonna be a STEP school near the base, but that's a little down the road."

"Steve—"

"I know," he said. "I'm not suggesting that you move, at least not now. Look, you dated a military guy. You married one. I think you knew what you were getting into. The fact is, I might see you guys more this way. No more long deployments. I can take three-day weekends."

She looked away, and when she looked back at him, her gaze was intense.

"I was fully prepared to be a single mother," she said. "I worked hard, I didn't complain, I kept my eye on the prize—and the prize is that boy, grown to be a good man. A successful man."

"Baby, I want that too," he said.

"I know you do," she said. "I also know you want to

be a damn astronaut. Even before you got that one little taste of space. Now…" She trailed off.

"Here's the thing," Hiller said. "I didn't say yes."

She paused and looked at him, her gaze softening.

"What did you say?" she asked.

"That I would think about it," he replied.

She was silent for a moment.

"Tell them yes," she said.

"I don't think—"

"No," she said. "Don't start. When you asked me to marry you, I promised myself one thing—that I would never give you cause to regret it. And I stand by that. You tell me that we can make this work, and I'll believe you. Then you have to do it, you understand?"

"Jasmine, I need you to be sure about this."

"Do I sound sure?"

"You sound like you want to beat my ass," he said.

"Well," she said, placing her hand over his, "I don't. Or maybe just a little."

He started to make a quip, but instead he laced his fingers into hers.

"I love you, Jasmine," he said. "I don't regret a second I've ever spent with you. Or with Dylan."

"I know that," she said.

*   *   *

Dikembe was at his father's bedside when he awoke. The older man's eyes searched restlessly for a moment before fixing on him.

"Bakari?" he whispered.

"No, Papa," he said gently. "I am Dikembe."

"Dikembe," he said. "My dear boy." Tears welled in his eyes. "They told me Bakari was dead," he said.

"Who told you, Papa?" Dikembe asked. "You've only

just awakened. You've been asleep for more than a month."

"*They* told me," he said, his voice rising. "*Mapepo. Les diables*. They…" He trailed off.

Dikembe knew—he had felt it. In their final assault, the aliens—every one of them—had fixed their terrible will toward his father, to try and kill him, extinguish his mind. In the end, it had been their single goal.

Having felt their touch, he could not believe they hadn't succeeded, even though none of them got close enough to the elder Umbutu to make physical contact.

"Bakari is dead, isn't he?" his father said. "My sweet boy."

"He is, Papa," Dikembe replied.

"Where is he? I want to see him."

"We had to bury him," Dikembe said. "The doctors were not sure when you would awaken."

Or if, for that matter.

"And the aliens? What of them?"

"They fell apart," Dikembe said. "Many remain, but they seem disorganized. As if their failure to kill you broke them somehow."

His father was silent for a moment.

"We will water the soil of this country with their blood," he said. "Bring me my elephant gun."

"Papa, you need time to recover."

His father placed a hand on his shoulder.

"I shall never recover," he said. "Not until they are all dead."

7

FEBRUARY
1999

Thomas Whitmore ran his hand through his hair and tried to put on a smile.

The nine members of the Chinese delegation did not smile back, but President Qian tilted his head. He was in his sixties, a dignified-looking man with sharp black eyes. Before the Fourth, he had been a junior member of the Politburo, but—as in the US—the vast majority of Chinese leaders had been wiped out in the attacks, and had been replaced by younger, less experienced people.

Whitmore glanced at his much smaller delegation, which consisted of two aides and David Levinson. He'd kept things minimal intentionally—he didn't want to even symbolically suggest a show of force. General Grey had argued for a military presence, given that ESD was driven primarily by the Army, but Whitmore had been able to persuade him that this approach would bear more fruit.

Now he just hoped he was right.

"Gentlemen," the president said. "I'm honored that you have invited me to meet you here, in New Beijing. I'm more than impressed at the progress you've made in rebuilding—China is an inspiration to the United States and, I dare say, to the rest of the world."

He paused to let the translator finish.

"I believe we know why we're here today, and I hope we can walk away from this with what can only be considered an historic agreement. After the groundwork we laid last year with other world leaders in Naples, this should be fairly painless."

Qian started talking, and the translator smoothly chimed in.

"You must understand, we have reservations about any agreement of this magnitude," he said. "There are a number of issues which remain unaddressed."

"Then let's address them," Whitmore said. "I'm not suggesting a static agreement, but a process, a process which will benefit us and ultimately the world. On that day, nearly three years ago, when every nation came together—"

"I've heard your speeches concerning unification," Qian said. "You are a stirring and persuasive speaker, and I do not disagree… in theory. What we discovered five years ago was that we have better things to do than fight among ourselves. That our responsibilities are not limited to China, but to the human race. Unfortunately, not everyone came to that same conclusion."

"If this has to do with your border dispute with Tibet," Whitmore said, "I think I've made my position clear on that."

"They made unprovoked attacks against our forces there, while we were still engaged in the ground war," Qian said, hotly. "How can you advocate the unification of humanity, and yet support a separatist faction at the same time?"

"As you must know," Whitmore said, speaking evenly, "the subject of Tibetan independence is a complicated one. It's our belief that the violent agitators were and are in the minority. I've engaged in negotiations with the Dalai Lama—"

"Yes, so we heard." The translator's tone was pleasant, but the Chinese president's was not.

"Look," Whitmore said. "You said yourself we shouldn't be fighting one another. The Dalai Lama is in favor of peace, even if it means he remains in exile. But I think, in light of the way our world is now, there must be some sort of compromise on the issue."

The Chinese president was silent for a moment.

Then he started speaking, in stilted but comprehensible English.

"There are no reporters here," he said. "No microphones, and until we have a final agreement, I must ask that no one in this room discuss this meeting."

"That is acceptable to me," Whitmore said.

"Ten years ago, what you suggest would have been unthinkable. China is old. Our leaders and government have changed over time, but China remains China. Once we were ruled by Mongols, but in a few short generations we made them Chinese. So it was with the Manchu, a few centuries later. But the aliens did not come to govern us. They would not have become Chinese. They came only to exterminate us, and they nearly did so—millennia of history, wiped away in a few days. We cannot risk that happening again."

He paused and took a drink of water.

"What I mean by this is that we are willing to make some compromises regarding our territories. This includes Tibet and Taiwan. However, we will not tolerate being bullied into any position."

Whitmore was surprised that Qian was so frank about the matter. He was all but saying that he was willing to play ball, as long as he and his government could save face.

"Can we talk about something else for a second?" David Levinson piped up.

Oh, God, Whitmore thought. Levinson was brilliant, but he was also a loose cannon. Over several objections, they had brought him along mostly for PR, and for scientific support. David had also insisted on being present, though. That might be good. As long as he remained on script, things would probably be okay.

But Levinson wasn't a very scripted kind of guy.

"David?" Whitmore murmured.

"No, I'm just…"

David pointed to a man in his mid-thirties—lean, square-jawed, wearing a People's Liberation Army uniform bearing the shield-shaped air force emblem.

"You," he said. "You're Lao, right? Lao Jiang?"

The man looked startled and glanced at his president. Qian nodded slightly.

"I am Lao," the man said.

"You're in charge of research and development, astronautics division, right? The thing in the desert? You're trying to build spaceships?"

Lao nodded cautiously.

"How's the anti-gravity coming?" David asked.

"David—" Whitmore said.

Lao shrugged and squared his shoulders. "We will solve that issue any day now."

"Yes," David said. "I'm sure you will—but you don't have to. We already did." He held up a disk. "It's all right here. It's yours."

"I don't understand," Lao said.

Whitmore did. "The Earth Space Defense initiative isn't about the United States, or about China—"

"Or Tibet," David put in, not quite under his breath.

"It's about getting things done in the most efficient way possible. That means both cooperation and compartmentalization. We share, and we don't waste effort trying to catch up with one another."

David cut back in.

"We're developing the technology to replicate—and hopefully surpass—their space-traveling ability, melding the best of our technology with the best of theirs. We've solved most of the major problems of low-acceleration anti-gravity, and we're picking up steam on stable fusion reactors. You guys, on the other hand, are somewhat ahead of us in adapting the aliens' quite impressive structural, integrative, and life-support capabilities."

"What makes you think this?" Lao demanded, this time forgetting to get the okay from his leader.

"It's called the Internet," David replied. "I'm referring to a paper published by two of your scientists, Long and Hui—"

"Yes," Lao said, more quietly. "I've seen the paper."

"So," President Qiang said. "You're suggesting we let you develop space-flight technology? While we work on what? Life-support systems?"

"No," David said. "We'll work on space technology, but our focus is going to be on building fighters. As we sort out anti-gravity, the fusion drive, and so on, you get all the specs. You won't be behind."

"And if we're not building fighters with this technology, what are we building?" Qian asked.

"Heavy lifters," David said. "Tugs. Transports. Prefab housing. That sort of thing."

"President Qian," Whitmore said. "Gentlemen. What we're suggesting is that your portion of this is the moon."

For a moment, they all stared at him.

"You're offering us the moon?" the Chinese president said at last.

"Just because we landed a few ships on it doesn't mean we own it," Whitmore said. "Nobody should own it—but wouldn't it be great if China was the country that developed it, built the base that's going to protect us all? The last thing we need is another moon race."

Qian looked at the other members of his group, then back at Whitmore.

"I cannot promise anything without discussing this with the Central Committee," he said. "But this is a very good start, Mr. President. A very good start indeed."

*   *   *

A week later, on Air Force One, winging over the Pacific, Whitmore patted David on the shoulder.

"You scared the hell out of me the other day," he said, "but it worked."

David smiled. "They've been Jonesing for the moon for at least a decade."

"You never cease to amaze me," Whitmore said. "You really should reconsider that directorship."

David shook his head. "Still not biting."

"I could issue an executive order," he said.

"I'll take my chances," David said. "Anyway, the real story here is you. I never would have guessed you could pull the world together so quickly."

"I'm not pulling it together," Whitmore said. "I'm helping it to pull itself together. Early in my first term I was accused of being weak, of compromising too easily. Of not sticking to my guns—but you know what? Compromise is what's going to help us survive. It's the lubricant that will make ESD work." He smiled bitterly. "And it only took three billion dead, and staring directly into the face of utter annihilation, to get the ball rolling. The politicians that survive in this environment are the ones who can convince their people they can make them safe, not the ones who quibble over the little things. The deck is stacked in my favor."

"Maybe so," David said, "but you still have to know how to play the game. There's always a joker in the deck."

Whitmore settled back in his seat. "It's almost embarrassing, isn't it?"

"What's that?"

"Us slapping each other on the back like this, when a few years ago you took a swing at me."

"Oh, I didn't take a swing," David said. "I connected."

"Yes, you did," Whitmore agreed. "I guess... I guess if I thought some guy was fooling around with my wife, I might have done the same."

"I was being stupid," David said.

"I'm glad things worked out with you and Connie," Whitmore said. "When you find someone you not only love, but who also has your back..." He trailed off.

"I'm sorry," David said. "It must be hard."

"It's just—I know she would have loved to see Patricia grow up. She was looking forward..." He found his throat starting to seize up.

"Anyway," he said. "Give Connie a hug for me when you get home."

"You mean Senator Connie," David said. "You can walk across the street and hug her yourself."

"Yeah," Whitmore said, "but I don't want to get belted again."

8

JANUARY
2001

"Here, Dad," Patricia said. "Let me help you with that."

At first she didn't think he'd heard her. It wasn't that unusual these days. She knew his sleep was still troubled, and the strain of trying to stay on top of everything, to get everything done, was taking its toll. He was, to say the least, preoccupied.

After a moment, his shoulders slumped a little, and he stopped trying to fix his tie. She saw that his hands were shaking.

"I don't know what's wrong with my fingers," he murmured.

"You've actually never been all that good at this," she said. She picked apart his attempt and then began retying it. "There," she said when it was done. "Perfect."

He smiled. "What would I do without you, Patty?"

"What's the matter?" she asked.

"I'm just nervous, I guess."

"You?" she said. "Nervous? The greatest orator of all time?"

"Don't overdo it," he said.

She patted his lapels. "You can do this, Dad. It's just one more speech."

He nodded and looked at her sadly. "How did you get

so grown up all of a sudden, Munchkin?" he asked.

"I'm only eleven," she said.

"It seems like yesterday that you were just eleven *days* old," he said.

"I'll try to slow down a little," she said. "Now come on."

When they reached the Oval Office, his aides took over. She took a seat in the back, behind the cameras, trying to remember to breathe, praying that nothing went wrong. It was almost over...

All too soon, the moment came, and the cameras started rolling. For what seemed like a long moment, her father just stared at them. Then his expression settled into his familiar, affable, slightly rakish lines.

"My fellow Americans," he began. "It has been the highest honor I have ever known or will ever know to have served you and served this country, both in the military and in this office. As a nation—as a world—we have suffered terrible loss and heartbreak, but we have also shown incredible resilience and resolve. This will not end when I leave office—your strength comes not from me or from any political leader, but from yourselves. Indeed, all of my strength these past years has come from you. Today, I address you one last time as president of these United States."

He went on, but she almost wasn't following the words anymore. Instead she watched his cadence, his countenance, intensity and honest sentiment. Her dad, through and through, still at the top of his game.

When he finished, there wasn't a dry eye in the room, hers included.

* * *

APRIL

Jake was celebrating his eleventh birthday when he saw that the new kid was about to get his ass kicked. He was in his secret place, in the cockpit of his fighter with a little piece of sugar cookie he had hidden in his pocket during lunch a week ago, the last time the noon meal had included a dessert. He didn't have a candle, but he had some matches, and he had some cedar bark he had twined together.

He was about to light it when he saw the kid cutting through the park on the way back from school. If Jake hadn't already known he was new, that would have been a giveaway—seven-year-olds didn't cut through the park. That was where the older kids hung out. Jake was big for his age, but even he tended to avoid the place this time of day.

He looked down at his little crumb of makeshift cake and improvised candle.

"Dammit," he said.

He climbed out of the cockpit and made his way down to the ground. Then he went after the kid, hoping he would find him before trouble did.

No such luck.

* * *

There were only two of them—Doug and Edwardo—but that was plenty. Edwardo was dumb, but he was built like a Humvee, easily the biggest kid in the school, despite being only fourteen. Doug was smaller, older, smarter, and by far the more dangerous of the two. Edwardo was a bully. Doug simply didn't care about anything—he didn't care if he got hurt or even if he died. Once, on a bet, he'd let Tony Chu burn his arm with a lighter. His skin was smoking before Tony lost his nerve and gave up. Doug never made a sound.

"What's up, kid," Edwardo said.

"Nothing," the boy said. "I'm just walking back to the dorms. Somebody said I could go through here."

"Sure," Doug said. His voice was soft, and a little reedy. He didn't *sound* dangerous. "You're the new kid."

"My name is Charles," the boy said.

"I didn't ask your name," Doug said. "Don't ever tell me anything I didn't ask."

Charles took a step back. He wasn't stupid—he knew something was wrong.

Jake took a deep breath, stepped from behind his tree and started toward them.

"Charlie," he said. "There you are. You dummy, I told you to go *around* the park, not through it." He grinned at the older boys. "Not the smartest tool in the shed," he said. "Come on, Charlie. You have that meeting with Mr. Marshall, right now. I'll get in trouble if you get lost."

Doug looked at him dubiously.

Jake had never had any trouble with Doug. As far as he knew, Doug barely knew he existed. Now he examined Jake through narrowed eyes. Jake met his gaze and smiled, or tried to. He wasn't sure he was successful. For a moment, no one said anything.

"Sorry," the little boy said. "Sometimes I don't listen." He inched back toward Jake.

Doug looked at the boy, then slowly turned his cold gaze back on Jake.

"You're sure about this?" he said softly.

It felt like ice water had been poured over him, but Jake nodded.

"Come on, newbie," he said to Charlie.

Edwardo started forward, but Doug put a hand on his chest.

Jake started walking, feeling like he had a bullseye

on his back. The kid followed him.

Once he figured they were out of earshot, he turned on the boy.

"Are you *mental*?" he snapped. "Don't ever cut through the park, especially not after school."

"But Danny said—"

"Danny Clausen? Red-headed guy?"

"Yes."

"He was trying to get you hurt," Jake said. "Or worse. Now I'm on Doug's radar, exactly where I don't want to be. Thanks."

The boy made a sort of hiccuppy sound. Jake looked back and realized he was crying.

"Hey," he said. "Don't do that."

"I can't help it," the boy said.

"Alright, look. Charlie?"

"Charles," the boy sniffled.

"No," Jake said. "It's not. It's Charlie, unless you want to get your head dunked in the toilet pretty much every day. I don't know where you were before this, but obviously things are different here. You need to get a grip on that."

"I was with my Aunt Betty," Charlie said. "In Portland."

"Why aren't you still there?"

"Aunt Betty died," he said.

"Oh." He paused. "So you've been living in a nice place—how many other kids at Aunt Betty's?"

"Just me."

"Okay," Jake said. "So most everybody here, we've been orphans since the Fourth. We didn't have an aunt to go live with. So things are different here. Mr. Marshall and most of the other grown-ups mean well enough, but there aren't enough of them to protect you. There's over a hundred kids here, and we're all on our own."

"But you helped me," Charlie said.

"I'm sure I'll regret it," Jake said. Charlie stopped walking.

"Come on," Jake said. "What are you doing?"

"I don't want to be here," Charlie said.

"Charlie," Jake told him, "none of us does."

*   *   *

The Darling Home for Boys and Girls had been a motel, back in the day. It was basically a two-story rectangle arranged around a courtyard that had once had a pool in the middle. Their first few months there had been spent filling the pool in with dirt to make a vegetable garden.

Jake took Charlie to the front office. Mr. Marshall wasn't there—he stayed in his room most of the time these days, alone with his vodka.

By the time they'd found the refugee camp—by the time they learned that against all odds the aliens had been defeated—his son Hank's leg infection had progressed to an untreatable point, at least in terms of what little medical care was available in the camp. Hank had died a few days after they arrived, and Mr. Marshall hadn't been the same since. It seemed like setting up the orphanage took the last of his willpower.

The Fourth had left a lot of orphans, and Jake knew that many of them still didn't have roofs over their heads. He was one of the lucky ones.

Nadia Lu was at the counter. Her hair was the color of steel and her eyes were tiny and utterly black. The old lady was nice if she wanted to be, but she could also come down like a hammer when the situation required it.

"Hey, Jake," she said. "Who's this?"

"Charles Miller," Charlie said.

"Charlie Miller," Jake corrected. "He says he doesn't have a room assignment yet."

"Uh-humm," Ms. Lu said, flipping through some paperwork. "No, I don't even have him on the list."

"I just got here today," Charlie said. "They dropped me off at school."

"They?" Ms. Lu said.

"Some guys," he said. "Ms. Patel and Mr. Smith."

"Patel and Smith, huh," Ms. Lu sighed. "Another unauthorized drop off." She looked at Charlie. "You'll stay in the shelter until we sort you out, Charlie. Show him where it is, Jake."

The shelter had once been Conference Room 4. The lettering was still there on the wall. Now it was crammed with cots and mattresses. It was where they put kids they didn't really have room for, so most of them were transient. Ms. Lu was probably already on the phone, trying to get some other place to take Charlie, because they were full up.

Jake left a frightened-looking Charlie there and went to his room. It wasn't exactly nice, but it was a lot better than the shelter. The rooms had windows, for one thing, and their own bathrooms. He shared his with three other boys. Shane, the oldest at sixteen, was plucking at his guitar when Jake came in, the opening bars of "Stairway to Heaven," which Jake was now hearing for about the two millionth time. They nodded at each other, but didn't talk. Jake unloaded his backpack and started on his homework.

Arkady came in a few minutes later. He was stout and dark-haired and talked louder than necessary.

"I can't believe you're bothering with that shit," he said.

"Busy," Jake said. "Studying."

"Why? Nobody cares if you do that. The teacher doesn't even care. She doesn't even read it."

"I care," Jake said.

"Oh, that's right," Arkady said. "You're suffering

under the delusion that you're going to *be* someone. A fighter pilot, right?"

"Well," Jake said, evenly, "I certainly won't be a pilot if I can't do math."

"You can't be one *period*," Arkady said. "We're fricken' orphans in a world full of orphans. You know how many people get into the STEP schools? Three percent, and almost all of them come out of private schools, or are homeschooled, or whatever. You don't have a shot."

Jake closed his book and stood up. "I don't know what's wrong with you, Arkady, but if you don't shut up, I'm going to take a shot—at your ugly face."

Shane put the guitar down. He stood to his full height, almost six feet, although it was a very lean and willowy six feet.

"Knock it off, Arkady," he said. "I know you've had a rough day, but leave Jake alone. And Jake, you sit back down."

Arkady dropped his backpack.

"Why don't I just leave, period?" he said, and with that he bolted back out of the door.

"What's wrong with him?" Jake asked.

"Marisol dumped him," Shane said.

Just like that. It was like someone had switched on a light inside of him.

"Oh," Jake said. "That's, uh… that's too bad."

Shane chuckled and picked up the guitar.

"Yeah, right," he said.

"What's that supposed to mean?" Jake said.

"You've had a crush on her since you were six. You need to let it go, son. She's four years older than you, and even if she wasn't, she's way out of your league."

That actually hurt more than what Arkady had said about his prospects of becoming a pilot, but he wasn't going to let on. Instead, he turned back to his studies.

* * *

After an hour or two, he realized he couldn't concentrate. He kept thinking maybe he should go find Marisol and see how she was taking the breakup.

He found her, on one of the benches in the corner of the courtyard.

Making out with Tom Lopez.

After that, he needed a walk. He slipped out of the courtyard and into the poorly lit parking lot, trying to push down his disappointment. He was so distracted, he nearly tripped over Charlie.

"What the hell are you doing out here?" he asked. Then he saw the boy had his backpack on. "What's this?" he demanded.

"I don't belong here," Charlie said. "I'm not even supposed to be here."

"Where do you think you're gonna go? You think there's someplace out there better?"

"Yes."

Part of him thought he should just let the kid go. He might land somewhere better. Probably not, but he might, and he would no longer be Jake's problem. Which he wasn't anyway, but...

It was no use.

"Charlie," he said. "Come with me."

He led the boy across the lot, through the abandoned plot that edged the park. The weeds were waist-high, and at the far end were a thicket and a half-finished strip mall. During the economic crash following the Fourth, a lot of things had been left half-built.

Charlie didn't say anything, just followed him through the maze, then to a ladder that led up to the roof. There, hidden in piles of sheet metal, roofing, and other unused building material he showed Charlie his greatest secret.

"What the heck is that?" the boy asked.

"It's my fighter jet," he said. "Get in. There's two seats." In the back of his mind, one of the seats had always been for Marisol, but he'd never worked up the guts to bring her here.

Charlie stuck his head in.

"It's not real is it?" he said. "It didn't fall out of the sky?"

"I built it," Jake said. "Get in."

Charlie climbed in, and Jake followed him.

"So this is the stick," Jake said. "That's how you control the plane. And this is the altimeter…"

The stick was the joystick from a video game, and the altimeter was a pressure gauge from an old fuel tank. The rest of the control panel was built of similar bits of electronic rubbish he'd been collecting over the years.

"Go ahead," Jake said. "Fly her. Pull back the stick and get us off the ground."

Tentatively, Charlie reached for the stick, then pulled back.

"*Vrroom*," Jake said. "And we're climbing to cruising altitude. Oh, man, look, Charlie—the bad guys are coming at one o'clock. Switch the radar to targeting. Right here."

Charlie flipped the switch.

"They're almost here. Listen, hear that? You've got a tone. That means you have a radar lock. Fire that missile."

"Okay," Charlie said. He was starting to smile.

"*Bamm*," Jake said. "You got it, man. Now let's take out some more."

"This is pretty cool," Charlie admitted.

"You wanna see something cool?" Jake said. "Watch this."

He flipped another switch, and this time a little screen flickered to life. He reached down and pushed in the hidden VHS tape, hoping the player still had some battery power.

The alien destroyer appeared, seen from a distance. Fighter jets were converging on it from all directions. They fired missiles, but unlike the time he had watched from the ridge when he was six, this time it was clear that the weapons were having at least some impact. There had once been a voice-over, explaining what happened, but his speakers were shot.

"Have you ever seen this?" he asked Charlie.

"No," the boy said. "Aunt Betty didn't want me to."

"So they're shooting their missiles," Jake said, "and they're working, but the ship is just too big. It's not enough, and they don't have that much time, because they don't know how long the shields will be down. And then the president himself, President Whitmore, gives it a try—and misses. Hits this thing here."

He pointed to one of the petals unfolding at the bottom of the ship.

"The aliens are about to use their primary weapon, kill everybody, and no one has missiles left. Except this guy."

He pointed to one of the planes flying toward the belly of the ship.

"But his missile won't fire. So what does he do? He flies his jet into their weapon. And—well, watch."

Jake was silent as the tiny plane charged up into the starship's primary weapon, as the cyclopean ship glowed, burned, and crashed.

He realized tears were running down his face.

"That guy," he said, trying to keep the quiver out of his voice. "Russell Casse. He took them down. He was an alcoholic and kind of a loser, but when it mattered, he was a hero."

"I've heard his name," Charlie said.

"Of course. Levinson, Hiller, and Casse. Who hasn't heard of those guys? And that's what I'm going to do," Jake said. "I'm going to be a pilot. Like Hiller. Like

Russell Casse. Casse was a nobody, and now everyone knows who he was. So I figure even orphans like us have a chance."

"Like us?"

"Yeah," he said. "You and me, Charlie. Any of us—but nothing good will come from running away. Understand?"

"I think so," Charlie said.

"Come on," Jake said, "let's go back. We have school tomorrow."

He took Charlie back to the shelter, and then went to the front desk. Ms. Lu was still there, looking tired.

"What is it, Jake?" she said.

"That new kid," he said. "Charlie."

"What about him?" she said.

"He can stay in my room."

She raised her eyebrows and put down the magazine she was reading.

"Jake, you've already got four in your room," she said. "That's capacity."

"He's little," Jake said. "He can sleep on the floor. Or I can."

She looked hard at him for a moment. Then her lips twitched in a small reluctant smile.

"If you get your roommates to sign on, we'll give it a try," she said.

"Don't worry," Jake said. "They'll sign on."

9

JUNE

As the light of early dawn stole across the desert, David rolled his bike out through the front door of his house, a house that two years before hadn't been there. It was by most standards a small house, although compared to the one he had grown up in, and especially his apartment in Manhattan, it seemed almost obnoxiously large.

Still, he approved of it. Although government built, it was constructed of something that at least resembled adobe and seemed at home in the Southwest. The nearly flat roof was covered in solar panels, so when he made his toast and eggs he had the pleasure of knowing he wasn't burning fossils.

Of course, there were fifty houses around it that were nearly identical, all situated on streets and avenues named for American states—his was on Pennsylvania Avenue. He'd had his pick, and had chosen it because it was at the edge of the development, with a backyard that blended seamlessly into the desert.

The houses weren't the only thing new about the region around what had once been called Area 51. When it went from being a covert facility to the now famous Center for Alien Technology, the research facilities had been vastly expanded, which meant many thousands more employees, many of whom worked mining the nearby alien wreck for raw materials and technology. The government had built housing and some facilities for the newcomers, but something else had happened.

Outside of the military boundaries of the base, a town had grown up. Displaced entrepreneurs from everywhere came to set up shop, building restaurants, grocery stores, movie theaters, bars, bowling alleys, daycare, schools and all of the other support structures of a small town. Almost daily some new shop opened, and just this year they'd held their first election for mayor and aldermen. Their first order of business had been to choose a name for the place, which no one seemed to agree upon.

All of this, of course, was several miles from where the actual work went on, and that included the base housing. In case something went *kablooey*. Which unfortunately wasn't that unlikely.

Still, it gave him a nice, long bike commute each morning to get his thoughts together.

* * *

Two hours later, David watched as the techs clustered around the device, doing last-minute checks on the hydraulics, the electrical connections, the coolant levels, and forty-nine other persnickety items of business.

"We, uh, ready this time?" he asked Singh.

Singh was twenty-something, the brightest in her class at his old Alma Mater, M.I.T. Her nose was a little crooked due to—as she put it—"an unfortunate cricket mishap."

"They say the sixth time is the charm," Singh replied.

"Who says that?" David asked. "I've never heard anyone say that."

The last of the technicians left the chamber, and David was left with an unobstructed view. There was no disguising what it was—despite its sleek, high-tech lines, the device screamed "cannon" just as loudly as anything that ever armed a man o' war. It was in a transparent polycrete chamber a hundred feet below the observation and control deck, aimed down a tunnel five miles long and a hundred yards in diameter which—when it wasn't being used as a firing range—could double as a gigantic wind tunnel.

David heard the lab's outer door cycle.

"Who is that?" he asked Singh, without looking back.

"It's Director Strain, sir," she said.

"It must be my birthday," David murmured, sotto voce.

"And Vice-President Bell," she added.

"And Hanukkah and Christmas," he said. Then he turned and put on a smile.

Director Strain's middle years were visible in his receding hairline and a comfortable paunch. That along with his round, jowly face and Midwestern politeness made him seem pleasant and avuncular. David had been working under him for two years now, and knew Strain was neither.

"Director," he said, shaking hands. "Mr. Vice-President. What an honor. Congratulations on the election."

"Thank you," he said. "Your endorsement was much appreciated."

But entirely unnecessary, David thought. Whitmore had convinced General Grey to run for president, with Bell grudgingly continuing on as vice-president. Seen as Whitmore's natural heir, Grey had bested former Secretary of Defense Nimziki in a landslide. What David didn't tell Bell was that he'd nearly skipped standing on the stage along with Grey during the campaign. Not because of the general, but due to his worries about Bell. No one questioned the need to spend a huge chunk of the budget on military research and development, David least of all. Nevertheless, Whitmore had insisted on—and usually got—programs to help those Americans being left behind, and on investing in the infrastructure of the future.

They needed scientists and engineers more than ever, and yet fewer kids were getting the education they needed to fill those jobs. More and more, applicants for those positions were coming from overseas.

There was nothing wrong with that in and of itself. The world was united and at peace in a way that no one in the last century—or any period in human history—could have dreamed of. But he worried about a two-tiered system developing. Bell was in favor of cutting money to education, not increasing it.

Bell approached the glass and peered down.

"So that's it?" he said.

"Well," David said. "It's a prototype, of course."

"I thought it would be bigger, given what it has cost."

"Well, eventually it will be bigger," David said. "Much bigger, but at this point it's wiser to keep them small."

Bell looked a little puzzled.

"How big is it?" he asked.

"It's, ah, a bit less than a meter long. About a yard."

"So is it actually useful as a weapon?" Bell asked.

"Sure," David said. "I wouldn't want to be standing in front of it."

"But could it take down one of their vessels?"

"Well, no. No, of course not," David said.

"I see," Bell said in a disapproving tone. "Well. Let's see it in action, then."

"Actually," David said, "this isn't a good time."

"What does that mean?" the director asked. "You said it was ready to test."

"Yes. To test. Run some current through it, see what the oscillation rate is so we can calibrate it a little more finely…"

"Can it or can it not be fired?" Bell said.

David took a deep breath.

"Theoretically we can certainly try to fire it," he said.

"Then do so," the director said.

There was a long moment of silence.

"Okay," David said reluctantly. "Dr. Singh, let's warm her up."

Singh went to the panel and started the checklist. The cannon reoriented slightly and began to glow an actinic blue. Then a green haze appeared around the weapon.

"What's that?" Bell asked.

"Energy shield," David said. "Just a precaution."

"What's the target?" Bell asked.

"A chunk of the hull from the wreck up there," David said. "Also behind an energy shield, about a hundred meters that-a-way."

"Ready," Singh said.

"Hang on," David said. He grabbed flash visors and handed one to each person in the room. "Better put these on," he said.

When everyone was outfitted, Singh started the final sequence.

David's visor darkened as a beam suddenly appeared, painting the cavernous tunnel in a blue-green radiance. He realized that he was holding his breath, and let it go. Maybe Singh was right, and the sixth-time business was really a thing.

The beam pulsed more brightly, faded a little, then swelled brighter still.

"Okay," David said. "Great test. Let's shut 'er down."

Before Singh could touch the controls, there was a sudden burst of light, and his flash visor went opaque.

"What the hell!" Bell yelped.

David cautiously cracked his visor, then pulled it off.

"It's okay," he said.

Bell pulled his visor off too.

"You call that okay?" he said.

The cannon was gone, and the polycrete cube that had housed it was shattered.

"That went pretty well, I think," David opined.

"*It blew up*," Bell said.

"Yes, that's one way of assessing the situation," David admitted.

"Is there another?"

David went to the console. "Let's replay the video feed from the target end," he said.

They moved to a screen and watched as the beam struck a chunk of destroyer encased in a green field. The field held for about three seconds, and then the target disintegrated.

"So it works," Bell said. "For one shot."

"That's why we don't make them bigger," David said. "Or just power up the big ones we found in the ship. The explosion you just witnessed packs just about as much punch as the A-bomb dropped on Hiroshima. If it wasn't for the containment field, we'd all be airborne particles right now."

Bell looked at the director.

"Is this true?" he asked.

"Yes," Strain said.

"See, making the cannon is easy," David said. "The same goes for most of their technology. We have a bunch of it sitting on top of us, and plenty more around the globe. We can harvest it—we can even grow it—but we haven't yet learned to duplicate it."

"What do you mean, 'grow it'?"

"Well—their technology isn't built out of bits and widgets. It grows, organically, like a plant, and the grown technology that powers everything—we still don't have a real handle on that. Their power source doesn't seem to generate or store energy so much as conduct it using some sort of subatomic oscillation. It's almost like they opened tiny wormholes through which to conduct the power. And that might in turn be linked to their telepathic communication. Most of their technology won't work unless they have two power-data streams, a result of their hive-think, most likely. Add to that the fact that everything about their tech is quasi-biological, which we also can't really replicate."

"English, if you don't mind," Bell said.

"Ah—fine. So the human nervous system has an electrical component, yes? Like a computer. Yet after decades of building better and faster computers, we're still not sure we can ever build a computer that acts like a brain. Or build prosthetic limbs that can be tied directly into the human nervous system and take commands from the brain…"

Bell stared at him impatiently.

"We're standard, they're metric," David said. "Times about a zillion. What we're building is necessarily a hybrid of us and them. As you can see, there are some problems we haven't completely solved."

"Can you solve them?" Bell asked.

"Sure, given time," David said.

"That's the problem, isn't it?" Bell said. "How much time do we have?"

"At this point it's impossible to say," David replied.

"Why?" Bell demanded. "We have their technology, we have thousands of them in captivity—yet we still have no clue as to where they're from or how long it took them to get here."

"No," David said. "And the really important question isn't where they're from. The real question is *how* they got here."

"I don't follow," Bell said.

"The universe has a speed limit," David said. "It's 186,282 miles per second. The speed of light. So even if you can travel that fast, it would take a little over four years to get from here to the nearest star. Odds are they weren't going anything like that fast, based on what we've seen of their drive capabilities. The mother ship was a quarter the size of our moon, a world unto itself. They might have traveled centuries, even millennia to get here, with whole generations being born, living, dying in the ship. If the distress call was limited to the speed of light, it could take centuries or more to reach them, thousands of years for them to answer it."

"I sense an 'or,'" Bell said.

"Or—there's always an 'or'—they have some way of breaking the speed limit, or at least going around it. In which case they could show up tomorrow."

Bell took that in for a moment.

"Assume they're going to be here tomorrow," he said. "Speaking of which—I'd like to see them."

"Them?" David said.

"The prisoners."

"Ah," David said. "*That* them."

* * *

"Each one has its own cell?" Bell asked.

"We initially thought it would help prevent them from taking collective action," Director Strain said. "We had some worries that keeping them in groups might allow them to somehow unite and amplify their telepathic powers. As it turns out, we might not have bothered. After they lost the ground war they became—quiescent. They haven't tried to escape or struggle in any way."

"Why keep them in their exoskeletons? As I understand it, without them they're not much of a threat—physically anyway."

"I would love to strip them down," Strain said, "but they can't survive long without their suits."

"You can't recreate the conditions on their ships?"

"As far as we can tell, after a certain stage of maturity, they're almost always in their exoskeletons," the director explained. "All we know for sure is that if we take them off, they eventually die."

"Why?" Bell asked.

David glanced at the monitors, which showed cell after cell of essentially motionless aliens.

"We don't know that either," David said. "I have a few ideas—"

"I don't want ideas," Bell said. "I want facts. Accomplishments. I want weapons that will blow anything that comes our way out of the sky."

"Yeah," David said. "It's just that, you know, facts and accomplishments usually start out as ideas. Kind of the way it works."

Bell's only reply was a nasty look.

"I've seen enough," he said. Then he turned and walked away.

10

APRIL

2004

Jake was underneath a '92 Honda Civic when the boss called his name. He slid out, wiping his oily hands on his coveralls. The radio was blaring Lynyrd Skynyrd's "Free Bird," and it was a little hard to hear.

"Yes, sir?" he said.

His boss was named Sam Franklin, but everyone called him "Frank." He was a big man, with a complexion almost as dark as the oil that streaked it. He was old enough to be Jake's grandfather, but the years hadn't slowed him down much, if at all. Jake doubted he could beat the old man in any form of physical contest.

"That's enough for today, Jake," Frank said. "You've hit the wall on your hours this week."

"I don't mind," Jake said. "I could use the money."

"We all could," Frank replied. "I'd like to give you more, but you're still in school, and there are laws about how much time you can spend on the clock—and before you say anything, let me tell you, you damn sure ain't quitting school."

"No, sir," he said. "I'm not planning on it." But he reflected that he might not have a choice—he'd failed the STEP academy entrance exam. He had one more shot at it, and then that dream was over. Then he might need the skills he'd picked up working in the garage, although he'd started the job for other reasons.

The orphanage was running in the red, and funds from the government were short. What funds there were had to be directed at the younger kids, so if you were seventeen and wanted new clothes more than once a year, you found a job. In his case, he was buying for two, because Charlie wasn't old enough for real work yet. It also cost money to get the study materials he needed for the entrance exams.

Then there was the car.

"Is it okay if I tinker with the Mustang?" he asked.

"Sure," Frank said. "That's on your own time. Just so we're clear, though—you've got a way to go before you pay that off."

"I understand," Jake said, "but when I do pay it off, I intend to be able to drive it out of here."

"Fair enough," Frank said. "So long as we're on the same page."

Jake worked another hour, tinkering with the Mustang, then washed up. He picked up a couple of burritos on the way back to the orphanage, and when he got to the room, he found it empty. So he settled in to do his homework, munching on the burrito.

Charlie came in a few minutes later, carrying something in a large paper bag.

"You've got a green chili special over on the table," he told Charlie.

"Cool," Charlie said. "I'm starving, and I heard dinner tonight was mystery meat casserole again. Last time I had the bubbles for two days."

"I remember," Jake said. "The bathroom was toxic. Hence the burritos." He nodded at the bag. "Whatcha got there?"

Charlie couldn't suppress a smile. "Happy birthday," he said.

"My birthday isn't until tomorrow," Jake said.

"I know," Charlie said. "I couldn't wait."

"Nice wrapping job," Jake observed.

"Well, I did my best."

"Okay," Jake said. "Give it."

Charlie laid the thing on the bed, and Jake took it out of the bag. For a minute he couldn't believe what he was seeing.

"Charlie, where did you get this?" he asked.

Charlie beamed at him. "I built it."

"You're ten, Charlie," Jake said. "How does a ten-year-old build a laptop computer?"

"I'm a really smart ten-year-old," Charlie said.

That was certainly true. Although several years younger than Jake, Charlie navigated his studies as well as he did, and in certain subjects—like math and electronics—Charlie actually outstripped him. It had ticked him off at first—just another joke from the Universe, with Jake Morrison as the butt. But without Charlie, he would be struggling a lot more than he was at calculus and trigonometry.

With a computer, his odds of passing the next test shot up. A lot.

"I found most of the parts here and there," Charlie said. "You wouldn't believe the stuff people throw away or leave behind. Anyway, it doesn't kick ass, or anything, but it can run some decent software. It's got a word processor."

"Nice," Jake said.

"And all fifteen sample tests," Charlie said. "You're welcome."

"Holy crap!" Jake said. "Where did you get those?"

"I found them on a website. They're from two years ago, so they were free. Better than nothing."

"Outstanding," Jake said, and he set the computer on a table. "Okay, show me how to work this thing." He frowned. "Is this the on–off switch?" he asked.

"Yep."

"But it looks like—"

"One of the switches from your old fighter control panel?" Charlie said. "It is. I've been saving it for something useful."

Jake was silent for a moment, remembering. Just a few days after he and Charlie met—after he had denied Doug and Edwardo their fun at Charlie's expense—Jake found his "fighter jet" in ruins. They must have followed him, just looking for something, anything, any way to hurt him. Or maybe they'd been trying to get him alone, and just stumbled across it.

In any event, Jake said nothing, did nothing. When Edwardo taunted him, he pretended he didn't have any idea what the bully was talking about.

"This is so fricken' cool," he said. "Thanks, Charlie."

"I wish I could have gotten the current tests for you," Charlie said, "but those are like two hundred dollars."

"I know," Jake said. "How do they expect us to get into the good schools if we can't afford the practice tests?"

"That's easy," Charlie said. "Kids like us aren't supposed to go to the good schools."

"Maybe not," Jake said, "but we're going to—and like you said, old tests are better than none at all."

1 1

JUNE

Catherine Marceaux lit a cigarette and crossed her legs, watching a man row a shell along the Loire River, then glancing at the menu of the Bistro Aronnax. The air was damp and a little chilly, the sky a swirl with high, lacy clouds. The breath of the sea moved up the river and through the streets. Nantes was no Paris, but then no place was—or ever would be again. Still, it had its charms.

She was glancing at her watch as the waiter arrived and asked if he could get her something.

"I would like a glass of Muscadet," she told him, "and some oysters, I believe."

"Very good, mademoiselle," he said.

She found that irritating. No, she wasn't married, but she was twenty-eight. She had a Ph.D. She wasn't a girl.

She finished the cigarette and was stubbing it out when Devin finally arrived, an apologetic look on his long, soft face.

"I thought I was about to be stood up," she said.

"Sorry," he said. "Can you believe it? The train was late."

"I can believe it," she said. "It's okay."

He hesitated, then bent down so they could kiss cheeks.

"Have you ordered yet?" he asked.

"Just now," she said. "You aren't that late. If you were

French, I might even consider you on time. But for an Englishman, I must regard you as tardy."

He smiled and pushed back his unruly chestnut hair. "It's good to see you again, Catherine. I was surprised to get your message."

"Well," she said, "I saw you were on the program for the conference tomorrow. I thought things would be too busy then, and hoped you would be here early enough to get together beforehand."

"I don't suppose this is from any sort of romantic inclination?" he said.

"I'm afraid not," she said.

"I thought not," he said. "Disappointing."

They made chitchat a bit, talked about some old schoolmates. Her oysters came, along with the accoutrements. Devin ordered the sole as Catherine tasted the surf of Bretagne on the half shell. After the meal, as they waited for coffee, she finally came around to what she wanted to discuss.

"I've been working with several patients," she said. "I can't name them, obviously, and it's not important—but they were all involved in the fighting after the alien ships came down. I wonder if you've done any of the same."

"Because I work for the Royal Air Force?" he asked.

"Just a shot in the dark," she said.

"You must see well at night," he said. "One of my patients was a pilot who was involved in that mess in the Middle East. I've one or two more. What you really want is a psychologist who works for Special Forces, though."

"I'll bear that in mind," she said, "but you'll do for a start."

"I'm always game for a start," he said.

"These fellows you worked with," she said. "Did they have anything in common? Anything striking?"

For the first time he looked a little uncomfortable.

After a moment of silence he responded.

"They all had a form of post-traumatic stress disorder," he said. "It's not surprising, given the things they saw and did."

"Half of the remaining population of our planet has PTSD," she said. "I was wondering about something else, something... different."

He nodded. "I know," he said. "I had three patients. Two were more or less what you might expect— nightmares, depression, sensitivity to certain triggers. The one fellow, though—how shall I put this? He said he had things in his head. Shapes, symbols, images..."

She leaned forward, feeling a bit excited.

"Did he draw any of these things for you?" she asked.

He raised an eyebrow and leaned back in his chair.

"It's why he came to me actually," he said. "He had become rather compulsive about it."

"What did he draw?" she asked.

"Symbols. Some of it looked like writing. And sketches of the aliens themselves, but the thing he was most obsessive about was just a circle with a line, or lines, through it."

Catherine took out another cigarette, lit it, then flipped open her notebook.

"Like this?" she said. She held it up.

"Yes," he said. "Remarkably similar."

"And could he explain to you what it meant?"

"Only that it was something to fear," he said.

She leaned back again and exhaled a long plume of gray smoke.

"Did you ever study mythology?" Catherine asked.

"The minimum," he said, a hint of suspicion in his voice. "You aren't about to go Jungian on me, are you?"

She smiled. "Not exactly. Do you know what animal is most universally considered magical or sacred across all mythologies, religions, and belief systems?"

"I'm sure I have no idea," he said. "And just as sure you're about to tell me."

"The snake," she replied.

"I don't follow."

"Dragons in the mythology of Old Europe, the feathered serpent in Mesoamerica, the Naga in India, the Rainbow Serpent of the Australian Aborigines—in almost all cultures serpents or serpent monsters represent the sacred or the demonic or both. They are freighted with supernatural meaning. They symbolize natural forces, and yet most of our symbols, you would agree, are more arbitrary. The cross, the Star of David, the little fish Americans sometimes put on the backs of their autos. Language itself, for that matter, where sounds are made to stand in for objects, actions, thoughts.

"To understand any of these things you must know the symbolic language they are composed in. It's not intuitive—it must be learned. But snakes—did you know that chimps have a specific call they make when they see a snake? It's a warning to the others. A chimp raised in captivity, if shown a toy snake, will react exactly as a wild one would. He has no practical experience with snakes, doesn't know what it is, hasn't been taught about it—but he has a reaction."

"I take it you're saying primates are hard-wired to recognize a snake as something special?"

"Yes," she said, trying to contain herself. "Yes, and in human cognition, the 'specialness' works out as something supernatural—a spirit, a god. It wakes up something very ancient inside of us when we see a slithering thing."

"The fear of being eaten, I would think," Devin said. "Small primates, living in trees—not a lot of tigers up there. But snakes—if you don't figure out what they are when you see one coming along the limb, you don't have baby primates." He shrugged. "Okay, but what does this have to do with the circle?"

"Like your man, my patients—and I have four—equate this symbol with terror. Does it frighten you?" She took another drag on her Gauloise.

"Not at all," he said. "It almost looks like a smiley face without eyes. Which could be creepy if you thought of it that way, I suppose. But really, it's very puzzling."

"Because it's not hard-wired into you," she said. "It is in my patients. Like the chimp and the toy snake, they don't know what it is, but it frightens them—and all of them had direct mind-to-mind contact with aliens."

"What do you think it means?" he asked.

"I don't know," she replied, "but I'm going to do my damnedest to find out."

12

Patricia found Dylan waiting for her outside of the school gate, looking oddly uncomfortable.

"Hey," she said. "What's up?"

He shrugged. "Not a lot," he said. "Where are you headed?"

She nodded toward the black sedan parked a block away. A Secret Service agent stood nearby, trying to appear as if he wasn't watching them.

"Home," she said.

"Oh," he replied. He looked down.

"So how's your dad?"

"He's doing fine," she said.

"Good."

"So," she said, after a moment. "I got my letter the other day."

"And?" he asked.

"I'm in," she said.

"That's great," he said.

"What about you?" she asked.

A grin spread across his face.

"Well, you had to know I aced the exam," he said. "I got my letter a couple of days ago, but I didn't want to say anything in case—you know—you flamed out."

"Flamed out?" she said. "Do you want to compare scores? Because we can compare scores, Mr. Please-Help-Me-With-This-Calculus."

"Look," Dylan said, "there's no need to get into a pissing contest here."

"You whipped it out first," she said.

"It's cool," he said. "We both got in. That's all that matters. And, incidentally—in a real pissing match, you know who would win, right?"

"Gross, but conceded," she said. "Anyway, we're both awesome. I'm sending my voucher to Mecklenburg. You can probably get a spot there too."

His face fell a little.

"Yeah," he said. "I'm not going to Mecklenburg. I'm going to Nevada."

"Oh?" She was disappointed, but didn't want it to show.

"My mom got a job at a hospital near the Center for Alien Technology, where Dad is stationed. We can finally end this long-distance-family thing. Mom's really happy."

"I'm sure you are too," she said.

"I am," he admitted. "I've really missed Dad. Being able to see him every day—that's gold—but... I'm going to miss being here."

"Yeah," she said. "I'll miss you too."

He looked up at her, and for a moment their gazes connected in a way that they just hadn't before. For a wonderful, terrifying moment she thought he was going to kiss her, but then he didn't, and they started walking.

She thought she felt relieved, but at the same time...

"So you're staying until the end of the school year," she said.

"Yeah," he said. "Then we make the move."

"I'm happy for you," she said. "And for your mom and dad." She paused, then added, "We'll stay in touch, and then we'll probably be in the ESD Academy together.

You're still planning on that, right?"

"I'm the son of Steven Hiller," he said. "I've pretty much got to be a pilot."

"I don't know that I have much of a choice either," Patricia said.

"Not true," he replied. "You could be president."

Jake sat on his bed, reading the letter again. He realized he had tears in his eyes. He was the only one in the room, and decided to keep it that way. He closed the door, locked it, and read the document once more. Then he returned it to the envelope.

He went to work, and tried to stay focused and on task, but his mind was racing at a million miles an hour. At the end of the day, he made a decision.

He found Frank in his little office lit by buzzing neon tubes.

"Jake," Frank said, "you were lucky you didn't lose any fingers today."

"Yeah," he said. "I was a little distracted, I guess. Listen—I'd like to go ahead and pay off the Mustang."

"You've got the money?" he asked.

"Yeah. Two hundred, right?"

"That's the balance," Frank said. He paused. "You know, there was a guy in here looking at that car yesterday. Offered me nearly twice what you're paying."

Jake's heart sank. "Mr. Franklin…"

"No," Frank said. "It's not that, son. A deal is a deal, and we shook hands. The car is yours. What I'm suggesting is that if you had a mind, you could make a nice profit on her. You should give it some thought."

Relieved, Jake nodded. "I'll do that," he said, but he didn't mean it. He didn't own very much—the clothes on his back, the computer Charlie built him, and a few books. This car was *his*. Something just for him.

He went home and read the letter again, then took to his books. He still had a few months of school left.

He didn't look up when Charlie came in. They were back to three-to-a-room now, and August, their youngest bunkmate, rarely showed up until bedtime.

He heard the bed creak as Charlie sat on it.

"How'd it go today?" Jake asked.

"Oh," he said. "You know."

Something in his tone made Jake look up. Charlie looked miserable. His lip was swollen and split, and the skin around one of his eyes was an angry red, suggesting that soon he would have a black eye.

"What happened to you?" he demanded.

"Yeah," Charlie said. "Don't worry about it."

Doug was long gone, and at least one rumor had him killed in a bar fight. But he'd left a legacy. There were always bullies.

"You got mouthy again, didn't you?" Jake accused.

"Oh, so this is my fault?" Charlie said.

"Of course it isn't your fault," Jake said. "It's never your fault when someone beats you up. Not unless you start the fight."

"I didn't start the fight," Charlie said. Then his mouth twisted a little. "Exactly."

"Okay, what does that mean?" Jake asked.

"It's just, I was talking to Mary Pettigrew—"

"That's Josh Pardo's girlfriend," Jake said. "Have I taught you nothing?"

"She's my age," Charlie said. "I think we might be soul mates."

"Really? You're twelve, man. You don't find your soul mate at twelve."

"It happens," he said, defensively.

"Yeah," Jake said. "What you're feeling is called puberty." He sighed. "So go on—you were talking to her."

"And Josh came up," Charlie said. "We had some words."

"What kind of words?"

"I might have suggested he had the brains of a banana slug."

"Well, that's at least true," Jake said.

"I know, right?" Charlie said. "But he didn't appreciate it at all. Then this happened."

"Charlie," Jake said. "You can't keep writing these checks your fists can't cash."

"I know," he said.

"No, I mean really. I usually get you out of these messes. That's…" He stopped.

"What?" Charlie said, perking up. "What happened?" Then he smiled, despite the busted lip. "Holy crap! You got in, didn't you?"

Jake pulled the letter from under his mattress and handed it to Charlie.

Charlie read it. "I knew you could do it," he said, beaming. "Way to go, Jake."

"Thanks," he said.

A bit of an awkward silence fell then, as Charlie took in what that meant.

"So, I'll test in, too, in a couple of years," he said. "I'll get into wherever you go."

"Sure," Jake said.

* * *

Jake put in his voucher for Casse, the STEP school in Nevada, and got his confirmation a few weeks later. He gave his notice at Frank's Auto Repair and put the finishing touches on the Mustang. He thought about the drive to Nevada, about arriving at the school under his own power in a car he'd half-rebuilt himself.

Arriving in style.

Yet the closer his departure day grew, the more he felt something was wrong.

About a week before he was due in Nevada a kid named Taylor came running up to say that Charlie was in trouble. Taylor was out of breath and freaking out a little, so Jake ran. What he found was Charlie backed onto a retaining wall that ran above the top of "the canyon"— an old drainage canal. It was a drop of about thirty feet. Charlie was balanced on the narrow wall, his back to the fall. Josh was advancing on him with a pocket knife. He had accomplices, Ryan and Li, and six or so kids who were just watching to see what would happen.

Josh wasn't like Doug, ice cold and hollow inside, afraid of nothing. He was more like a volcano ready to erupt at any moment.

Charlie saw Jake, but Josh's back was to him.

He didn't think about what he did next at all. He picked up a piece of concrete rubble, walked up behind Josh. Josh must have heard him coming, because he turned around, but the expression on his face was puzzled, not comprehending even as Jake smacked him in the ear with the heavy chunk.

He didn't make a sound at first. He just fell, dropping the knife and clutching at his ear. Jake bent over and got the knife, then went to the wall to help Charlie down.

About that time, Josh sucked in enough breath to start screaming.

Jake glared at Josh's accomplices and the spectators.

"You guys are all assholes," he said. "You were just going to watch him force Charlie to fall?"

None of them said anything, but they all got out of his way when he led Charlie past them. Nearby, Josh was sobbing like a baby.

*　*　*

For the next few days, Jake wouldn't let Charlie go anywhere alone, and if he stayed in the room, it was with the lock and chain on. Charlie was uncharacteristically obedient. A punch in the face was one thing, but falling into the canyon might have been fatal—and Josh knew it.

Josh, who now had a cauliflower ear.

Jake hadn't expected to get in trouble with the headmaster, and he didn't. Very likely no one had even reported the incident.

A day before he had originally planned to leave, he went into the room. Charlie was reading something or other, with his feet propped up on the wall, next to an aging poster of F-18s flying at a city destroyer.

Jake tossed a used suitcase on the bed next to him.

"Pack up," he said.

"What?" Charlie asked. "Why?"

"You can't stay in the STEP dorms because you aren't enrolled in the school," Jake said. "I called, but you can't. So I found a group home that has room for both of us, not too far from campus. It's not free, but I think I have enough money to cover the first six months. After that we'll figure it out."

Charlie blinked.

"You're taking me with you?"

"Are you not following me?" Jake said. "Keep up."

Tears welled in Charlie's eyes.

"Okay," Jake said. "Don't start that again." But Charlie

couldn't stop, and after a moment, Jake went and put an arm around him.

"It's gonna be okay," he said.

"I don't wanna hold you back, Jake," he said. "I'll be okay here. Really."

"I'm sure," Jake said, "but you're all I have, Charlie. You're my only family, and anyway, how am I gonna pass without you explaining my homework? I'm not leaving without you. Look, I've already got these."

Charlie took the proffered piece of card stock.

"Bus tickets?" he said, sniffling. "What about your car?"

Jake shrugged. "Cars are overrated," he said. "The bus is how all the cool kids travel."

14

MARCH

2006

David watered the plants on his patio, and then inspected his rock garden. He had never had much use for lawns, and in the rain-starved desert Southwest it seemed almost criminal to attempt one, but he liked plants and taking care of them. He had become a fan of cacti, which came in all sorts of crazy forms, and in the past few years he had also taken up bonsai, using as stock the hardy species native to the region—pinyon, mountain mahogany, and so forth.

After a bit of watering and pruning, he went inside and made himself a drink. Almost as if on cue, Connie drove up. He poured her Scotch and met her at the door. She was carrying something.

"Hey, what's this?" he asked.

"Just a little something I picked up for you," she said. She held it toward him, a very nice, very traditional bonsai tray—rectangular, flat, jade green.

"Is it my birthday?" he asked. "Did you do something—you know—naughty?"

"No," she said. "Just celebrating the both of us being home at the same time. That doesn't happen a whole lot. And for a whole month!"

"Um," he said, and gave her a kiss and then took the

tray. "And this, uh, planted in it?"

"Well, I know you like local species," she said.

"Sure, sure," he said, "but this is sagebrush." He looked at her questioningly.

She laughed. "Yeah. I uprooted it on the way home. It's just a joke."

"No," he said, wagging his thinking finger. "No, it's not a joke—it's a challenge."

"Seriously," she said. "I didn't want to pick out a plant for you so I just got... that. I thought it would be funny."

"It deserves a chance," he said, eyeing the scraggly plant. "I see potential." He set the planter and the weed on the table and reached for his drink.

"Don't forget," Connie said. "You're picking up your father at the airport in an hour."

"Forget?" he said. "Of course I didn't—that's today?"

"Yep."

He sighed and set his drink on a coaster.

"Rough day at work?" she asked.

"The usual," he said. "Things are getting pushed through too fast. I thought things would get better once Bell was out, but this guy President Jacobs brought in—Tanner—he's a piece of work. There was this..." He stopped.

"You know what?" he said. "Never mind. Are you going to go with me to get my father, Senator?"

"On your bike? Or did you learn to drive in the last few weeks?"

"Don't you have, like, a driver? He'll have luggage."

"Well, but I gave Jeeves the evening off," she said. "Along with my butler and the kitchen staff. But I guess I could drive you."

* * *

"This is nice," Julius Levinson said, looking around the living room. "You've been here, what, five years?"

David felt slightly trapped as he watched Connie beat a retreat to "freshen up" before dinner.

"About that, Pops," he agreed.

"So this is the first time I've seen the place. Very nice. It reminds me of your Aunt Rachel's house on Long Island. Manhattan gets blown up, and Long Island is spared. Who could know?" He peered down the hall. "You could have got something bigger," he said. "Who knows? It's just the two of you now, but—"

"What? Are you planning on moving in with us?" David said.

Julius frowned. "You know what I'm talking about, I think. You two aren't getting any younger."

"How about a drink, Pops?" David said.

"Again he ducks the question."

"I didn't hear a question," David said.

"Just some water," Julius said. "Don't go to any trouble."

"It's no trouble," David assured him. "There's this little knob you turn. It's like magic."

A few minutes later, they were on the patio at a small café table. Julius looked around at all of the bonsai.

"These pots are too small," he said. "You'll stunt their growth."

"That's sort of the point, Pops," David said.

"Look at this one," Julius said, gesturing at the sagebrush. "Some sort of weed, I think."

"Yeah," David acknowledged. "So what was this big news you mentioned over the phone?"

Julius paused and rubbed his hands together. "I'm very excited," he said. "I've been thinking about it for a long time. I'm a humble man by nature. I don't make too much of myself, but after all of these years I think, why not? The world deserves to know."

"Know what, Pops? What are you up to?"

"I'm writing a book," he said.

"Book? What kind of book?"

"I'm not sure about the title yet. I have some ideas. I'm thinking of calling it *How I Saved the World*."

David regarded his father for another moment.

"You know what?" he said, finally. "I think I'll go freshen my drink."

15

AUGUST

Ms. Park, the chemistry teacher, reminded Jake of a crane. Long-limbed and graceful on the one hand, but with dark cold eyes that seemed to contain very little emotion or empathy on the other. In this she stood in stark contrast to the coding teacher whose room Jake had just come from, where the jovial Mr. Lenhoff seemed prepared to offer a hug at the least sign of stress.

"You will now choose lab partners," she said, after some twenty minutes of dry, soulless lecture. By the time Jake had turned his head to look, more than half of the class had partnered up—many of them had been here for a year already, or were locals and so knew one other.

Jake did notice a girl looking his way. She wasn't smiling, but she seemed to sort of have a question mark over her head. And she was pretty, with brown hair cut in bangs and a little spray of freckles around her nose. He was about to signal her when someone tapped him on the shoulder.

He glanced up to see a boy about his own age. His frizzy hair was shaved very short.

"So," the fellow said. "I'm new here and from the looks of it, you are too. Want to partner up?"

Jake glanced back at the girl, but she wasn't looking at him anymore.

"Sure," he said, wondering why this guy didn't seem to know the rule that you were supposed to pick a girl for your partner, preferably someone hopelessly out of your league, so some sort of screwball romance could evolve. So the movies told him anyway.

"My name is Dylan," the boy said.

"I'm Jake," he replied.

"Where are you from, Jake?"

"I was born in L.A."

The boy grinned. "No kidding? Me too." His face quickly sobered. "Were you there, when…?"

"I was at summer camp," Jake said. "My parents dropped me off a couple of days before."

"Did they make it out?" Dylan asked.

Jake realized he had been asked that question more times in the past few days than for most of the balance of his life. Living in an orphanage, it was more or less a given that your parents didn't "make it out." Out here it was a valid question, albeit one he didn't enjoy answering.

"No," he said. "Or if they did, they never managed to find me."

"I'm sorry, man," Dylan said. "I didn't mean to bring up bad memories."

Jake shrugged. "To be honest, I barely remember them," he said. "I was six." He pointed with his nose. "We'd better set up our station. Ms. Park is giving us the stink-eye."

They moved into the lab and found an unoccupied spot. Jake noticed the girl still didn't have a partner, but Ms. Park was pointing a guy in her direction.

"So how about you?" Jake said.

Dylan smiled. "We lived on a hillside, so I actually saw the ship arrive. I was pretending to shoot at it with my toy laser gun. I had no idea."

"I saw it too," Jake said. "When the Knights took their first run at it."

"When they lost," Dylan said.

"Yeah."

Now Jake felt obligated. "So your parents?"

"They're fine," Dylan said. "We lived in D.C. for a while, and then my dad got a job here a couple of years ago. Mom wanted me to stay in the D.C. school, but when I got in here, we moved."

"Cool," Jake said. "I guess we have a few things in common, then."

"I guess we do," Dylan said. "Oh, man, she's looking at us again."

They turned their attention to the experiment.

* * *

It was no accident there was a tech school in the town of 51. The community had grown up outside of the military boundaries of the Center for Alien Technology, which employed thousands of scientists, engineers, and technicians. People like that demanded good schools for their kids, and here they had gotten one. It stood just off the border with military housing, and although it had dorms, a lot of these kids—military or not—lived with their families. The group home Jake had found was about a kilometer from campus.

Walking back after school, Jake noticed the girl from class, sitting on a bench at the bus stop, reading a book. Her eyes flicked his way for a second, then back to her book.

Great, he thought. Should he just walk past without saying anything? Play it cool? That would be his strategy.

"Hey," he said involuntarily, and he flinched.

She looked up. "Hey," she said.

"So, you're waiting for the bus?"

What am I doing, he wondered. Could he have asked anything dumber?

"No," she said. "This is how I amuse myself. I watch people get on and off the bus while I pretend to read."

"Okay," Jake said. "I know it was a dumb question. So."

He started to walk on.

"I wasn't being sarcastic," the girl called after him. "That's actually what I'm doing. There's not a whole lot interesting going on around here, in case you haven't noticed."

Looking back, Jake tried to get a read as to whether she was still making fun of him, and decided it didn't matter.

"Anyway," he said, and he started off again.

"How is it," she asked. "Consorting with royalty?"

That turned him around. He took a few steps toward her.

"What do you mean?" he said.

"You're going to tell me you didn't know?" she said.

"I'm going to tell you I have no idea what you're talking about," Jake replied.

"Your lab partner," she said.

"Dylan?" he said. "What about him?"

"Dylan *Hiller*," she said. "Son of Steve Hiller."

He struggled with that for a second.

"*The* Steve Hiller," he said.

"Yes. You really didn't know?"

"No. I had no idea, and he didn't say anything."

"Didn't watch a lot of TV growing up, did you?" she said.

"We only had one in the orphanage, and there was always a fight over what we were going to watch—so, no."

"Orphanage," she said. "Okay. Well I guess that makes me feel a little better."

"How so?" he said.

"Well, you were giving me the eye," she said. "The 'I'm desperate here, I guess she will do' eye. Or maybe that doesn't make me feel better. I thought you skipped over me to go with the famous kid, but if you didn't know who he was—"

"Dylan asked me first," he said. "That's all that was going on there."

"You could have lied and told him you already had a partner," she said.

"But—" Jake found he was becoming very confused, very quickly.

"Now I'm stuck with David Bustard," she said, "who is—put nicely—a lump. His parents must have paid someone off to even get him in here."

"You're making my head hurt," Jake said. "What's your name?"

"I have that effect on people," she said. "My name is Emily."

"I'm Jake."

"Well, Jake, nice to meet you," she said, "and nice being your last choice for lab partner."

That seemed like it should be the end of the conversation, but he found his feet wouldn't move. After a minute he figured out it was because he had something to say.

"For the record, that 'look' you saw wasn't a look of desperation," he informed her. "It was more of a 'she's really cute' look. I was actually disappointed when Dylan asked me."

She frowned a little bit, and for the first time since the conversation began, she suddenly didn't seem to be in control of it anymore. Which felt kind of good.

"Well," she finally said. "I guess that's different, then."

He saw a bus coming in the distance.

"Sit down," she said. "Quick. Don't blow my cover."

"What?"

"Just do it!" Emily said.

He took a seat, as requested, acutely aware of her presence only a foot away. The bus pulled up, three people got off, and then it drove away. The former passengers walked off in different directions.

"What do you think?" she asked, once they were gone.

"Of what?" he asked.

She sighed. "Okay—the guy in the suit? Corporate spy. And did you notice there's a pale area around his wedding band? He has two families in two different states, and they don't know about each other. His wedding rings are two different sizes. He was wearing the smaller of the two just now."

"Ooooo-kay," Jake said.

"The lady in the plum-colored dress?" she said. "Dominatrix."

"She's, like, sixty," he protested.

"She's wearing a corset under the dress. Did you notice the one weak eye? In private she wears a monocle."

"I don't even want to know about the guy in the Hawaiian shirt," he said.

She looked a little horrified. "No, you don't," she said. "We shall not speak of him."

He continued to sit there for a moment.

"Is this literally the only thing to do around here?" he asked.

She seemed to think about that for a while.

"There's a place in town that shows old movies for a dollar," she said.

"Oh," he said. Then he cleared his throat. "So, Friday?"

"Okay," she said. "Right here, six o'clock."

She turned her attention back to the book, and after a moment he mumbled a goodbye and continued home, wondering exactly what had just happened.

* * *

Dikembe was kneeling, reading the tracks in the damp understory of the forest. They were deep in the south, probably beyond the borders of the country his father had invented, moving into the Congo basin. It was supposed to be the last hunt.

Part of him refused to believe it.

Since his brother's death, nothing had been the same, including the aliens. They never again showed the level of organization they had shown before. Over the years they became increasingly aimless. Some fought, especially if they were in a group, but many seemed hardly aware they were being slaughtered. But there were so *many* of them. The ship, after all, had been more than twenty-four kilometers in diameter.

For the nine years since his brother's death, Dikembe had hunted. His ability to almost *smell* them had deepened over time, deepened in them all. From a decade of butchery, his arms had grown as hard as the steel of his machete. He felt, at times, like some sort of automaton, a robot that did only one thing.

So he hardly dared hope that it was nearly at an end.

No one had seen one for almost a year—and then, a few days ago, a report came from a village on the edge of the rainforest.

The jungle seemed to explode in front of him, as the vegetation ripped open and the aliens came swarming at him and his men. Without a sound, he launched himself forward, sliding beneath the legs of the first, a maneuver now so practiced it took no thought at all. His machetes, honed every night to a keen edge, did their work, as did those of his men, and they did it in almost unearthly silence.

There had been a time when the men cried out with fear or anger or jubilation as they came at the foe, but

that had been ground out of them long ago. They saved
their breath for the fighting. These aliens fought better
and harder than any he had encountered in many years.
A few still had energy weapons and tried to use them,
although to little effect.

As he struck one down, another loomed over him,
and he realized with a start that it was larger than the
others, larger than any alien he had ever seen. It looked a
little different, too, although he didn't have time to reflect
on why, because its tentacles struck him in the ribs and
sent him sprawling. He rolled and came back to his feet,
finding it hard to breathe, reckoning that he must have
broken ribs and hoping the newly sharpened edges of
bone hadn't pierced his lung.

He sliced off the tentacles that were reaching for
him, and backpedaled. He ducked behind the trunk of a
massive tree and darted around it. The alien was already
turning, but too slowly. He slashed at its back, severing
the rest of its flailing tentacles, and then cut into its head.
It required three chops as opposed to the usual one, but
the exoskeleton finally split.

He felt the monster trying to get into his thoughts,
something none of them had managed to do for a long
time. His legs tried to seize up, and he felt a deep despair,
as if he had failed in something profoundly important, a
failure for which there could be no forgiveness…

Then Zuberi slashed the thing inside of the exoskeleton.
It died, and only the echo of its pain remained.

"You're okay?" Zuberi asked.

"Yes," Dikembe murmured, shaking it off.

"This one was different, don't you think?" Zuberi
asked.

"It was," Dikembe agreed. He moved in for a closer
look. The creature inside the ruined armor was a different
hue than the others, a dark mottled green. Its head was

bigger, too, proportionally. Thicker, the shield more widely flared. Zuberi's weapon had severed its neck, but above its left eye was a sort of pucker.

"Looks like a scar," Zuberi said. "An old bullet wound, maybe. What do you think it was?"

"The last one," Dikembe said. "That's all I care about. It was the last."

*   *   *

That afternoon, he brought the news to his father.

"It is finally over," he told him.

His father shook his head.

"It will never be over," his father said. "For me, it will never be over."

16

Rain Lao had barely had time to settle into the cockpit when the guy was suddenly all over her, putting his hands places they had absolutely no business being. He wasn't rough or anything, but she still didn't like it. She pushed him back, irritated.

"You said we could go flying," she said.

"There's lots of ways to fly, baby," he said.

"Well, I want to literally fly," she said. "In this plane."

"Maybe," he said. "Maybe in a little while."

She had sort of known the guy was a creep. He was probably ten years older than her, and she'd caught him leering more than once, even though she was almost always wearing her school uniform. She should have known better.

"Well," she said. "Could you at least maybe close your eyes for a second? I'm shy."

"Now you're talking," he said. He closed his eyes and put his hand over them.

"Don't peek," she said.

Then she braced her back against the passenger side door, put both feet against his hip and pushed him out of the open pilot-side hatch. He yelped and fell to the ground. She yanked the door shut, locked it, and then turned her attention to the controls. He started yelling and banging on the door, and she ignored him.

Giving the instruments a quick check, she started the plane, a two-seater used almost entirely for crop dusting. Its single prop began to spin, became a blur, then nearly invisible. She eased the plane forward and turned onto the single, unpaved runway.

The fellow chased after. He was still yelling, but she couldn't hear him anymore, which was good, as he had been becoming increasingly more profane.

As she sped down the runway, he diminished in her rearview mirror, and she put him out of her mind as the plane rotated up and leapt into the sky. She knew she was grinning ear to ear. It had been far too long since she had flown.

This was a perfect day. The fields of winter wheat spread out beneath her, a quilt sewn of autumn colors. She took a few slow lazy spirals, gaining altitude, and then turned due south. The radio started yammering for her to turn around and land, but after a bit she switched it off.

It occurred to her that she had finally lost her mind, that the rural backwater of a nowhere place had finally driven her insane. Nevertheless, she felt sane, better than she had in a long time.

Because she was flying.

She didn't remember how old she was the first time her uncle had taken her up. Young. She *did* remember the first time he had let her take the stick—she'd been ten. Of course, he was always right there, ready to take control if she screwed up, but she never did—or at least she didn't think she had. He had pronounced her a natural.

By eleven, he was letting her take off. But then her Auntie Far had moved to the sticks, and she never saw her uncle anymore. Now Auntie Far was with the new guy, and Rain hated him.

She passed the small airport every day on the way to

and from school, staring longingly at the planes. She'd asked if she could fly one, but they didn't take her seriously—or even pretend to until today.

In a little over half an hour, she saw it, the gigantic disk of the ship her father died fighting against, lying on the remains of the city of Wuhan. Although their move had taken them to within two hundred kilometers of the place, Auntie Far had refused to take her there to see it.

Rain banked, trying to imagine what it had been like, the hundreds of alien fighters filling the air, the desperation of the human pilots who knew they only had moments to act in order to save, not just themselves, not just China, but the human race. If just one of the destroyers had survived long enough to get its shields back up…

She tried to imagine her father's last thoughts as an enemy fighter locked onto him and transfigured him and his plane into a cloud of plasma.

Rain wasn't even sure she remembered him—she had only been four. She thought she remembered his face, but that might be because of the photographs her aunt kept. She believed she remembered his voice, but that too might be something she'd dreamed up over the years, because his voice in her head sounded so much like her uncle's. Of course, they had been brothers, so that might account for it.

She flew lower, almost skimming the nightmare surface of the dead monster.

All around the circumference of the destroyer she saw what appeared to be a swarm of ants, as if it was a titanic cookie, and they were biting pieces off to take back to their nest. Correcting for scale, of course, the ants were men and women—but the analogy wasn't entirely inapt. They were recovery and mining crews, salvaging alien tech and materials from the crash. She saw a series of what might be some sort of chemical plants, storage buildings and structures for which she couldn't venture a guess as to their functions. What she found a little surprising was that in ten years they had barely made a dent in the thing.

Then she saw them—first from the corner of her eye, coming in from her three o'clock. Jet fighters, a pair of them.

"Hi, fellows," she said, waving, knowing that of course they couldn't see her or hear her. She wondered what it was like to fly a jet, outpace sound itself. She continued to watch, wistfully, thinking that soon they would be beyond her sight.

Then she realized they weren't just training or on patrol—it looked like they were headed straight for her. When she changed course and they corrected to follow, she became certain. One of them fired a burst of tracers across her twelve as it streaked by, the wind from its passage almost causing her to stall.

"Hey!" she shouted. "Are you serious?"

She turned on the radio.

"... final warning," it was saying. "You are over restricted airspace. Land immediately."

The jets were turning back.

She put the small plane into a dive. Everything went light. She knew if they fired their missiles there was nothing she could do, and she could only hope they didn't think she was worth it.

Almost to the ground, she pulled up—nearly too late, but she whooped in delight as the field rushed by her at almost two hundred klicks an hour. The jets passed again, far overhead, but now they were turning to make a run at her. It was time to stop fooling around.

She gained a little altitude and spotted a dirt road. She lined up with it, then eased back, or thought she did, but her nose went high and she stalled. The plane struck the road, hard. The landing gear snapped and the craft was suddenly skidding on its belly. A wing struck a telephone pole, and spun the plane twice before it roughly settled into a ditch.

She unbuckled and climbed out of the crumpled aircraft and walked a safe distance away, in case it took a notion to catch fire. She looked around, and saw little but fields in every direction, although the top of the spacecraft was still visible on the horizon.

Nowhere to hide, even if there was a point in doing so.

She took a seat on the bank of the ditch, lit up a cigarette, and waited for them to find her. The first to show up were a couple of guys in the blue uniforms of the People's Police, probably from some nearby hamlet. They examined the plane, and then looked over at her.

"You there," one of them said. "Did you see the pilot? Which way did he go?"

She blinked. It hadn't occurred to them that the only person anywhere near the wreck was the pilot—because she was a girl. She probably could just tell them she was on her way home from school, and that a tall man with a Minjiang accent had run off thataway. She'd be able to skate out of this whole thing.

But it irked her to be so easily dismissed. Why? Because of her age? Because she had a skirt on?

"I'm the pilot," she said.

"Don't joke, girl," the officer said.

"Not joking," she replied.

He stared at her for a moment. "What were you doing flying a plane?"

"It seemed like a nice day for it," she said.

About that time she heard the helicopters coming, and knew she wouldn't have gotten away with the other thing, anyway.

"How old are you?" the policeman demanded.

"Thirteen," she told him.

"Not such a good pilot, I guess," the other man said, kicking at the wreck.

"I think I did okay," she said. "It's the first time I ever landed on my own."

The helicopters began settling in the field. These weren't locals, either.

"Man," she sighed. "These guys really can't take a joke."

* * *

They took her someplace, confiscated her I.D. and everything but her clothes, which a female officer searched carefully.

"A girl your age shouldn't be smoking these," the officer told her as she took Rain's cigarettes and lit one for herself. They took Rain's fingerprints, and a little blood.

Then they put her in a little gray room and asked her a bunch of questions. She answered them honestly, trying to keep her composure, but the fact was she was starting to get a little worried. Her plan had been to return the plane—landing it somewhere near its hangar, and then proceed home on foot. She'd expected some trouble from the local cops, but this—this was starting to get a little scary.

Especially after two days passed. She hadn't been charged with anything, and since the first day no one had spoken to her other than to offer her food and drink. The third day, a man in the uniform of an Earth Space Defense lieutenant showed up. He had a thin face and seemed very stern.

"Come on," he said.

"Where are we going?" she asked.

"You're going home," he replied.

He took her to a helicopter, and an hour later she was home.

* * *

Auntie Far was a mess. She couldn't even talk to her at first. New Guy just kept comforting her and giving Rain evil looks.

Auntie wasn't really her aunt. Due to the old one-child policy, if you had an aunt or uncle they were usually really old. She was lucky to have a real uncle. Of course the policy had ended after the alien attack, but it would still be a few years before aunts were commonplace.

Auntie Far was really a cousin on her mother's side, but Rain's mother and Far had been close. Rain had been visiting Auntie Far while her mom was attending a conference in Beijing. Her mother had died there, when the destroyer incinerated the city.

Rain went into the kitchen and cooked herself some noodles with preserved mustard greens and black bean paste. It had been a while since she'd had anything good to eat. She had just finished when Auntie Far came into the kitchen. There wasn't much to it—a gas cook surface with two burners, a sink, and a small table with two chairs.

Her "aunt" joined her at the table. She was still a relatively young, nice-looking woman—as Rain's mother would have been, were she still alive.

"I'm sorry, Auntie," she said. "I'm not sure what I was thinking."

Far took her hand. "I love you," she said. "I know you didn't want to come here. I know you liked the city. But I have family here, and work. We weren't making it in the north."

"And New Guy doesn't like me," she said. "He wants a child of his own."

Auntie Far's face became very still.

Rain was already regretting saying it.

"Auntie…" she began.

"No," her cousin said. "Rain—I love you. When your mother and father died, I gladly took you in. But I cannot handle you anymore. You're on a path that leads nowhere good. I have failed you, and so we must try something new."

"New?" Rain said. "What do you mean?"

"Pack your things," Auntie Far said. "Everything you think you'll need. You leave in the morning."

"For where? For how long?"

"I can't talk about this anymore," she said.

"Auntie!"

"Pack," she said.

*   *   *

A car came before the dawn. The driver stowed her bags in the trunk without any comment. Auntie watched silently, until it was time to go.

"It's for your own good," she said, as they hugged goodbye.

Rain wanted to plead to stay, or at least part of her did, but on one level she was too angry. Whatever place her aunt was sending her to, it was less for Rain's good than for her own, of that she was sure. Auntie Far wanted to get on with her life, and it was clear she couldn't do that with the anchor of a teenager around her neck.

So Rain got in the car feeling stiff, and still angry, and she was sure she would feel that way for the rest of her life.

It was a very long car ride to the nearest real airport, and by the time she got there she had nodded off a few times. The driver escorted her in, made sure her tickets and documents were in order, and left.

She saw that she had three transfers, and that her final destination was a place called Jiuquan, in Gansu Province. She had never been particularly good at geography, but she thought it was in the northwest somewhere.

Then she was flying again. She liked it a lot less when

she wasn't at the controls, but it was fascinating to watch the landscape roll by and change beneath her, from the fields, plains, and snaking rivers of the heartland to progressively drier, rougher-looking terrain, until she began to see the bones of the earth poking through its green skin. Then there was more bone than green—just desert and the isolated swaths of vegetation surrounding rivers. She had never been to the desert before, and she wasn't sure which she felt most—anticipation or apprehension.

She didn't get to see much of Jiuquan—as she debarked a man in an ESD pilot's uniform met her and escorted her to yet another plane, this one not much larger than the one she had stolen. Within twenty minutes they were back in the air, and the landscape became really severe.

"Where are we?" she asked the pilot after a while, not really expecting an answer. He was young, maybe no more than twenty, and had an accent she didn't recognize. Pleasantly, he also turned out to be a little more talkative than the car driver.

"Inner Mongolia," he said. "That's the Gobi Desert you see below you."

Mongolia?

"Where are we going?" she asked.

He appeared surprised. "You don't know?"

"Not really," she said.

He pointed up ahead, where she now could see a massive spread of human construction and tall, narrow towers that seemed somehow too spindly to be inhabited.

"Dongfeng Aerospace City," he said.

Dongfeng, she thought. *East Wind.*

He did a turn around the enormous city in the desert, lined up with a runway, and began his descent. She watched as huge hangars, rocket gantries, and industrial facilities grew larger and whipped past. The place was lousy with military aircraft, from fighters to gigantic transports. They touched down, and even before the door was open she recognized the uniformed man watching her arrival.

"Uncle Jiang!" she shouted.

* * *

"You have no idea how close you came to a prison sentence, young lady," Lao Jiang scolded Rain. "I had to ask for favors, which I am loath to do—you've no idea how this has put me out."

"I'm sorry," she said. "I was upset. I wasn't thinking—"

"No," he said. "You weren't, but you're going to start thinking right now. My brother's daughter isn't going to grow up to be some sort of hoodlum ne'er-do-well. Do you understand?"

"No," she said. "I don't. All I wanted to do was see where he got shot down, what he was fighting—"

"Did it help?" he asked. "Is he any less dead?"

"No," she said softly.

"I understand your anger, and your sorrow," he said. "I—wish I could have been more available to you these past few years, but I've been promoted. It's hard for me to get away from this place at the moment."

"As for that," Rain said, "why are we in the middle of the Gobi Desert, Uncle Jiang?"

"We're building," he said.

"Building what?"

"Our future," he replied. "You'll learn about that later. For right now, listen to me. You may have noticed the size of this place. There are a lot of people here, and many of them have families. There is therefore a school here—which you will attend. You will not cut class, you will work hard, and you will not joyride in any of the fighter jets."

"I don't think I can fly a fighter jet," she said.

"Nonsense," he replied. "You can fly anything you

want. You can *do* anything you want. But if you don't straighten up, you won't get the chance. You want to fly again? Then earn the privilege. Fly for China."

It dawned on her then that she wasn't *actually* in trouble.

"You're proud of me," she said.

He looked outraged.

"For stealing?" he snapped. "For flying into a restricted area? For crashing a plane?"

"For walking away from it," she said. "You never really taught me to land, remember?"

He glared at her, but she swore one side of his mouth twitched up.

"Come along," he said. "Let's get you settled in."

"Hey, Steve," David Levinson said. He held out a bottle of wine. "Housewarming present."

Steve examined the bottle. "Alright," he said. "Champagne. Classy. This'll go great with the foie gras I'm grilling out back."

"It's like beer, but more expensive," David said. "Goes with anything."

"Y'all come on in," Hiller said. "Hi, Connie." He and Connie exchanged a brief hug, and by then Jasmine was at the door, and they made a complete round of greetings.

"The place looks different," David said, looking around. "More..."

"Like a woman lives here?" Jasmine said. "Less like a frat house basement?"

"Those are exactly the words I was looking for," Levinson said. Then he did a slight double take. "Dylan?" he said. "Holy smokes."

Hiller turned as his son arrived in the foyer.

"Put on a little height, hasn't he?" Steve said.

"And put in some testosterone," David said. "Is that stubble? Are you trying to grow a beard? How old are you now, thirty?"

"Just seventeen," Dylan said.

"And the low voice?" Connie said. "Where did the low voice come from?"

"It happens," Jasmine said. "All too quick it happens."

"Let's get out of the door," Steve said. "The grill's getting ready out back."

"What can I get you to drink?" Jasmine asked.

"Why don't we go ahead and crack the bubbly?" Hiller said. "It's been, what, four years since we were all together? That's worth a little celebration."

*   *   *

It was almost too chilly for the Hawaiian shirt and shorts Hiller had chosen as his attire for the event, and it would only get cooler as the evening moved on. But when a man had a nice hot charcoal fire going, and hamburger patties waiting for the coals to be just right, he had to look the part, even if it was November.

He had tried grilling during the summer, the year after he moved here. Once. From that he learned that when the mercury read one hundred and six, and humidity was more or less zero, you had no business with a spatula in your hand unless you were inside, with the AC cranked, flipping pancakes.

The moon was a white ghost in the bright Nevada sky. He looked at it wistfully for a moment.

"Soon," he said. "You and me."

He checked the coals and thought they needed another few minutes. He got his glass and sat with the others on the patio, where they'd pulled rattan chairs up to a table with an umbrella.

"I was just asking Dylan how the STEP is," Connie said as Hiller arrived.

"I wanna hear the answer to this myself," Hiller said. "I

need an update. Kid won't even let me do his homework anymore."

"You can do my homework anytime you want," Dylan said. "Just don't turn it in. I'm trying to get into the ESD Academy, remember?"

"Ouch," Hiller said. "Didn't we have that talk about father–son solidarity and the, you know, correlation of that to access to the car keys? Cuz I thought we had that talk."

"Dad has been very helpful in supporting my studies," Dylan said quickly. "Anyway, the school is great. Hard, but I knew it would be. Still, it's kind of rough. Back in Virginia I was at the top of my class. Here—there's a lot of competition."

"My boy is up to the challenge," Jasmine said.

Dylan looked a little embarrassed.

"The thing is, I came in with all kinds of advantages. Most of us at the STEP school did, but others, like my buddy Jake—he's my lab partner in chemistry—he really had to work to get here. His parents were in L.A. when—you know. He grew up in an orphanage."

"A lot of kids your age did," Connie said.

"Yeah. Kind of makes me appreciate my own circumstances," Dylan said. "I've got a mom and a dad. I had pretty good schools coming up. I think Jake was mostly self-taught. He sticks out a little."

"Well, it sounds like he's motivated," Hiller said.

"He wants to be a pilot too," Dylan added.

"Oh, well that's too bad," Hiller said. "You'll never be friends with that chump."

"Why do you say that?" David asked.

"Well, you know—pilots," Hiller said. "Bunch of self-important jerks."

"Oh, right," David agreed. "Absolutely. Dylan, listen to your father."

"I always do," Dylan said.

"See?" Hiller said. "That's that solidarity I was talking about. Also—don't forget you said that."

"This is sort of what Connie was—I'm sorry, Senator Levinson—was talking about on TV the other day," Jasmine said.

"Oh, you saw that?" Connie said.

"Yeah," Jasmine said. "You seemed a little, well…"

"Frustrated?" Connie said.

"I was gonna say pissed off," Jasmine said.

"Yah," Connie agreed. "The big news is that the whole country—the whole world—is united, right?"

"That's the story," David said, "and we're all sticking to it."

"The fact is, we're only on the same page about priority number one," Connie said. "After that—well, Congress is still Congress. You would think that the education bill would be non-controversial, right? We need pilots and engineers, scientists of every kind, and yet educational opportunities are shrinking for most of our kids. 'The focus is on quality, not quantity'—I know that's Jacobs' favorite line, and he can prove by example that the STEP schools turn out great students. But we could have *both*—very good schools, and lots of them, for a fraction of our GDP."

"Well," Jasmine said, "I thought you were very articulate, and I think that other guy was a condescending jackass."

"You get used to that if you're a woman in Congress," Connie said.

"Honey, you get used to that if you're a woman anyplace but the kitchen," Jasmine said.

"Excuse me," Hiller said. "I think those coals ain't gonna wait. Besides, I hear me a girl power conversation about to happen."

"Let me help you with that," David said.

"That's all good," Hiller said. "You know your way around a spatula?"

"Maybe not all the way around," David said. "Just about halfway."

"Just as well," Hiller said. "You don't take another man's spatula from him—not in his own backyard. That there is sacred."

He stepped over to the grill, cleaned it off again, then started placing the burgers on the rack, which made a pleasant sizzling sound and released an even better aroma.

"Smell that?" he said. "That's the smell of America." He glanced over at David, trying to decide whether to get into it or not for a second or two before wading in.

Here goes…

"So when are you gonna have something for me to fly?" he asked. "I haven't been grounded this long—well, ever."

David looked pained.

"I've got Strain, Tanner, and Jacobs all over me about this," David said. "Now you too?"

"I get it," Hiller said. "They're pushing hard."

"It's not the hard," David said. "It's the *fast*. Those people we lost in the tunnel last month—"

"Was *not* your fault," Steve said.

"Nooo… yes it was. Because I knew we weren't ready for Beta. I should have refused, I should have walked out."

"You should be the damn director," Steve said. "Everybody knows that."

David opened his mouth to reply, but instead he waited a beat and then shrugged.

"Yeah, well," he said, "as many times as I've butted heads with these guys, I don't think I could do that now even if I wanted to."

"You know what you sound like?" Steve said. "You sound exactly like a man who wants the job."

"Well, you know how some people are," David said, after taking a sip of champagne. "Always wanting what they can't have. Now that I can't have it—"

"Bullshit," Hiller said. "You're a hero. You're the guy who saved us all. Me being able to fly that thing—that was nothing without you. Everything would have been for nothing if you hadn't done that thing with the computer virus. You just need to remind people who the hell you are."

"Maybe," David said.

"So," Hiller said. "Seriously. A whole 'nother year?"

"Don't be in a hurry."

Hiller nodded, but then he pointed to Dylan and Jasmine, and waved his spatula at the sky.

"They're coming back, you know that, right? E.T. phoned home. They're coming for us again. For my wife and my son. I get that you want to take it slow. You're probably right. I'm just getting nervous, you know? It's like a countdown."

"I know," David said. "I know, but I've got something that will keep you busy for the next few months, anyway."

"Yeah?"

"Uh-huh. The Chinese are getting antsy too. We're sending you over there to start their training program. The hybrid fighters may not be ready, but the simulators are ready to go, and the same tactical simulations you've been doing with our older jets is better than nothing. They asked for you."

"Well if they *asked* for me," Hiller said, "I reckon I'd better go." He pointed his spatula at David. "But you think about some of the stuff I said, okay? You're David Levinson. You need to get off your ass and own that."

"I'm a lease to own kind of guy," David said. "Less chance of buyer's remorse."

18

FEBRUARY

2007

It was easy to lose track of time kissing Emily. She was eminently kissable, had maybe the perfect mouth for it, and her face looked great in close up. So when Jake finally thought to look at his watch, he got a rude surprise.

"Crap," he said. "We're gonna be late."

She nibbled on his ear, which drove him crazy, and not in a bad way.

"So?" she murmured.

"So I told Dylan I would be there."

She sighed. "Fine. If you would rather be with Dylan…"

"Well, you're going too," Jake said. "Right?"

She touched her forehead to his. "Can't we just celebrate here?"

It was tempting, especially when she said it in the low tone of voice… but he didn't like to go back on his word.

"I told him I would be there," he said.

"Fine," Emily said.

"What's wrong?" he asked.

"What's wrong?" she said. "You have no idea? Nothing occurs?"

Jake wasn't as clueless as he made out to be, but he didn't see the point in starting the discussion she wanted to have. The celebration was all about Jake and Dylan being accepted into the Academy. Which meant that next fall, they would be leaving 51. He and Emily had been together for nearly a year, and it was starting to feel serious. There was a conversation that needed to happen, but he wasn't ready for that yet.

"Is this about my other girlfriends?" he said.

"Oh, shut up," she said. "Let's go meet Dylan and what's-her-name."

"Terry," he said. "Her name is Terry. We'd better move, we're supposed to get Charlie on the way."

"Of course we are," Emily said.

* * *

Their destination was Sean Thompson's house. His parents were only rarely home before midnight on weekends, and even when they were they were fairly *laissez-faire* about what went on in the basement game room—which wasn't usually anything particularly out of line. Tonight, though, Sean had somehow procured a few bottles of champagne. Jake hadn't spent a lot of time drinking, and Dylan practically never touched the stuff, probably from fear of disappointing his parents. Jake usually eschewed because he didn't want it to interfere with his studies. But school had gotten him where he wanted to go, so he figured a little indulgence wouldn't hurt.

Champagne, as it turned out, was pretty good.

Things started in high spirits. Charlie looked a little uncomfortable, since he didn't have a date. Sean and his girlfriend, Melissa, were working seriously at getting drunk. Emily asked Terry slightly barbed questions, and Dylan waxed poetic about the virtues of the Academy. Terry asked him questions about his famous dad, which left Jake without much to say.

So finally, he decided to change the subject.

"Pool," he said, pointing at the table. "Two out of three. Five bucks."

"You're on," Dylan said. "Rack 'em."

"Why don't we play doubles?" Terry asked. She was a pretty girl, heavily freckled, with curly auburn hair. Her suggestion was met with a moment of profound silence.

"Oh, no," Emily said, taking the other girl's hand. "Just walk away from the table. You don't want any part of that."

"What do you mean?" Terry asked. "It's just pool."

"These are two of the most competitive men you're ever going to meet," Emily explained, "and if you're on a team with one of them, and God forbid you miss a shot. . . Let it go. Let them bang their penises together by themselves."

"She means figuratively," Dylan said. Toggling his finger between him and Jake. "This thing here is strictly platonic."

"Whatever," Emily said.

Jake narrowly lost to Dylan in the first game, but that didn't worry him too much. He usually hit his stride in the second match, and the bubbly was making him feel loose and confident. It started well, with him breaking and sinking three balls before missing a shot.

That, however, was the high point of the game. He missed one shot he really, really shouldn't have, and began to get frustrated. Then, next turn, he scratched, allowing Dylan to set up for a substantial lead. It didn't help that Terry cheered enthusiastically every time Dylan made a shot, but Emily remained silent on his behalf, chatting instead with Sean and Melissa.

He noticed somewhere along the line that Dylan hadn't had much to drink at all.

Mama's boy, he grumbled to himself.

"Sandbagged me," he grunted.

"What?" Dylan said.

"Nothing," Jake said. "Two out of three?"

"Dude, that *was* two out of three." He reached for his glass. "How about a toast?" he said, pouring a little of the champagne.

"That sounds good," Jake said, still irked.

"To us," Dylan said. "To the Academy."

"To me and you," Jake said.

They clinked and drank. Jake reached for the pool cue.

"Let's go again," he said.

Dylan shook his head, sat down and pulled Terry onto his lap. She giggled.

Jake stood red-faced for a moment, then fell back onto the couch next to Charlie. He poured himself some more champagne.

"Dude," Charlie said, *sotto voce*. "You maybe shouldn't drink any more of that."

"You know what?" Jake said, refilling his glass, and producing one for Charlie. "I want to make another toast." He wobbled to his feet. "To my buddy, Charlie. Without him, none of this would have been possible. For me, anyway, cause I didn't have—you know—parents, much less famous ones who saved the fricken' world. Or, you know, money, or a fancy school. But I had Charlie. To you, Charlie."

"Jake," Charlie said. "Ease up."

It was too late. Dylan was already walking toward the door.

"Jake!" Emily said.

"Ah, goddamit," Jake said, as the door closed. "Just hang on, everybody. I'll fix this. I'll be back."

*   *   *

"Dylan," he called, once he was outside. "Hold up."

But Dylan wasn't walking. He was just standing there, waiting.

"Do we have a problem?" he asked. "Because I thought

we were friends, but now it looks like we have a problem—
with, what—me having parents?"

"I'm sorry, man," Jake said. "It's the champagne. You
know I'm not a big drinker."

"Alcohol doesn't come up with things like that," Dylan
said. "It just makes it easier to say them. You know, I'm
sorry about your parents. I know you had it harder than
me, but that doesn't mean everything comes easy to me.
I've worked just as hard at this school as anyone."

"I know," Jake said. "I was being stupid."

Of course, Dylan lived at home and didn't have to
work after school…

He knew he didn't need to go there.

"Come on," he said. "You're my buddy. Let's just go
celebrate. Maybe Emily's right, maybe we should just watch
TV or something. We are assholes when we compete."

"Well, you are anyway," Dylan said, but Jake could tell
he was joking now.

"Okay," Jake agreed. "Dial the competition back for
tonight. Be chill." He slapped Dylan on the shoulder.
"Remember that time with the motorcycles?"

"It was a wonder we weren't both killed," Dylan said.

"Yes, it was," Jake said. "Let's go back in before they
think we're making out or something—and no more pool."

He turned and started for the door.

"We could play darts," Dylan said.

"Hell, yes," Jake said. "Darts. Prepare to meet your
doom, Hiller."

* * *

"Now that's what I call a great wall," Steve Hiller said,
staring down through the cockpit glass at the arid
landscape and the snaking line of ancient masonry that
bisected it.

Seated to his right, Lao Jiang sighed and said something in Chinese.

"Oh, you've heard that one before?" Hiller said.

Lao looked surprised. "You understand Mandarin?" he said, in English.

"No," Hiller said, "but I get the general tone. I apologize. Sometimes my mouth gets a little ahead of the rest of me."

"Ah," Lao said. Hiller wondered if he was embarrassed. Lao was hard to read, except when he lost his temper. When that happened he tipped a little toward the crazy side, something Hiller could sort of appreciate.

"What do you think of the controls?" Lao asked, after a moment.

"Handles like a dream," Hiller said. "Although I'm used to something a little smaller and much faster."

They were at an altitude of two kilometers in a freighter prototype. It was more than a hundred meters long, and nearly half as wide, but not very deep. The underside was mostly powerful hydraulic landing gear and massive anti-gravity thrusters. When the vessel was in use, cargo would be secured to the platform, with the freighter functioning not unlike a sea-going container ship. The bridge and living quarters were contained in a raised tower toward the front of the craft.

Hiller wasn't just playing nice in praising its response. Considering its mass, it maneuvered beautifully—just very, very slowly.

"How many of these are you building?" Hiller asked.

"We think four will be enough," Lao said. "At least in the first stages. It's a bit of—what's your term?—a work around. Since a fully functional hybrid engine continues to elude us, we thought we could get a start using only the anti-gravity component, which seems more... stable."

"As in doesn't blow up?" Hiller said. "Yeah, I get it.

Although I think we're closer to the whole banana than you might expect."

"I've seen the latest updates," Lao said. "The fusion component remains volatile."

"Sure," Hiller said, "but we've come a long way. Meanwhile you guys over here are kicking some serious ass. I've got to say, I'm impressed."

Lao turned away—Hiller suspected so he could hide a grin.

"It only has an anti-gravity drive?" Hiller asked.

"It has some traditional chemical engines for emergency maneuvering in the event of a loss of power," Lao said, "but substantially, yes. The speed of the ship is very slow, of course. Think of it almost more like a balloon than a spaceship—it doesn't travel upward quickly enough to encounter any sort of problem with atmospheric resistance, so it needn't be streamlined—and it keeps going up once it's out of the atmosphere. It will proceed toward the moon at a leisurely pace."

"Slow boat," Hiller said. "Doesn't push anything into the danger zone."

"Not even close," Lao said. "This craft is probably safer than any aircraft ever built."

"Didn't they say that about the Hindenburg?" Hiller said.

"If they did, it was a stupid assertion," Lao said. "A huge container filled with propellant? There's no analogy here."

"That's just me kidding again," Hiller said, turning the craft again. "Although when it gets down to it, this thing does remind me of a dirigible. Who knows, maybe one of these days we'll be taking solar system cruises on one of these bad boys. Playin' space shuffleboard, watching the rings of Saturn…"

"Not on this ship," Lao said. "It's made for a strictly one-way journey."

"Oh, really? Just from here to the moon, and that's it?"

"That's correct," Lao said. "The thrusters are powerful enough to decelerate for a moon landing, but not strong enough to re-enter the Earth's atmosphere at a safe speed. We could have made them stronger, and the ships more aerodynamic, but at much greater cost. As it is, each of these ships and the cargo they carry will furnish material to build the moon base. Now Mars and Saturn—that's going to require the fusion drive, but that fortunately is not my problem."

"Yeah," Hiller said. "We'll let the French and the Russians worry about that. Say, will this thing do a barrel roll?"

"Regrettably not," Lao said.

"Okay," Hiller said. "Just thought I'd ask."

Lao shifted his seat a bit, to better face Hiller.

"I want to thank you for your participation with our pilots, Colonel Hiller. It has been very good for their morale."

"I've enjoyed working with them too," Hiller said. "They're a talented bunch of kids. If the bad guys come nosing around for another tussle, they're going to get some serious attitude from you guys—just like last time."

"That's kind of you to say," Lao said.

"Hey, I call it like I see it."

Lao nodded. Then an uncomfortable sort of expression appeared on his face.

"I wonder if I might impose upon you for a personal favor," he said.

"Let's hear it," Hiller said.

"My niece—you're something of a hero to her. If you wouldn't mind meeting her, perhaps give her some encouragement. She plans to be a pilot."

"That's not even a favor," Hiller said. "That would be my pleasure."

* * *

"David," Director Strain said. "Please, have a seat."

Strain's office was something of a testimony to space flight. Portraits of Yuri Gagarin, Neil Armstrong, John Glenn, and several other early space explorers adorned his walls, and his bookshelves were cluttered with scale models of various spacecraft, from the earliest Soyuz up through the space shuttle.

On his desk was a small mock-up of the hybrid fighter they were currently working to produce. It looked very much like a fighter jet, but conspicuously lacked jet engines—instead, it sported twin anti-gravity fusion engines underneath the wings and behind the landing gear. It hadn't been in the office the last time David had been there, which was only a handful of days earlier.

"So, David, how are things?" Strain asked.

"Depends on the things," David said. "Do you want me to sort of ramble, or do you have something specific you want to know about?"

"Specifically, I want to know about that," Strain said, gesturing at the model fighter.

"I think it's coming along nicely," David said. "A little more slowly than some would like…"

"A *lot* more slowly than some would like," Strain said. "I'm getting more and more pressure from the administration to at least have a test flight."

Here we go again, David thought. *Be diplomatic.*

"I understand the hurry," he said, "but we have to get this right. We have a new mathematical model that's extremely promising, but it's going to take some time to move from theory to engineering. If everything goes well, I think we can easily schedule a manned test around this time next year."

"I don't think you do understand," Strain said. "They

want a ship ready for a manned test flight by the ESD Spring Expo."

"What?" David said incredulously. "No! That's arbitrary. We don't build things to the schedule of—a… a *show*. A three-ring circus! We fly it when it's ready."

"David," Strain said, "a lot of people are hurting because we're putting so much into the ESD. Social programs are on life support. Most people are just getting by, and taxes are sky-high. There are elections coming up. There's already a slate of loonies waiting to run who want to defund us or drastically cut our budget. What if they manage to attract voters? The people need to see that we're producing results."

"We *are* producing results," David said. "I dare anyone to say we aren't."

"Well, they want this particular result," Strain said. "Because it's photogenic. It's sexy. People will get it."

"Who is 'they'?" David demanded.

"Tanner. President Jacobs. The Joint Chiefs of Staff. Congress."

"Oh," David said. "That 'they.'" He shook his head. "You have to tell them no," he said. "April is too soon. A few months more, at least. Maybe we can launch during Oktoberfest. Or Rosh Hashanah. And let it be a drone."

Strain pursed his lips and nodded slightly.

"Okay, David," he said. "Have it your way."

* * *

The next day, he found out what *Okay, David. Have it your way* meant, when his passkey no longer admitted him into the hybrid development area. At first he assumed it was a glitch, but when he went into the system to try and fix it, he saw he was locked out of that too.

"Sonofabitch," he said under his breath. "They did it, the bastards."

His first impulse was to go at Strain, but twelve seconds of reflection told him that was pointless.

So he dialed up his secretary.

"Get me on the next flight to Washington," he said.

19

Secretary of Defense Tanner had a receding hairline and shocks of gray hair at his temples. The expression on his face usually read as *no trespassing* or *do not enter*, and that was certainly the case today.

"David," he said. "I wish you had set this meeting up in advance. You can't just jump on a plane unannounced, and expect to be seen at the White House."

Oh yes I can, David thought, but he sensed it was better not to say it out loud.

"Where's the president?" he asked instead.

"Very busy. And Vice-President Lanford is out of the country. I'll have to do, and I don't have that much time myself."

"I've been taken off the hybrid project," David said. "Why?"

"You could have asked Director Strain that," Tanner said. "Saved yourself a flight."

"It wasn't his idea," David said. "I actually think he knows better, but he's too much of a coward when it comes to his job."

Tanner's already low eyebrows drooped lower.

"There are reports that you've been holding things up," Tanner said.

"Holding things up?" David sputtered. "No. It's called 'proceeding with caution.'"

"Too much caution, in our estimation," Tanner said. "The problems with the cannons have been worked out. Why is this taking so long?"

"Because this is more complicated," David said. "Antigravity does funny things at the quantum level, and that has an effect on all of the systems—including the power source and the reliability of the fusion containment shield. And there isn't a person riding on a cannon. If one of them becomes unstable and goes bang, it has a force field to contain it."

"The Chinese have flying dreadnoughts," Strain said. "We're starting to look bad."

"You want a fighter that can't break the sound barrier, I can give you that right now," David said. "And since when is this about national pride? This is an international effort, yes?"

"You have plenty of other responsibilities—"

"Not like this," David said. "You at least have to give me oversight. If you rush this through just for the sake of publicity, someone is going to get killed. Again."

"Levinson," Tanner said ominously, "I seem to remember hearing that you were offered the directorship, back when. You didn't want it. That means you're not in charge—you're part of a chain of command, and that chain of command is telling you to step away from this. Now."

"You can't—"

Tanner glanced at his watch. "That's your ten minutes," he said. "Have a nice flight home."

* * *

Dikembe pushed the jeep to its limit, banging along the unpaved road, hoping an axle didn't snap. A small herd of wildebeest darted from his path, and a few vultures flapped heavily from the limbs of an acacia tree. Up ahead he saw the border outpost, and a cluster of human figures.

He laid on the horn.

When he pulled up a moment later, he saw with relief that everyone in the little group was still standing. They— and the armed soldiers pointing rifles at them—turned at his approach.

"What is this?" he demanded. He recognized some of the men held at gunpoint. They were residents of a nearby village. He didn't have time to count them, but there were fewer than a dozen of them.

"They were trying to desert the republic," one of the soldiers said. "We have standing orders concerning such matters."

"Sir," one of the men said. "We were not leaving. We were hoping to get work in Kisangani, to provide for our families. We planned to return. We would never desert the republic."

"I know you," Dikembe said. "Guillaume, is it not? You were with the army. You were there that day when we broke them."

"Yes, sir," he said, "but I was injured. I still serve in the reserves, but I have no pension and no work. They say there is work in Kisangani."

"Not for you, traitor," one of the soldiers said.

"Yes, and you?" Dikembe said. "What is your name?"

"Mosi, my prince," the soldier replied.

"What nonsense," Dikembe said, waving it away with the back of his hand. "I am not a prince, not by any stretch of the imagination."

Mosi looked chagrined.

"Sir," he began, "your father—"

"Yes, I know," Dikembe sighed. "Did you fight with us that day, Mosi?"

"No, Prince. I was only twelve."

"It's a miracle you weren't drafted anyway. Mosi, these men are heroes of the state and have done nothing wrong. Release them."

"We are under orders to execute runaways," Mosi said.

"I am aware of that," Dikembe said. "But look at them. They are your countrymen, your people. Their fathers and yours were in cradles together." He drew his sidearm. "And if that's not enough, I'm telling you, stand down. You will have to shoot me before you murder them."

Mosi stood strong for a moment, but then he sighed and signed for his men to lower their weapons.

"We will suffer for this," he said. "We may die ourselves when your father hears what happened here."

"That is why no one will speak of this," Dikembe said. "That is why my father will never know."

He turned to Guillaume and the rest.

"You men come with me," he said, and he walked a short distance away. The men followed.

"You saved our lives," Guillaume said, after they were out of earshot of the soldiers.

"You were lucky," he said. "I was listening on their radio band. You must be more careful."

"I cannot watch my children starve," the man said.

"I understand that," he said. "I will have some supplies brought to your village. After that, I will see what can be done."

*   *   *

After seeing the men back to their families, Dikembe returned home, the hollow growing in the pit of his stomach.

Much had changed in the last eleven years, and none of it for the better. His father had done what he said he would. All of the border crossings now proclaimed the territory as the Republique Nationale d'Umbutu. Dikembe himself had been drafted to design the flag, which depicted the stylized head of an alien with two machetes thrust through it, against a star and a red background. Two such flags fluttered on his jeep.

The house—the place where he had grown up—was now the statehouse of Umbutu, and had been suitably painted to proclaim it so. This despite the fact that the old central government had attempted reconciliation several times. Aid organizations offering to provide medicine and food were turned away as well. Each day seemed to bring less hope than the last. Dikembe thought that things would get better once the aliens were all dead.

Instead they had gotten worse.

He found his father in his room, fully dressed in his military attire, lying on the bed.

"My son," Upanga Umbutu said. "Come rest with me." It seemed as if his father had aged several decades in the space of one. His hair was grayer, the lines of his face set deeper, but it was more than that.

Reluctantly Dikembe got up on the bed and lay on the brightly patterned coverlet. A ceiling fan beat overhead, pushing the hot summer air around the room. His father took his hand.

"Do you remember?" he said. "When you and Bakari were little, how we would lie like this in the heat of the afternoon, one of you on each side of me?"

Dikembe did. Back then, his father had been a busy man, always working, often gone for many days at a time to the capital or some hot spot. When he was home, however, he always took an hour to rest with his boys. They might talk of their day—more usually they took a nap—but he remembered how protected it had made him feel, how loved.

"I'm not a little boy anymore," Dikembe said.

"I know," his father said, "but sometimes I need my little boy. Both of my little boys."

Dikembe was silent, thinking. Quiet moments with his father were few these days. Should he merely receive it as a gift, or look at it as an opportunity?

People were hurting. His people.

"Father," he ventured after a moment. "It's been a year since the last of the aliens was killed. Isn't it time we rejoined the world?"

His father closed his eyes, and Dikembe wondered if he would ignore the question.

Then his lids fluttered open.

"That world is not for us," his father said. "None of them are to be trusted. That is all so clear to me. This is our place. We must protect our people."

"Our people are starving," Dikembe said. "Some are being executed for trying to find work."

"For deserting their country," his father said. "Disloyalty cannot be tolerated. We must be strong. We must face them down, these monsters that killed my Bakari." It wasn't the first time his father had said something like that, but it stirred a bit of horror in Dikembe, because he feared what it meant.

"They are dead, Papa," Dikembe said. "All of them."

"They are not," his father said. "They live on, inside and outside of our borders. They may look human, but they are not."

It was too much. Dikembe started to rise, but his father gripped his hand harder.

"I have heard rumors," he said, "that my son has been interfering with the work of the Home Guard."

So he knew, or thought he knew. Dikembe had always been aware that it would only be a matter of time before his activities were noticed by the old man.

"You made me a general after the war," Dikembe said. "They are under my command, are they not?"

"To be clear," Umbutu said, "they are not. They answer only to me—as do you. Do you have plans to usurp me, son? Is this what all of your scribbling has brought you to?"

"No," Dikembe said, feeling a chill pass through him. "I have no such intentions. You are my father."

"You would not be the first son to murder his father for his own gain," the old man pointed out.

"I wish you could not believe such a thing about me," Dikembe said softly.

His father sighed. "I don't, of course, my dear boy," he said. "I'm sure you would not have the stomach for it."

*   *   *

"So this is what you learned at Oxford?" Zuberi asked, glancing around the cluttered little room Dikembe thought of as his studio.

"It helps me clear my mind," Dikembe said. "You know what I mean. I'm trying to draw the things they forced into my brain."

"Why relive that?" Zuberi said. "I was tortured only a tenth as much as you were, and I do my damnedest not to think of it, ever."

"That doesn't work for me," Dikembe said. "I think I'm hoping if I draw these things enough, I will eventually get them out of my head. But I have to get them *right*, you know, exactly right—and that hasn't happened… yet. So I draw on. I think it keeps me sane."

Zuberi, gazing at the alien symbols and paintings, some of which were so abstract as to be inchoate even to Dikembe, seemed skeptical—until his eye rested on one particular sketch. It was one of the simplest, a circle with a line through it.

"My God," Zuberi said. "What the hell is that?"

"I call it *Fear*," Dikembe said.

"It's disturbing as hell," Zuberi said. He turned away from it.

"I know," Dikembe said. "But why?"

*   *   *

Whitmore greeted her at the door. He looked well enough, a little older, and a lot more relaxed.

"Connie," he said. "It's good to see you. Come on in, have a seat. Irene will bring us a little lunch."

They sat at his kitchen table. The maid brought coffee.

"David doesn't know I'm here," she said.

"Is that such a good idea?" he said with a little smile. "Considering."

"No, this is more about his pride," she said. "I don't want him thinking I'm trying to fix things for him."

"What *are* you doing?" Whitmore asked.

"I'm trying to, uh… fix things for him," she said. She explained the nature of the problem, and the former president listened without much comment until she was done. By then, chicken salad sandwiches had appeared on the table. As they ate, Connie noticed a picture on the wall.

"Wow," she said. "Is that Patricia?"

Whitmore nodded. "Yes," he said. "Seventeen. Can you believe it? She'll be attending the ESD Academy next year."

"Dylan, too," Connie said. "That'll be nice. To have someone you know in a new place is always a good thing."

"Sure," he said.

"And you—you've been keeping busy," she said.

That was true. It was the rare day that Whitmore didn't appear publicly in some capacity, whether lecturing crowds about the importance of the ESD or acting as a sort of ambassador, celebrating the achievements of the organization around the globe. In some ways he was still more the public face of America and the global alliance than President Jacobs or anyone else in the current administration.

"I like to stay busy," he said. "This place gets a little lonely if I just sit here, and there's so much left to do."

"They say you keep pushing back against the idea of a presidential library."

"Of course," he said. "That's an exercise in vanity. We've got kids in the country without enough to eat. I'm turning donors toward funding schools and existing libraries, and if they feel the need to stick my name on them, fine. But if I'm to have a legacy, I want it to be that we'll never be caught flat-footed again."

He took a breath.

"Sorry, sometimes I forget when I'm talking to an old friend. Connie, I'm not sure I've told you how proud of you I am. I always thought you were cut out for something big, and you've proven it. You've become a real power to reckon with on the Hill."

"Thank you," she said.

"This thing with David," he said, "I don't know how much help I can be. Jacobs is the sitting president, and I can't be seen to get in his way."

"I wasn't thinking of anything public or overt," she said, "but you know David. He's usually right about these things. You may not be in office, but you still have a lot of influence."

"And you want me to use it."

"Yes," she said. "For David. He's earned that."

"Yeah," he said, "you're right. I'll poke around quietly, drop some hints, have a conversation or two. I can't promise anything, though. What you have to understand about me is that what I do these days isn't really politics.

It's more like cheerleading, and I enjoy it—God knows I enjoy it more than backroom deals and trying to wrangle votes from Congress. I was never really cut out for that."

"Yet you did it," Connie said. "You'll certainly go down in history as one of the greatest presidents."

"Yeah," he said. "The president who saw three billion people die on his watch."

"No," she said. "The president who brought us all together so it can never happen again."

"I hope that's true," Whitmore said. "I really hope you're right. Not about how I'm remembered, but—"

"I know," she said.

20

APRIL

Before Rain became a resident of the Gobi Desert, she had imagined that all deserts were hot. This might have been because she'd paid little attention to geography lessons when she was younger, and possibly because the image her younger mind had summoned at the word "desert" was the Sahara.

The Gobi was high desert, and in the winter it could be very cold indeed. Depending on the winds, it could be cool even in summer, but on this late day in April it was unseasonably warm, nearly eighty degrees as she walked the dusty path from the school toward the apartment she shared with her Uncle Jiang. She stopped to slip off her shoes and dangle her feet in the cool water of the Ruo River, and gaze off at the scruffy hills west of town.

West, over mountains and plains, forests and finally an ocean, to America, where she was *not* going tomorrow. Of course, from here it was probably quicker to go east— or no, north, over the pole. It didn't matter. She would still be here, eating noodles with mutton, not hamburgers.

She watched a dragonfly hunt in the reeds. Across the shallow river, younger children laughed as they played tag among swings and jungle gyms. East, in the desert, the gigantic ships loomed, nearly ready to go to the moon.

She wished she could be on one of them, or at least go with Uncle Jiang to America, but she wasn't yet fifteen. Uncle Jiang assured her that her time would come, soon enough, but it seemed to be taking forever, each month crawling along like a snail.

She pulled her feet out and let them dry, which happened quickly in the arid air. Then she slipped her shoes back on and went home.

There she found Uncle Jiang packing, which just made her all the more jealous. She had an apple and a glass of water, and then went to her room to do homework. She paused to look at the framed, autographed picture of Steve Hiller, and collapsed on her bed.

She hadn't yet opened her books when she heard a slight rapping at the door.

"Yes, sir?" she said.

Uncle Jiang stayed in the doorway, looking a little uncomfortable.

"How was school today?" he asked.

"Good," she said. "Nothing to complain about."

"Well," he said. "That's fine."

"Is there anything else?" she said.

He paused another moment. "I know how much you wish you could come with me," he said. "To see the test flight. I'm sorry that it isn't possible. This is state business, and it wouldn't look right to bring nonessential personnel along."

"I understand," she said.

"However," he said, "I've arranged for you to view the event remotely."

"I was planning on watching it in the common room in the compound," she said.

"Yes," he said. "You could do that, or you could watch it here, in the apartment."

"How can I—" Then she hopped up and flew past him

to the next room. There, hanging on the wall, was a flat-screen TV.

"You got a TV," she said, unbelieving. "You, Lao Jiang, got a TV." Her uncle *despised* television. He believed it was the greatest existing underminer of civilization, and that it turned human brains into boiled jellyfish.

"If I see the slightest slip in your grades, it goes out, do you understand?" he said.

"I understand," she said. "Oh, thank you, Uncle Jiang."

"Well," he said. "You've done very well since you've been here. You've followed my rules without fail—at least that I know of."

He glanced away, out of the window.

"Ms. Li will keep an eye on you while I'm gone," he said. "If you wish to have a friend or two over to watch with you, that should be fine. It's a morning launch there, so it won't be too late here, but bear in mind you have school the next day."

"I will, sir," she said.

*　*　*

It had been a long time since Patricia had been on Air Force One, and her memories of the aircraft were indelibly marked by the confusion and terror of their flight from Washington, of the flames and smoke of the city's destruction by an alien destroyer. At six, she hadn't been clear on what was going on, only that grown-ups were frightened, and crying, and yelling at each other. But her father had been there, and that had helped.

He was here now, too, riding at the invitation of Vice-President Lanford.

She watched the barren but beautiful desert terrain as they began their descent, and forced herself to continue watching as the ruins of the wrecked spaceship came into view, now as much a part of the landscape as the volcanic cores and ragged uplifts that characterized the region.

"I get why they want to have the Expo here," she told her dad, "but it still gives me the creeps."

"Our first victory," he said. "It's hard to believe it's been almost eleven years." His eyes shifted to her. "It's hard to believe you're shipping out to the Academy in a few months."

"I'm having a little trouble believing it myself," she said.

"Have you settled on a major?" he asked.

"I'm still considering," she said. "I'm leaning toward poly-sci."

"Your mother would be proud of you," he said. "I know I am."

"Thanks, Dad," she said.

The fact was that she barely remembered her mother. Of course there were plenty of pictures and video to remind her, and biographies to read. And Dad, always Dad with his stories. Patricia wanted to remember, to fill the sadness that did linger, the remainder of the little girl trying to comprehend so much at once. So she could talk to her father about her, because she knew he would like that.

This time, however, she let it fall into silence and watched the desert arrive.

*　　*　　*

"That's truly a thing of beauty," Secretary of Defense Tanner said, touching the smooth metal of the prototype. Colonel Steven Hiller stood by in the hangar as Tanner and Vice-President Lanford examined the craft.

"She is attractive, Mr. Secretary," Hiller acknowledged. He meant it—it gave him shivers just looking at her.

Lanford turned to him. The vice-president was a striking woman in her late forties. She carried herself with an effortless air of competence. She had hazel eyes and dark brown hair, and was wearing a black suit.

"I'm given to understand, Colonel Hiller," she said, "that you have some problem with the test flight."

"Yes, ma'am," he said. "With all due respect, the little problem is that there's not going to be a test flight."

"I beg your pardon?" Tanner said.

"I'm not putting any of my pilots in that thing until David Levinson gives it the once-over, and has the test performance record to evaluate."

"Colonel Hiller," Tanner said, "you're skating toward insubordination."

"Sir, if one of my pilots is in danger, I'll skate all the way up that hill and back down it again."

"First of all," Tanner said, "they aren't 'your' pilots, Colonel Hiller. Secondly, Director Strain assures me this ship is ready to go."

"Why was Levinson removed from the project?" Hiller asked.

"Colonel, I know the two of you are friends—"

"Friends? We flew an alien spacecraft into their mother ship and blew it up. If it weren't for David, none of us would be having this conversation. The fact that we're friends is so, so not the point."

Tanner took a step forward, frowning dangerously.

"Colonel, you were on record yourself saying that you thought he was dragging the project out unnecessarily, that his approach was too timid."

"I never said 'timid,'" Hiller said. "There's nothing timid about him. Careful, yes. A little obsessive, sure. Especially when it comes to other people's lives."

"Colonel—" Tanner began, but the vice-president interrupted him.

"I see no reason to deny the colonel's request," she said. "He would feel easier about the test flight if Levinson approved the craft, so why not give Levinson access?"

Tanner's mouth pressed into an upward arc.

"The test is in two days,' he said.

"Well, then," Lanford said, "he'll have a day and a half with it."

21

The town of 51 was bustling as people arrived from all over the country, there for the ESD Spring Expo. The event had begun in 2004, in the months following the Army's adoption of alien weaponry, partly as an attempt to quell public reservations about use of alien tech. It had been successful, and in the following years had developed into both a showcase of the latest advancements and a conference at which scientists, engineers, and mathematicians came to put their heads together.

Attendance by the general public had been down the last few years, but following the announcement that the Expo would feature the test flight of the first fully operational hybrid fighter, it quickly became a sold-out event. Many who couldn't get tickets were camping out in the surrounding desert, hoping to get a glimpse of the ship taking flight.

Due to the crowds, it took Dylan a little longer to reach the hotel where most of the dignitaries were staying. The lobby was awhirl with color and alive with the sounds of languages from around the world. It took him a few minutes to pick out Patricia, dressed casually in jeans and a halter top. She had been cornered by a reporter and seemed to be giving an interview. She saw him at about the same time, and her expression said "Help me."

As he closed the distance, one of the camera crew noticed him. He said something into his face microphone, and the camera turned.

"And here's Dylan Hiller," the reporter said. She was a young woman with short red hair. "You two have been friends since childhood," she said. "How does it feel to be reunited for this momentous occasion?"

"Well, we keep in touch," Dylan said, "but we've got some catching up to do."

"Has your father made a decision about who is going to pilot the alien-hybrid prototype?" the reporter asked.

"I don't know," Dylan said, "but if you want to ask him, he's right over there."

She turned to look, as did the cameraman. Dylan grabbed Patricia's hand and began to move away quickly.

They were both laughing as they burst out onto the street.

"Hey, you," Patricia said. They exchanged a hug that felt way more awkward than it should have.

"Place has changed a little since we were kids, huh?" he said.

"To say the least," she said. "I don't recognize anything."

"Well, anything you would recognize is probably off-limits to us these days," he said, "but I can give you a tour of the new stuff."

"That sounds fun," she said. "I've got until five, and then Dad is giving some sort of press conference, and he wants me there."

"Sure," he responded. "Come on."

They congratulated each other on getting into the Academy, and talked a little about what they thought it would be like. Now and then he pointed out a new landmark, but quickly realized that although a lot of building had taken place, most of the most interesting stuff was underground.

"So, I guess your dad is proud you're going to be a pilot?" she said.

"Well, he always said he'd be proud of me whatever I chose to do."

She looked at him a bit skeptically.

"Do you believe that?" she asked.

He thought about it for a moment.

"I believe he thinks he means it," he said, "but every time I say I want to be a pilot, like him, he gets this certain look, and I know it wouldn't be quite the same look if I wanted to be a librarian or a haberdasher or something."

"Haberdasher?" she said. "You're going to hurt yourself, using words like that."

He smiled and shrugged. "Risks of a decent education. Anyway, I think the world sort of expects me to be a pilot."

"Didn't we have this conversation two years ago?" she said.

"Yeah," he said. "Right before we both went off."

It was weird. On one level he felt like he knew Patricia really well, but there was something different—a distance, an awkwardness. She didn't even look the same. She looked grown up. Which she was, and he probably looked different too.

He spent the next half hour working up his nerve.

"So," he finally said. "While you're here—would you maybe like to go out?"

It sounded dreadful even as he said it. He didn't have trouble asking girls out. It was kind of his thing—it was keeping one around that he wasn't so good at. And yet, the words just seemed to clunk out of him like bricks.

Her eyebrows rose slightly. "Do you mean like on a date?" she said, a little uncertainly.

"Well—maybe," he said. "What do you think?" But he could already tell from her apologetic expression.

"I think I have a boyfriend back in Virginia," she said.

"Oh," he said, suddenly wishing there was a deep hole he could step directly into. "Yeah, of course you do."

"What's that supposed to mean?" she asked.

How could *that* be the wrong thing to say? He thought he knew something about girls. Patricia was raising serious doubts.

"Well—look at you," he said. "You're smart, fun—the complete package."

"Okay," she said. "Now you're making me blush. Can we change the subject?"

"Absolutely," Dylan said, eager to do so. "Changing subject in five, four, three, two, one… What do you think about green chili pizza?"

"I'm sure I'm at a total loss on that subject," she said.

"Well," he said, "let me educate you. There's a place right up here. My buddy Jake works there. He's going to the Academy too, so you should meet him anyway."

*   *   *

Jake knew he had seen the girl before, the moment she walked into Pizza 51, but he couldn't for the life of him place where. She had honey-blond hair, dark eyes, and a very nice smile that went straight through him and left his toes tingling.

One thing he was certain of—she wasn't one of the local girls. There weren't that many of them, and he would have noticed her for sure.

Dylan was on his phone when they came in, so Jake just did his best to look friendly.

"You must be Jake," the young woman said, sticking out her hand.

"That's me," he said, shaking it. "And you—I know you. From—ah—somewhere."

"Really," she said. "Have we met?" From the way she

said it, he knew they hadn't, and she was having some fun with him.

"No," he said. "No—TV maybe? Magazines? Are you a model?"

"Dylan didn't tell me you were so smooth," she said.

"I'm not smooth," Jake said. "Completely unsmooth. Just confused."

"She's Patricia Whitmore," Charlie piped up from the corner table, where he was doing his homework.

Of course she is, Jake thought, giving himself a mental smack in the head. Dylan talked about her all the time, and naturally she would be coming to the celebration. There was no way Dylan could resist bringing her around to show her off.

"Thanks, Charlie," he said. "That didn't make me look stupid at all."

"My pleasure," Charlie replied. He didn't look up.

"So," Jake said. "You're in town."

"You're very in the moment, aren't you?" Patricia said. "Not thinking ahead, not thinking back just... right there. I like it." Was she flirting with him or making fun of him? He couldn't tell, but whichever it was, he didn't want her to stop.

Dylan put his phone back in his pocket.

"Sorry," he said. "That was Mom. She wants me to pick up a few things for dinner. Did you guys introduce yourselves?"

"In a roundabout way," Patricia said. "So Dylan says I should try the green chili pizza."

"It's the specialty of the house," Jake said. "I'll get one started."

"You're off shift in five minutes," Charlie said. "I just saw Ronnie pull up."

"Good," Patricia said. "You can join us, then, Jake. You too, Charlie."

* * *

The pizza came out and Ronnie took over, so they adjourned to the long table in the back. Dylan pointed out that Patricia would be joining them at the Academy as well.

"That's great," Jake said. "Congratulations."

"I'm going too," Charlie chipped in.

"What? This year?" Patricia said. "How old are you?"

"I'm twelve," Charlie said. "So I won't get in this year, of course. But I'll get in."

"He will," Jake said. "Smart as a whip."

"Do your parents work at the Center?" she asked.

"Um, no," Charlie said.

"Charlie and Jake are sort of—orphans," Dylan said.

"Oh," Patricia said. "I'm sorry."

"It's okay," Charlie said. "You're sort of a half-orphan, so you can be in the club."

Jake kicked at Charlie's feet under the table.

"Well… okay," Patricia said. "So where were you, when it happened?"

"Summer camp, outside of L.A.," Jake said.

"So, Patricia and I were right here," Dylan said.

"I think they probably know that story," Patricia said. "I'd like to hear more about Jake and Charlie. Did you guys know each other before?"

"It's really not all that interesting," Jake said, but then Charlie started in on how he met Jake, and although he had the urge to try and shut him up, he realized that Charlie was making him sound pretty good. Dylan, on the other hand, looked a little like he had eaten something sour. Maybe he had other places he wanted the conversation to go.

"So what now?" Patricia asked Charlie. "What are you going to do when Jake goes to the Academy?"

"I'm in a good group home," Charlie said. "I'll go to school here and get in the Academy as fast as I can. I've already picked a major—astronautical engineering."

"That's pretty cool," Patricia said. "So you want to build spaceships?"

"Maybe," Charlie said. "Or repair them."

The bell rang on the door, and Emily came in. She was wearing her yellow sundress and black boots, one of his favorite outfits. She swept her gaze across the little group, and Jake found himself pushing his chair back a little without knowing why.

"Jake?" she said. "What's going on?"

He remembered then that he was supposed to meet her at the coffee shop after his shift.

"Oh, man," he said. "I'm sorry. I got distracted. You'll never guess who Dylan brought to see us."

"Patricia Whitmore," Emily said. "I can see her. She's sitting right there."

"Ah, yeah," he said, standing. "Patricia, this is Emily."

"Nice to meet you," Patricia said. "Would you like to join us?"

"Would I, Jake?" Emily asked.

"Absolutely," Jake said.

*   *   *

Later, when Patricia and Dylan left, Jake and Emily walked Charlie home, and then they turned toward her house.

"So," she said. "Patricia Whitmore."

"Yeah," he said.

"Royalty, like Dylan."

"She seemed okay," he replied.

"Uh-huh. Why didn't you introduce me as your girlfriend?" she asked.

"I—well, I guess I thought it was kind of obvious."

"No," she said. "It wasn't. It wasn't obvious at all. You didn't kiss me, or hold my hand, or call me honey, or anything like that."

"Huh," he said.

"I am your girlfriend, aren't I, Jake? Has something changed since the last time you told me you loved me?"

He stopped walking and turned to face her.

"What kind of question is that?" he asked. "Of course you're my girlfriend. What's wrong with you?"

"Is she going to be at the Academy, too?" she said.

He paused, wondering if he could tell her no and get away with it.

"Yes," he said. "Look, I don't have the hots for Patricia Whitmore. She's Dylan's friend—I was just trying to be nice."

"You forgot me, Jake," Emily said. "We're still within walking distance of each other, and you forgot me. What's it going to be like when you're off at the Academy?"

"Emily," he said, "I love you. You know that."

Her eyes were wet, but she wasn't actually crying. "How's this going to work?" she asked. "I've got another year of school left, and I won't be going to Colorado, we both know that."

"Why not?" he said. "You could get a job there, or go to another school."

"You're asking me to follow you to Colorado?" she said.

Jake realized that was exactly what he'd just done.

"I'm just saying if we love each other, we can work something out," he said.

She was quiet for a moment. "I really do love you, Jake," she said. "I don't think you know how much."

He kissed her then, and they were still kissing when they got to her house.

"You can come in," she said. "Mom's on the night shift all this week."

"Okay," he said, feeling a little weak in the knees. Emily's father had left when she was twelve, so they were alone in the house. Not for the first time, but…

They landed on the couch, and things moved forward. Way forward. More forward than they ever had before.

"What are we doing?" Emily whispered.

"I… I don't know," he said.

"I want to, Jake," she said. "I want to make love with you."

Jake found it a little hard to breathe, much less talk.

"But you said—you've always said…"

"Forget what I said," she said, and then kissed him again.

* * *

Later, they lay together, and he felt her heartbeat against his chest and stroked her long brown hair.

"I'm glad," she said. "I wanted it to be you. I want it always to be you."

"You're not sorry we didn't wait?"

She sighed. "Wait for what, Jake?"

22

"Well, what's the verdict?" Hiller asked.

David looked up from his laptop, where he was desperately scrolling through the data from systems testing.

"There's no verdict," he said. "It's a hung jury."

"Will this or will not this thing fly?" he asked.

David raised his hands in a gesture of helplessness. "It's not enough time," he said, "and some of these test results are missing data. It's sloppy, Steve."

"But have you actually found anything wrong?"

David studied his friend's expression for a moment.

"No," he finally said. "I haven't found anything wrong—but that doesn't mean there isn't."

"You can be damn frustrating when you want to be, you know that?" Hiller said.

"That's the point," David objected. "I don't want to be frustrating. I would love to give you a straight answer." He sighed and ran his fingers through his hair. "According to what I see here—it should be a go."

"Great," Hiller said. "Perfect."

"Only—why don't you tell your pilot to just use basic anti-gravity. Don't kick it into high gear."

"Okay, see, you're doing it to me again," Hiller said. "How's it gonna look if in front of twenty thousand people the ship just sort of eases up into the sky?"

"Ah, not you too," David said.

"David," he said. "Tanner and the president say this thing is going to fly in the morning. I can tell them no, but it's probably going to cost me my job, and I like my job. So do I tell them no?"

"Tell them whatever you want," David said. "I just hope your pilot knows what he's doing."

"He does," Hiller said. "Because he's me."

"What? Wait, Steve, no!"

"After all this, you think I'd put anyone else in that seat? No way in hell."

David wanted to object further, but he knew Steve well enough to know when his mind was made up. He just hoped that this time the feeling in his gut was indigestion.

He watched Hiller leave, then continued going through the data.

*   *   *

Charlie found Jake sitting on the stoop of his group home with what might have been the most hangdog expression he had ever seen.

"Wow," he said. "What the heck? Something go down between you and Emily last night? She seemed kind of pissed that you forgot her."

Jake shrugged. "I guess she was," he said.

"Did you two break up?"

"What? No. Why would you think that?"

"You look like a kid who just had his lollipop taken away," Charlie said. "That's why."

"Yeah," Jake said. "I guess I'm just rethinking the Academy."

At first Charlie just thought he'd heard him wrong.

"Rethinking?" Charlie said. "What does that mean?

You're gonna change your major?"

"No," he said. "I'm thinking about not going at all."

Now Charlie was sure Jake was joking—but the punch line never came. What had happened overnight? At the restaurant, he'd seemed so enthusiastic, joking with Dylan and Patricia about who would be the "top gun."

"That's crazy, Jake," he finally said. "It's all you've talked about since I met you."

"Right," Jake said. "Because I was a kid when we met. Kids aren't realistic. They all think they're going to grow up to be superheroes or trillionaires or whatever. Do you know how long it took me to admit to myself that my parents were dead?"

"I've still never heard you say it outright," Charlie said.

"Well, they are," he said. "They're dead. Deceased. Gone."

It took him aback a little. Jake was always the guy that held out for hope. He was never quite going to believe his parents were dead until he saw the bodies. But now he sounded... resigned.

"Okay," Charlie said, "but what does that have to do with the Academy?"

"I barely made it in," Jake said. "Odds are I won't make it all the way through, anyway, and if I do I probably won't make it into flight school. Dylan and Patricia— they've got families cheering them on. The whole damned *country* is cheering them on."

"You've got me," Charlie said.

"Exactly," Jake said. "I've got you, and I've got Emily, and that's it. If I leave here—"

Then Charlie suddenly got it.

"Wait," Charlie said. "Emily? Did you guys...?"

Jake got a funny expression on his face.

"You did," he said. "You did the deal. Knocked boots. Which—Emily was actually *wearing* boots."

"Keep your voice down," Jake said.

"Wow," Charlie said. "What was it like?"

"It was—mind your own business!"

"Okay," Charlie said, trying to frame the situation. "So if you're using me as an excuse to stay here, it is my business. It's this thing you've got with wounded birds, Jake."

"Wounded birds?" Jake said. "What are you talking about, Charlie?"

"You want to be the hero," he said. "Like when we first met. You saw me as a wounded bird who needed nursing back to health. Emily—look, I like Emily. She smart, and she's pretty, she's got stuff in all the right places, but she's a wounded bird. Her father didn't die, he *left*. And her mother is a little on the crazy side. And everybody but you thinks she's a little weird. So you want to give her what she needs, which is love, I guess. If you go away, you won't be the hero, you'll be the bad guy. The guy that abandoned the little kid who needed him. The guy who abandoned the girl, just like her father did—and you can't stand the idea of being that guy."

"What do you know about any of this?" Jake snapped.

"I know you," Charlie said. "You had a candle's chance in a hurricane of getting into school here, but you never doubted you could do it. It was what you wanted because it was a step toward what you know you have to be. And then you put it all in jeopardy by bringing me along."

"I brought you along because I didn't want you to get hurt," Jake said. "You haven't been a burden."

"Whatever. I won't be. I'm going to school here, I'm going to the Academy, where I'm probably going to whip right past you, by the way. I don't need you to take care of me, and neither does Emily. If she loves you, she'll let you go."

"It's not that simple," Jake said.

"Well, I'm just a kid," Charlie said, "but it seems kind of simple to me."

"Like I said," Jake replied. "Kids are unrealistic."

* * *

That evening, Dylan and his family had dinner with President Whitmore and Patricia. The conversation stayed light, nostalgic at some turns and hopeful at others. There was a good deal of back-patting and doting on him and Patricia. It was a little embarrassing, but it made him realize something.

He was the son of a stripper and the adopted son of a Marines pilot, and yet somehow, against all odds, the folks to whom he felt the next closest kinship were an ex-president and his daughter. It was the most unlikely extended family imaginable, but somehow in a world full of terrible loss, something new had come together.

Like the world itself.

It made him feel—big.

But it also left him confused, and tonight a little sad. In the back of his mind, he had always imagined that there was something more between him and Patricia than friendship, or even kinship. That they were sort of meant to be together. She had a boyfriend, but that wasn't necessarily a permanent situation—he'd had girlfriends, but he'd pretty much thought of them as placeholders until he and Patricia were together. In fact, in the restaurant, Patricia had been flirting almost as if she didn't have a boyfriend.

But not with him. With Jake.

Which meant, boyfriend or not, she didn't feel about him the way he felt about her.

It seemed somehow unfair, which he knew logically was stupid, but this wasn't a subject he was all that logical about. Maybe all it needed was time back together, which they would have plenty of once they were at the Academy.

After dinner, Patricia and her dad went back to their hotel, and he and his parents returned home. He said goodnight and had just settled into his bed to read a book when his father rapped on the door.

"Not doin' anything embarrassing in here, are you?" his dad asked.

"No," Dylan said. "Just trying on my pink ballerina outfit. Come on in."

Steve Hiller came in and sat on the bed.

"Big day tomorrow," Dylan said. "Flying the prototype."

"It ain't so big as all that," his dad said. "Just another day."

"Whatever you say," Dylan said. "Seems like a big deal to me."

His dad shrugged, but Dylan knew how excited he was to get back into space again. He talked about it all the time.

"Hey," his father said. "Have I told you lately how proud I am of you?"

"Almost every day," Dylan replied.

"I did, huh? How about that I love you?"

"That, too," Dylan said. The older man smiled, but it was a serious sort of smile, not the one that announced some smart comment.

"I just—I always wanted to do right by you, Dylan," he said. "You and your mom. I can't tell you what a pleasure it's been being your father. The one thing I would change about my past is that I'd have married your mother sooner."

He sounded almost too serious, and it worried Dylan a little. He felt a lump form in his throat as he remembered the day he had been given the ring to hold, told to make himself useful. How important he'd felt.

"Well," Dylan said, "you did okay. I could never ask for

a better dad. I only hope I can be half the man you are."

"You're your own man, Dylan," he said. "You're not half of anything. You know what I always say."

"Yeah," Dylan said. "Passion and conviction."

"And I will always be proud of you. You remember that when you get to the Academy."

"Okay," Dylan said.

Then his dad was grinning the other way.

"Of course, me and your mom are gonna make a scene, aim for maximum embarrassment when we take you there. Your mom's gonna be all 'my baby' and I'll be like, 'Don't forget your stuffy and your pj's, son.'"

"Oh, please, no," Dylan said with mock dismay.

"Alright," his dad said. "Give me a hug. I've got an early start tomorrow."

"Good night, Dad," Dylan said. "Kick ass tomorrow."

"You can count on that."

23

APRIL 27

David lifted his head, blinking, and wondering where he was for a moment before realizing he'd fallen asleep at his desk. He checked the time.

"Shoot," he said. It was eight in the morning. It had been about six when he put his head down, just for a second.

He went to the small lavatory in his office and shaved. Then he changed into the suit he kept in his office for those days he might unexpectedly need one. No one was in the staff room—they were all at the Expo—so he made himself a half a pot of strong coffee, drank a cup, and took one to go.

The launch was at eleven in the morning. By his watch, it was already eight-thirty. He had to hurry. Gulping down his coffee, he took his bicycle in one hand and began guiding it toward the elevator.

Outside, the day's events had already begun. Whitmore was on the loudspeaker, talking about the ESD, about how it was continuing to bring the world together, about how all of the sacrifices everyone was making were going to pay off in the end. Now and then the speech was punctuated by the distant roar and applause from the audience in the hastily erected arena.

Traffic, usually unknown in the area around the Center,

was a nightmare. Some streets were closed, others were temporarily designated one-way. He wove in between the cars, hoping he still had time.

*   *   *

At about five in the morning, Hiller kissed Jasmine carefully, so as not to wake her, and then swung himself out of bed. He sat quietly on his patio, watching the eastern sky turn the color of coral, sipping his coffee. Then he got up to go to work.

"Did you think you were just going to sneak out of here without saying goodbye?"

That was Jasmine, in her robe, pouring some coffee for herself.

He shrugged. "I figured you needed your rest after last night. You're not as young as you used to be."

"Please," she said. "I get a better workout doing the dishes."

"I've got one for that," he said, "but I ain't going there."

"Yeah, you've got a joke for everything," she said. "After all these years you still think you're all that."

He opened his arms and took her in.

"That's because after all these years, I still am all that," he said.

She hugged him, hard, and he expected a comeback, but if she had one, she kept it to herself.

"Gotta go to work," he said.

"So I heard," she said. "Be careful up there, Steve."

"Just another day at the office," he said.

He kissed her. "I love you."

"Yeah, I know," she said softly. "I love you, too."

*   *   *

When Hiller got to the hangar, the H-1 was still inside, with the techs running down the pre-flight checklist. He stepped over to her and ran his fingers over the metal of her hull.

"We're going to make history, you and me," he told the sleek machine. "And when those bastards come back, we'll show 'em Earth is the last damn place they ever want to mess with."

Then he put on his flight suit and went through his personal checklist.

After a while, they started rolling the ship out onto the strip.

*   *   *

"This is so fuckin' awesome," Charlie said.

Jake gave him an elbow to remind him whose company they were in.

"Sorry, ma'am," Charlie told Jasmine Hiller.

"It's okay," she said. "I've heard a lot worse—but you should still watch your mouth."

"Yes, ma'am," Charlie said. "But it is awesome."

It was hot for late April, and Jake caught himself squinting, as if that would help him see through the heat-distorted air rising from the desert floor. It must be worse for the majority of the crowd, who were watching from a distance of five miles, but Dylan had wrangled them sweet seats in a hardened bunker that was much closer. Patricia and her father were there, too, and the vice-president and a lot of people Jake didn't know.

"Ms. Hiller?" someone said. Jake saw it was a national reporter—the guy with the sideburns. He had a camera crew behind him.

"Yes," she said.

"Would you be fine for a quick interview?"

"Sure," Jasmine said. "But when that plane rolls out—"

"I understand," he said. "It'll be quick."

She stood up and stepped into the aisle, pulling Dylan with her.

"Ms. Hiller, how do you feel about your husband piloting the first hybrid fighter?"

"Well, I'm proud, of course," she said. "Nobody can fly like my husband."

"Any worries?"

"Worries?" she said. "Steve flew a broken-down alien wreck into space and blew up the mother ship, and still made it home in one piece. Like he said to me this morning, this is just another day at the office."

"What about you, Dylan?" the reporter asked, moving the microphone. "I hear you're planning on following in your stepfather's footsteps."

"Dad has really big shoes," Dylan said, "so I don't know about that. But he is my inspiration. I'm starting at the ESD Academy this fall, and I'm planning on going to flight school after that. Hopefully, I'll be flying one of those." He pointed, and the camera swung around.

"Here it comes," Jake murmured.

It was sleek and beautiful, even through the rippling air. Jake felt a thrill that started at his toes and ran all the way up his spine.

"Just look at that." He squeezed Emily's hand, and she squeezed back, shooting him an odd, thoughtful glance.

"Yeah," she said. "I see."

Then, slowly, she unlaced her fingers from his.

He looked at her, but she wouldn't meet his gaze.

Outside, the fighter rolled out a little further and stopped. Distant figures swarmed around it for a while, and then one-by-one they retreated back into the hangar.

*   *   *

Hiller shook hands with the techs as they came back in. He waved as they boarded the elevator that would take them deep into the bedrock.

And he was alone.

He looked out at the waiting ship, remembering the countless hours of simulation, thinking how good it was going to be to actually fly something fast again. When he'd signed up with ESD he hadn't really understood how much time he was going to spend at a desk, or doing public relations, going over performance evaluations. Life was like that—if you were good at something, you often got promoted until you weren't doing what you were really good at.

He squared his shoulders.

"Whew," he said. "Okay, let's go do this."

"Steve!"

He turned at the familiar sound of David's voice.

"Hey," he said. "What are you doing here? You know I'm solo, this time. No sharing the glory with some computer nerd."

"Yeah, well, I'll have to live with that," David said. He looked out at the waiting craft. "You sure about this?"

"I'm good at flying," Hiller said.

"Well, yeah," David agreed.

"It's what I should be doing. To tell you the truth, I've been hankering to fly this thing. Your misgivings just made it easier for me to justify climbing into the cockpit."

"You're welcome?" David said uncertainly.

Hiller patted his friend on the shoulder.

"Gotta go," he said.

"No, wait." David fished into his pocket and pulled out a pair of cigars. "I didn't want you to leave without your victory dance."

He proffered one of the cigars, and Hiller realized with a start that he had left his own cigar back in the locker room.

"Wow," Hiller said. "Man, you saved the day. I was about to go without one." He read the label, smelled it. "Okay," he said. "Now that's what I'm talking about."

"Not 'til the fat lady sings," David said.

"That's right," Steve said. "See? I *did* teach you something."

"You and me," David said. "Right here, when you get back."

They shook hands, and then Hiller began walking toward the plane.

* * *

A general cheer went up in the room as Steve Hiller emerged from the hangar and started toward the aircraft. He opened the cockpit, climbed in, and closed it.

Jake realized he was holding his breath.

* * *

Hiller looked over the controls, remembering the first time he'd been in an alien spacecraft, eleven years ago.

It was hard to believe it had been that long.

These controls looked much friendlier. He might almost have been back in his F-18, but he knew what was under the hood was going to make all of the difference. He wondered if Chuck Yeager had felt like this in the X-15, the rush of excitement and adrenaline that made him feel almost like he was twenty again. He looked up at the hot, blue sky and knew there were stars there, and that he would see them soon.

"Colonel Hiller," Control crackled over his headphones. "You have a go."

"What, no countdown?"

There was a brief pause.

"If you want one..." the controller said.

"Nah," he said. "I'll just wing it—so to speak."

He flipped on the power, watched the systems come on line.

"Everything looks good," he said. "Engaging anti-gravity."

The ship lifted slightly. Her landing gear was no longer on the ground, and it began retracting into the belly of the craft.

"Okay," he said. "Let's see what she'll do."

Unaccountably, he remembered his last flight with Jimmie, his best friend until an alien fighter turned him and his plane into ash. He remembered the little speech Jimmie made on the way to the destroyer, to lighten the mood.

Or, as the good Reverend would say, "Why we are on this particular mission, we'll never know. But I do know, that, here today, the Black Knights will emerge victorious, once again."

"This one's for you, Jimmie," he said.

* * *

The fighter didn't take off like a plane, didn't coast down the runway. One second it was on the ground, and the next instant it wasn't, accelerating in a broad curve up toward the heavens with incredible speed.

In an instant it was almost too small to see, but the tracking cameras continued showing close-ups of it as it soared toward space.

The cheering in the bunker was almost deafening.

* * *

Hiller felt the grin stretching on his face. The ship handled like a dream, better than the alien craft its technology was based on. He felt a ferocious pride as the Earth dwindled below him.

Then a light started flashing on his panel. The stick began to quiver in his hand.

"Colonel Hiller?" Control said. "We're getting some funny readings from the fusion interface."

"A knock-knock joke is funny," Hiller said. "This isn't funny." He engaged the coupling compensator, but the reading continued to increase.

"Colonel Hiller—"

"Just hang on," Hiller said. "I'm on it. Just a little bump in the road."

24

FEBRUARY

2012

"Hiller," the voice in his ear said. "Make course correction as instructed."

"Understood," he said, checking the flight plan and then banking to adjust.

Mountains rolled by beneath him, wrinkles in the crust of the Earth. He glanced off to his three o'clock and saw another H-7 fighter nosing through the high-altitude atmosphere. A third flew off to his right, although since they were synched up in speed, it didn't look as if either fighter was actually moving.

"Change orientation," the ground instructed.

"Copy. Patricia, why don't you take point for a while?"

"Sounds good to me, Dylan," she said.

He dropped back and let her enter the lead position in the triangle.

"Coming up on second mark," she said. "Let's take them up to six klicks."

They cut up through the clouds like knives through butter, with hardly a bump at all. To Dylan, it all seemed a little unreal. A thousand simulations didn't add up to one true flight, and even though he knew that all of the bugs had been ironed out of the hybrid vessels—that if he screwed up too much Control could fly the ship like a drone—he still felt the danger of being so far above the ground.

He liked it.

He had wondered—so many times—if he would fail his father. It seemed so much more important now not to do so. More than ever it felt as if everyone was watching him, waiting for him to slip up.

He could do this—and he could do it with passion and conviction.

"Okay, boys," Patricia said. "That's it for today. Let's take it back to the crib, nice and easy."

* * *

Once back on the ground, the three of them posed for a picture next to Dylan's craft. Then they went out for a beer.

"To our first flight," Dylan said, and they all raised their glasses. "A hell of a good time. Let's hope our scores are good."

"Good?" Jake said. "They're gonna be great."

"I got us a little off-course—" Dylan began.

"Two degrees," Patricia said. "It's nothing."

"I can't wait until we get to take them into space," Dylan said. "Those things are awesome."

"I'm definitely in love," Jake said.

Dylan glanced at his friend, then at Patricia, wondering if Jake was still talking about the H-7s, or if he had moved on to another topic.

Patricia still had the boyfriend, right? Still, Dylan felt a little dip in his mood.

He wished powerfully and suddenly for the person he most wanted to share this with.

"Guys," he said, "excuse me a minute. I need to make a phone call."

"Sure," Jake said. "We'll be here."

* * *

Jake watched Dylan step outside. When he turned back to Patricia, he saw the smile had abandoned her face.

"Something wrong?" he asked.

The smile came back, but he knew it wasn't real.

"It's not the time," she said. "Tonight's our night."

"Come on," he said. "We're wingmen now. Wing people? Wing somethings."

"It's going to sound stupid," she said, "and typical."

"I doubt that," Jake said.

"Dale and I... kind of broke up."

It was a hard moment for Jake, because what he actually wanted to do was get up on the table and dance. It took every ounce of willpower not to grin like a lunatic.

"Well, that's huge," he said. "You guys have been together since high school."

"Yeah," she said. "Six years."

"Oh, crap," he said. "You're not crying. Don't do that."

Even with the tears, though, she didn't look sad. If anything, she looked angry.

"Actually," she said, "we didn't 'kind of' break up. Last week when we talked, he told me he loved me, and all the usual stuff, how he couldn't wait until I was home on leave. Yesterday he told me he was engaged to someone else."

"No, he didn't!" Jake said.

"Yeah," she said. "Apparently he's been seeing her for a while."

"Man, I am so sorry," Jake lied. "That guy is an idiot."

"Well, I was in love with him," she said. "What does that make me?"

Available, Jake thought.

"Steadfast," he said. "You could have had your pick of any guy in the Academy."

"Oh, stop it," she said.

"And Dylan—"

Now she did look a little sad. "He's too much like my brother," she said. "Listen, don't tell him about this, not yet. I couldn't handle it right now if... if he tried to, you know..."

"Yeah," he said. "I get it."

He realized that probably went for him, too. Did she know? Had he let on? Dylan was kind of obvious, but Jake thought he had his feelings under control, and he knew it wasn't a good idea. Two officers, in flight school together. In fact, it was a really bad idea.

Take two steps back, Jake boy, he thought. *Maybe three.*

*   *   *

The phone rang twice before she picked it up.

"Hi, Mom," Dylan said.

"Hey, baby," she replied. "How'd it go?"

"It went good," he said. "I think it went great."

"That's my boy," she said. "And I know you're not hot-doggin'."

"Keeping it simple," he said. "Staying safe. How are you doing?"

"I'm fine," she said. "Doing really well, keeping busy. In fact I go on shift in about an hour."

"Well," he said. "I just wanted to tell you how it went."

"You know I always love to hear from you," she said. He thought he heard a faint catch in her voice, and a long silence followed.

"Mom?"

"It's okay," she said. "I was just thinking how proud— how proud your dad would have been of you."

Dylan felt his own throat constrict, remembering the H-1 prototype, reaching toward the sky, hurtling up like a reversed meteor—and then a sky full of light, and incomprehension, denial, grief. In a nanosecond, the man he called his father had ceased to exist, and an entire planet went into mourning.

"Damn, Mom," he said. "Now you're gonna make *me* cry, too, and I'm out with the guys."

"What makes you think I'm crying?" she said. "And don't use profanity. I raised you better than that."

"I think I heard a 'damn' from you every now and again," he said.

"You do as I say, not as I do," she said. "Anyway, you go be with your friends. You don't need to be calling an old lady on your day of triumph."

"It's a small triumph, Mom, if even that."

"Son," she said, "you celebrate it all—the little ones and the big ones. It's called counting your blessings, and sometimes that's what gets you through. Now go on."

"Okay," he said. "I'll see you in two weeks."

"Yeah," she said. "I'm looking forward to that."

* * *

From the other side of the room, Dylan saw Jake and Patricia leaning across the table toward each other. They appeared to be in a deep discussion about something, but when he walked up they turned his way.

"The president call again?" Jake asked.

"No," Dylan said. "Someone much more important. My mom. What's up? Looked like you guys were deciding the fate of the world."

"Well," Jake said. "Sort of. We took a vote while you were gone."

"What vote was that?" Dylan asked.

"That whoever wasn't in on the voting should buy the next round."

"Damn, I missed *another* vote?" Dylan said. "It's like this happens every time I leave the table."

"Looks like it," Jake said. "You know what I'm in the mood for? That really expensive beer they have on tap here."

"I actually think they have a thirty-year-old single malt behind the counter," Patricia said.

"I'm thinking a really expensive Irish Car Bomb," Jake said.

"First off," Dylan said, "you can't technically make an Irish Car Bomb with Scotch. Or IPA. And B, if I'm buying, I pick the drink."

"Oh, crap," Jake said. "This could be bad. It's not going to have fruit and a little umbrella in it, is it?"

"Jake," Patricia said. "Don't provoke him."

About four minutes later, as Jake stared at his Singapore Sling and she at her Jaeger shot, Patricia poked a finger at Jake.

"I told you not to provoke him," she said.

Dylan smiled and sipped at his own drink.

"The Scotch was a good idea, Patricia," he said. "Smoky, peaty—nice. How's that Jaeger?"

"It's cough syrup," she said.

"I call it democracy in action," Dylan said. "So, what next?"

"How about a little pool?" Jake said.

"Oh, no," Patricia said. "Absolutely not. I see either one of you near the pool table or the dart board or even Ms. Pac-Man, I'm calling it a night right now."

"Patricia, this isn't like in the Academy—" Dylan began.

"I know it's not," she said. "This is flight school, where any little thing can get you washed out. And I am not getting sent home because you boys can't control your testosterone."

* * *

"President Whitmore?"

Thomas Whitmore realized someone had been trying to get his attention for a while. He shook his head, but it wouldn't clear.

"Yes," he said. "Who is it?"

"Agent Vega," the man said. "Sir, you weren't answering. I took the liberty of opening the door. I was worried that something had happened."

"No," Whitmore said slowly. "Agent Vega," he said.

"Yes, sir." Vega was a short, compact man with a big man's presence. He was staring at him uncertainly. "You're okay, then?"

Whitmore realized several things at that point. He was in his pajamas, standing in the bathroom of his house in Virginia—but it seemed to him that a minute ago he'd been somewhere else, somehow. He also realized that Vega was staring past him, gaping at the mirror above the sink, where Whitmore had been carefully smearing shaving cream.

"Does this look right to you?" Whitmore asked him.

"Sir?" Vega said. "It looks like a circle."

"It does," Whitmore said. He shook his head. "It's not right."

"No sir, I guess not," the agent said.

"What time is it, Agent Vega?"

"It's just after ten in the morning, sir."

"Didn't I have that thing at nine-thirty?" Whitmore said.

"Yes, sir," Vega said. "That's why I was becoming worried."

"Right," Whitmore said. "I guess you would. Is there any coffee?"

"I'll have Ms. Tallman bring some," the agent said.

"No," he said. "I'll have it at the kitchen table."

*   *   *

After his coffee and some apologies over the phone for missing the breakfast meeting, he went for a run, and in the daylight, in the fresh air, he began to realize how out of it he had been. How long he had been standing at the mirror.

The nightmares were getting worse, too, more vivid. For long years—for almost a decade they had nearly gone away. But now...

He probably should see someone about it, he decided. If he was missing meetings, then it was time. He had a physical coming up anyway.

When he got back from his run, he'd put it on his agenda.

*   *   *

David arrived home late. The sun had long set into the desert horizon and the stars were clear and cold overhead. He pushed his bike into the hall and leaned it against a wall. Then he went out back to water the plants, his usual routine.

He stopped in front of the prize of his collection, a gnarled, thick specimen, the one he called *Old Man Leaning into the Wind*. He remembered it as he first saw it, the scrawny unpromising stick of sagebrush in his new pot. But David had been stubborn, and persistent. So had the plant.

"Hey, my friend," he said. He took a pair of tweezers from his pocket and used them to trim it back a bit by plucking the delicate leaves and fine stems.

"There," he murmured, when he was done. "Was that so bad?" He spread the tips of his fingers and brushed it very gently.

Once back inside, he reflexively took down a glass and reached for the Scotch, and then remembered he had poured it all out, months ago. The temptation to just finish the bottle, buy another one, and finish that had been too great. He couldn't go down that road. He had responsibilities.

Instead he had tap water, and he sat alone on the couch and he felt her absence. The lack of Connie.

This time, saving the world wouldn't be enough to get her back. He would have to rewind time itself, to the moment before the teenager in the SUV decided to send a text to his girlfriend, before he coasted through a red light at nearly eighty miles an hour. They had tried to comfort him by saying she probably never felt it, never knew what was happening. But he knew Connie would have wanted to see it coming.

Now Nevada had a new Senator, and he had a vacuum in him as big as outer space that he hadn't even begun to fill.

25

MAY

The Gobi Desert dwindled below her as Rain pushed her fighter to the limits of the unassisted anti-gravity drive. The horizon became a curve, a dome, part of a circle, and then the great desert was just a sandy smudge on the continent. Blue sky faded to black, and the lights of deep space stared at her.

Space.

She had been flying for a year now, but this was her first trip out of the atmosphere, and she felt immensely privileged to be—at twenty-one—the youngest person, let alone woman, to go into space. The runner up was a Russian named Titov, who had been twenty-five.

Part of it, she understood, was the way China traditionally picked pilots for training. They were chosen in high school, based on various qualities, not the least of which was party loyalty. Training began immediately after high school. In many countries, like the U.S., this wasn't true—four years of college were required before flight school.

Since Uncle Jiang took her under his wing, she'd had many advantages. Her father was a hero of the Alien War, albeit not a prominent one—just one of the scores who died attacking the destroyers. Her uncle was a highly placed government official. Most believed he would be given command of the moon base. And since arriving at Aerospace City her grades had been near perfect, her conduct spotless.

As far as she could tell, the "incident" when she was thirteen had somehow been forgotten, expunged from her record.

The fighter was all spaceship now—there wasn't enough atmosphere to give the wings anything to do. She watched the moon rise as she continued to accelerate, and against the sphere of it she could now make out a silvery spot, tiny at first, but growing quickly in size as she approached it.

Eventually the shape of it was evident; the last of the gigantic transport vessels on its dawdling one-way trip to the lunar surface. The rest were already there being unloaded and pulled apart for use in construction.

She approached the giant ship closely so her onboard cameras would get a good look. Space was big, and she hadn't come near the big ship by happenstance. It was a part of a mission that was largely public relations. She was to be not only the youngest pilot in space, but also the youngest to circumnavigate the moon.

As she whipped past the freighter, it flashed its floodlights at her in greeting.

Then it was behind her, and the moon was all she saw.

The first moon ships had relied on chemical rockets, their fuel both finite and heavy. They burned hard leaving Earth and then coasted, decelerating constantly as the Earth's gravity pulled them back, going just fast enough to enter the influence of the moon's gravity—at which point they began falling toward the moon. The trip took them about three days.

She had no such restrictions. Her ship had a power supply that was essentially unlimited. She could maintain a speed or even accelerate continuously, cutting the flight time from days to hours.

She wasn't going crazy, though. There were still dangers—like the enormous debris field left behind by the alien mother ship, that either hadn't yet been permanently claimed by the Earth or the moon, but had instead settled in a sort of tug-of-war zone.

"*Chang'e One.*"

She was so absorbed in her instruments, at first she didn't understand that someone was talking to her over the radio.

"*Chang'e One,*" the voice repeated.

"*Chang'e One,*" she said. "This is Lao."

"*Chang'e One,* we have a situation. One of our pilots on a low-orbit run has experienced a malfunction. You're the closest craft to his position. Please divert while we try to determine a fix for his malfunction."

Rain looked back at the moon and allowed herself a mental shrug. Her craft was named *Chang'e* for the legendary moon goddess, whose story was—at best—somewhat bittersweet. For Rain, Chang'e would have to wait.

"Give me his position," she said.

She had to begin shedding velocity immediately until she would be able to turn and actively accelerate toward the Earth—which on the face of it, felt a little crazy. She watched her home of twenty-one years wax larger, and then began to kill her speed. AG drive or not, if she overshot and hit the atmosphere, things could get ugly fast.

It took about an hour to find the pilot and manage a trajectory that put her within about twenty meters from and relatively stationary to his H-7. But it was a trajectory, not an orbit—they were already beginning to reenter the atmosphere.

The ship was different from hers only in call sign. All

of the fighters were built in America and then painted according to the specs of the countries into whose service they went.

"Pilot," she said. "This is Lao. What's going on over there?"

"You tell me," he said. "My AG thrusters aren't online."

"Okay," she said. "Hang on."

She maneuvered using small fluctuations in the AG field until she was looking at the dorsal surface of his fighter. She spotted something immediately—a shiny patch and what looked almost like icicles trailing along the hull, back toward the rear of the craft.

"You've got frozen coolant coming out of the jacket," she said. "Something must have punched through."

"I didn't feel anything," he said. "Rain, is that you?"

She recognized his voice. "It's me, Heng," she said. "I don't see a hole—it must have been pretty small. Control, are you copying all of this?"

"Affirmative," the voice came. "We have his telemetry, but some of his internal systems are down. Can you confirm if the fusion chamber is uncompromised?"

She remembered the horror of watching Steven Hiller's ship explode. She had shaken hands with him, he had signed her picture. She'd had something of a crush on him.

Since that time, there hadn't been another accident. If Heng's fusion component went critical, however, there now might be two more—even with shields up, she might not survive the sheer kinetic impact of an uncontrolled fusion explosion. Heng certainly would not.

She checked the readings, rechecked them.

"Control," she said. "Fusion containment is uncompromised, but his AG units are fried. I'm getting nothing from them."

"That's what we expected," Control said. "We're working on a fix."

"Control, we're at ninety klicks," she said. "We've already passed the Kármán Line."

That wasn't a problem for her, at least not yet, but it meant that gravity was accelerating Heng's ship toward the Earth, and the atmosphere was starting to put up a fight. She could still easily return to space, but without engines, Heng was about to become a meteor. His shield would help shed the heat of reentry and keep the ship from tearing apart, but the g-forces in the cockpit would be deadly.

Then there was that sudden stop at the end...

"Is there any way I can tow him with my EVA line?"

"Negative," Control said. "We've thought of that. The tensile strength of the cable isn't great enough."

There followed a silence in which Rain stared at her controls, thinking furiously. There had to be something she could do. She couldn't just let Heng die.

"What are the odds?" Heng said softly. "Space is so big."

"Hey, stay cool," Rain said. "We'll think of something." Her fighter began to vibrate, however, and the heat sensors on the hull were starting to get worried.

"I'm sorry I spoiled your moon trip," Heng said.

"You haven't spoiled anything," she said. "Control? What have you got?"

There was a long pause.

"*Chang'e One*, your orders are to establish a stable orbit."

"I can't just let him fall!" she protested.

"Captain Heng, you're going to make a dead stick landing," Control said. "We'll try to talk you through it."

Rain looked over at Heng, and saw the resignation on his face. Like her, he had run the dead stick simulation over twenty times—landing without power, using only the aircraft's ability to glide. In simulation, no one had ever managed it, even with a fully functioning computer—not from space, anyway. The velocity was just too great.

"Control, there has to be some other way," Rain said.

"Captain Lao, achieve orbit. That is an order."

"It's okay," Heng said. "I can do this. I'll see you on the ground."

Both craft were bucking now, and their noses were beginning to glow.

"I'll buy you a beer," she said.

"I'll let you," he replied.

"It's just like landing a space shuttle," she told him. Only it wasn't. The old shuttles came into atmosphere in a sort of belly flop, using their blunt, shielded undersurface to build up a shock wave to protect them from the worst of the heat. They achieved and maintained the right angle using steering jets until they were deep enough in the atmosphere for their wings to become useful.

The H-7s were meant to reenter under power.

And Heng was coming in at a bad angle, anyway.

"Good luck, Heng," she said softly, feeling more and more helpless as she saw a stream of hot gas begin to form a trail behind him.

*   *   *

The hybrid transport flew so smoothly that David could close his eyes and imagine he was on a train. It was in essence a middle-sized jet that had been retrofitted with AG drive and an energy-propellant system. It wasn't capable of space flight, but it made ground-to-ground travel swift and painless.

For people who didn't mind leaving the ground.

For David, it was still a horror show.

Fortunately the flight from the Center for Alien Technology to the Centre Spatial Guyanais was only about a three-hour jaunt in the company ship. Being the director of the ESD had its perks.

He had been director now for five years, and wished desperately he had taken up the task earlier. If he had, Steve Hiller might still be alive—but he had avoided the responsibility until it was too late.

Tanner and Jacobs had opposed him, of course, but that opposition was never made public, and there wasn't much of a fight when he pointed out that he could either expose their complicity in rushing to test a design before it was ready, or they could put him in charge. That Whitmore stood with him on the issue hadn't hurt.

More than a decade of the most intense military spending in the history of the planet had been starting to take its toll on the morale of the average person. They had just seen one of their heroes go up in a fireball of the technology that was supposed to save them, which they were paying for in a hundred ways. The administration needed David Levinson on their side, and they knew it.

Strain was their scapegoat, and he accepted his lot without complaint, resigning in disgrace. It wasn't entirely fair, but then if Strain had had the guts to fight them in the first place, probably none of this would have been necessary, so David couldn't work up much sympathy for him.

He took off from a desert and landed in a jungle, or near one, anyway. Like most functioning space facilities on Earth, the site in French Guiana that serviced France and most other European nations had grown considerably over the last decade or so. He had been here only two years before, and hardly recognized it.

Max Martell he easily recognized, however. He was short, dark-skinned, in his sixties with a startling shock of white hair and a mild, even demeanor.

"Director Levinson," Martell said. "So nice to see you again."

"Likewise, Max," David said. "Looks like things are jumping here."

"We're doing our best to stay on schedule."

"I saw the timeframe was looking like, what, three years? That's fantastic."

"Phobos in two, maybe three—a functioning defense system on Mars in three to four," Max said. "I hear the Russians are pushing ahead on the Rhea project."

"Yes," David said. "Things are looking up. If the bad guys don't come back, we're all going to look pretty silly."

He stopped when he saw the expression on Max's face. His wife and two-year-old son had been in Paris.

"Sorry, Max, you know me. Mr. Sensitive. I'll be as happy as anyone if this all turns out to be for naught."

"Well, it's not for nothing anyway, is it?" Max said. "Clean power sources, anti-gravity—carbon emissions are way down. Automakers think that within a year or two they can produce affordable cars with crash shields..." He trailed off, and now it was his turn to look mortified.

David brushed past it. "You're right," he said. "We're doing well. Now let's go explain that to the people who write the checks."

If the aliens did come back, and wanted to strike a crippling blow to the ESD, the place to start would probably be the ESD Spring Expo, which was what brought him to French Guiana. Despite—or perhaps because of—the disaster that had cost Steve Hiller his life in the 2007 Expo, the event had continued to grow, becoming truly international. Leaders from the European Union, China, Russia, Saudi Arabia, Indonesia—every major and minor nation engaged in the collective defense initiative was represented, both as a public show of support and engagement and as a practical matter of sorting out priorities.

For David, politics was the least interesting aspect of the Expo, although it was unfortunately what he spent most of his time doing. What he really enjoyed were the presentations, the solid and just-crazy-enough-to-work applications individual researchers and research teams had worked out, hypotheses regarding the aliens themselves, where they were from, what the nature of their last signal was, and speculations about alien civilization in general. The budget for SETI had been quintupled and they had vastly better tools for probing the heavens in search of alien transmissions.

Tantalizing evidence presented itself, was analyzed, and was largely shot down as irrelevant. Even though they now knew beyond debate that humans weren't alone in the universe, they still didn't know where the aliens had come from. Space was too unimaginably vast.

In short, it was the largest meeting of space and technology nerds on the planet. About eighty-to-ninety percent of what was heard at the panels was rubbish, but there were always a few moments of real genius, too. The problem that had been the cause of Hiller's death was definitively solved by a lone mathematician working out the intricacies of the subatomic oscillation in the grown energy source. For him, it had been a purely mathematical problem, something he was working on only because it intrigued him. For the ESD, it was the final breakthrough they had been looking for.

He sat in on a general discussion about progress on the moon base, along with Commander Lao Jiang and several of his project engineers. They had already established a minimal presence on the lunar surface. In terms of power it was already self-sustaining, and within a few months, as the water-mining operation came up to speed, they would be able to produce oxygen through electrolysis.

"On a related note," Lao informed the audience in his conclusion, "as we speak, one of our hybrid fighters is on a course which will circumnavigate the moon. It will be the first truly long-range test of the craft and their ability to defend the moon base until the cannons are in place."

"Is it true the pilot is a relative of yours?" a reporter asked.

"I'm pleased to confirm that," Lao said. "She is my niece. My brother—her father—died on the Fourth, defending the world against the enemy. However, Rain wasn't chosen for this honor due to her birth—she finished at the top of her class in flight training. I am very proud."

"And she is only twenty-one, is that correct?" someone asked.

"Also correct," Lao said.

That opened the floor for a rising tide of questions. Lao linked a newsfeed to the projector, which was updating the progress of the Chinese mission to circumnavigate the moon. David took the opportunity to duck out of the back door and escape the reporters. Inevitably, though, there were a few waiting. He waved them off with a few polite comments, and then, turning to beat a hasty retreat, slammed into someone.

"Oh! Ah, I'm terribly sorry," he began, reaching to help the dark-haired woman back to her feet.

"It's okay," she said, skootching up to her knees so she could pick up a ream of papers she had just spilled from a folder. "I suppose I may have been standing too close."

"Here," he said, kneeling. "Let me help you with those." He collected several of the loose sheets. All seemed to be sketches or paintings of a circle. One looked like a smiley face sans eyes.

They both straightened up as he handed them to her. She was probably in her late thirties, but there was something waifish about her. Her hair was long and brown, her dark eyes large and animated. She looked a bit familiar.

"Director Levinson," she said.

"Yes," he said. "How do you do?"

"My name is Catherine Marceaux," she said. "*Dr.* Catherine Marceaux."

"Oh, right," he said. "Yes. You're the psychologist."

"Psychiatrist," she corrected.

"Sorry," he said. "You wrote a book or something, didn't you? On alien behavior?"

"My specific interests are in the interaction between the human and alien psyche," she said. "I would very much like to bend your ear for a bit. Is this a good time?"

David didn't get a chance to answer, because the room behind him erupted into bedlam.

"Excuse me for a moment," he said, and he ducked back into the conference hall. He pushed past Lao, who was furiously barking into a cell phone.

Everyone was staring at the projection screen.

David turned his own attention that way.

"Houston," he said, "we've had a problem."

26

"Screw this," Rain muttered under her breath. She engaged her engines and fired herself toward Heng like a bullet.

"*Chang'e*... what are... doing?" Control demanded.

The communications were already breaking up due to the ionization caused by her entry into the atmosphere. Heng's fighter was engulfed in white flame. She saw he had somehow managed to turn belly-down—which was a good start—but the angle was too steep, and his craft was beginning to yaw dangerously. If he spun, it was all over.

The comm crackled again, this time unintelligibly.

Rain plunged on, her ship tremoring as if it was having a seizure. The force field automatically tripped on, but it caused too much wind resistance so she overrode it until she managed to overtake Heng, and then pass him. By that time they were at twenty kilometers above sea level.

She flipped the force field back on and began to decelerate, knowing that what she was doing was more or less insane. But it was the only thing she could think of.

Heng's ship hit her, much harder than she had expected. His craft glanced off. Everything started to spin, and for a moment she had no control at all—she didn't know where the horizon was. Finally she was able to kill her rotation, and saw that he was still above her.

This time she managed to ease up under him and start putting on the brakes—with his ship piggybacked on hers.

There was no way she was going to be able to kill their velocity in time. The AG thrusts weren't powerful enough to decelerate two ships, not at the speed they already had achieved, and not with the ground so near.

Fifteen kilometers.

Ten...

Seven...

Her instruments were going crazy.

Then her right AG thruster went dead.

"Well, that's not perfect," she murmured. "Heng? Can you hear me?"

"Yes," he said. "What the hell?" His voice was staticky, but the most intense part of the ionization was behind them.

Her other thruster cut out.

"Time to use your wings," she told him. "Get off my back."

"Copy," he said. "For the record—you are the craziest person I've ever known."

"I really want that beer," she said.

He lifted off of her, and she immediately engaged her rudder and wing-flaps and banked, hard. The idea was to kill more of her speed by using the atmosphere—sort of like running switchback down a steep slope rather than straight down it—but they were already so near the surface it was anyone's guess how this little jaunt would end.

She banked again, cutting a long "S" shape through the sky, scanning the terrain below for someplace to land, but all she saw was mountains, coming up fast.

One kilometer.

She turned hard to avoid spattering against a peak, and then hit a column of air. She felt momentarily weightless as the craft dropped, uncontrolled, for twenty meters before slapping back against a thermal. She dodged another cliff side and saw treetops coming up fast.

This is going to hurt, she thought. It seemed like the time to eject. What that would be like at this speed, she didn't know. Besides, that would be sort of like losing.

Then she was past the trees, and land like a table top appeared. She pulled up her nose, full flaps. This time her landing gear didn't break right away—instead she hit tail-first so the AG units took the hit and broke off. She skipped, came down on the gear. *Then* they broke. The *Chang'e One* plowed a furrow through the short grass and came to a stop.

Dots dancing before her eyes, Rain desperately checked the fusion containment and found that it had shut down quietly. After the explosion that killed Steven Hiller, that part of the plane was arguably the safest, at least in theory.

"Heng?" she said.

Nothing.

She looked around, and across the plain, maybe two kilometers away, she saw a huge column of smoke rising.

"Heng, do you copy?" she said, urgently.

"Yeah," he finally replied. "Had to eject. I'm hung up in some trees. You?"

"I'm well," she said. "My ship has seen better days."

"Where the hell are we?" he asked.

She checked her instruments.

"North America," she said. "Montana, I think."

Off in the distance, she saw what she thought might be a herd of buffalo.

Her comm crackled again.

"Captain Lao?" It was Control. By the sound of it, the signal was bouncing off a satellite.

"Yes," she said. "I'm on the ground and unhurt."

"I'm patching Commander Lao through," Control said.

She quickly snatched off her headphones and held them a few centimeters from her ears as Uncle Jiang went off furiously for about two minutes, seemingly without taking a breath. When he settled down a little, she put them back on.

"… multi-million dollar vehicle!" he said, then there was silence.

"Commander Lao," she said. "Aren't you supposed to be in French Guiana?"

"Yes," he answered. "I'm on my cell phone."

"Are we being broadcast, sir?"

"No," he said. "Right now it's a private line."

"Then I love you, too," she said. "I'm afraid I'm still having trouble with landings, but I think you'll agree I did better this time."

He sighed audibly enough that she could hear it.

"There are choppers on the way to recover you and Heng," he said. "Say nothing of your insubordination, do you understand? And try to stay away from reporters until we're ready."

"Yes, Uncle Jiang," she said.

"And just for the record," he said, "what you just did was perhaps the stupidest thing I've ever seen. Also the bravest."

"Thank you, Uncle Jiang."

"It was not a compliment," he said.

But she could almost sense the faint grin on the other end of the line.

*   *   *

"Drilling?" David said.

He glanced around the room, from face to face. There were exactly four people present. One was a man named Lucien Ondekane, a refugee from the National Republic of Umbutu. Another was a South African intelligence field operative, a young woman named Molly DeBoer. Number three was Secretary of Defense Tanner, and David made four. Tanner had summoned him from a discussion on quantum uncertainty and AG fields, just as it was getting interesting. That was after everyone calmed down about the Chinese pilot, and things started rolling along back on schedule.

He hadn't seen the French woman again, and he felt rude for having left her hanging. He had checked the program and saw she was speaking, but her presentation conflicted with his schedule.

As for his current discussion, it was... kind of interesting. Probably more interesting than whatever psychobabble an attractive—well, a ridiculously attractive—psychiatrist had to offer.

Ondekane started speaking in French, and DeBoer began a running translation.

"He says the ship didn't crash, that it landed. They fought the aliens for ten years. . ."

"Yes, yes," David said. "We know all of this. Skip to the drilling."

She said something to Lucien, who nodded and started again.

"Once it was over, they found a huge hole in the ground, so deep that they couldn't see the bottom, so deep that the monsoon rains didn't fill it up."

David frowned. "That's... not typical. Ask him if he knows why."

Lucien wasn't sure. "There are many rare and precious metals in the region," he said.

"Sure," David said, "but that can be said of many of the other locations as well."

"Maybe their primary weapon misfired," Tanner suggested.

"No," David said. "Think about it. New York, London—more than a hundred cities they fired their primary weapon upon. Nowhere did it dig a hole. It wasn't designed that way. Their primary weapon was meant to do what it did—depopulate huge swaths of urban area. Reduce cities to rubble. Unless…"

"Unless what?" Tanner asked.

"Maybe it was set on stun."

"What the hell does that mean?"

"Maybe the primary weapon was a multitasker. We only saw one setting. After all, in no other ship was the weapon intact. It's how we beat them, by blowing them up."

"Or maybe that ship was just a one-off," Tanner said. "Maybe it had a different mission and a different tool set."

"We're pretty sure it's the same ship that took out Lagos and Kinshasa," David said. "So it did the other thing, too. You see what this means. We've got to get in there."

"We've been trying diplomatically for years," Tanner said. "They refuse."

"Maybe it's time to get undiplomatic," David said.

"I'll take it up with the president," Tanner said, "although I don't really see the relevance. We've got their cannon, we've put their technology to good use. We have a base on the moon and soon we'll be on Mars and the moons of Saturn. It doesn't matter what they were doing a decade and a half ago. What's important is that we stop them from doing anything at all if they come back."

"There's something here we don't know," David said. "What we don't know very certainly can hurt us."

"Like I said," Tanner replied, "I'll take it up with the president."

Lucien suddenly started speaking again, quietly, his tone flat and hopeless. DeBoer stared at him, listening but saying nothing.

"What?" David asked.

"He says do not go there," she said. "It is a place of evil spirits and madness, and if you go there you will only be infected by it. You will let it loose on the world."

* * *

Dikembe swept his gaze over the troubled ground, wishing not for the first time that he could simply get in a jeep and drive away, leave his country, go someplace and paint for the rest of his life. As a question of practice he could, of course, do that, but he knew if he did he could never come back.

For years he had been flattering himself that he was making a difference, that he was the one person standing between his father and the people. He had helped the starving, in many cases aided those without hope of survival, enabling them to escape into nearby countries. Now he was starting to doubt that he had had any effect at all.

The problem, in a sense, was *uchawi*.

In England, speaking to a young literature major, he'd made the mistake of translating the word as witchcraft, following the practice of English anthropologists of the last century. Witches, he was stridently informed, were merely women who held to the pre-Christian beliefs of the land, who worshipped nature or the Great Mother and such. It was the Patriarchy that named them witches and attributed evil doings to them, trying to keep women in their place.

So perhaps it was a problem with the word, and the freight it carried in the English and not the concept. The fact was, people all over the globe believed that sickness and misfortune weren't naturally occurring things. If you became ill or died suddenly it was because someone—or something—was practicing *uchawi* against you. This was a belief that was still strongly held by many of his people, even in the face of modern science and medicine.

His people were not at all unique in this regard—even people in the most technologically advanced countries like the United States had faith healers or relied on mystical explanations for traumatic events. Yet here, the deep-rooted belief in spirits and sorcerers of ill will had become all mixed up with the aliens. When somebody was sick, or acted badly or did anything that conflicted with the tenets undergirding his father's brutal regime, they were said to be infected by one of the thousands of alien spirits that now dwelt in the dark recesses of the land.

Killing them all, it seemed, had done little to decrease their influence.

Such things were happening elsewhere as well. He had lately read a book by a French psychiatrist, in which she theorized that contact between humans and aliens showed a residual effect. She had interviewed and studied the transcripts of conversations with people from all around the world—any place human and alien had come face to face. She conjectured that part of this residual contact was the absorption by humans of alien semiotic structures, of the symbols by which they understood and negotiated the universe.

The author, Catherine Marceaux, had applied on three occasions for a visa to enter the Republic of Umbutu to conduct her studies amongst his people. His father, of course, had denied the visas.

Some clear-thinking people believed that co-opting traditional superstitions was a thing his father had done with foresight, in a clinical, calculated move to validate his rule. In reality, Dikembe had been forced to admit years ago that his father was quite mad. He surrounded himself with seers and charlatans, protected himself with magical charms. He saw enemies even in the faces of children.

The place Dikembe stood now only made that all the more clear.

"How many?" he asked Zuberi.

"Around a hundred," his old friend replied.

Dikembe felt numb. The bodies had been thrown into a wide, dry creek bed, and from the looks of it a bulldozer had then pushed dirt over them. Whoever had done it was either stupid or didn't care—when the rains came, most of the dirt had washed away, so that now one could see the shapes of corpses here and there, exposed arms and legs. Vultures had been picking at what they could reach, and in fact vultures had led hunters here, men hoping to find a dead elephant or giraffe from which to scavenge.

Instead, they had solved the mystery of the missing village. It was not the first mass grave Dikembe had seen, but it was the largest.

"How can this go on?" he asked himself.

"How can we stop it?" Zuberi said.

"We stand up to him," Dikembe said.

"You could do that," Zuberi said, "for all it would accomplish. But if I were to say a wrong word, they would start with my wife, and then my children, and they would do it in front of me. You understand that, don't you? I'm risking far too much in even showing you this."

"Surely…" Dikembe said. "Surely there must be those even inside of his guard who understand that he is mad, who can see the ruin he is driving us to."

"What are you suggesting?" Zuberi said. "A coup?"

Dikembe didn't answer that. He didn't need to say it aloud, and Zuberi didn't need to hear it. It would only make things harder on the both of them. It wasn't that he hadn't considered it, but he kept hoping that things would somehow get better. For a while it almost seemed like they would. His father showed moments of clarity, became more susceptible to reason for a time. But that had been an illusion. Things were getting worse. The voices in his own head, quiet for so many years, were whispering again. It was happening to others, especially his father, who now sometimes spent weeks in seclusion and at other times went on sudden tours of the country, dressed in uniform, draped in ornaments created from alien bones and exoskeletons.

It was getting worse, and Dikembe realized that it was time to stop putting it off.

Something had to be done.

27

JULY

Patricia expected her father to answer the door the way he always did, but instead she found herself smiling at Agent Vega.

"Hey," she said. "Is Dad here?"

"Yes, Ms. Whitmore," the agent replied. "He isn't up yet."

"Isn't up?" she said. "It's eleven o'clock. He's usually up before six."

"He's been sleeping in a little more often lately," Vega said.

"Well, I'll surprise him," Patricia said. She put down her bags and went back to his room. The curtains were drawn, and the light was dim.

Shock stopped her in her tracks.

"Dad?" she said.

He was sitting up in the bed, staring off at nothing. For a second she was six years old again, and he had just wakened from another nightmare—but it was much more than that. His hair was nearly completely gray, and his face was so stubbly he must not have shaved in three or four days. His room—always spare and neat, the product of his military background—was a mess.

He turned toward her slowly.

"Marilyn?" he said.

Patricia froze, her throat tightening. Marilyn was her mother, and she had been dead for sixteen years. She didn't know what to say.

Then the look on his face changed as he understood his mistake.

"Dad—"

He put his hand to his forehead.

"Munchkin?" he murmured. "Patty?"

"It's okay, Dad," she said. "You must be tired."

"You're so much like her," he said. He looked confused. "What are you doing here?"

"I'm on leave for two weeks, remember?"

He nodded, but it was as if he was still half asleep. "Yeah," he said. "God, it's good to see you. Come give the old man a hug."

After the greeting she sat next to him on the bed.

"What's going on, Dad?" she asked.

"These damned meds," he muttered. "Half the time—"

"Meds?" she said. "For what? I haven't heard anything about this."

"Well, you know, I sort of hoped it would go away."

"Why don't we get you up and get you some coffee, and you can tell me about it?" she said.

He nodded. "Alright."

"I'll go get the coffee started."

*   *   *

He showed up half an hour later. He'd put on a robe, but he hadn't shaved. In the light streaming through the windows he looked even worse than he had in the darkened room. He looked old, and lost, and fragile.

Faded.

It scared the hell out of her.

He sat down and flashed a reasonable facsimile of his famous crooked smile.

"So how is flight school?" he asked.

"No, Dad," she said firmly. "We're going to talk about you first. What meds?"

He rubbed his forehead with his fingers.

"Nothing is really helping," he said. "I don't think they know what they're doing. I think some of it makes it worse."

"What's wrong with you?" she said.

He sighed and looked at his finger as he scratched it in a circular motion on the table.

"I'm, uh—they won't quite use the word psychosis around me, but some of the drugs are... about that. And depression. I checked." He looked up from the table, and his eyes had a sort of pleading. "I'm not crazy, Patty," he said. "I'm not. But they're in my head, and I can't get them out."

"They?" she said.

"The aliens," he said. "The goddamn aliens. In my head—and not just when I'm asleep, not just when I close my eyes. Sometimes it's like they're projected from my eyes onto the wall, onto other people's faces. There are other things I see, or think I see, that are hard to describe." He bent toward her. "You remember when you were little?"

"The nightmares," she said. "They went away."

"Slowly," he said. "I was a little shaky for a couple of years, but I managed it. I was okay, and it got better. I almost forgot about it. But now it's all come back, and I don't know why. Neither do the doctors."

"Dad..." she began. "Since when? When did it start coming back?"

"A few months ago, a year. I'm not sure," he said. "It was little at first, like a cricket in my brain, but now..."

"So when I came home last time?" she said, and he nodded.

"It comes and goes," he said, "but when it comes, it always comes a little stronger."

"Why have you been hiding this from me?" she asked.

"You've got enough to worry about," he said. "I know how rough flight school can be. There's nothing wrong with my memory. Sometimes I wish there was."

As he talked, he seemed to be getting better. His eyes became more focused, his expression more like what she was used to. He asked her about flight school again, and she answered as best she could through the cloud of distraction. When he came to the topic of Dale, she took a deep breath.

"Yeah," she said. "About that. That's kind of over."

"Since when?" he asked.

"A few months ago," she said.

"So now you're hiding things from me?"

"Sure," she said. "You should be used to that. The things I don't tell you—"

"Could fill a shoebox," he finished, smiling. "I'm sorry, Patty. I'm sorry I'm not one hundred percent for your visit. I really have missed you."

"I missed you, too," she said. "The breakup wasn't that long ago. I thought I might as well wait to tell you in person."

"For the record, I never liked Dale," he said. "No ambition. I mean, you don't have to want to own the world, but having a goal of some sort would be nice."

"Well, apparently he was ambitious enough to maintain several girlfriends at once," she said.

"You want a little accident should happen to him?" her father said, in his best Vito Corleone impression. Which was terrible.

"Nope," she said. "Moving on. Besides, my new ride is

a bona fide killing machine, so if the mood strikes me—
pow."

"So is there a new guy?" he asked.

"No. Every other guy I know right now is a pilot," she said. "You know how that is."

"Not really," he said. "Not a lot of women pilots back in my day."

"Well, it's not a good idea, flight school romance," she said.

"So there *is* somebody," he said.

"What?"

"You made the face," he said. He sounded fine now. It wasn't so bad. Whatever was going on with him, he would snap out of it. He always did.

"I know what face you're talking about, Dad, and I did not make it. I haven't made that face since high school."

"No, I've seen it since," he said. "When we were out in Nevada, for the test flight…"

She realized with a start he was about to say something about Jake, and she knew she would blush. He didn't, though. He trailed off, and his eyes became a bit vacant, the sparkle suddenly gone.

"Captain Hiller," he murmured. "He died there."

"He was a colonel, Dad," she corrected gently.

"My God," he said. "They got to him, somehow."

"Dad?"

"The aliens," he murmured. "I always knew they would get their revenge."

"It was an accident," she said. "A problem with the fusion containment."

"What about David Levinson? Is he…?"

"As far as I know he's fine," Patricia said, her own spirits beginning to flag. "He's the director of the Earth Space Defense, remember?"

"I asked him to do that," Whitmore said. "We needed

to unite the world around a common goal."

"You did," she said.

He shook his head. "It isn't done," he said. "They're out there. We have to be ready." He looked up. "Patty, David has to be warned. They got Hiller. Now they'll come for him." His voice was rising, edging toward hysteria. She put her hand on his.

"It's okay," she said. "I'll let him know. We'll be ready. Did I tell you about the new fighters? They handle like a dream—like nothing you've ever flown before."

Her talking seemed to calm him down, so she kept going. Finally he got up and kissed her on the head. "Let me shower, clean up, Patty. We'll go out somewhere. That Italian place you like, maybe."

The last thing her dad needed at the moment was to be in public. "I'm tired, Dad," she said. "Long flight. Why don't we have sandwiches for lunch, then order in for supper? Maybe watch a little Letterman tonight."

He smiled faintly. "We watched Letterman the night before they came. I don't remember who the guests were. Good thing he was on vacation at his place in Montana," he said. "That sounds good, Patty."

"Feel free to shower, though," she said. "And a shave wouldn't hurt you either."

*　　*　　*

She cornered Agent Vega the next day.

"Who knows?" she demanded.

He fidgeted a little.

"Just me and the other agents," he said. "The house staff. His doctors."

"Yeah," she said. "And whoever they blabbed to."

"Secret service doesn't 'blab,' ma'am," Vega protested.

She stepped a little closer.

"Agent Vega," she said, "I was more or less raised by the secret service. I have nothing but the highest respect for you, but all of you are human, and humans talk. I know, because I'm one too. From now on, I need to know what happens here. What meetings he has and with whom. Any public appearances he might have scheduled, anything like that. "Do you understand?"

"Yes, ma'am, but with all due respect, you're not going to be here all of the time."

"I know," she said. "I'm going to hire some sort of chief of staff, someone who can make the minute-to-minute decisions."

"That's what we're doing," Vega said. "Our job is to protect him, and not just from bullets."

"Can you honestly tell me you don't feel understaffed?" she asked. "That you have this all under control?"

He pursed his lips, and after a few seconds shook his head.

"No," he said.

She nodded. "You'll vet whoever I hire. Maybe a retired agent? Let me know if you think of anyone."

"I'll ask around," he replied.

*　　*　　*

"Holy crap, Dylan," Jake breathed. "We did it."

"Come again, Saber Two," Control said.

Jake cleared his throat. "Sorry, Control, that was just me sneezing."

"What he means to say," Dylan cut in, "is that we've achieved orbit."

"Very good, Saber One. Proceed toward training course."

Jake glanced off to his right, where Dylan's sleek fighter was a shadow against the larger shadow of the Earth, visible only by its running lights. The Earth wasn't entirely dark, though—here and there were glowing patches, like distant jumbles of Christmas lights. He wondered what it would have looked like in 1995 when New York and Mexico City, Beijing, Mumbai had still been down there.

He switched to their private channel.

"Just to clarify," Jake said, "holy crap, Dylan, we're in space."

"Yeah," Dylan said. "We are that. Patricia is going to be pissed off. Our first run upstairs while she's on leave."

"She'll get over it," Jake said. "Once we explain—over and over—how awesome it was."

"Okay," Dylan said. "Let's focus on the mission now. No more small talk."

"Yeah, yeah," Jake said. "I don't see anything yet. Do you?"

"Nope," Dylan replied.

Jake continued to marvel at the blaze of the heavens. An eye-hurting light appeared on the Earth's horizon, and his cockpit glass adjusted.

"Sunrise," he said. He watched the bright point of the sun spread a crescent of blue, green, and white on the rim of the world.

"I've got something," Dylan said.

"Coming from where?"

"Where do you think?"

"Those sneaky bastards," Jake said. "Yeah, I see them now." There were four of them, and they were coming straight out of the sunrise, making it impossible to spot them visually—but visually wasn't the best way to see things up here anyway. They had instruments far more sensitive than the human eye.

"Let's get turned," Dylan said. "Otherwise they'll be all over our tails. Nice and easy, just like in the simulator."

It was nothing like the simulator. The bad guys weren't

pixels, they were drones programmed to behave like alien fighters. That was space out there, as well, and a really long fall if anything went wrong, as it had for the Chinese pilot a few months earlier.

"I've got a lock on one," Dylan said.

"I've got the one on your three," Jake said. He fired a burst, watched it stream into the rising sun. A stutter of green light from Dylan crossed his.

"Hits," Dylan said. "Shoot, there are two more coming from behind us."

"Your call," Jake said.

"Go get 'em. I'll deal with these."

The wings of their craft were useless in space, of course, but the anti-gravity drive wasn't, especially with a gravity well as big as the Earth right below. Jake's craft whipped up and around. The attackers behind him were below instead, and closing fast on Dylan.

"Yee-hah!" Jake cried as he dove toward the planet, firing his energy weapon. One of the enemies was rocketing straight at him now. Jake strafed the one on Dylan's tail and then went into a tight turn, trying to avoid the simulated green death streaming by. Then they had passed each other, so near that Jake suspected they were about a meter away from causing the automatic safety gear to kick in. The ESD wasn't in the business of losing expensive spacecraft in training exercises.

Jake turned hard and kicked on the fusion drive, at the same time breaking and turning with the AG thrusters, reversing his course almost instantly. The acceleration compensators didn't quite absorb all of the g-forces, so for a moment he felt as if he had an elephant sitting on him. As the spots behind his eyes cleared, he saw the bogie coming back down his throat.

He fired.

"He shoots!" Jake hollered. "He scores!" Then he

turned to find Dylan and the other three attackers, but his screen indicated that all of them had been destroyed. They hadn't, of course—drones were expensive, too.

That meant Dylan was down.

Jake was the last man standing.

* * *

Dylan hardly spoke on the way down, although Jake tried to draw him out a few times. Finally reentry and landing took all of his attention.

It wasn't until later, at the bar, with a drink in each of them, that Jake tried to nudge Dylan again.

"Come on," he said. "It was three against one, and you got them all."

"And they got me," Dylan said. "That never happened in the simulator."

"Well, the real thing takes some getting used to," Jake offered.

"Yeah? You seemed to do just fine," Dylan said, hunching over his drink.

"Beginner's luck," Jake said. "Shake it off. Next time, right?"

Dylan took another drink of his IPA.

"What if I wash out, Jake?"

He sounded serious.

"What?" Jake said. "That's crazy talk."

Dylan lowered his voice. "You know what killed my dad?" Dylan said. "It wasn't the explosion. It was being Steve Hiller, the guy that did something impossible and saved the world. One of the guys, anyway. After that, he wasn't just a guy, you know. He was *the* guy, and Dad took that seriously. He carried that weight even after it got too heavy for him, and he climbed into a ship he didn't trust because that was what he was supposed to do.

"Now that he's gone… it feels like it's all come down on me. Like if I fail, I'm not just failing myself—I'm failing everybody."

"Dylan," Jake said. "Buddy. You aren't going to fail. You'll probably be first in the class. Well, second in the class—I'll be first."

Dylan didn't smile.

"That was a joke," Jake said.

Now Dylan did smile, a little. "No it wasn't," he said, "but thanks."

"What was it you told me your dad always said? If you're passionate about what you do, if you do it with conviction, you can never fail."

"Never fail *him*, is what he meant," Dylan said. "I can passionately and with great conviction let everyone else down." He straightened and leaned back in his seat. "God, Jake, I miss him," he said.

"I know," Jake said.

"Listen to me," Dylan said, rolling his eyes. "This must sound really stupid to you. I mean you—"

Yeah, Jake thought. *At least you had somebody like that in your life, if only for a while.*

But that wasn't what Dylan needed to hear at the moment, and Jake knew it. There was a flip side to that, too. He could barely remember his parents. That pain was far in the past. If he had been as close to his father as Dylan had been to his, and lost him—well, he had trouble imagining it.

"It's not stupid," Jake said. "I get it."

Dylan nodded. "Thanks," he said.

"You're just not used to losing," Jake said. "You don't take it well."

"Look who's talking," Dylan said.

Jake nodded, then raised his glass.

"We didn't lose. As a team, we won. So here's to the team."

"To the team," Dylan seconded.

28

JUNE

2013

Dikembe locked eyes with the man in the tent. Outside, the sky was weeping gently upon the savanna. The west was a cloud of orange light nestled on one side of a cottony gray vault.

The man's name was Weiss. He would give no first name, and he would not say for whom he really worked. He was stocky, blunt-faced with close-shaven hair that was nearly all black, despite the fact that he must have been at least fifty.

When Dikembe began trying to collect men for the mission, he began outside of the country, quietly recruiting mercenaries, for two reasons. First, anyone he enlisted from his own country might be an informer for his father. Even if they were not, word might get around to someone who was. The second reason was that if they failed, at least it would not be his countrymen dying.

As he recruited, Weiss had simply shown up. He did not seem like a mercenary, and did not claim to be. To Dikembe, he gave the impression of being more like some sort of spook—CIA or something. In the new world order he wasn't sure how that worked. Whether he worked for an individual country or for the Earth Space Defense coalition.

A lot of people wanted to get their hands on the ship. He was a little surprised Umbutu hadn't ever actually been invaded.

It appeared as if Weiss had been hanging around the area, waiting for wind of any sort of uprising or instability. Then he was just *there*.

"I want to be perfectly clear about this," Dikembe said. "I do not want my father killed. I want him taken out of the country, but he will be alive when this happens, and he will remain alive. Also, I don't want any unnecessary deaths amongst my people. I will let you into my father's compound and deal with what guards I can. You will come in, take him, and then we will leave."

Weiss nodded. "How many soldiers in the compound?" he asked.

"On the order of thirty," Dikembe said. "The exact number changes, and there are several checkpoints along the way."

"The trick will not be getting in," Weiss said. "It will be getting him out. Have you considered using helicopters? I have several at my disposal."

"Do you have any with force fields?" Dikembe asked.

"No. Such vehicles exist, of course, but no. That would make this whole thing much less… quiet."

"Then no," Dikembe said. "My father's guards are armed with energy weapons, and they will easily shoot down any air support."

"Even if your father is in the chopper?"

"No, of course not," Dikembe said.

"Then can't we steal a republican chopper to get him out?"

"That's worth considering," Dikembe said.

"Well, then," Weiss said. "Let's go over the photographs and consider our options."

* * *

As he approached Upanga Umbutu's rooms, Dikembe tried to remember better times, but it had become difficult. Those years seemed so distant, the images he was still able to conjure as antique as sepia photographs.

He stopped before the little shrine that had been erected in the hall, dedicated to Bakari. He stared at the picture of his brother for a moment, recalling the last time he had seen him alive, his final words. What would Bakari have to say about what Dikembe was about to do? Would he be proud or ashamed—or, like Dikembe, deeply conflicted?

He heard the chatter of gunfire begin outside. The two guards outside the door clutched their weapons.

"The compound is under attack," Dikembe told them. "You, go help secure the perimeter of the house. And you, Enzi—I must move my father to a secure location. Go and alert the helicopter pilot. Quickly."

"Yes, Prince," they both said, and ran off to do his bidding.

So far, so good. The mercenaries, to all appearances, were assaulting the gate. That would draw almost all of his father's men to the front of the house. The helicopter pad was in the back.

He pushed open his father's door. The old man was standing in front of a mirror, dressed in his uniform. Dikembe was fairly certain he slept in it now.

"They're coming for us, aren't they?" his father said. "They took my lovely Bakari, and now they have come for you, Dikembe. And for me."

"The helicopter is out back," Dikembe said. "We will withdraw to the installation in the south. We can hold them off from there."

"I feel them," his father said. "Like rats in my skull."

"Papa, come along."

His father's eyes rolled about and his mouth worked without sound. Dikembe took his arm and guided him through the house, out of the back door, to where the chopper was warming up. He had to force him to duck down as they drew near. As he helped his father climb into the back, he saw that one of Weiss's men was at the controls. His father did not notice, of course.

So far, so good, he thought again. *All according to plan.* The helicopter lifted in the darkness. Dawn was only an hour away, but she was shy yet, still hiding in her damp robe of night.

"I have dreamed many things," his father said, his voice almost singsong, as if reciting an old epic. "So much has been foretold. The day of return is at hand." He turned to Dikembe. "Do you understand?"

"I'm not sure what you mean, Father," Dikembe said.

"At first we fought them, and believed with our souls that they were dead, and yet from beyond death they still hunted us. Their ghosts hunted us, stalked us from the shadows beneath our feet, in the waters, in the very temples of our skulls. They lay in wait for us beyond our borders, in the abhorrent world beyond, and for years I— even I did not understand. The wise men and women who counseled me also failed to understand. Only now, as I dream my waking dream, is all finally revealed."

His voice became soft and measured, the tone of it totally sane—if not for the words. It was like a man describing the garden in front of his house.

"What is that, Father?" Dikembe asked. "What do you understand?"

Dawn was breaking, a watery gray line in the east. They had probably already crossed out of Umbutu. It was all but over. He hoped that no one had died, but that was probably too much to wish for. He knew the blood would stain him forever, but he also knew he had done the right thing. Perhaps with help, his father could get better, become more like the man he had once been.

"Hunter and hunted," his father said. "Predator and prey. I thought they were our enemies, that they came here to kill us."

"They did come here to kill us, Father," he said. "They slaughtered billions."

"No," his father shook his head slowly. "They are our other halves. They are us and we are them. It's only fighting that fact that causes the pain. We must rejoin them. Only then will any of us be whole again."

Although his words were mad, Dikembe felt a sort of creeping horror, because it also made a certain sense. If he just gave in to the voices…

"No," Dikembe said. "It cannot be true."

"But it is, and now they have come for you, as they came for Bakari, and for me. We shall all be complete at last."

The helicopter descended, approaching the treetops. Beyond, on a small field, Dikembe saw a circle of armed men.

His father's men.

"I said once that you did not have it in you," his father said. "I now see I was wrong, but all will be well, my son."

Dikembe drew his sidearm and pointed at the pilot.

"Do not land here," he said.

Then he felt a sharp pain in his side. His father grabbed his arm, and with terrifying strength twisted the gun from his grasp. Dikembe felt a wave of weakness flow through him, and in shock, he realized he had been stabbed.

The treetops were close. He hurled himself from the helicopter at the nearest one.

*   *   *

When David had last seen the moon base in person it had resembled a bunch of half-assembled office furniture more than it did anything coherent. There had been enough going on to declare it operational. Now, however, it was very nearly complete, although one key element was missing. The base was laid out in concentric circles around a central hub. The hub contained a socket where one day, hopefully in the next few years, a gigantic cannon would be emplaced.

"Set her down gently, will you?" he asked the pilot, a young woman named Celeste who wore her hair clipped short. She made him feel like if they got in a fight, he wouldn't do that well. Not that she seemed angry, or mean. She just seemed… efficient.

"We're already down, sir," she said.

"Oh," he said. "That was very… smooth. Kudos."

Minutes later, in the hangar, he was greeted by a young man wearing the Chinese version of the ESD uniform and escorted to what would look like an ordinary meeting room were it not for the thick but transparent wall which afforded a stunning view of the lunar landscape—made all the more spectacular by Earthrise.

It wasn't anything he'd ever imagined seeing in his lifetime—not in person. It came up quickly, a ball of alabaster and cobalt, and unlike a rising moon, it cast no glow in the sky, since there was no atmosphere to scatter its light. It seemed smaller than a rising moon, due to the lack of an atmospheric lens on the horizon. It was beautiful, and lonely, and seemed to David as fragile as a glass Christmas ornament.

"You know the first photo of the Earth from space was supposed to make us all forget our petty differences and join together. End war and all of that."

David turned at the familiar voice.

"President Grey," he said. "So good to see you. It's

been a while. I heard you were taking a well-earned rest."

Grey's bushy eyebrows and what remained of his hair was now completely white, and he seemed to have shrunken a little bit, but his presence remained undiminished.

"I was," Grey said. He waved his hand to take in their surroundings "But I thought I had earned the right to see this, and President Lanford agreed. I came up on a transport a few days ago, with your advance crew. Eighty-two years old, and here I am on the moon. Seems impossible." He nodded toward the airlock. "I watched you land. Thought I'd say hello."

They shook hands.

"How are you, David?" the former president asked.

"Oh, I'm doing alright," he said. "Considering the fact that I'm in a little bubble of glass and steel surrounded by a vacuum, inundated by deadly radiation, and my insides feel like someone pumped them full of helium and champagne bubbles."

"It shouldn't be anything new to you," Grey said.

"Ha," David responded. "I avoid this whenever I can. I came up here to cut the ribbon in '09, and this is my first time here since."

Grey's voice softened. "I was so sorry to hear about Connie," he said. "She is very much missed."

"Yes," David said. "The flowers you sent were beautiful. I don't think I ever sent a thank you card. I don't think I sent any."

"It's understandable," Grey said. "When I lost Amelia, it felt like my whole life ground to a halt. Like my own history had disappeared."

They watched the Earth continue to rise against the blaze of stars.

"It was all bunk," Grey said.

"What's that?" David asked.

"The picture of the Earth—the idea that if people saw

the truth, that our national boundaries aren't 'real,' that there would be peace on Earth."

"No," David said. "No, that took the massacre of roughly half of the world's population in under two days by our unexpected friends. It seems like the thing we respond to best is fear."

"That's what gets us moving, anyway," Grey said. "I'm proud of what we've done here. I'm an old warrior, but I'd sure like to see our warriors put out of a job. Yet I wonder sometimes—what if they don't come back? What united us was a common enemy, a remorseless inhuman foe beyond our ability to comprehend. But if fifty, a hundred years pass, and that common enemy doesn't come back? What happens to all of these weapons then?"

"I don't know," David said. "There are brush fires here and there, but this is the longest the human race has gone without a major war or genocide or police action taking place since—well, the Stone Age. Maybe we could, uh, get used to it. Maybe if we actually *had* a hundred years of universal peace, it wouldn't even occur to us to fight each other again, and we could turn all of this technology and drive toward going out there. Finding new worlds, cleaning up *our* world—whatever we want."

Grey clapped him on the back. "Son, I hope you're right… and I hope we get the chance to find out."

"This isn't a private party I hope?" someone said.

"General Adams," Grey said.

Joshua Adams was the senior American Army official with the ESD, third in command behind the president and the secretary of defense. He was a quiet, intense man with a receding hairline and eyes the color of gunmetal. He looked vaguely tired, as if he hadn't been sleeping well. David caught Adams glancing at the transparent wall, and when he did his brow furrowed, as if he felt out of his element.

As quickly as the expression appeared, it flitted away. He reached out, and David took his hand. The grip was somewhat painful.

"General Adams," David said, trying not to grimace. "I've read the reports of what you encountered in the Atlantic in '96. Very impressive—it's a miracle you survived."

"It wasn't exactly my idea of a vacation," Adams replied, and he glanced again at the vista. "I can't say this is much better. We did what was needed though."

With him was Lao Jiang, commander of the moon base.

"What do you think, Director?" Lao asked.

"I like what you've done with the place," David said. "But when the Russian place opens on Rhea, that's gonna pull from your demographic. Everyone's gonna want to gaze at the rings of Saturn while they sip their lattes."

Lao looked a little puzzled.

"He's making a joke," Grey said. "With David, you have to get used to that. Hell, I thought he was joking at first when he told us he wanted to fly up to the mother ship."

"I think I understand," Lao said. "My English is still far from perfect."

"Your English is very good," David said. "A lot better than my Mandarin. My apologies."

"You flatter me," Lao said. "May we talk?" He indicated the table and chairs. "President Grey, I would be very honored if you would join us."

"Thank you," Grey said. "I'd be pleased to."

"As you suggested," Lao said, "we've been busy. We have a functioning command here, but we are fragile by nature. At the moment I feel like something of a sitting duck, as you say."

"Well, that's part of why I'm here," David said. "We're working on the cannons back home, but I need to have a look at your infrastructure, to get the place up to speed. We don't want to blow all the fuses the first time we try her out."

"I remember you said something about building the cannon here," Grey said. "What happened to that?"

"Eventually we will," David said. "You should see the monster we have on the drawing boards. As a matter of practicality, though, we've been able to harvest intact cannon from many of the wrecked destroyers. Now that we've solved the problem of the energy source—and now that China has built this next generation of what I have to say are really neat tugs—we can afford to schlep a few of them up here—as well as to Mars, when that's ready, and eventually Rhea. After that we can talk 'new and improved.'"

"How long before the cannons are ready?" Adams asked.

"We're on track for early 2016," David said. "We can't take any chances there, but in the meantime we can get your defensive shields running."

"We're also planning on bringing up some tactical nukes in the next few months," Adams said to them all. "They're equipped with gear to match the alien shield phasing and slip right through their defenses." He nodded toward the entrance. "The first one came up on the same tug as Director Levinson."

"Wait, what?" David said. "Why didn't I know about this?"

"We informed your office," Adams said.

"That there would be a nuke coming up," David said. "*Not* that I would be sitting next to it." He rubbed his head. "That settles it. No more flying coach. First class, from here on out."

29

Dikembe was only vaguely aware of hitting the tree, of thrashing for a handhold, of limbs whipping his body, the final hard stop on the ground. After all of that he somehow got up and began running.

His mind had shut down, but his body knew what to do. He stayed in cover of the trees, knowing he had no chance at all if the helicopter spotted him. He knew where he was now—near one of the military compounds—and he remembered that the terrain grew hilly and more deeply forested to the south, where the savanna began blurring into highlands.

Stopping for a moment, he used a piece of torn shirt to try and staunch the flow of blood from his wound, while still trying to wrap his head around the fact that his own father had stabbed him.

He heard the chopper fly over and crouched in a thicket, then continued along a creek that was rapidly becoming the aqueous spine of a swamp. He kept to the margins of it, away from open water, hoping he wouldn't meet a crocodile—or worse, a hippopotamus. The helicopter passed again, farther away this time.

The soldiers could chase him on foot, he knew, but none of their ground vehicles could follow him where he was going. So it was only men he needed to outrun.

What had happened? Weiss's man had to be in the pay of his father. What of Weiss himself? Was he part of the conspiracy to entrap him as well? There was no way of knowing.

All he knew was that if he'd ever had a chance to stop his father, he had missed it. The only option that remained was to escape, perhaps bring the horrors occurring in his homeland to the world's attention, make the case for an armed intervention by the United Nations. It was probably what he should have done in the first place.

Perhaps he was a little mad, too, and certainly the victim of his own hubris.

*   *   *

Day passed into night, and he no longer heard the helicopter. He continued beneath the light of the moon. It was full, and sometimes when he looked up he felt a tremor of fear without knowing why. Then he realized it was because it resembled the thing he kept drawing, the circle with the line through it.

That was another thing to put on his "to-do" list—find this French psychiatrist, Marceaux. He had a few things to tell her.

Lost for a time, he had to nap in the forest—never a pleasant thing, even when you weren't bleeding off and on from your ribs. But in morning's light he was able to find the old cabin. It had been built by a Belgian hunter two generations ago, but he and Bakari had stumbled across it in their explorations. Dikembe hadn't been there in years, and by the look of the place, neither had anyone else.

He found a few of the canned goods they had once stored there, and opened them with his knife. The expiration date on everything was long past, but that was the least of his worries. There was a spring of clean water nearby—probably the reason the Frenchman had chosen this spot. There he cleaned his wound, which wasn't nearly as deep as he feared. With any luck, none of his organs had been nicked, and he wasn't going to die of peritonitis.

Then, temporarily sated and refreshed, he began to plan his escape.

* * *

Patricia pocketed her phone, feeling drained. They had been training in high-g emergency flight for three days, and now this. It was suddenly all too much.

"Hey," Jake said. "What's the matter?"

They were off duty, walking in the park along the old canal, a greenway of tamarisk, Russian olive, and willow. It was one of her favorite places. She missed the verdancy of the east, and this was the closest she could come to it out here. She had taken to jogging here when she was off duty, and lately Jake usually joined her.

She and Jake had been spending a lot of their free time together, which wasn't unusual—they had been hanging out since Academy days. In the past, Dylan had almost always been present, too. Something had changed, though, and when she was forced to think about it, she knew what it was.

She liked Dylan, loved him even.

But there was something about Jake...

Not that anything had happened. Not that anything *could*, given their circumstances. Since her breakup with Dale she hadn't dated anyone else. She wasn't sure she was ready to, and Jake was good company. He made her laugh, and at times he made her feel... other things.

Ordinarily she wouldn't answer a call mid-run, but when she saw who it was, she knew she had to.

"I think I'm done running for today," she said. "You go on."

"Are you okay?" he asked, standing nearby.

"It's just all the training," she said. "It's messing with my inner ear."

Jake nodded as if he accepted that, but then he looked back up.

"Because, it really seemed like that phone call…" He left it hanging for her to pick up, or not.

She didn't.

"Are you applying?" she asked instead.

"For what?" he said.

"What do you mean, for what?" she said. "Legacy Squadron."

Legacy Squadron was the shiny new thing. A squadron composed of the best pilots from the various countries who formed the collective ESD effort. It was being hailed as the "point of the spear." Detractors called it a propaganda stunt, which Patricia agreed it clearly was. However, it was the best kind of propaganda—the kind that promoted something true.

That the world was finally united.

"Oh, hell yeah," he said, but then he sobered a little. "It kind of sucks, though. I mean, it puts me up against you and Dylan. Only one of us can make it in."

"Right," she said. "Or one of the approximately forty other people who will apply from the U.S. You can't worry about that. You want it, you have to go for it."

"Is that right," he said. "Fine. I'm sure you'll kick my ass anyway."

She smiled, knowing it wasn't true. The truth was, it was probably going to be Dylan. It wasn't just that Dylan was a great pilot—it was who he was, what he represented.

The same was true of her, to a lesser extent, but it wouldn't do to tell Jake that. And who knew? She had been wrong before, about plenty of things.

"Go on, finish your run," she said. "I'll be okay."

"That's alright," Jake said. "I'm a little tired myself." He smiled. "Talked to Charlie today," he continued. "Kid is kicking butt at the Academy."

"Was there any doubt?" she asked.

"Not really," he said.

She remembered when she had first met Charlie and Jake, when Charlie told their story. She had always known that—relatively speaking—she and Dylan had had it good, but the way those two had struggled, stood up for each other, watched each other's backs. It was what she wanted. Someone like that.

"He's so funny," Jake said. "There's this girl a year ahead of him, and he's in love with her, of course. He's always been like that, aiming a little too high."

"Maybe he figures you have to aim high to hit high," she said. Their hands brushed, and almost without thinking she took his. An instant later, she wondered what the hell she was doing, but it seemed so natural.

"Uh, Patricia," he said, and he turned toward her.

Then she knew it was about to get too real, too fast.

"The phone call was about my father," she said, gently untangling her hand and looking down at the path as she began walking again.

"Oh?" he said. "Is he okay?"

She knew she shouldn't say anything. She hadn't even told Dylan, but the secret was eating a hole in her.

"Jake, this has to stay between you and me," she said. "You can't tell anyone."

"Sure," he said. "Of course."

"My father hasn't been well. Last time I was home I had to hire someone to help take care of him. That was who the call was from. Apparently he left the house without telling anyone. The secret service didn't find him for hours."

"When you say 'isn't well,'" Jake said, "what do you mean?"

"They don't know," she said. "Some of his doctors think it's some weird form of PTSD, a dissociative disorder, psychosis… you name it, they've tried it on. He hears voices. He sees things that aren't there. He's paranoid, he forgets things…" She realized that she was crying. She stopped walking and balled her fists at her sides.

"I'm sorry," she said.

"No, it's okay," Jake said. "Patricia, I'm so sorry."

"He's just—everyone thinks of him as this great man, this monumental figure, but to me he's just Daddy, you know? The guy that used to tuck me in. He called me Munchkin. And I'm losing him."

"He *is* a great man," Jake said. "There's no question of that."

"But how will people remember him now?" she said. "I can't stand that he might be remembered like this, on top of everything else."

He put his hands on her shoulders as they began to shake. Then he slowly pulled her in for a hug. She buried her face against his shirt, and for a time that's all she did. She felt exposed, embarrassed, and protected, all at the same time.

"It'll be okay," he said.

"How?" she replied. "I don't know how it can be okay."

He just held her a little tighter. She felt his heart beating in his chest. In that moment she wanted to lift her head, look him in the eyes, see what he was thinking. What would happen.

Instead she reluctantly pushed back from him.

"I'm sorry you had to listen to all of that."

"No," Jake said. "I'm happy you felt you could talk to me. I know we joke a lot, Patricia. I know I do. But I want you to know that if there is ever anything I can do, any way I can help—I'm here for you."

"I know that, Jake," she said.

Then she kissed him, because she didn't care anymore. She knew it was wrong, that it was a problem, that nothing good could come of it. And she simply did not care.

For a moment he was so surprised he didn't respond, but then he did, carefully, thoughtfully, and, Jake being Jake, playfully. When they finally broke to look at each other, he grinned.

"Do you have any idea how long I've been wanting to do that?"

"Of course," she said. "Since we met."

He blinked and raised up a little.

"Oh *really*," he said. "When we met the first thing you thought was, 'This guy wants to kiss me'?"

"A girl knows, Jake. I was disappointed to learn you had a girlfriend."

"But you had a boyfriend," he said.

"That's true," she said. "I'm horrible."

"We're both horrible," he said.

"Completely," she said, as he bent to kiss her again.

*   *   *

Dikembe woke the next morning, cold, stiff, living pain in every joint. His side felt like it was on fire. The skin around the wound was puffy and red and the only part of him that felt hot. Groaning, he roused himself and went to the spring.

He surprised a red-flanked duiker that was drinking the clear, cool water. Its head jerked up in alarm, and then the tiny antelope dashed off into the bushes. Overhead, in the leafy tops of the bush mangos and khaya trees, a troop of vervet monkeys chittered a protest at his presence.

He washed his wound again, gritting his teeth against the agony. He cupped his hands and took a drink, then another.

Water was perhaps the chief constraint on his plans. He could go for a while without eating again, but not without water. He didn't know how long it would be before he ran across another source from which he could drink without becoming ill. It might be a long time if he went south or west. North, and he would be back on the savanna, too easily seen from the air. That left east, and the mountains.

It would be hard going, especially wounded, but clean water would be easier to come by.

He sat with his back against a tree, trying to focus. What else did he need? Antibiotics would be nice. He could carry a little water in the tins he had emptied out. A machete would be good, a gun even better. There were some villages in the foothills. They might help him.

Yet if they did, and they were found out…

He remembered the mass grave.

No. He would have to avoid villages until he crossed the border.

He wasn't going to get any stronger, only weaker. The sooner he left, the better. So with a groan he rose from his resting place, realizing as he did so that the tree he had leaned against was an mvule, which some held as sacred and others thought of as being possessed of evil spirits. Either way, it was considered best to avoid them.

Like so many things, it was too late for that.

Dikembe returned to the cabin and began loading what little there was of use into an old rucksack. When he turned to go, he saw a shadow outside, and froze in place.

"It's me, old man," a voice said. "Zuberi."

Dikembe leaned around the corner and saw it was indeed his old friend, leaning against a tree.

"Remember?" Zuberi said. "I came up here with you and Bakari, now and then. We had some good times."

"You shouldn't be here," Dikembe said. "If my father learns you are here…"

"Let me worry about that," Zuberi said. "You're wounded. I brought medicine."

"Leave it," Dikembe said. "I can make use of it."

"Just let me do this for you," Zuberi said. "Then I'll disappear." He motioned. "Lie on the table in there."

Grudgingly, Dikembe did as he was told.

"I should have known you would try something like that," Zuberi said as he examined the wound. "And that you would not invite me."

"Your family," Dikembe responded. "I would not put them at risk."

"I understand that," Zuberi said, "and I appreciate it." He made a clucking sound. "This is getting infected," he said. "You won't make it two days."

"I will," Dikembe said.

"Your whole family," Zuberi said. "So hard-headed." He irrigated the wound with alcohol while Dikembe throttled a scream. Through tears of pain he saw his friend produce a hypodermic.

"Antibiotic," he said. "I have more you can take by mouth."

Dikembe hardly felt the sting of the shot.

"What happened to the others?" he asked.

"Your mercenaries?" Zuberi said. "Mostly massacred, I'm sorry to say. The old man knew somehow. He always knows. Maybe he's right, the voices in his head—do you have them, Dikembe? I thought they were long gone, but I've begun to have the dreams again."

"Yes," Dikembe said. "I have them, but I don't think my father had any sort of supernatural instruction. I think I wasn't careful enough in choosing my mercenaries. The helicopter pilot was supposed to be with me, but he was really in my father's pay. There may have been others. He let my trap for him become his trap for me."

"Yes, perhaps," Zuberi replied. "Even in his madness, he is as clever as always. I'm going to sew this up, okay? It won't be a very good job."

"Just hurry," Dikembe said. He was feeling suddenly torpid, as if moving his limbs was the most difficult thing in the world to do.

He was surprised at how distant the pain felt when Zuberi began passing the needle through his flesh. He watched him sew, reminded by the long strand of catgut of a spider weaving a web.

"Zuberi?" he said.

"Just relax," Zuberi said.

"That was no antibiotic," Dikembe said.

"No," Zuberi said. "It wasn't. I'm sorry, old friend. This was the best I could do for you."

Dikembe tried to roll from the table, but everything was going light, and Zuberi was holding him down, an apologetic look on his face.

Then miasma, falling, darkness.

30

SEPTEMBER

For a long moment Jake thought his friend was going to hit him. Dylan vaulted out of his cockpit, and was actually shaking with fury. He braced to take the punch. Nearby, the final ship of the squadron settled onto the tarmac. Jake's own H-7 was behind him, and Dylan had come down only a few meters away, dangerously close.

The moment passed. Dylan's fingers unclenched.

"What the hell was that?" he demanded.

"What?" Jake said. "You mean the part where I saved our asses?"

Dylan jabbed a finger at him. "I mean the part where I told you to do one thing, and you did something else," he said.

"Well," Jake said, "maybe it's because the thing you wanted me to do would have gotten me shot out of the sky, leaving what was left of the squadron wide open from the back. The 'something else' I did gave us the win."

"That's not the point," Dylan said. "I was designated leader for that run."

"And you made a bad call," Jake countered.

"I had a plan," Dylan snapped.

"Then you should have shared it," Jake retorted. "Because from where I was sitting, I didn't sense a plan."

"I think you're trying to shave my points," Dylan said. "Make me look bad. You want the Legacy Squadron spot for yourself."

For a moment, the accusation left Jake breathless.

People were starting to notice them.

"Okay," he said, slower and softer. "First of all, no, I wasn't trying to make you look bad. I've never done that, I never would do that, and you freaking know it. Second, yes—hell yes, I want the Legacy Squadron spot. I'm not going to bow out just because you think you're supposed to inherit the position."

"What the hell does that mean?" Dylan demanded.

"You know exactly what it means," Jake said. He started walking off, already wishing he hadn't said it.

"You know what?" Dylan said. "My father saved the world. Patricia's father saved the world. What did yours ever do?"

Jake stopped in his tracks.

"Really?" he said.

"You went there first," Dylan said.

"No," Jake said. "I didn't go *there*. That's a whole different place—and maybe this isn't about what just happened up in space, huh? Maybe this is about something else. Someone else."

"Shut up," Dylan said. "Let's get off the tarmac. People are staring."

Jake began walking again, steering them clear of everyone else on the tarmac. Dylan paced him. It didn't take him long to break his own imperative.

"You don't deserve her," Dylan said as they exited the hangar.

Here we go, Jake thought.

"And you do?" he said.

Dylan didn't answer, but Jake knew—had known from the moment he and Patricia let him in on their relationship.

Patricia thought it would go better if they did it together. All that had done was delay this conversation. His comments about their respective fathers made it all pretty clear how Dylan thought things should be.

"Dylan," he said, "if you have something to say, say it."

"Emily," Dylan said.

"What about her? We haven't been together in years."

"You destroyed her," Dylan said. "You took her virginity, and then you left her."

That stung. He'd known even in the moment that making love with Emily was a bad idea, that it was important to her, that she would think of it as a promise even if she didn't say so. He hadn't exactly been thinking with his head at that point, and he regretted it.

"She broke up with me," Jake said.

Dylan wagged a finger at him.

"Yeah, but she would have taken you back in a second," he said. "She was testing you. She wanted to see if you would fight for the relationship. Not only didn't you fight, you took off running."

"She told you all this?" Jake asked.

"In several long, painful crying jags," he said. "She wanted me to talk to you, try to convince you to come back."

"What can this possibly have to do with Patricia?" Jake demanded.

"Emily thought Patricia was the reason—she thought that you were in love with her. I told her that was stupid, that you guys had just met. Now I think she was right. If you told Emily you loved her and then did that to her, you can do it to Patricia—and I don't want to see her hurt."

Jake took his time to reply.

"You know," he said, "I know I didn't handle the Emily thing very well, and you're right, I was relieved when she broke up with me. I did know she would take me back, but if I had stayed with her, I wouldn't have had a future. I wouldn't be flying.

"That's all I've ever wanted," he continued. "And yeah, maybe when I first met Patricia I saw her as part of that future, the one I couldn't have with Emily. But I did nothing about it, not then and not later. Not until Patricia was single, anyway, and not until I knew she felt the same way."

Dylan absorbed that quietly—by that time they had reached the locker rooms, where the conversation would be anything but private. They changed out of their flight suits and took a shuttle to the dorms.

Once they were in the room, Dylan started up again.

"You're endangering your career," he said. "That's fine if you want to do that, but you're also endangering Patricia's."

"I know that," Jake said. "Don't you think I haven't thought about that?"

There was a light knock on the doorframe, and they both turned. The door hadn't shut all the way, and to his dismay Jake saw Patricia standing there.

"You guys should maybe have the door shut when you have these heart-to-hearts," she said.

"Hey," Jake said. Then he noticed she had been crying. He rose and went to her. "What's wrong?"

She closed the door gently.

"I saw you guys come in," she said. "I guess I should have given you more space, but I didn't know you were fighting. I'm pretty sure I know what it's about, and let me assure you both—no careers are in danger."

"What do you mean?" Dylan asked.

"I've resigned from flight school," she said.

"Why?" Jake said. "Because of me? You should have talked to me, I would have—"

"No, Jake," she said, taking his hand. "It wasn't about you. Or us."

"Then why?" Jake asked.

"It's my dad," she said softly. "He needs me. I need to be there with him."

"It's worse?" Jake said.

"Yeah," she said. "It is, and I've put off doing this for too long."

"But—what will you do?" Dylan asked. "You owe the ESD some time. You can't just walk away."

She smiled, but it was a transparently false one.

"I can, actually. Turns out I'm Patricia Whitmore. I'll still be military for a while, but I'm going to be an aide to President Lanford. I majored in poly-sci with a minor in communications, remember? And I've been swimming in the political pond most of my life. I can be close to Dad that way."

"I can't believe this," Jake said. He would rather Dylan had hit him. It couldn't have hurt as much.

"When do you leave?" Dylan asked.

"End of the week," she said.

* * *

"So?" Julius Levinson said, as he sat on the couch. He put his hands on his knees and leaned forward. "Have you read it?"

That was fast, David thought. The driver had only dropped his father at the house two minutes before. Luggage down, brief hug, review please.

"It's good to see you, too, Pops," David said. "How was the trip out?"

Julius's thick eyebrows shot up. "It's very fancy, first class," he said. "Warm towels. Who knew? But the kosher meal—meh. Still, much better than coach. Not exactly Air Force One, but it'll do. So, eh—thanks for the ticket."

"You should see Air Force One now," David said.

"They've made… improvements."

His father was looking around, as if trying to spot something. "It's all the same," he said. "Nothing's changed."

"Well, you know I'm not home that much," David said.

"Yes, I know. Very important person, you are. Flying to the moon, for goodness sakes. How was the kosher meal on the spaceship?"

David didn't feel it was particularly politic to mention that he hadn't kept kosher since he was eighteen, and that among his in-flight meals there had been a ham-and-cheese sandwich.

"It was, you know—space food," he said.

"It's not healthy, this," his father said, gesturing around. "You know I loved Connie like a daughter, but David—it's been four years. This place is like a museum."

"It doesn't feel like four years," David said. "It feels like last week. Like yesterday, actually."

"You need to move on," Julius said. "I'd still like grandchildren, you know."

David sighed and rubbed his forehead.

"Pops, sorry to disappoint you, but I think at this point that's really not on the cards."

"Son," Julius said. "I'm not disappointed in you— but a man can dream, can't he? Anyway, you need companionship, David. A man doesn't need to live alone."

"You've been alone since Mom died," David said.

"We're not talking about me," Julius said. "And in fact, I'm very busy, too. Did you know, they're talking about sending me on a book tour? What about that? Me, on tour."

"Well, that's very exciting, Pops—I'm glad for you."

"The thing is," his father said, "I think you should come with me. Levinson and Levinson, the father and son who saved the world. What do you think?"

What David was thinking was that he would rather have all of his teeth pulled without anesthetic, and that he couldn't say *that*, and that he needed time to come up with some plausible excuse to *for the love of God* not do that.

"You know what, Pops?" he said. "Why don't we talk about this over a big steak? There's this new place in town that's amazing."

"David, it's only four o'clock," his father said.

"Rrrright," he said. "But—early bird special."

His father narrowed his eyes and shook an index finger at him.

"That's very smart," he said. "Just let me go shave."

* * *

"There's no early bird special?" Julius said to the waitress.

"No, sir," she said patiently. She was nice-looking, with dark, curly hair, maybe thirty, maybe a little younger.

"I guess I was mistaken," David said. "But that's fine, we're here. Order whatever you want, Pops—the sky is-the limit."

"Here are your menus," the waitress said. "I'll get your drinks. My name is Rachel, and I'll be your server."

"Rachel," Julius said. "May I ask you something?"

"Certainly, sir," she said.

"This is my son. Maybe you've heard of him. David Levinson. Flew up into space and blew up the alien mother ship."

"Yes, sir," she said. She smiled at David. "I've seen you on TV."

"That's nice," David said. "So you—"

"And he's single," Julius said. "Can you believe that?"

"Dad—" David said.

"Are you single, Rachel?" his father persisted.

She blushed. "Well, yes," she said.

"Such a shame," Julius said. "Two such good-looking people…"

"Dad!"

"I'm just trying to help."

David smiled at the waitress. "I'm sorry about that, ah—Rachel. My father doesn't have what most people would think of as… boundaries."

"It's okay," she said. "I'll get your drinks."

"What?" his father said, as she walked off and David glared at him. "What's wrong with her?"

"Well, to start with, she's probably less than half my age."

"Well, if I'm going to have grandchildren… you know. Look at Michael Douglas and that lady he's married to. It's not unusual. Why, in the Torah older men and young women—"

"Let's just—what do you want to eat?"

"Don't rush me," Julius said. "I haven't looked at the menu yet."

"I know," David said. "You've been too busy trying to set me up with the wait staff."

"Okay," his father said as he picked up the menu. Then he promptly put it back down again.

"About this tour," he said. "I'd really like you to come. We can spend some time together, get to know each other better."

"We know each other pretty well," David said.

"You know what I mean," Julius said.

He sighed. "Pops, I just—I have a very full plate. I'm supposed to be six places at once, all of the time. Taking— how long is your tour?"

"Two weeks," he said.

"There. Two weeks. I just can't do it. If it were a day or two, maybe."

"Okay," his father said.

David blinked. "What? Okay what?" he asked.

"You'll do two days with me. Two appearances. It'll be fine." He opened the menu again.

David raised a finger, wondering what exactly had just happened.

"I think I'll have the Ribeye," Julius said.

* * *

Later, when the waitress brought the check, it had her name and phone number on it.

"See?" Julius said. "You think the old man is mashugana."

Back at home, David tore up the receipt and put it in the recycling bin.

* * *

For Jake, it was a long week. He called Charlie, who—as he'd told Patricia—was blazing through the Academy like nobody's business. Not only had his grades and test scores allowed him to start a year earlier than most, he was on track to finish more than a year early.

"I've met my future wife," he told Jake. "She sits across the room from me in my engineering math class."

"This isn't still the one from last month is it?" he asked. "What was her name, Karen?"

"Katrina," Charlie said. "No, that didn't work out. This is a new girl."

"So what's this one's name?" Jake asked.

"She looks like an Isabella or maybe a Colleen," he said. "Outside chance of an Amber."

"So when you say you've met her, you mean you've *seen* her," Jake said.

"Well, and there's my dreams," Charlie said. "I'm

probably going to ask her out, like, tomorrow."

"Well, good luck with that," Jake said.

"You sound a little down," Charlie said. "Something going on?"

"Actually," he said, "Patricia is dropping out of flight school."

"Well, that's too bad," Charlie said. "I…"

The line went silent.

"Charlie?" Jake said.

"Oh. My. God," Charlie said. "You've been playing tonsil hockey with Patricia Whitmore, haven't you?"

If Charlie's only prominent quality was his almost eerie ability to cut right through what Jake said to what was percolating underneath, Jake would have probably strangled him years ago. Fortunately, he had other qualities—but it was still annoying.

"Ah. Sort of," Jake said.

"Has Dylan beaten the crap out of you yet?"

"First off," Jake said, "there is no universe in which Dylan Hiller can beat the crap out of me. But no, he's not exactly happy about it. Not that it matters anyway, not with her leaving."

"Think so?" Charlie said.

Jake had done almost nothing but think about the question Charlie was alluding to, and he was tired of it.

"You know what?" Jake said. "Tell me more about Amber."

"It's probably Isabella, the more I think of it," Charlie said.

*　*　*

Jake met Patricia outside of the gate about an hour after he was off duty. He had been trying to imagine how the goodbye would go, and had settled on being heroically stoic and supportive. The other alternative involved him on his knees, begging her to change her mind, probably with a few tears thrown in.

Not a good look.

When he arrived at the rendezvous, he didn't see her at first. Not until she honked the horn, and he realized she was inside a jeep.

"Come on," she said.

"What's going on?" he asked.

"Just get in," she said.

He did as she asked, and after a second's hesitation, gave her a kiss. Then she stepped on the gas and the base was dwindling behind them.

"This isn't the way to the airport," he noticed.

"Very observant," she said. "I told you I would be done with flight school at the end of the week, not that I was leaving. I'm staying through the weekend."

"Oh," he said. "So where are we going?"

"We're going to be alone," she said. "No more sneaking around, no more pretending. I've rented a cabin up in the mountains."

Jake felt as if his vocal cords were frozen.

Alone? In a cabin in the mountains?

"But I didn't pack," he finally managed.

"I didn't want to spoil the surprise," Patricia said. "I stopped in town and got you a few things."

"If you got me lingerie, I can't promise I'll wear it," he said. "I'm really, really self-conscious about my body."

"You'll wear it and be happy, or you don't get the chocolates," she said.

"Damn, woman," he said.

"Damn what?"

"I'm the guy," he said. "I'm supposed to be doing this stuff."

"Okay, let's assume that's in the least way a valid point.

Were you planning on impulsively taking me someplace for our last weekend together?"

"I was... there may have... not... been a plan," he admitted.

"Exactly," she said.

"In my defense, I thought you were leaving today."

"Noted," she said. "Now sit back and enjoy the road trip. Turn on the music there."

He hit the start button, and Robert Plant's "Big Log" began playing.

"No!" he said.

"Oh, it gets better," she said. "We've got Stones, we've got Dire Straits, Hendrix, the Who—three hours of hand-picked classic rock."

"That's awesome," he said. "I love you."

She looked at him, then.

"I mean, the music, I love—hey, you're going to drive us off the road."

She turned her attention back to driving. Robert Plant started singing.

My love is in league with the freeway...

"Patricia," he said.

"Yes?"

"I do love you."

She drove for a moment or two without comment.

"You know, Jake," she said, "I'm starting to think I love you, too."

He sat through the rest of the song, wondering what to say next. The Kinks came on.

"So how is this gonna work?" he asked.

She glanced back at him, a bittersweet expression on her face. "Don't ask me," she said. "I did the long-distance thing for five years, and it completely fell apart on me."

"I'm not him," he said.

"I know you're not," she said. "Look. Just set the long-distance thing aside for the moment, okay? Let's treat this weekend like it's our last. Like the world ends on Monday. After that, we'll see. After all, we might not even be—you know—compatible."

"Oh," Jake said. "I'm compatible."

"I'm just saying," Patricia said.

"One hundred. Percent. Compatible."

"We'll see," she said.

"Yes, we will," he said.

31

APRIL

2014

David was in Lisbon for the tenth annual Xenology Conference when he bumped into Dr. Catherine Marceaux for the second time.

Literally. He was checking his phone messages and turning a corner in a crowded corridor when he tripped and ran into her from behind. It wasn't much of a collision, and she seemed more-or-less prepared to ignore it until she recognized him.

"Director Levinson," she said.

"We have to stop running into each other like this," he said.

"I don't know," she said. "It's the only way I seem to be able to contact you. Your staff seems quite adept at screening your calls."

"My staff sometimes doesn't know what's good for them," David said. "I had no idea you've been trying to get in touch."

She smiled a bit skeptically.

"I, uh, read your book," he said. "One of them."

"Oh, yes?" she said. "What did you think?"

"It was, well, very interesting," he said. "Not entirely up my alley, even though the chapter on recursive feedback loops and computing language I found very interesting. It resonated with some of the things I'm working on."

"Are you suggesting a collaboration of some sort?"

"What? No. I was just saying—"

"Look, I've frightened you again," she said. "I was joking. What I meant was, would you like to discuss this someplace quieter?"

"Quieter?"

"The bar, perhaps? Over a drink?" She looked at him, somehow serious, sarcastic, and playful at the same time. She was also gorgeous.

A drink wouldn't hurt, would it?

*   *   *

David made a face when he tasted his drink.

The hotel bar had a theme of some sort, although David had a little trouble discerning what it was. It involved a fair amount of vintage neon advertising American beer, old cigarette posters featuring a cowboy, an antique gas station sign with a green brontosaurus on it, and several stuffed armadillos… among other things. The bar itself was covered in pale blue Formica.

"What's the matter?" she said.

"I ordered a martini," he said.

"Let me see."

He handed her the glass and she took a small sip.

"Yes," she said. "That's what you have. A martini."

"It's just vermouth on ice," he said.

"Oh, you wanted an *American* martini," she said. "Shall I go ask for that?"

"Do you speak Portuguese?" he asked.

"Some," she said, "but the bartender is French, anyway."

"I'm okay with this," David said, although he really wasn't. "I'll know better next time."

"Shall we talk shop then?" she asked.

The question set him at ease, because he had begun to worry that he was on a date. He hadn't dated anyone since Connie died, and he still wasn't really sure he was ready. Not that it mattered—he was so busy there wasn't any time for such nonsense anyway.

They talked for a while about her book and the theories she outlined in it. She wanted to know if he knew of any persons she might interview who had experienced alien contact. He did, of course—President Whitmore and Dr. Okun both came to mind. Okun, the former head scientist at Area 51, had been used as a mouthpiece by one of the aliens. It nearly killed him, and now, seventeen years later, he was still in a coma.

The president's contact with the aliens was classified, however, as was Okun's very existence. Still, he ventured to ask if she was aware of other examples of catatonia induced by alien ESP.

"Yes," she said. "There's a full range actually. Some died during or soon after their contact. Others were rendered catatonic for varying durations. Still others seemed hardly affected."

"How do you account for the differences?" he asked.

"I can't find a single consistent correlate," she said. "It appears to have to do with the individual, how long the contact was, how intense. Here's the interesting thing though." She paused.

"Yes, what's that?" he asked.

She leaned forward across the table, so their faces were much nearer.

"Some of them are regressing," she said.

"Regressing?"

"Yes," she said. "Many of my subjects report having experienced night terrors, difficulty sleeping, confusion and so forth for a short time after their contact. In most cases, this faded over time. They felt more normal. In the last few years, however, there seems to be a general trend of worsening symptoms."

"Do you know why?" he asked.

"No," she said. "It's quite frustrating. I was wondering if you might have a theory."

"Nothing I can think of," he said.

"The captive aliens—" she said "—have they shown any sort of change?"

He laughed. "They're playing dead, all of them. Nothing new there."

She sighed and leaned back.

"Would it be possible for me to examine them?" she asked. "The aliens?"

David had been as diplomatic as he could about her book. Although it did raise a few interesting issues, for the most part it didn't seem much like *science* to him, but rather more a kind of storytelling that wasn't easily subjected to testing or verification. He found he was liking her though. So instead of going with a flat "no," he decided to be slightly more encouraging, in a way that wouldn't actually be a lie.

"That's a tough one," he said. "We only allow access to them in drips and drabs. You'll need to write a proposal, and it will need to somehow fit with the Earth Space Defense goals. I'll see what I can do."

She nodded. They went on to discuss the Umbutu situation, and David had to admit that he hadn't made any headway there. The old man was utterly inflexible, and launching any sort of invasion remained out of the question. If the heavy hitters in the global coalition were seen to be behind something like that, it could be looked upon as a new form of colonialism—which could in turn weaken trust in what was at the moment a very popular organization.

He got his American martini, and then another, and three, and soon they were no longer talking business, exactly, but had spun off into a discussion of what consciousness really was. She seemed to hold with Hofstadter in saying that what people referred to as consciousness was actually a powerful symbolic system whose most potent symbol was that of selfhood, of identity. That led to whether any part of a person's "self" survived death, and then somehow they were on the subject of old movies.

What he really noticed about the conversation, what really impressed him, was that while she asked about him—his childhood, his education—trivial details seemed to delight her—she never once brought up the big day, the Fourth of July, the trip to the mother ship, Hiller, the president—none of it.

She smiled at him a lot, and touched his hand when she laughed sometimes. He thought he was probably looking outright foolish, and although on one level he wanted the night to go on, on another he did not.

Another finally won.

"Well," he said. "This has been really nice, but I've got an early morning."

"*Bien sûr*," she said. "I understand."

"Good. Good," he said. "Well, okay."

She stood up and reached for him.

"Um—" he started.

Then she kissed him on both cheeks.

"This is how we say good night in France, yes?"

"Yes," David said. "Right. Good night."

He started to turn away, but four drinks were bubbling through his veins and he was feeling as if he ought to say something. He just wasn't quite sure what it was.

So he decided to just open his mouth and see what came out.

"Tomorrow," he said. "Would you like to, I don't know, get together or something?"

"Huh," she said. She looked thoughtful.

"What about this," she said. "I know a little about Lisbon. Tomorrow afternoon I'll take you on a walking tour. You can buy me dinner."

David nodded, feeling like he had some sort of obstruction in his throat.

"That sounds great," he said.

*   *   *

Lisbon was nestled up to the sea, but most of the city sat on hills steep enough to make San Francisco—what had been San Francisco—look like a flat plain. One particular incline was impressive enough that, more than a century ago, the city had constructed a gigantic elevator—the Elevador de Santa Justa—to transport passengers up and down it.

"It's a work of art as much as it is a machine," Catherine said, waving at the iron neo-Gothic arches that climbed upward from their vantage point at its base. "It was designed by a student of Gustav Eiffel—you know, the man who designed the Eiffel Tower."

Her expression took a melancholy turn, and he understood why. As he would never see the Empire State or the Chrysler Building—or the original Statue of Liberty—she would never again see the original Eiffel Tower, the Sacré Coeur, the Arc de Triomphe. When New York had still been a place, he'd thought of such tourist attractions as just that, too hokey to go see himself. Now, they were poignant symbols of a city and a way of life forever vanished.

They entered the elevator, manned by an old fellow with a rather stern expression. Inside it was paneled in wood, mirrors, and windows. The controls were brass, and for a moment David felt as if he was inside some kind of invention from a Jules Verne novel. The lift took them to a balcony and café, where they drank coffee and looked out over rust-red terracotta roofs toward the sea, and watched Sol sink nightward.

Soon thereafter they went to a fado club and listened to music that he could only think of as some sort of Portuguese blues. Instrumentally it was mostly guitar, played in a particularly percussive manner, and the vocals wailed, rose and fell like gentle weeping. Yet there was also a sort of triumphant thread in it. Although he understood none of the words, it made him feel sad, cathartic, and uplifted all at the same time. Part of this was probably due to the freely flowing red wine.

They snacked on sausages and cheese, and when Catherine deemed him drunk enough, they had a large bowl of tiny snails. He had eaten escargot before—this wasn't that. Escargot were sort of rubbery gray balls slathered in butter and garlic. These things looked exactly like the small garden snails he remembered from growing up, antennae and all. They were steamed, and death had fixed their necks in a fully extended position, and they were eaten by using a straight pin to pluck them from their shells.

Once he gagged the first few down, he had to admit they were pretty good. Again, the wine helped.

They danced, which he had not done since God knew when. They talked, about everything and nothing. It had been a very long time since he had gotten to know somebody, anybody, to explore another person as they explored him. It was like being seventeen again, and it was quite honestly an experience that he had never really expected to come across again.

He was delighted and terrified.

Finally, he walked her to the door of her room and when she leaned up to kiss his cheek, he shifted his head and met her with his lips. She uttered a throaty little chuckle and then kissed him back. He took her in his arms and pulled her close.

After a moment, she took out her room key and opened the door. Then she took him by the hand and led him inside.

*   *   *

He woke to his phone alarm going off, and stirred, groaning a bit.

Then he realized where he was, and remembered. He slowly turned to look at the other side of the bed and found Catherine there, smiling enigmatically, her hair pleasantly mussed, her eyes not fully open. She looked beautiful.

"Oh," he said. "Good morning."

"Is that important, the sound your phone is making?" she asked.

"Sort of," he said. "I've got a flight in about two hours."

"So you're just dashing away?" she said.

"Well, it's an ESD transport," he said, "and I'm the boss, so I don't have to show up early for baggage check and screening. I have time for a cup of coffee, at least."

"That's not exactly what I was thinking of," she murmured.

*   *   *

Afterward there was still time for coffee, some hard rolls and cheese. They exchanged contact information, and when it was finally time for him to go, they shared their most awkward kiss.

On the plane, he began wondering what he had done.

He felt guilty, remembering the last time he and Connie had made love. He hadn't known it would be the last time. If he had known, if he had seen it coming—if she had died of cancer, or something predictable—would it have made a difference? Would it be so hard to let go if he had been able to tell her goodbye?

But he hadn't, and he couldn't.

He watched the gray Atlantic far below. People—his father in particular—had been urging him to get on with his life, but did that necessarily mean a new lover, or a new wife? Catherine was smart and beautiful and acerbically funny. He should be happy, counting the days until he saw her again, worried that she wouldn't call. Instead he just felt guilty. Empty.

Connie had been the great love of his life. Maybe for him, there would not—could not—be another.

One thing felt certain. If there ever could be another, it wasn't now. No matter what his father said, no matter what he had briefly thought he felt last night—it was too soon.

A few days later, when Catherine called, he reached for the phone—and then didn't answer it. He didn't know what to say or how to say it.

* * *

Dikembe didn't know how long he had been in the hole, enveloped in darkness. He had first tried to keep track by counting the number of times he slept, but without night and day to set the pace, he soon became uncertain about the count.

After a certain point he didn't care.

The hole was a concrete shaft about two meters in diameter. Food and water came down in a bucket on the end of a rope, apparently at night, because even then there was no light. Unable to see them, he identified the bucket and its contents by touch.

In the first few days of his captivity, he had made a grab for the rope and tried to climb up it. Whoever was at the end of it let him ascend a few meters and then simply let go of the rope.

After that the food and drink stopped coming for what seemed a very long time. Then, one night, a new rope came down. He ate and drank and placed the containers back in the basket. The rope was withdrawn. The bucket also served as his latrine, although when the food had been withheld, he had been forced to use a portion of his floor, which didn't make things any more pleasant.

And so it went. He dreamed terrible dreams, asleep and awake. Tried to think of happier days, of his time in Oxford. Everything had been new then, life a broad river taking him somewhere brilliant. His only responsibilities in those days had been to himself, and he had stayed in England after school, might have stayed there forever. Even after the aliens came, he could have stayed, returned to Oxford for that matter.

But something in him knew he had to come to the place where he was born. For what? To watch it die of a human disease? To see his father metastasize into the very thing they had fought so hard against? To end his life at last in darkness?

He spoke to himself. He sang, and listened as his voice reverberated in the tube. He shouted and screamed and pounded on the concrete at times. He cursed Zuberi, and promised to kill him and the family he held so dear, but even that finally passed. What would more killing accomplish?

His wound healed—someone must have given him antibiotics, or perhaps they were in the food. He did jumping jacks and calisthenics and boxing footwork, punching into the darkness, sometimes to the point of exhaustion. He felt himself thinning, becoming less and less. Not physically, but inside. Despair rode on his shoulders, heavier every moment, and he knew that soon it would break him.

On one occasion when the basket came down it contained not only the usual fufu and water, but small, cylindrical objects. Most of them were quite smooth, but one was not—it had a flared end, and a little stud, and when he pushed the stud something happened, and he shut his eyes, because they hurt.

It took him several long, deep breaths to understand what was happening, that he was holding a small penlight and seeing something for the first time since Zuberi's face had blurred into nothingness.

As his eyes adjusted, the ugly concrete wall and the filthy floor seemed like the most beautiful things he had ever seen.

It could be improved, however. Because the rest of the cylinders were pieces of colored chalk.

He took the chalk and began to draw, feeling like a cave painter at the dawn of human history, at that crucial point when something changed in humans, when they began using symbols and language to understand their world. To depict themselves and the animals around them for the spirits and one another to see. To bend sight and mind and hand into creation.

He started off trying to fashion a world for himself, a boundless savanna populated by giraffes and elephants, skies full of clouds, birds, and wind to bend the acacia trees. And yet somehow when he formed them on the concrete they weren't the same as he remembered. The giraffes had the huge slanting eyes of aliens and were mottled gray and black. Their horns multiplied and formed a mane of squirming tentacles. He drew hyenas with flat, flaring heads but no mouths. Instead of birds and clouds his sky was populated with suns and full moons and round stars, all with lines bisecting them.

He went quickly at first, but then he began to conserve the chalk, to work less representationally and more essentially. He spent a long time on every line, curve, and dot as his drawings grew increasingly abstract—until one day he realized that he had just drawn a jumble of symbols that looked like the writing they had discovered in the alien ship. Furthermore, he thought he knew what some of them meant.

It was also possible, he realized, that he was going mad. He wondered who had sent him the gift—his mother? It seemed unlikely. Perhaps it wasn't a gift at all, but a sort of taunt, something that would eventually be taken from him, to drive him to utter hopelessness.

He didn't care, because he had them now. He kept going, even as his supply of chalk diminished and the penlight grew fainter, day by day. When he ran out of space, he erased something, and thought of it as a sort of ritual, the way the Navajo people of the American Southwest erased their sand paintings before dawn.

He had no dawn, so he made his own. He was God, making, unmaking, remaking the world. By the time the light finally failed and the chalk was all gone, he needed neither, but continued to paint with his fingers, in the darkness.

32

SEPTEMBER

The alarm that announced the training drill came right in the middle of dinner mess. Jake and Dylan looked at each other over their food, then bolted up from the table, racing toward the Steven Hiller hangar and the hybrid fighters it housed.

Alarms were blaring outside, too, and ground crews were rushing to their positions. The new surface-to-air cannon were already warming up. It was a full-on drill, a test not just of the pilots, but of everyone in the base.

Jake gave Dylan a fist bump and then mounted his fighter and dropped into the cockpit. There were twelve fighters in Lance Squadron. Jake listened as each one ran through a short checklist. Then Control came on.

"Pilots, good day. We have bogies inside of the orbit of the moon. You will see their present trajectories on your instruments. Your objective is not to engage, but to avoid enemy fliers and neutralize the much more immediate danger of an attack upon our moon base."

Three other squadrons were involved—Claymore, Javelin, and Saber. Along with Lance, they represented the last pilots in the North American bracket who were still in competition for Legacy Squadron.

Of course, no one in the upper echelons was officially

admitting it was a competition, but the media was, and the pilots all knew.

Okay, Jake thought. *Team player. Whoever they make Lance One...*

"Captain Hiller, you will lead your squadron as Lance One. The rest of you will see your call signs register on your display."

Jake got Lance Two, of course. He tried to bite down on his disappointment, the unfairness of it. To put everything away but the flying.

"Lance Squadron," Dylan said. "Let's go."

They rolled out onto the runway, and then Dylan's ship leapt into the air.

* * *

As Dylan watched, the hangar named after his father dwindled, and he remembered that day again—the climb, the roar of the crowd, the flash of light.

"I wish you could see me, Dad," he said, in barely a whisper. Then he pushed to forty-five degrees and increased the thrust. Behind him, Lance Squadron formed up like a flock of geese.

The sky went from azure to indigo to black in a matter of moments. The ship shuddered as it battered through the atmosphere, then the sensation subsided, and finally vanished.

"All squadrons," Control said, "our long-range telemetry is down. You will have to proceed using only your own instruments."

"And there's the curve ball," Jake said.

He was right—things had just become much more difficult. Even in a ship like this, you couldn't just point at the moon and go—you had to aim for where your target was going to be when you got there. At the moment, the moon wasn't even in line of sight, but on the other side of the planet.

Dylan started calculating a flight path, while keeping mindful of the approaching enemy fighters.

"Lance One," his headphones crackled. It was Jake, coming over their internal channel—the other squadrons couldn't hear them.

"What is it, Lance Two?" Dylan said.

"Submitting a flight path," Jake said.

"You?" Dylan said. "You did some math?"

"Hey, I'm more than just smoking good looks," Jake said.

Dylan stared at the plan as it appeared, and a little grin started on his face.

"You realize this is certifiable," he said.

"Yeah," Jake said. "It's also gonna work."

Jake's plan involved doing something spacecraft usually worked very hard *not* to do, but the more he looked at it, the more Dylan liked it. Except for one teensy point.

"If we get through the first part," Dylan pointed out, "that puts us in the thickest part of the mother ship debris field."

"Yeah, but that's good," Jake said. "It'll make it harder for the bogies to track us. You know they're going to turn around and get right on our tails. As an added bonus, the other squadrons won't know where we are, either."

Dylan considered, running a few calculations of his own.

"It's a good plan, Jake," he admitted. "If we make it through, it could get us to the lunar target well ahead of the others. Just—stick to it, okay?"

"You bet, Lance One."

Dylan switched back to the group frequency.

"I'm sending the flight plan," he said. "Lock and load."

"Holy crap," Lance Five said, a minute or so later. "Are you kidding?"

"Anyone gets in real trouble, you know the drill," Dylan said. "This is gonna be a cakewalk."

The early training missions had been pretty safe, as such things went. Lack of real weapons, the presence of force fields, massive telemetry data to protect against impacts. The computers on the ground could still take control of the fliers if they needed to, so even after ejecting, odds were good that the fighter could be brought under control.

These drills, though, were pushing the boundaries of both the machines and the pilots, and the danger was increased, as well. Without real aliens shooting at them, blinding their instruments, cutting them off from ground control, they were still considerably safer than, say, the Blue Angels had been, performing their aerobatics back in the day. Still, he and the rest of Lance Squadron were definitely about to leave the comfort zone.

He took his heading, accelerating with his fusion engine, aiming at the edge of the world. A series of blips appeared on his long-range radar.

"We've got bogies," he said. "Looks like ten of them."

"I see them, Lance One," Lance Eight confirmed.

"Got 'em," Lance Twelve said.

"On my mark, long range missiles," Dylan said.

"I'm locked," Jake said.

"Away," Dylan said.

The small but deadly missiles streaked out ahead of them, quickly becoming tiny points of actinic light. They were, of course, unarmed. He watched as they bent in an arc toward the approaching drones. The "alien" formation suddenly changed direction, like a school of fish.

"They're flanking our spaceward side," Lance Six said.

"We were expecting this," Dylan said. "Maintain heading and acceleration. Do not break off to engage."

As the fighters hurtled toward the atmosphere, the rim

of the moon became visible beyond the Earth's horizon. Dylan watched the aliens positioning themselves like a flying firing squad, with Earth's atmosphere as the wall against which they were backed. Two of them were missing, taken out by missiles. The others had managed to shoot down the projectiles before they came into range.

Then they appeared visually, along with the inevitable lances of green light stabbing outward.

His ship started bucking a little as he entered the upper atmosphere.

"They've got a lock on me," Lance Five shouted.

"Just hang on a few more seconds," Jake said.

"Keep tight," Dylan shouted as he watched the planetary horizon begin to flatten dangerously.

"Coming up on ninety klicks," Jake said.

"I can't shake it," Lance Five said. "It's right on my tail."

"They're tracking me, too," Lance Three said.

"Hold on," Dylan said. Then, "Noses up!"

When reentering the Earth's atmosphere, the angle of descent was crucial. If the approach was too deep, the forces of reentry could crush and incinerate a spacecraft. Hit too shallow, though, and it was like a flat rock hitting the surface of a pond—the ship would skip right off of the atmosphere. That was very bad in the old days, with limited fuel, if what you were trying to do was land, but this wasn't the old days, and they weren't trying to land. They were trying to cut the corner as closely as possible.

The fighters slapped into the atmosphere with a force that rattled Dylan's bones right through the inertial compensators. The stick felt suddenly sluggish, as if he was trying to steer through molasses. Then he was hurtling along a new trajectory, a few degrees north of being parallel to the Earth below.

Another few seconds, and they had returned to a relative vacuum.

"One more time," Dylan said. "Then we're flying straight. Lance Five?"

"They got me," Five said.

"Three?"

"Nope, they missed me and cashed out in the atmosphere," Lance Three said.

"Ouch," Jake said. "Those drones are expensive."

"They should have made them smarter, then," Dylan said. "Not our worry right now. Let's do that one more time."

They dove again, skipped again, and then the moon was fully visible. The blips simulating alien ships fell well behind them, but they weren't giving up—they were still coming, just taking a longer route.

"Sending course correction," Dylan said. "We're a few degrees off."

Then they kicked their fusion drives to high and lit the sky.

*   *   *

"Entering the debris field," Dylan said. "Heads up, everybody. Watch your radar, but use your eyes, too. We have the sun behind us—that'll help."

Technically, they had already been in the debris field for a while—it was huge—but they were only just entering the part of it that was statistically dense enough to pose a real risk. Dylan wished for functioning energy weapons rather than the training lasers, which were no stronger than flashlights.

If the space flotsam helped protect them from being discovered by the enemy, it also made it more difficult for him to detect the opposition—including the real enemy, the other squadrons. He could see the lunar face, but he still didn't know the target, although it had to be somewhere near the moon base.

His radar showed him most of the bigger chunks well before he was in danger of hitting them, but the little ones could be just as nasty at these speeds.

"Crap!" someone shouted.

"Who is that?" Dylan said.

"Lance Three," the pilot replied. "I just got dinged, that's all."

"How does everything look?" Dylan asked.

"I'm okay," Three said. "Just a scratch."

"Okay, but check your engine readings every few minutes."

"Will do."

They had crossed in hours what it took the Apollo missions three days to traverse. In theory, everyone else was way behind them, and they were nearly out of the worst of the debris field. They still had no lunar target, though, and since the satellite net was supposed to be down, they'd have to find it themselves.

"Bogies!" Jake shouted.

Just appearing on Dylan's radar, they must have been lying in wait at the edge of the debris field, but now they were powered on and screaming their way forward, energy weapons slicing through the perpetual night.

It seemed as if they were coming from everywhere.

"Evasive maneuvers," Dylan said. "Two and Three, you're with me—everyone else buddy up in counting order."

"We've got four of them behind us," Jake said.

"Round the world," Dylan said. He went into a tight climb relative to the lunar surface. Jake and Fiona in Lance Three were off either of his wings.

The hybrid fighters were faster than the original alien ships, and they were maneuverable too. His anti-gravity thrusters were starting to complain, but he managed to drop in behind the alien flight group as they continued to pursue Jake and Fiona. He lined them up and started taking them out. One banked rapidly and arced back toward him, but his beams played across it, and the simulator became inert.

Then he had several on his tail. Jake and Fiona were turning to help, but in his gut Dylan knew they didn't have time. He dove toward the lunar surface, whooping like a madman, and turned sharply just before plowing into the surface, going a Nap-of-the-Earth or, in this case, Nap-of-the-Moon, speeding along about ten meters from the barren landscape.

One pursuer took the bait and followed him as he dipped in and out of craters and jagged around lunar mountains, but the other enemy craft kept its high vantage, taking the occasional shot and keeping track of him for its brother.

His sensors told him he had registered a non-lethal hit in his wing. *Just a flesh wound.* Then he saw that he was approaching an open plain. He pulled back the stick and turned up, just as more laser fire went by.

"Ah, shoot," Fiona said. "I'm out, but I got your eye-in-the-sky, Dylan."

"Thanks, Three," Dylan said. "I owe you one."

Another near miss blazed by, and he began veering randomly to present a harder target.

"Lance Two? Jake?"

"Right here, buddy," Jake said as his fighter emerged over the lip of the last crater and pelted the enemy on his tail with green light.

"Squadron report," Dylan said.

Of the twelve, only five were still considered operative. Most of the enemy was gone, but Twelve, Eight, and Six were driving those that remained away from the moon.

"Find that lunar target," Twelve said. "We'll keep these off of you."

* * *

"I think I see it," Jake said.

The dogfight had taken them pretty far from the moon base and eaten up a good bit of their lead over the other squadrons—maybe too much.

"Yeah, I see it, Lance Two," Dylan responded.

Jake's radar showed a blip approaching the base, something larger than the fighter drones. He gained a little more altitude, glancing down at the rugged pockmarks of the moonscape below. A cluster of radar signals appeared, coming from the near side of the debris field.

"What's that?" Jake said. "More aliens?"

"Claymore Squadron," Dylan said. "Dammit, they're closer than we are now."

Heart pounding, Jake checked his readings.

"No," Jake said. "We can do this. We just have to push it, that's all. They have to decelerate to keep from whomping into the moon. Big Mama there is about fifty klicks from the base. We're lower than that…"

"So we can accelerate," Dylan finished. "It's gonna be close."

As they pushed their H-7s to their maximum acceleration, Jake felt like a comet, like a missile, like nothing he had ever known before. None of it was real, but it felt real, and they were kicking ass. All they had to do was pull off this last little trick.

This was what he had worked for, fought for, and he knew now that he could never get enough of it. Let the real aliens come back, let them try. He would fly rings around them and blow them out of the sky, and he would do it in Legacy Squadron. It didn't matter what the world thought.

He believed. Charlie believed.

"Buddy," Dylan said. "You need to trim back. You're on a possible collision course with Claymore Three."

"He'll blink," Jake said.

"What if he doesn't?" Dylan said. "This is a training mission."

"I can do this, Dylan," Jake said. "I can take the shot."

"No," Dylan said. "I can do it, and without ramming into one of our own."

"It's my shot," Jake said. "Dylan, I can see it. You're still too far away." He had visual contact with a silver sphere that almost screamed "target." He began trying to get a lock. Meanwhile, Claymore Squadron also came into sight.

Whatever the target was, it seemed to have some sort of field that was preventing him from locking on. Which just meant he had to go to visual and get closer.

"I've got it, Jake," Dylan said. "Peel off."

Jake ignored him, concentrating on the target. He began firing his laser, hoping to establish a range, use the lasers to paint the target for the missile, rather than radar.

Claymore Three was getting very large in his two o'clock, very quickly. He cut to the left to get out of its way—and it followed him.

"What the—"

He suddenly realized that Claymore Three wasn't an H-7—it was a drone.

Another little twist in the test.

He fired his missile and rolled desperately, but it wasn't enough. Emergency shields on both craft flashed on as they nicked each other and both went wildly out of control. He saw stars and craters, spinning around him, but he pulled back on the stick and kicked it hard, still trying to stabilize. Saw the target and made that his axis, gradually killing the spin.

He realized his missile had missed, and began arming another.

Suddenly a fighter cut in front of him.

Dylan.

"Get your craft under control," Dylan said. "I have this. That's a direct order, Lance Two."

For a moment, Jake almost didn't comply. Then, cursing to himself, he dropped back, watching helplessly as Dylan took the shot and won the day for Lance Squadron.

He knew he should be happy they'd won. Maybe he would have enough time on the way back to convince himself of that.

But he doubted it.

As they turned back toward Earth, however, his mind drifted toward other things. To Patricia, wherever she was, whatever she was doing. He wished he could talk to her, but their communications were limited to Control and the other participants in the drill.

Their most recent phone conversation had left him a bit worried. Nothing in particular that she said, but just the general tone. As if maybe she was having second thoughts about the whole long-distance thing. Or maybe he was just reading that in.

He would see her again in thirty days.

It was going to be a long month.

*   *   *

Some of Patricia's earliest memories were of the National Mall, but like most childhood memories, they were distant, full of color but little detail. Two images remained clear, however.

One was of her father, standing with his back to the Lincoln Memorial, his face and the face of the statue at nearly the same angle. The other was of her mother, in a blue dress, with her hand touching the wall of the Vietnam Memorial, pointing out a certain name to her.

What she remembered more vividly was seeing the Mall rebuilt, watching wasted landscape made green, construction crews that numbered in thousands and lived in temporary government housing that was now long gone. It still wasn't finished—the construction was ongoing, but the big push was over.

The original mall had been the product of accretion, adding monuments one at a time over a period of roughly a century and a half. The new one sprang up of a piece, the Washington Monument completed at about the same time as the Vietnam War memorial. And like the White House, the new National Mall was bigger than the old.

Patricia looked out from the podium at the enormous crowd, gripped her father's hand, and wished she was anyplace else.

"In this place," President Lanford was saying, "we have memorialized the dead of our great leaders, made material the symbols of our ideals—and yes, paid tribute to those who fought and died on behalf of this country. Today we add a new monument in memory of what is without any doubt the very darkest moment of this nation—and of the world. It would be impossible to write the names of everyone who died in what was also our shortest war, even if we knew them all. If we cannot speak their names, though, we can still honor them, and honor those who fought so hard to preserve those of us who remain."

The cheer was nearly deafening, and her father squeezed her hand, hard. She looked up at him, saw something like panic in his eyes.

"It's okay," she whispered in his ear. "I'm right here. Just a few more minutes."

"President Whitmore?" Lanford said. "Would you do the honors?"

She had to let go of his hand then, as he stepped to the microphone. She saw him straighten a little as he faced the crowd.

You can do it, Dad, she thought, with more prayer than confidence.

"It is my great honor to stand before you today," he said. "Those of you who remember me may also remember me as being a bit long-winded. If so, don't worry, I'll keep it brief."

A little ripple of laughter traveled through the crowd.

"I only want to say this," he said. "This monument is more than a memorial, or an elegy made concrete. It is also a celebration of our accomplishments since that day, and the bright hope of our future." He paused, and she saw a vacant look pass over his face. Then he cleared his throat.

"My fellow Americans," Whitmore said, "my fellow citizens of the world—I give you the Fourth of July Monument. I declare it open to the nation and to the world."

Patricia let out the breath she had been holding.

He'd made it.

The monument was surrounded by what the tech people called an optical phase screen, a spin-off of force field technology. So up until that moment, they had been looking at something like a reflective surface, albeit one that flowed sluggishly, as if it were made of mercury. That suddenly vanished.

She had seen the plans for it, but the reality was something else again.

The monument was an enormous sphere, or more precisely a globe, with each continent and island fashioned in fine detail. No national or state boundaries were present, but each city that had been destroyed in 1996 was signified by a small, five-pointed star. The globe itself was dark and burnished, but the stars were of some brighter material. So too were the words etched in the oceans and seas, connecting the continents to one another. It was one phrase, written in every script and language on Earth.

We're going to live on.

Like everyone else, she was looking at the monument when her father staggered back and lost his footing. By the time she realized it had happened, a young secret service man had caught him.

"No, no, no..." her father was whispering.

Patricia looked around. Had anyone seen?

"Let's go," she told the agent. "Help me get him to the car."

"Yes, ma'am," he said.

They were halfway there when Patricia saw from the corner of her eye McKenna Morgan from FOX News. The reporter and her crew were almost running, trying to catch up with her. So someone had noticed after all.

"Get him there," she told the agent. "Don't let anyone talk to him."

"Okay," he said.

Patricia spun around and placed herself in front of the approaching crew.

"Ms. Morgan," she said. "So nice to see you."

The other woman dithered for a moment, then nodded to her crew. She held up her microphone as the camera light came on.

"I'm here with Patricia Whitmore, daughter of President Thomas Whitmore, and aide to President Lanford. Ms. Whitmore, just a moment ago, we saw President Whitmore fall. Is he okay?"

"He's fine," Patricia said. "He had a muscle cramp in his calf. You know how those hurt."

"Can you comment about his health in general?" the reporter pushed on. "Can you confirm or deny the rumors of his illness?"

"I don't know what rumors you're referring to," Patricia said, "but he saw his doctor last week and got a clean bill of health."

"Can you explain, then, why he's become so reclusive lately?"

"My father was at the center of the world's attention for a long time," Patricia said. "I think he has earned the right to some privacy and some peace and quiet. I'm sure your viewers will agree."

She saw more reporters were on the way.

"If you'll excuse me," she said.

"Wait—" the reporter began, but then the agent was there, taking her arm.

"This way, ma'am," he said, as behind her a wall of secret service formed.

"Thank you, Agent…"

"Travis, ma'am," he said.

"Thank you, Agent Travis," she said.

In the car, she found her father still white faced and mumbling. She took his hand.

"It's okay, Dad," she said. "We're going home." She wanted to cry, but she fought it down, for his sake.

"I can't," he said, voice breaking. "I can't."

"I know," she said, and she made yet another decision she had been putting off. No more appearances. If she had her way, the public at large had just seen the last of President Thomas J. Whitmore.

She intended to have her way.

33

OCTOBER

Jake stood in the White House foyer, feeling uncomfortable in his class-A uniform. A steady stream of humanity swirled around him, as if everyone was on some sort of important mission. Maybe they were. He felt conspicuous in his lack of motion. He glanced at his watch and saw she was five minutes late.

Maybe this had been a mistake. They hadn't seen each other in four months. Maybe...

"Damn, I love a man in uniform. If I didn't have a boyfriend, but heck, it's not like he's here..."

She had somehow snuck up behind him.

"Listen, lady," he said. "I know everybody thinks us fly-boys are easy, but—well, who am I kidding? We *are* pretty easy." He reached for her.

"Whoa," she said. "Not out here."

She led him through the grand corridors of the nearly completed White House. He felt a little put-off. She'd been the one to talk about coming out of the shadows, not having to hide anything anymore. What was going on?

"Sorry I'm late," she said. "My meeting with the president went long."

"So you couldn't tell her, 'Hey, the love of my life is waiting downstairs, so get to the point, lady'?"

"Listen to you, with all of your assumptions," Patricia said. "'Love of my life.' Really."

"So I'm not the love of your life?" he said.

"You got an audition," she said. "I never said you nailed the part."

He tried to find a comeback for that, but his brain wasn't working right. He felt like there was sort of a cloud in there. This wasn't going as he'd expected, so he decided to change the subject.

"I've gotta say, I never thought I'd end up here—in the White House."

"I never thought I would be back," Patricia said. "But here I am."

"It must have been interesting, growing up here," he said.

"Oh, very," she said. "There's nothing more interesting to a seven-year-old than a bunch of politicians and lobbyists."

"Well," he said, "now that you put it *that* way." But he remembered the stories. How she and Dylan slid down the banisters, eluded secret service in elaborate hide-and-seek games, stole ice cream from the kitchen. To hear Dylan tell it, they'd had a ball here.

She ushered him into a small office and closed the door. He noticed a picture of President Whitmore and the first lady on the desk, and a photo of him, Patricia, and Dylan, posed against a hybrid fighter—the shot taken after their first flight together. The picture hadn't been taken that long ago, but already it seemed like a window into a different universe.

"This is my office, such as it is," she said.

"It's nice," he began.

"You need to kiss me immediately," she said.

For some time after that, neither of them said anything.

"Fine," she said when they came up for air. "You can have the part."

*   *   *

At dinner that night, over Italian, she asked him about the series.

"They're framing them as special-training missions," he said, "but everyone knows they're really tests. A lot of pilots have already dropped out, some others have been cut. I'm hanging in there, and so is Dylan."

"So I heard," she said. "He called me the other day."

"Really?" he said.

"Okay," she warned, "don't you start. You've got no reason to be jealous."

"Who said I was jealous?" he said, but sometimes, when confronted with exactly how much history Patricia and Dylan had together, he felt, well, something. It didn't help that Dylan had told him to his face that he wasn't good enough for her. Or that she didn't seem willing for their relationship to be public, probably because no one else would think he deserved her, either.

He was used to losing things, and people. It was a central feature of his life. But he couldn't stand the thought of losing Patricia.

"Well, you shouldn't be," she replied. "So when does this finish up? When do you know?"

"They gave us all leave," he said. "Time to relax, get a little sloppy. When we get back, there's no timetable. Dylan thinks it will be a series of emergency scenarios where they wake us up in the middle of the night or whatever."

"Are you nervous?" she asked.

"No, not really," he said.

She looked at him skeptically.

"Okay, yes," he said. "I get high technical marks, but for some reason they seem to be under this impression that I have trouble with authority."

"Impression?" Patricia said. "Why on earth would

anyone get such an impression? You're so dutiful, respectful, self-controlled."

"Now you're just being mean," he said.

"Jake," she said. "I love you—I hope you know I do— but this squadron they're putting together, it's not about who has the best technical flying skills. It's supposed to be the living embodiment of global cooperation. A team. A well-oiled machine. You have no idea how much the top is building this thing up."

"So you think I'm screwed?" he said.

"No, that's not what I'm saying," she said. "But, step back a minute. Your lifelong dream was to become a fighter pilot, right?"

"Yes," he said.

"Mission accomplished. Would it be so bad if you stopped killing yourself to get into this PR firestorm, and just became captain of a kick-ass squadron of your own?"

He looked at his pasta for a moment, trying to parse out what she was saying. He pushed it around a little with his fork, and then reached for his wine.

"You think it's going to be Dylan, don't you?" he finally said. "No matter what?"

"You're putting words in my mouth," she said. "Jake, I believe in you. I believe you can do this, and I have always told you so."

"Then why are you suggesting—?"

He realized his tone was a little sharp, so he took five and started again.

"Yes, I've always wanted to be a fighter pilot, but if you're going to be something, why not be the best at it?"

"There's more than one way to be the best, Jake. Don't confuse the hype with the reality. Just because Legacy Squadron is going to get all of the public attention, it doesn't make any other flight group less important. Nobody even knew who Russell Casse was, remember?"

As she said it, the day he first met Charlie flashed through his mind, when he'd shown the younger boy his "fighter jet." He had encouraged Charlie to believe an orphan could do anything, aspire to anything. He'd used Casse to make his point—not that Casse was an orphan, but that he was a nobody.

"That's all pretty easy for you to say," he said. "You grew up on television. Everybody knows who you are."

"It was an accident of birth, Jake. Are you going to hold that against me? And anyway, it's not all that it's cracked up to be. You think it was fun, being a teenager, having my every move scrutinized, having the very clothes I was wearing judged in front of the whole world?"

"I guess you and Dylan can commiserate on that subject."

She was silent, dangerously silent.

"You know," she said at last, "one thing I liked about you from the beginning was that you weren't from my world. You weren't born to privilege, you had to work for everything you got, and it was hard, and yet at the end of it you still had this big heart, this ability to love. When I saw what you and Charlie had, what you meant to each other..." She stopped and then looked at him. "If this is an issue, you need to tell me right now."

"I don't want it to be an issue," he said, "but it seems like you're trying to keep me sort of a secret."

"We're in public right now," she said.

"Twenty miles out of town."

Her voice dropped to a furious whisper.

"Look, if this is about me not jumping your bones in the vestibule of the White House, you have to understand a few things. My father is getting worse, and I don't want to draw attention to him. Which means not drawing attention to myself. That's difficult enough to do as it is, in the job I've got. So, no, I don't need the news rags speculating anymore about my love life than they already do, okay?

"Yes, I want to keep you under the radar, for now. That has nothing to do with how I feel about you, but if you can't handle it, I don't know if this can work. It's hard enough, the long-distance thing. If we're just going to argue every time we do see each other—is this how it's going to be?"

"No," he said. "No. I get it. Okay? I've just really missed you, and things are getting really tense back at the corral, and you're right. I want to enjoy the time we have together."

"It's okay," she said. "We probably should have talked about some of this stuff a long time ago."

"Probably," Jake said. He paused and cleared his throat. "So this whole laying low business. Does that mean we won't be, uh...?"

She smiled. "I have secret service at my disposal, Jake. Plans have been made."

34

NOVEMBER

On the day the sky appeared, Dikembe didn't know what it was, but he feared it, the circle of light. He crouched at the side of his cell, face to the wall, unable to bear the brightness and the sensations it sent crawling through him. He tried to think what it could mean.

After what seemed like a long time, he heard a voice.

"Dikembe," it said. "Take the rope, Dikembe." It was the first human voice he had heard in a very long time—and it was also the last voice he had heard.

"Zuberi?" He turned to look up, and saw the silhouette of a head appear in the brilliant blue disc. His eyes were adjusting.

"The rope," Zuberi said.

Dikembe saw, then, that a rope had been let down. It had a loop tied in the bottom. He regarded it for a long moment.

"No," he said. "This is some sort of trick. I do not trust you, Zuberi."

"It isn't a trick," Zuberi said. "I'm letting you out."

"Why?" he demanded. "You put me here."

"Does it matter?" Zuberi asked. "Aren't you tired of being in that pit?"

Dikembe stood up, stretching to his full height, realizing

Zuberi was right, that it didn't matter. In a way, he supposed, he was safe in the hole. It meant his father still wanted him alive—but what did it mean if his father wanted him out?

He could not bring himself to give a damn.

So he put his foot in the noose, thinking it might just as well be his neck. Then he grabbed onto the rope.

"Ready," he said.

Something began pulling him up. When he reached the lip of his prison, he saw the line was fastened to a winch on a jeep. They were in open country. He didn't see anyone but Zuberi.

Dikembe climbed out of the hole.

"Dikembe—" Zuberi began. It was as far as he got. Dikembe hit him below the waist, lifted him high and dumped him head first to the ground. Zuberi took the impact with his elbows and kicked at Dikembe's chest. Rage had such a hold on him that Dikembe hardly took note. As Zuberi scrambled backward, trying to stand back up, Dikembe threw himself bodily on the man, slamming at his face with his fists. He connected and felt the crunch of cartilage, heard Zuberi cry out in pain. His betrayer covered his head with his arms as Dikembe continued to pummel him.

Dikembe finally realized that Zuberi wasn't struggling anymore. Panting, he looked down at the bloody, brutalized face.

"Are you done?" Zuberi asked through split lips.

Dikembe relieved him of his sidearm.

He put a round in the chamber.

"Why?" he demanded.

"Because you would be dead, otherwise," Zuberi said. "They would have caught you and they would have killed you."

"You don't know that."

"I do," Zuberi said. "When I brought you in, however,

I was able to speak to your father. To plead with him to spare your life."

"Spare my life?" Dikembe said. "So I could live down there? What were you thinking?"

"Well, I admit it wasn't ideal," Zuberi said, "but it gave me time. Your father trusts me completely now, and so eventually I was able to arrange this."

"And what is this?" Dikembe asked.

"A rescue," he said. He winced and touched his bleeding lip. "There is enough gas in the tank for you to reach the border. I happen to know of one crossing which is not well-guarded today. You have food, water, and currency. And some clothes."

"And you?" Dikembe asked. "How will you explain my escape?"

"You beat me up," Zuberi said. "You took my sidearm and killed my men."

"What men?"

"They're behind the jeep," he said.

Dikembe strode around the vehicle and saw them, both shot to death.

"It couldn't be helped," Zuberi said. "If it matters, they were two of the men responsible for the massacre. I chose them very carefully."

Dikembe felt sick. He was having a hard time gathering his thoughts.

"In this story of yours—how did I get out of the hole?" he asked.

"Ah," Zuberi said. "Your father sent me for you. My orders were to take you out." He spit some more blood. "Are you going to shoot me, or may I stand up?"

Dikembe motioned for him to stand.

Zuberi got up, touching his face gingerly. "You've at least made my story seem quite plausible. I could hardly have done this to myself."

"Why did my father send for me?" Dikembe asked.

"Because he wants you to attend an execution," Zuberi said. "Your own, in fact."

Dikembe let that sink in. He had suspected it, of course, but to hear Zuberi say it was a different mule altogether.

"Why now?" he said. "Why not earlier?"

"He had a dream or something," Zuberi said. "Some sort of revelation. I'm not sure if you're aware of this, but your father is really quite mad."

"Yes," Dikembe said. "That thought had entered my mind."

Zuberi reached into his pocket and pulled out some car keys.

"Here," he said. "You had better get going."

Dikembe took the keys.

"Should I drop you off somewhere?" he asked.

"No," Zuberi said. "I'll walk. It's not really that far, and it will look more authentic if he sends someone out here to have a look."

He stuck out his hand and attempted a grin, although it was obvious that it hurt.

Dikembe took it. They shook.

"I am sorry I did you harm, old man," Zuberi said. "I did not want to see you die."

Dikembe nodded. "Take care of your family," he said.

Zuberi smiled a bloody smile, and then walked away. Dikembe put on some of the clothes, and then got behind the wheel.

*   *   *

The kilometers scrolled by on his dashboard. Dikembe still squinted at what was only ordinary daylight. Despite the clean clothes, he smelled wretched.

The grasslands extended to each horizon, and he felt

tiny, alone. It seemed almost too big after his time in the hole. Even in the light, rolling through the green grass and a sky like turquoise, the dark savanna of his drawings remained with him. He felt that if he got out and scratched the bark of a tree, he would find a nightmare beneath it.

He forced himself to look forward, to a flat in England, by the sea. Or perhaps a sunnier place, like Spain. A house that was mostly glass, with plenty of light. Some canvas, a sketchbook. Somewhere quiet, but not *too* quiet, where he could rejoin the stream of humanity.

He came to the border crossing. As promised, it was unguarded, and soon the sign declaring the National Republic of Umbutu was in his rearview. An hour or so later he pulled over at a truck stop. It was the usual informal affair, with a few cots and a little restaurant under a round arbor. Children were playing in the red dirt, and an old man sitting out front waved and greeted him in English.

Dikembe asked him if there was a shower, and there was—a gravity-fed affair in back. He took his time cleaning himself up, and when he was done he was amazed by how much better he felt. His spirits rose further when he sat at one of the small tables and was served chicken stew heavily laced with cumin and a lukewarm 33 Export beer.

The old man came over with a beer of his own and started chatting. Had he come from Umbutu? Dikembe answered that he had not, but from farther east. He asked the old man what he knew of Umbutu, and was regaled with tales of monsters, murder, and cannibalism. Dikembe hoped that the last wasn't true, but the rest of it, although exaggerated and distorted, contained large grains of truth.

A few more men joined them as the shadows lengthened. They laughed and joked and talked about their day. For Dikembe, it was surreal—he had almost forgotten that people lived this way, just being ordinary. He wondered if his Oxford mate Brian was still alive, and if so what he was doing. Whether they would have anything to talk about if they ever met again.

He wondered where Hailey had ended up. Probably not on the yacht anymore. She would be around forty now, probably married with a few kids.

He might be able to track Brian down. Hailey would be more difficult, since he couldn't remember her last name, but the owner of the yacht probably had an accounting of its employees. The point was that it was all out there, a planet mostly at peace, a world he had only been able to observe through a tiny crack in the wall.

He took a cot and slept more soundly than he had in many years.

*   *   *

The next morning, back on the road, something began to itch at him. Something didn't feel quite right. He was avoiding something—and then he finally understood what it was.

Zuberi. Why hadn't he rescued Dikembe sooner? Why had he waited until his father made the decision to execute him?

The answer was simple. Because whatever he said, Zuberi knew that in freeing Dikembe he was putting himself at risk, and he had not been willing to take that risk until there was—in his mind—no other choice.

Dikembe pulled over to the side of the rutted dirt track that passed for a road and turned off the engine. He got out and looked across the manioc fields that bordered the road, toward the blue distance he had put behind him. He looked ahead, where the fields were cut by a line of palms of some sort. He sat on the jeep for a moment, feeling the heat from the sun on his face, taking in the great dome of the sky that—only yesterday—he had all but forgotten.

Then he got back into the jeep and started it again. He drove forward until he found a small crossroads that allowed him to turn around, and started back the way he had come.

35

This time the border was not unguarded. Four men with assault rifles watched Dikembe approach. He stopped short of the checkpoint and got out of the vehicle.

"Stop there," one of the men said.

Dikembe sized them up.

"You," he said, pointing. "You are Mayele. You fought with my brother in the Salt Ridge battle. You fought alongside me when we cleared the lowlands."

"That is true, my prince," Mayele said.

"Don't listen to him," the apparent leader said. He was young, with wide-set eyes. He wore the insignia of a captain. "He is not a prince. The president has declared him a traitor and an outlaw, and that he is possessed by the demons."

Dikembe ignored him, and instead turned his attention to a big man, who also bore the alien tattoo and hash marks on his arm.

"And you," he said. "Jelani. I saw your brother and his family safely out of the country. You are aware of this."

Jelani's gaze dropped, as if to study the chalky dirt of the road.

Dikembe took a step forward. The captain brought his rifle to bear.

"You," he said to the captain. "What's your name? I don't know you."

"Faraji," the man said. "Stop there."

"Faraji," Dikembe said. "Put down your gun."

"I will not," Faraji said. He motioned with his hand. "Take him prisoner," he told the others. "Don't any of you remember? He conspired against our country."

"I conspired against my father," Dikembe said, "because he is mad and he is destroying you, all of you. I've been across the border. There are no monsters out there, and the only monsters in Umbutu are those we have made of ourselves. Faraji, you were too young to fight, so you never knew their touch. Never learned to hunt them by sensing how they hunted us.

"I have known that. Mayele and Jelani know what I mean, and they remember what it was like to follow their princes into battle—the twins of Umbutu. What it was like to fight to save your people rather than to repress them." He looked at the two men he knew. "It was a different feeling, wasn't it?"

"Yes," Jelani said softly. "It was." He raised his rifle and pointed it at the captain. "Faraji," he said. "Lower your weapon."

Mayele made his decision and covered the fourth man, who hadn't said anything. That man dropped his weapon, but Faraji's gun was still pointed at Dikembe's heart.

"Put it down, son," Dikembe said. "None of us need die here."

"I will not betray Umbutu," the captain said.

"You betray nothing," Dikembe said. "I have come to see my father. I will not meet him as a prisoner, but as a son come of his own free will. Step aside."

"Faraji," Jelani said. "You are fixed to marry my sister. I do not want to kill you, but if you murder my prince, I will put you down like a dog."

Faraji's lips tightened across his teeth. Then slowly, slowly he lowered the weapon. Jelani took it from him, and his sidearm as well. They also disarmed the other man, who had yet to speak.

"Do not harm them," Dikembe said. "We are all one people. We should not be killing each other."

"What should we do?" Jelani asked.

"Make sure they don't have any radios," he said. "Take their jeep and follow me. By the time they can walk to an outpost, it won't matter anymore."

*   *   *

The village of Zuberi's birth was only a few kilometers from the capital. It was a small place, with less than a hundred houses, most thatched with grass although a few were roofed in tin. The streets were dusty with red dirt, and the children playing in them fled at the approach of the jeeps.

Memory served Dikembe well—he had little trouble locating Zuberi's house. When he approached, Zuberi's eldest son, Moke, came to the door. He was fourteen and looked frightened, but also determined.

"Moke," Dikembe said. "Is your father home?"

Moke's eyes widened as he recognized him.

"No, my prince," he said. "He is at the capital, with your father."

Dikembe noticed someone approaching from behind Moke—a man in the uniform of his father's Home Guard. Dikembe drew his pistol.

The man looked surprised, and cut his eyes. Following his gaze, Dikembe saw the assault rifle leaning against the wall on the inside of the house.

"Don't, brother," Dikembe said.

"I know who you are," the man said.

"I have no quarrel with you," Dikembe said. "Come out of the house." From the corner of his eye he saw Jelani come up on his right. That seemed to do it—the guardsman held up his hands and stepped across the threshold into the harsh sunlight.

"Is your father here?" Dikembe asked Moke again.

"No," he said. "It is as I said."

"Then ask your mother to come out," Dikembe said.

Moke vanished into the house and returned in a few moments with Eshe, a small woman with pleasant, round features.

"Dikembe," she said. "How can this be?" She took a step back, as if fearing he wasn't who he said he was.

"Eshe," he said. "Do you remember who kept watch by the granary the first time you and Zuberi—"

Her eyes went wide.

"Hush," she said. "My children are here." But she looked relieved.

"Has this man hurt you?" Dikembe asked, nodding at the guardsman.

"No," she said, "but I am afraid of him. He says my husband sent him, but I do not believe it."

"Don't listen to this woman," the guardsman said.

"Well?" Dikembe said, moving to confront him. "What were your orders?"

"I won't tell you that," the man said.

"No?" Dikembe said. He took three quick steps and clubbed the man in the nose with the butt of his pistol. The guardsman cried out and staggered back. He tried to flee but Jelani was there, and knocked him off his feet.

Dikembe chambered a round.

"What are you doing with my friend's family?" he asked softly. "You have exactly one chance to answer me. Then I shoot your kneecap."

"Wait," the man gasped. He was having trouble

breathing for all the blood coming from his nose.

"I'm listening," Dikembe said.

"Your father fears Zuberi may be disloyal. I was sent here to—make certain of his loyalty."

Dikembe nodded. That was what he'd thought.

"Handcuff this man," he told Jelani. "Eshe, get your family together and pack anything essential. Jelani, you are to take them through the checkpoint. Find them lodging across the border. Mayele, you go with him. Take this man, too, and leave him along the roadside. Alive."

"Yes, my prince," Jelani said. "But what of you?"

"You've already served me very well, my friend," Dikembe said. "You've done your part. Stay with Zuberi's family and keep them safe until you see him or me again."

"God keep you, my prince," Mayele said.

"And you," Dikembe answered. He began walking toward his father's compound.

"You're not taking the jeep?" Jelani called after him.

"No," Dikembe said. "It's a nice day to walk."

"My prince, it's fifteen kilometers," he said.

"I've been in a hole for months," he said. "I can use the exercise." He had drawn quite a crowd now, and many of them came forward to touch him. He shook their hands and patted the boys and girls on the head.

"Where are you going, Prince Dikembe?" one of the boys asked.

Dikembe squatted down in front of him.

"I am not a prince," he said. "I am just a man, and I am going to see my father, who is also just a man."

*   *   *

"Keep it real up there," Dylan said, as he and Jake fist-bumped.

"Always," Jake said. He looked confident almost to

the point of swaggering, but Dylan knew it was mostly a bluff. Deep down, Jake had to be as nervous as he was.

The trials had been getting more and more difficult. Some pilots had dropped out because they couldn't handle the stress. Others were eliminated in the hops themselves. Now there were only eight still in the running for the North American slot in Legacy Squadron.

Like the moon run, a lot of the Earthbound tests had pitted squadron against squadron, with points awarded to the members to create rankings. A few had been simpler—like the time they had been challenged to make a series of high-speed maneuvers over open ocean while practically skimming the swells. There, pilots had been eliminated individually.

You just never knew, not until they announced it.

He took a deep, steadying breath and climbed into his cockpit, wondering what was in store this time. He checked his instruments, wondering how different the new H-8s would be that Legacy Squadron would fly. Probably not very in the cockpit, but he'd heard crazy things about their speed and maneuverability.

He glanced over at Jake, who seemed to be studying his instruments as well. But then he saw the other man was holding something, a little rectangle. His picture of Patricia, the one he kept in the cockpit.

Dylan still didn't quite know what to make of that—partly because he tried his best not to think about it. Jake was a good enough guy, but Patricia deserved something better than good enough, and he figured she would have realized that by now.

His radio suddenly came to life.

"Alright," the flight officer said. "Final training hop. Grand Canyon Run, winner takes all."

For an instant, Dylan's mind went blank. The Grand Canyon Run was a flight simulator program they'd done back in the first year of flight school. It was a sort of homage to his father, who had survived a dogfight with an alien fighter by luring it into the canyon.

What...? Then Dylan got it.

"Crap," Jake said. "This is going to be fun." Obviously Jake got it too. Their H-7s leapt up almost at the same time, quickly followed by the other six.

Getting there will be half the battle, he thought. It would be the only part of the flight where he could fly full-throttle. He turned his nose in what he thought was the right direction while playing with the nav computer to get his bearings. Some of the others were taking it more cautiously, plotting their courses before coming to speed.

Dylan went full throttle, hoping the vector in his gut lined up pretty closely with the one his flight computer would give him in a few moments.

The Grand Canyon. How many times had he heard his dad tell that story?

"You can simulate it all you want," he'd told Dylan, when he was in flight school, "but the real thing—that there's a beast."

* * *

Winner take all, Jake mused. No more points for teamwork, no more holding back. It was a race, pure and simple. A race he could win.

In the simulator they had always entered the canyon from the west, just as Steven Hiller had in his legendary flight from the ruins of Los Angeles, so he set his flight path and throttled up. About that time a stream of target data started coming in, and he realized things weren't as simple as he'd thought.

The Grand Canyon was wide at the top, many kilometers across in some places, a few hundred meters in others. A pilot could drop ten meters below the rim and fly through the whole canyon without any worries.

He should have known it wouldn't be that easy.

New figures appeared on the screen. Depth goals—points in the vast, twisting chasm where they would be required to fly just meters above the Colorado River. Down there, things could get much, much narrower.

"This is gonna be like nothing we've ever done," he said. "Parts of that thing are so tight…"

"Keep your shields up if you're worried," Dylan shot back.

"Yeah," Jake said. "Sure will. Thanks for the advice." But he had no intention of keeping his shields up. Shields used power, and they created drag when deployed in an atmosphere. Shields would make him slower, and today he was going to go *fast*.

He sped over Lake Mead at over Mach 2, and seconds later was in the canyon. By that time one of the pilots—Martin—was lagging so far behind it was hard to see how he could catch up. The others, however, were now tightening in toward each other. Jake was slightly ahead of the pack, followed closely by Moffett and then Dylan.

Jake's nervousness began to melt away as he took his first dive. It was a straight stretch, but down near the river the walls closed in pretty tightly. He wondered what it had been like to do this with an enemy shooting at you, and his estimation for the late Steve Hiller rose a notch, even though it had always been pretty high.

Flying in space was far easier than this. There was much less to slam into. Once he hit his depth, he decided to stay low and save time for the next descent. Behind him he saw Dylan trying to pull around Moffett, but the likeable southern boy wasn't having any of that, maneuvering in front of him each time. Jake could imagine his friend's frustration, and it brought a little grin to his face.

The canyon took a sharp bend, almost too sharp. He saw Tong and Kerry above, at a safer altitude, beginning to pass, and increased his speed slightly. They were going to have to come down in a minute to hit their mark.

"Morrison, Moffett," Dylan's voice came over the radio. "Let's keep those guys up there."

"Now that sounds like a plan," Jake said. He took the H-7 right to the top of the next altitude goal, as did the two behind them.

"You'd better clear out," Tong said. "I'll go right through you."

"You can try," Jake said.

He heard Tong cursing, not quite under his breath.

Jake, Dylan, and Moffett maneuvered wildly through the narrow chasm. As Moffett had been denying Dylan the chance to pass on the right or left, they were now keeping Kerry and Tong from descending to the altitude required by the test.

"Kerry, Tong, you're both out," the flight director said.

Jake whooped. "Good call, Dylan," he said.

"Thanks," Dylan replied. Then he flipped his fighter so one wing was pointed skyward and another toward the canyon floor, and rushed past Moffett. He then jetted right past Jake, pulling into the lead. Moffett yelped in surprise and broke hard, nearly hitting the wall. He recovered by climbing and climbed too high, putting him out of the contest as well.

Jake swore silently. The canyon opened back out a bit and he pushed the H-7 hard, but Dylan still had the lead when it began to tighten again.

36

Each step he took along the packed red dirt of the road made Dikembe feel curiously stronger, as if the land itself was lending him strength. He knew the exhilaration was probably some sort of delusion caused by months of sensory deprivation, and intellectually he knew this wasn't likely to end well for him.

In a way, that no longer mattered.

He tried to fix an image in his mind of his father, years ago, before the aliens came. He had been stern, fiercely proud of his name and lineage, a strong leader who demanded respect. There was—in those days—more to him than that. He was a man who believed that his obligation to his people was greater than theirs to him, that a ruler's courage could be measured by the burden he was willing to bear, rather than how much he could make his people do. He was a man who loved his children, the father who wanted his boys to grow to be strong and wise.

His father was still those things, but they had all been bent into strange and terrible shapes. Some part of Dikembe had always believed his father would get better, become at least something of the man he had been. In the space of what Dikembe experienced and what he dreamed of—that was where anger lived, where it transfigured into hatred.

Dikembe did not want to die hating his father, as much as he detested what the old man had become.

The empty road took him on toward what he could only think of as his destiny—a concept he had once rejected. As a young man he had believed he had free will, could do anything he wanted, walk any path he saw, *make* the path. Now, at last, he understood it wasn't so.

Perhaps it was surrender to that that made his steps so light.

As the compound came in sight, an odd thing began to happen. People began emerging from trails and side roads onto the highway. At first just a few, but then their numbers grew, and he realized that many more were arriving from behind him. He recognized many from Zuberi's village. They were mostly women and children, although he made out a few elders in the growing crowd. They surrounded him, some singing, most looking terrified.

"What is this?" Dikembe finally asked. In his mind's eye he saw messengers from Zuberi's village—on foot, on bicycles—spreading out through the countryside, telling of Prince Dikembe's mad march toward the executioner.

"My prince," one boy said. "We do not intend that you should die. We will go with you."

The boy's words filled him with an almost unbearable pride for his people. The land seemed almost to swell beneath his feet. He gazed around at the faces, young and old, and he loved them all—began to understand how such love might drive a man to madness.

"Listen to me," he said. "My father is not the man we once knew. He will not hesitate to order his men to attack you, and that I could not bear. Please, for my sake, return to your villages."

A woman broke through the crowd, and he saw to his dismay that she was Eshe, Zuberi's wife, followed by her children, and flanked by Mayele and Jelani.

"They are not his men," Eshe declared, in a voice more carrying than he had known she possessed. "They are our husbands, our fathers, our sons. Our country has descended into madness and misery. There is no place left to go. If our men are willing to shoot us, what is the point of living on?"

The crowd stirred at her words. Some began to shout.

"You must not do this," Dikembe said to Eshe. "I cannot have your deaths on my conscience. This road I must walk alone."

"No," Jelani said. "We will walk it with you, my prince. To the end."

Off in the distance, the doors of the compound opened. A tank and several other vehicles appeared. He was out of time.

"Go," he shouted at the crowd.

No one budged.

He sighed. "Any of you with arms," he said, "put them down now. Please. We must not give them an excuse to open fire. Do not shout or carry on. Let me speak to him."

His father stood up from the hatch of the tank, just as he had done in the final assault on the aliens. He wore the flayed exoskeletons of several aliens and a necklace made of their bones. His Home Guard surrounded the tank, marching on foot. In one of the two armored Humvees, Dikembe saw Zuberi. He did not appear to be armed.

The tank rumbled to a stop, and his father peered at him from behind dark sunglasses.

"These men around me," he said, gesturing, "they believed you had gone away. Abandoned Umbutu."

"That was my intent," Dikembe said. "When your men pulled me out of the hole you put me in, they were not prepared for what I had become. Perhaps they expected a broken man. That they did not find—isn't that true, my old 'friend'?" He gestured toward Zuberi, at his bruised and swollen face.

"I am aware of Zuberi's failure," the old man said. "And I know why you came back. It is because you understand what you must do, just as Bakari did."

"What did Bakari do, Father?" Dikembe asked.

"He joined his other half. He became whole."

"My brother," Dikembe said, "was killed by a stray bullet."

"There are no stray bullets," his father said. "There are no accidents, and chance is a phantom without substance. We all have a place and a purpose."

"I remember a man who taught me that my place and purpose was in service to my people," Dikembe said. "A man who taught that one should never place oneself above the needs of those he rules. Of the man who taught me these things, I no longer see any trace. I see instead a man caught up in the vision of his own greatness, his own importance. A man whose pride has eaten him and taken his shape. I see a man who has become what he once hated, and that is what these people around me see. Your people, Father. You loved them once."

His father gazed at the mass of people behind Dikembe as if seeing them for the first time.

"See what you have done," he said. "See what you have done."

He motioned with his hand.

"Zuberi," he said. "Come here."

Zuberi didn't hesitate. He climbed from his vehicle and walked over to the tank. Dikembe's father handed Zuberi a handgun.

"Go to my son," he said.

Zuberi crossed the few meters with measured strides.

"Zuberi!" Eshe cried from behind.

Zuberi's expression was flat, hard to read.

"Give my son the gun," Umbutu said.

Zuberi handed Dikembe the weapon and stepped to the side.

"What do you think?" his father said. "You believe you can kill me? It isn't possible, you know—but perhaps I am wrong. Let me see, once and for all, what kind of son you are."

The wide world seemed to shrink as Dikembe felt the grip of the gun in his hand, the weight of it. He chambered a round and raised the pistol. Several of the guards brought their weapons to ready.

"No, no," Umbutu said to them, motioning them to lower their rifles. "Let him."

Dikembe put his father in the sights.

Then his father took off his sunglasses, and Dikembe saw him—really saw him.

His eyes were pools of misery and madness—and hope. In that instant, Dikembe knew it wasn't a trick of some kind. His father was pleading with him. This was something he hadn't seen before.

Those who believed in *uchawi* were wrong. Madness was not a demon or a spell that entered a man from the outside. In his father's eyes he saw it all—the man he had been, the man he could have been, the man he was. For each of those versions of his father, there was a sort of reflection of who he, Dikembe, had been, could have been, still might be.

For his father, there was no "still might be."

Dikembe put his finger on the trigger. His hand was shaking. His father stared into the gun barrel, unflinching.

Dikembe lowered the gun and saw the disappointment in his father's eyes, followed swiftly by anger.

"Again you fail me," he said. "Zuberi, take the gun."

Zuberi reached for it.

"Come along, old man," Zuberi whispered. "Give it to me."

Dikembe surrendered the weapon.

"You did your best," Zuberi said, still under his breath. "There is no shame."

"Zuberi," the old man said. "Send my son to be reborn with his ancestors."

* * *

Jake banked right, but Dylan was there, keeping him from passing. He couldn't go over him—the next depth goal was too close.

As he counted it, four pilots were already out. He executed a dizzying series of banks, all the while glaring right at Dylan's tail.

Where are the other two?

The flight officer answered his question a moment later.

"Lebos and Blankenship, you're out. Hiller and Morrison—looks like it's down to you two."

"Okay, then," Jake said. He pushed right up, but Dylan was flying as fast as the craft would go in Earth's atmosphere—at this altitude, anyway.

"Why don't you just give up, Morrison?" Dylan said. "You'll never catch me. Number two's gonna have to be good enough for you."

It sounded like his usual banter, but in that instant Jake knew it wasn't. As far as Dylan was concerned, there was no version of his world where Jake could beat him.

He was wrong.

Dylan was a good pilot, but he wasn't as good as everyone thought he was. He was still coasting on his father's reputation, and Jake had been forced to take that, all of these months, to settle for feeling like second place. Because, of course, the son of Steve Hiller had to be the best. It only made sense.

Jake could've made the shot in the moon run. He knew he could have. Dylan had used his rank to stop him. To keep him in his place.

But second *wasn't* his place. Not this time.

The canyon took a turn, and a brief window opened up.

"We'll see about that," he told Dylan. "Passing on your left."

"Negative, Morrison," the flight officer cut in. "There's not enough room."

Jake saw how tight it was, but he knew he could make it.

"Don't worry," he said. "I got this." He pushed the stick a little further, and began pulling around before Dylan could get in his way.

"*Dammit*, Jake," Dylan snapped. "I'm the ranking officer! What the hell are you—"

Dylan stopped in mid-sentence.

The next moment was a long one. The craft were so close to the same speed that it almost seemed as if they were standing still, but the canyon was a blur. Jake wondered why Dylan thought he could give him orders when they were in the middle of a free-for-all.

A reply formed on his lips—

—and something hit him.

Or, rather, he hit something. Dylan's wing. His friend's fighter spun, utterly out of control, but then Jake had to put everything he had into not crashing.

It was instinct more than anything else that kept him from slamming into the canyon wall. Over the radio, he heard Dylan shouting in what sounded like sheer panic, and he fought his own, banking hard.

"I'm going down!" Dylan yelped. "Eject, eject, eject—"

As Jake came around, he saw Dylan's fighter explode against the canyon wall.

* * *

Zuberi raised the pistol and took a few steps back. Dikembe locked his gaze on him and prepared himself as best he could.

Then, suddenly the crowd moved to engulf him, form a wall around him, Eshe and her children among them.

"Didn't you hear me, Zuberi?" Umbutu shouted. His Home Guard shouldered their rifles and took aim.

Zuberi took a step forward.

"No," Dikembe said, pushing the hands away from him. "Back up, all of you. This must be as it must be." He fought his way free and for a moment, faced with all of that firepower, they fell back. He was alone, in the open.

"Do it now, Zuberi," he said. "Before they come again."

Zuberi nodded. He raised the weapon.

Then he turned and shot Dikembe's father, once, twice, three times. Dikembe saw the impacts on his uniform, but the final bullet went in just to the side of Umbutu's nose.

There was a thunder of arms, and Zuberi staggered as bullets and plasma rays tore through his body. A few went beyond him, striking people in the crowd. Dikembe, horrified, started forward, and so did everyone else.

For a moment everything froze, and the only sounds were the whimpering and cries of the wounded.

Upanga Umbutu toppled from the tank, rolled down the side, and thudded unceremoniously to the ground. Dikembe took a step toward his father, but the Home Guard turned their weapons toward him.

Again his people surrounded him, and he felt their strength as his own. He saw Zuberi draw his last breath, as his wife and children ran to him.

He pointed his finger at the Home Guard.

"Put your weapons down," he said. He saw the uncertainty in their eyes, and so he walked up to them. "Put them down and walk away," he said. "Or will you murder what remains of your people in the service of a dead madman?"

The man he was nearest to dropped his weapon, and then, in a matter of seconds, they all did.

Dikembe went to his father then, but it was far too late. His father's final words to him would always be, *Again you fail me.*

37

DECEMBER

Jake showed up for the hearing in his class-A uniform, feeling very alone. No one seemed to want to look at him, much less talk to him.

Things were moving fast. Dylan's crash was only a week in the past. Jake had been under house arrest during that time, not allowed any communication with anyone. He wished he could at least talk to Patricia and Charlie, to try to explain things, but he also wondered if it would do any good. Patricia wanted a low-key relationship, and right now, he was probably news.

The investigation had taken place immediately and internally, and the brass were working hard to minimize everything in the press. According to his counsel, they were likely to do one of two things—crucify him to make him an example, or try to quietly make him go away. Either way, even though there were several more training scenarios to go, he wasn't going to be in them, and Legacy Squadron had gone from being within reach to utterly impossible.

He saw his judge advocate approaching—Second Lieutenant Dalton. He was a sandy-haired fellow with a weak chin, younger than Jake, and—if it was possible—seemed more nervous.

"Right this way, Lieutenant," Dalton said.

Jake had expected a courtroom, but instead he was led into an office occupied by a single man—Lieutenant Colonel Mitchum.

"Sir," Jake said.

Mitchum was in his late sixties, a compact man with piercing black eyes and a quick temper. Jake had made it his business to avoid the lieutenant colonel's scrutiny until now—not always successfully.

"I'll keep this brief," Mitchum said. "I have persuaded the powers-that-be that an article thirty-two hearing is—how can I put this? A bad idea. It would only drag something out that we want to put behind us as quickly as possible. In part, you can thank Lieutenant Hiller for this—he refuses to sign a complaint against you, and his only testimony is that you made a profound misjudgment. From what I have seen of the data, I would tend to agree, but bad judgment comes in a variety of scents—and in your case, it stinks. I don't know what sort of ax you were grinding, Morrison, and I don't care, but it ends now."

"Yes, sir," Jake said.

"You'll finish flight school, but I'm reassigning you. You're too dangerous to fly a fighter."

He'd known it was probably coming, but it still felt like a kick in the gut.

"Understood, sir," he said.

"No snappy comeback?" Mitchum said. "No sarcastic comment?"

"Not today, sir," Jake said.

"Then you're dismissed."

"Thank you, sir."

* * *

It was cold outside, and the light was fading. In the deep indigo to the east, stars were appearing. He watched as an H-8 took flight from behind the distant hangar. He followed it as its running lights quickly dimmed with distance. He sighed.

"You really screwed up," a familiar voice said.

"Patricia?"

He turned to find her watching him from a few meters away, bundled in an overcoat.

"Hi," she said.

"How—?"

"I wasn't able to get in touch with you for a week," she said. "You didn't think I would wait any longer, did you?"

"I thought—"

"Don't think, Jake," Patricia said. "Not your strongest attribute."

He studied her for a moment, trying to read her. Was she angry? Disgusted?

"I did screw up," he said finally. "I just wanted it so much…" He trailed off.

"That doesn't justify anything, does it?" he blinked when he saw her expression. "What?" he asked.

"They sat on it for three hours, Jake," she exploded. "For three hours I knew that there had been a crash, that a fighter had been destroyed. For three hours I thought one or both of you could be dead."

"I'm sorry," he said. "I'm sorry I didn't call, but they wouldn't let me."

"I know," she said.

He reached for her again, but something stopped him, and he dropped his hand by his side.

"Patricia," he said. "Look. I'd understand if you didn't…" He couldn't quite finish.

She frowned. "You think I flew all the way out here and waited around in the cold to *dump* you? Morrison, sometimes I think your head isn't set on straight. Stop moping already and kiss me."

He stared at her for a heartbeat or two and then he did that, and for a while nothing seemed to matter. Then Patricia drew back a little.

"It's cold," she said. "Let's go get a drink and a bite to eat."

"Are you sure?" he said. "I'm not too popular around here these days. It's a small town. People may see us together. Word might get around."

"Yeah," she said. "About that. Turns out I don't care nearly as much about that as I thought I did. Not after—well, priorities change. I'm not ashamed of you, Jake. You made a mistake, a bad one. It could just as easily have been Dylan who made it, the way you two go after each other, but it's not the end of the world, is it?"

He took that in and nodded.

"I won't be flying fighters," he said. He squeezed her hand. "But I guess, at least—"

"At least?" Her eyebrows jumped up and she pulled her hand away. "Hang on there. You don't think I'm some kind of consolation prize, do you? Because if that's how it is, I guess I *did* fly out here for nothing."

"No!" he said. "Patricia, God no. I've wanted to fly since I was a kid. It's the first thing I remember wanting, the last thing I thought about every night before I closed my eyes. Until I met you. After that I thought—I *knew*—you were my future. At first I believed that was because you were going to the Academy too, that we had shared goals. But since you left flight school I realized—it's not about that. It's about you. About how I want to be with you. If I had to choose between being a pilot or being with you, I'd stay grounded for the rest of my life."

"The rest of your life?" she said, after a little pause. "That could be a while."

"Yeah," he said, taking a deep breath, "but I don't see a rest of my life without you in it. When I try to, I draw a blank."

It hung there for a minute, and despite the chill he felt as if he was sweating. Then she smiled a little. To Jake, it felt like the sun rising.

"I know what you mean," she said.

"You do?"

Yes," she said, and she kissed him again. "Now let's get in out of the cold."

"Right," he said. He took her hand and they started walking.

After a few steps she looked up at him.

"You know you're going to have to do that again, right?" she said. "With a ring and flowers. And use the actual words, posed as a question."

"Yeah," Jake said, "I get that."

*   *   *

Jake met Charlie at the airport with his bags.

"Valedictorian," Jake said. "I knew you could do it, Charlie. I wish I could have been there to see you walk."

"That's okay," Charlie said. "To tell the truth, it was pretty boring, all in all."

"That's the way I remember it," Jake said. "So are you ready for flight school?"

"Followin' in your footsteps, bro," he said.

"Yeah," Jake said. "That's not a very good idea. Better you follow in your own footsteps—or, whatever, you know what I mean."

"Hey," Charlie said. "At least you didn't get court-martialed or anything."

"Looking on the bright side these days?" Jake said.

"Why not?" Charlie said. "We made it."

Jake snorted. "You made it. I've flown the last fighter I'm ever going to fly."

"But you are going to fly, right?" Charlie said.

"Sure," Jake said. "If you want to call it that. I'm assigned to tugs."

"That's, ah—that's great," Charlie said.

"Don't even—" Jake said. "But look, it's my fault. I blame no one."

"Really, not even a smidgen?"

Jake struggled with that. It was his fault, sure, technically, but if Dylan had pulled away, just let him have it...

That was pointless. He'd nearly killed the Chosen One. Charlie was right—he was lucky not to be in prison, much less still in the service.

"How is Dylan?" Charlie asked.

"I don't know," Jake said. "Physically okay, I guess, but he's not talking to me."

"And Patricia?"

Jake couldn't keep from grinning. "That's still good," he said. He clapped Charlie on the shoulder. "You know what? You're right. We did okay for a couple of orphans, and at least one of us is going to fly a fighter."

"I don't know," Charlie said. "I hear all the cool kids are piloting tugs."

EPILOGUE

2016

Rain rose early, dressed, and reached for her flight jacket. She held it for a moment, not quite believing it was hers. She ran her fingers along the seams of the Legacy Squadron patch.

Everyone seemed to think it had been easy for her, that it was inevitable she would represent China in the international unit—but to her, it was still unbelievable. Inside her there still lived that little girl, bitter over the loss of her parents, angry at the universe, the arc of her life bending toward ruin. If it hadn't been for Uncle Jiang, she knew things would be very different at this moment. Very few people her age even had aunts or uncles, so she had been more than lucky.

She put on the jacket and went outside. It was still dark, and the moon stood nearly straight overhead. She looked up at it, tracing the familiar face of the satellite with her gaze, focusing at last on the spot where the moon base was. Without a telescope, she couldn't see it, of course, but she knew it was there, and so was Uncle Jiang. It felt almost as if he was looking down on her.

Soon she would be there herself, with her new squadron, and she would see him again.

She made her way across the frozen ground to the

hangar, where the guards recognized her and waved her through. She continued on until she found it, her ship.

"Ms. Lao," someone said. "You're up early."

She looked down and saw that it was one of the mechanics, an older fellow whose name she did not know. He seemed to be fiddling with one of the engines.

"Hello, sir," she said. "Is anything the matter?"

"No," he said. "I'm just making certain that she's ready for her next flight. I've been assigned as part of your ground crew."

"I'm sorry," she said. "Would you tell me your name?"

"It's Lu, ma'am," he said.

"I appreciate your attention, Lu. I'm honored you chose my ship to maintain."

"The honor is mine," he said, sliding out from beneath the H-4 and standing up. "In fact, I asked for the assignment."

"Why?" Rain asked.

"It was my great honor to crew for your father on his last flight," Lu said. "I believed he would wish me to serve his daughter. He talked about you so much, and your mother, May. He would be very proud of you."

At first, Rain didn't know what to say. She just looked at him.

"Thank you," she said finally. "And thank you for telling me."

"It's nothing," he said. "What are you doing up so early?" he asked.

"I just wanted to see it," she said. "I'm trying to think of a name."

"Names are important," Lu said. "They were to your father."

"Were they?" she said, surprised, wondering how he could know that.

Lu nodded. "The last plane he flew was an old Shenyang

J-8. It was about sixteen years old, not even close to state-of-the-art. We lost most of our better jets in the failed attacks on the destroyers. I did my best with it, updated some of the radar equipment—but it all had to be done so fast. I was very young. I sometimes wonder, if I had been a better mechanic…" He trailed off. "I'm sorry," he said. "You don't want to hear an old man rambling."

"No, wait," she said. "You were saying something about names."

"Oh," Lu said. "Yes. He named her *Beautiful Wind*."

"*Beautiful Wind*," she repeated. "*Meifeng*."

Lu nodded. "I remember thinking at the time it was an odd name for a plane."

In the flicker of that moment, she saw in the space behind her eyes her father's face, that face she once believed she had forgotten. Beside him, a woman smiling down at her.

"It was my mother's name," Rain said softly. "He usually just called her 'May,' but it was really Meifeng."

Lu looked a bit chagrined. "I hope I haven't brought up unpleasant memories," he said.

"You haven't," she said. "To have any memory of them at all is a blessing. Thank you."

She bowed to him, and then went back out to look at the stars.

* * *

Dikembe lay in bed, knowing he was awake, unable to move anything but his eyes. He didn't know where he was, only that he'd been dreaming strange and horrible dreams, and that they had followed him from the waters of sleep into the night air. The darkness seemed filled with unseen presences lurking just beyond what he could see and hear, hints of strange, liquid eyes and a babble of nearly intelligible voices.

He couldn't turn his head, but *it* came to *him*, entering his frozen field of vision a little at a time. It was like a moon rising, but then he began to see the score across it, and his heart hammered in his chest. He wanted to close his eyes, to scream, to push the terror inside of him away. He thought he knew fear. He thought he had mastered it. But this was the worst, the brightest terror he had ever known.

Then his mind finally found his body, and it spasmed as if an electric shock had been run through it. His legs kicked involuntarily as the paralysis broke, and he fell heavily from the bed onto the hardwood floor.

When he looked back up, there was nothing there.

Groaning, he pushed himself up and pressed his hand to his forehead. He threw on a robe and made his way from the room, down the hall, to what had once been his father's office but which now belonged to him. He turned on the lamps, but not the overhead lights.

Dikembe began to draw. He drew until the daylight filtered into the atrium and cocks crowed in the town. And finally, after so many trials, one came out right, or so close to right that it sent a surge of fear through him just to look at it.

Then he got up for a cup of coffee and sat on the veranda, bathing in the morning light, trying to put distance between him, his nightmares, and the thing he had drawn.

Yet the peace he sought did not come, not even momentarily, for as he turned his gaze to the monstrous ship that yet squatted on the savanna beyond the walls of his compound, he saw that something was not right. It took him a few moments of staring before he realized what it was. Then he leapt up and called for his guard to assemble the vehicles—and as they did so he quickly donned his uniform. He took his seat in one of the trucks, and in a few moments they were racing down a dusty road that was all too familiar.

They came to the edge of the hill—the one his father had come over in the tank. The day he lost his brother to death and his father to madness. From there he stared out at the massive ship, quiet for so many years.

"Gather the army," he said. "Bring every heavy weapon we have, and do it quickly. Evacuate the nearby villages."

He held up his hand, and he saw that even in the daylight it took on a bluish tint.

This time it was going to be different. He wasn't going to make the mistakes his father had made.

This time, the world would know.

* * *

When the woman's face appeared on the screen, at first David Levinson didn't recognize her. But then she smiled.

"Director Levinson," she said. "How are you?"

"Patricia?" he said. "Is that you?"

"It's me," she said.

"Ah… It's been a while. You've grown up."

"So they tell me," she said.

He paused a moment, trying to think of something to say.

"I hear you're working for the president." He could see from the background that she was in the White House. It was impossible not to think of Connie, in her suit, always in motion, always with a purpose.

"Yes, I am," Patricia said. "To what do I owe the pleasure, Director?"

"Right," he said. "Well, I've been trying to get in touch with President Whitmore— -with your dad, and I've kind of been getting the runaround from his staff."

Patricia's expression changed a smidge, and only that. She suddenly seemed more guarded.

"Dad has been keeping to himself lately," she said.

"Is he okay?"

"He's fine," she assured him. "Is this about something important?"

David thought about lying and telling her it was, but he didn't quite feel up to it.

"Not really," he said. "I just haven't talked to him in a while. I thought I'd see how he was doing. Catch up."

"I'll tell him you called," she said. She looked a little uncomfortable. "I wish I could chat more myself, but you know how things are around here."

"Oh, yes," David said. "Here too. Always busy. Just give him my best, will you?"

"I will do that," she replied.

An instant later, he was looking at a blank screen.

He sighed and sat back in his chair. Through his window, he watched as a flight of H-7 trainers took to the sky.

He wondered how the world could be getting so much bigger and so much smaller at the same time. Every day, it seemed, they made some new leap forward in technology. There were now human beings on Mars and the moons of Saturn, and the world itself had come so far. Tomorrow the big cannon was going to be emplaced on the moon base and maybe—just maybe—humanity could begin to give a sigh of relief.

But Connie was gone. And Steve Hiller. And so many others who had died on the Fourth or since. Now Whitmore seemed to have withdrawn from the world.

David was the director of the greatest organization in the solar system, and yet he suddenly realized that he didn't really have anyone with whom to have a conversation, unless it was about work.

Except his dad.

Had it come down to that? He loved his father, but if he called him, he would have to fend off yet another request to go on some talk show or press junket with him.

Tomorrow was going to be busy. Probably he should just go home and get some rest.

He got out of the chair and was reaching for his jacket when his secretary buzzed him.

"Yes?" he said. "What is it?"

"You have a call, sir," he said. "From a Mr. Umbutu. He says it's urgent. Shall I put him on hold?"

David blinked and stared at the screen for a moment.

"No," he said. "Hell no. Put him on. I've waited a long time for this."

*   *   *

Fifteen minutes later, he was airborne, trying desperately to keep the pasta he'd had for lunch where it belonged. This time it wasn't airsickness. If what Umbutu had said was true, things might be about to become…

Interesting.

ABOUT THE AUTHOR

John Gregory Keyes was born in 1963 in Meridian, Mississippi, to Nancy Joyce Ridout and John Howard Keyes. His mother was an artist, and his father worked in college administration. When he was seven, his family spent a year living in Many Farms, Arizona, on the Navajo Reservation, where many of the ideas and interests which led Greg to become a writer and informed his work were formed.

Greg received a BA in anthropology from Mississippi State University, and worked briefly as a contract archaeologist. In 1987 he married Dorothy Lanelle Webb (Nell) and the two moved to Athens, Georgia, where Nell pursued a degree in art while Greg ironed newspapers for a living. During this time, Greg produced several unpublished manuscripts before writing *The Waterborn*, his first published novel, followed by a string of original and licensed books over the following two decades.

Greg earned a Masters in anthropology from the University of Georgia and completed his coursework and proposal for a PhD, which thus far remains ABD. He moved to Seattle, where Nell earned her BFA from the University of Washington, following which they moved to Savannah, Georgia. In 2005 the couple had a son, Archer, and in 2008 a daughter, Nellah. Greg continues to live with his family in Savannah, where he enjoys writing, cooking, fencing, and raising his children.

His original novels include the "Age of Unreason" historical fantasies and the "Kingdoms of Thorn and Bone" epic fantasies, while his licensed fiction includes *Star Wars*, *Babylon 5*, *Dawn of the Planet of the Apes: Firestorm*, and the official movie novel of *Interstellar*.

ACKNOWLEDGEMENTS

Thanks to Dean Devlin and Roland Emmerich, foremost for providing me such a fun sandbox to play in, but also for their comments and advice on the manuscript as it developed. Thanks also to Mike Ireland, Marco Shepherd, Nicole Spiegel, and Ryan Jones. Very special thanks to my editor, Steve Saffel, and to Josh Izzo for making sure everything pulled together, and to the entire team at Titan Books and Titan Comics, including Nick Landau, Vivian Cheung, Laura Price, Natalie Laverick, Miranda Jewess, Beth Lewis, Chris Teather, and Tom Williams.

INDEPENDENCE DAY RESURGENCE

OFFICIAL TIMELINE

FIRST CONTACT (Roswell, NM, 7/47): An extraterrestrial craft crash lands near a ranch in Roswell, New Mexico. The US military launches an investigation.

SILENT ZONE (Nevada Desert, 1970s): Dr. Brackish Okun arrives at Area 51 to work with the NSA and CIA on the study of the New Mexico ship.
(*THE COMPLETE INDEPENDENCE DAY OMNIBUS*)

ARRIVAL AND ATTACK (Middle of Atlantic, 7/2/96): A massive alien mother ship enters Earth's orbit, deploying 36 city destroyers to annihilate the world's largest cities. Within 48 hours, 108 cities are reduced to ashes.
(*INDEPENDENCE DAY: THE ORIGINAL MOVIE ADAPTATION*)

EARTH STRIKES BACK (Nevada Desert, 7/4/96): Earth's nations launch a globally coordinated counterattack, destroying the alien mother ship and eliminating the extraterrestrial threat.

WAR IN THE DESERT (Saudi Arabia, 7/4/96): Military pilots in the Saudi Arabian desert witness the destruction of Jerusalem and engage in a hand-to-hand assault with

extraterrestrial crash survivors.
(*THE COMPLETE INDEPENDENCE DAY OMNIBUS*)

TERROR FROM THE DEEP (Atlantic Ocean, 7/5/96):
A functioning extraterrestrial craft is discovered beneath
the Atlantic Ocean. An investigation—headed by Captain
Joshua Adams—is implemented by the U.S. military.
(*INDEPENDENCE DAY: DARK FATHOM*)

THE WORLD REBUILDS (11/30/96): Aside from a small
pocket of resistance in an isolated area of the African
Congo, the alien threat has been neutralized—and the
world begins to rise from the ashes. Reconstruction starts
as the great cities, monuments, and landmarks of the
world are slowly restored to their former glory.

LEADERS UNITE (Royal Palace of Naples, Piazza
del Plebiscito, Naples, Italy, 3/17/98): Centuries-old
conflicts and political distrust are dissolved to create an
unprecedented unity among the nations of the world.

EARTH SPACE DEFENSE FORMED (Geneva,
Switzerland, 5/25/98): Following the newly established
global peace alliance, the United Nations creates the
Earth Space Defense program (ESD) to serve as an
early warning system and united global defense unit. In
conjunction with this announcement, the ESD launches a
worldwide publicity and recruitment campaign.

F-22 ADDS ALIEN TECH (Elmendorf Air Force Base,
Anchorage, Alaska 1/8/99): ESD applies recovered alien
shield technology to an F-22 Raptor to understand how
they can better integrate other alien technology into
future full Hybrid Fighters. This light experiment will
serve as the foundation for the dramatic innovations that

the ESD delivers nearly a decade later.

PRESIDENT WHITMORE'S FAREWELL (Washington, DC, 01/15/01): After two terms in office, President Thomas Whitmore makes his final address to the nation, clearing the way for the newly elected President William Grey.

CONGO GROUND WAR CONTINUES (Democratic Republic of the Congo, Africa, 8/10/01): A faction of aliens continues to hold out in a remote part of the African Congo—the survivors of a stranded city destroyer. The ESD repeatedly offers their support and assistance to the local government, but is met by aggressive refusal. (*INDEPENDENCE DAY: CRUCIBLE*)

U.S. ARMY ADOPTS ALIEN WEAPONRY (El Paso, TX, 10/23/03): Applying new data from recovered alien weaponry, U.S. Army scientists make dramatic advances in applying their findings to military applications.

ALIEN PRISON RUMORS (Area 51, NV, 2/7/05): Rumors of a top-secret alien prison below Area 51 start to gain traction with the general public. ESD officials offer no comment regarding the legitimacy of these reports.

WORLD MOURNS COL. STEVEN HILLER (Area 51, NV, 4/27/07): While he is test-piloting the ESD's first alien-human hybrid fighter, an unknown malfunction causes the untimely death of Col. Hiller. He is survived by his wife, Jasmine, and son, Dylan. (*INDEPENDENCE DAY: CRUCIBLE*)

ESD MOON BASE OPERATIONAL (2/21/09): Monitored from its command center in Beijing, China, the Earth Space

Defense Moon Base opens. Designed with both offensive and defensive weapons capabilities, the moon base is the first of several planetary bases designed to monitor our solar system for potential alien threats.

PRESIDENT LANFORD ELECTED (Washington, DC, 1/20/13): Elizabeth Lanford, the forward-thinking former vice president under President Lucas Jacobs, is sworn in as the 45th president of the United States, becoming the first woman in history to hold the office.

NEXT GEN HYBRID FIGHTER UNVEILED (Tokyo, Japan, 8/19/14): The next generation of hybrid alien–human vehicles and weapons systems are introduced, after years of research and development from ESD scientists around the world. One of the standouts is the H-8 Global Defender hybrid fighter.

HONORING 20 YEARS OF GLOBAL UNITY (Washington, DC, 7/4/16): "As we remember the last 20 years, we must also look to the future. The world has rebuilt stronger than we ever imagined and we must promise ourselves, as well as future generations, that we're never caught off-guard again. We must continue to work together to secure the future of the human race—for as long as we stay united, we will survive."